CITY OF
DEVILS

CITY OF DEVILS

DIANA BRETHERICK

First published in Great Britain in 2013 by Orion Books,
an imprint of The Orion Publishing Group Ltd
Orion House, 5 Upper Saint Martin's Lane
London WC2H 9EA

An Hachette Livre UK Company

1 3 5 7 9 10 8 6 4 2

A CIP catalogue record for this book is
available from the British Library.

ISBN (Hardback) 978 1 4091 2790 1
ISBN (Trade Paperback) 978 1 4091 2792 5
ISBN (Ebook) 978 1 4091 2793 2

Typeset at The Spartan Press Ltd,
Lymington, Hants

Printed in Great Britain by
Clays Ltd, St Ives plc

The Orion Publishing Group's policy is to use papers that
are natural, renewable and recyclable products and made from
wood grown in sustainable forests. The logging and manufacturing
processes are expected to conform to the environmental
regulations of the country of origin.

www.orionbooks.co.uk

*To my mother Patricia and in memory
of my father Philip Bretherick*

Prologue

Turin, October 31st 1887

Giuseppe Soldati stopped suddenly and sniffed the air as if he was a beast on the trail of its prey. He could smell some-thing tart and unpleasant that reminded him of sour milk. He looked around to see if someone was following him but it was difficult to tell. The narrow lane was winding and there were plenty of hiding places. As he peered into the darkness, he could see his breath forming small clouds of vapour in the cold, damp air. Soldati was accustomed to the night and its secrets and he sensed that he was not alone. Despite this he could see nothing, which, he supposed, was hardly surprising given the lateness of the hour. As if to confirm it, he heard the bells of Chiesa di Santa Teresa softly chime in the distance. It was midnight. He shook himself and hurried on, heaving the small sack that contained the spoils from his night's work higher onto his back. He stopped again. This time it was

I

more than just a smell. He could hear it quite clearly in the stillness of the night even though it was little more than a whisper.

'Giuseppe Soldati . . .'

He pulled the sack round and clutched it to him. He had worked hard for his ill-gotten gains and he wasn't about to lose them to a fellow thief. Every instinct told him to run – and yet he was curious. Who would be calling out his name at this time of night?

'Giuseppe Soldati,' whispered the voice again, more urgently this time. It seemed to come from nowhere as if it was a spirit – perhaps of one of his victims returned from the grave to seek vengeance. He gulped and crossed himself but God offered no protection.

He moved away cautiously, his eyes moving from side to side like an agitated reptile. By now the sense of being followed was almost overwhelming. He was surrounded by shadows that seemed to lurk down every alley and in every doorway as if waiting for him to pass before leaping out at him. Once or twice he thought he could hear heavy breathing – almost like panting. But when he stopped to listen all he could hear was his own breath and his heart beating ferociously as if it was burrowing through his chest in a bid to escape.

Soldati set off once more, telling himself not to be a fool, that it was simply a case of his imagination playing tricks on him in the darkness. But then his name was called for a third time.

'Giuseppe Soldati . . .'

Somewhere between a whisper and an incantation, the words seemed to hang in the air as if waiting for him to snatch them away. He came to an abrupt halt and looked around him, trying to work out exactly where the voice had come from. Before it had been behind him but now it seemed to come from everywhere so he did not know whether to run forwards or retrace his steps. As he swivelled in confusion, first this way then the other, he thought he could hear laughter. Soldati started to move forwards but then a figure stepped out of the darkness and blocked his path. He turned to run away but he was not quick enough.

His last thought, as he felt the garrotte tighten around his throat, was not of his family or acquaintances – who all loathed him. He didn't even ask himself why he was being murdered. He knew perfectly well there were plenty who wished him dead. Instead, ever the professional criminal, he wondered why his killer needed a knife. He could have sworn that he had glimpsed a tell-tale glint of metal as the noose was slipped around his neck with the deftness of the skilled assassin. Then the final blackness descended upon him and for Soldati it ceased to matter.

It was just as well that he did not live long enough to find out the answer to his final question. The knife was put to work in such a hideous fashion that those who later saw the body were quite unable to put the image from their minds.

Soon the dense Turin fog swept in from the river and surrounded Soldati like a clammy shroud. His attacker had long since melted into the mist and he was left, propped up against a monument that was dedicated to the dead, like a sacrifice to an unnamed idol. A fitting end, for Giuseppe Soldati's last resting place in the Piazza Statuto was reputed to be the black heart of the city, a point of pilgrimage for Satanists, the location of the gates of Hell itself. The monument was topped by a stone angel that stared down at the corpse below with an expression that might have seemed strangely malevolent for a creature of God. For Lucifer, though, whose likeness it was said to be, it was more than apt.

1

Tests of compression show rapists, brigands and arsonists to be stronger than murderers and robbers, who are in turn stronger than forgers and thieves.   Lombroso, 1884, p 209

Turin, November 1st 1887

It was torture . . . or at least that's what it looked like. A bearded, thickset, middle-aged man stood in the centre of a large room in his shirtsleeves. He was manipulating a younger man into a fearful looking contraption with leather buckles, dials and metal spikes. It was not a straightforward process. The younger man did not fit easily into the equipment and there was a certain amount of grunting and cries of pain as he was pushed this way and that.

James Murray stood half hidden, watching in the doorway. He ran his hands through his thick dark hair as he always did when he was trying to work out something that perplexed him. After a moment or two he leant forward, as if to get closer to the scene being played before him, his brow creased with concentration.

He weighed up the evidence, just as he had been taught to do by his tutor Dr Bell when he was studying to be a doctor in Edinburgh. Everything indicated that he had stumbled on a medieval torture chamber, except in this case, despite his evident discomfort, the subject seemed happy enough to comply. The older man was still having some difficulty in sliding his companion into the correct position. Seeing James, Professor Lombroso, for so he turned out to be, beckoned him over.

'You over there – give us a hand, won't you? This is clearly a task for two rather than one!'

James obeyed and under the older man's direction held the subject by the shoulders, steadying him whilst the various straps were fastened.

'Now all that is required is the calibration of the dials and we can start the experiment. Perhaps you could assist by recording the results, as you have already been so helpful?'

James nodded. He had not expected his chance to come so soon and he was somewhat apprehensive. But this was at least one of the things he had come to the University of Turin for – hands-on experience of the new science of criminal anthropology, and it was an opportunity he could not turn down. Being in a foreign city had already lifted what had become his natural state of gloom and now, despite some reticence in the face of something unfamiliar, he was exhilarated at the chance to be a part of something that previously he had only read about. The professor gestured towards the equipment.

'Now, young man, what you see here is a measuring device. You see this oval in the centre?'

James nodded and moved closer to inspect it.

'Touch it. What does it feel like?'

Professor Lombroso looked at him, bushy eyebrows raised. James leaned forward and put his hands round the oval, expecting it to be cold and unyielding. Instead it was soft and flexible. He nodded as if he had been expecting it all along.

'It bends.'

'Exactly! You see it's made of a pliant metal. Our subject here has to compress and pull at it so that we can test his strength. Off you go, Ottolenghi.'

The subject grunted as he pushed and pulled. Beads of sweat started to appear on his forehead. He stopped and mopped his brow with a handkerchief.

The professor urged him on. 'Come, my friend. Keep it going or we won't get a decent measurement.'

Ottolenghi gave a rueful grin and started again. Lombroso looked over his gold-rimmed glasses at James. 'Now what I need you to do is to keep an eye on these dials and call out the numbers on them as accurately as you can. Do you think you can do that?'

'Yes, sir,' James replied confidently.

'*Eccellente*! Now I will record the data and with a bit of luck we'll get there. Keep going, Ottolenghi!'

Ottolenghi, now a deep red colour, continued with his labours and James called out the numbers on the dials, hesitantly at first and then, as they went on, with more certainty. After a number of attempts the experiment was finally completed. Ottolenghi looked relieved that it was over. He was drenched in sweat by his exertions and was clearly exhausted. There was a good deal of handshaking and nodding and expressions of gratitude as the participants inhaled their own, perhaps not entirely deserved, sense of achievement.

As all of this was taking place, out of the corner of his eye James saw the door open and a woman enter the room. She was tall and slim with long dark hair tamed into a loose braid that hung down her back, giving her an exotic air. She had on a sober grey dress that, worn by any other woman, might have been described as dowdy but on her it somehow seemed to enhance her beauty. James blushed slightly as she stared at him with her large brown eyes, a half smile playing about her lips as if she was mocking him. She moved towards the professor and began to whisper in his ear. He started to smile and nod, glancing over at James. Finally he spoke.

'*Dottor* James Murray, I presume? You are clearly impatient to begin your studies! Sofia here tells me she left you in one of the empty exhibits rooms but when she returned to collect you she found that you had already gone off in search of excitement!'

James bowed his head in acknowledgement. 'Professor Lombroso, I apologise. I was eager to explore the museum.'

Lombroso looked at him through narrowed eyes as if weighing him up.

'Indeed, Dr Murray. Well, such curiosity is commendable and your arrival was timely. I prefer to conduct my experiments personally whenever I am able and it is obvious that you are going to be a great help in that endeavour.' The young man who had been the subject of the experiment coughed meaningfully. 'As of course Ottolenghi here already is.'

Ottolenghi was tall and gangling with a large, dome-shaped forehead and small round glasses perched on the end of his nose. His arms were long and swung about as if he didn't know quite where to put them. It made him seem awkward which was somehow comforting. He grinned amiably and extended a hand. James seized it gratefully, feeling instantly at ease with him.

'Salvatore Ottolenghi at your service. I look forward to

working with you.' James returned his smile, happy to see a friendly face.

'Ottolenghi is my chief assistant and will be your fellow student whilst you are here, assuming that you meet the requirements. But we shall soon see whether or not that is the case,' Lombroso said.

Suddenly James felt a little nervous. The excitement of participating in an actual experiment had made him temporarily forget the purpose of this visit, an interview with the professor for the position of assistant. Ottolenghi gave him a sympathetic smile. Presumably he had once been in the same situation and James felt reassured to see that someone at least had survived the selection procedure unscathed. His new landlady had kindly informed him that Lombroso was said to be a difficult man to please.

Lombroso turned to the woman. 'Sofia, could you bring us some refreshment in a moment or two?'

She nodded and left the room. James could not help but watch her retreating form. Their first encounter as she had showed him into the building had been . . . unusual. She was handsome, of course, and a little older than him, in her late twenties, perhaps. But it was more than that. She had looked at him in a way he'd found disconcerting. As she greeted him at the front door he had noticed that her large dark eyes had travelled the length of his body and she looked directly at him, holding his glance in a way that seemed not only incongruous for a servant, but also blatantly inviting.

'Sofia is my housekeeper,' Lombroso said firmly.

Ottolenghi smiled in amusement and winked at James. Lombroso looked over his spectacles at them. 'Ottolenghi, I believe you have some duties to perform. The consignment of skulls from Madagascar – they need to be checked.'

9

Ottolenghi nodded. 'Indeed, Professor. I will attend to it directly.' He looked over to James, as he was leaving and gave a short bow. 'See you again, I hope.'

Lombroso stroked his luxuriant beard thoughtfully. 'So, Dr Murray, before we take refreshment what would you think to a tour of our little museum of criminal curiosities?'

'I would be delighted, Professor.'

Lombroso smiled his satisfaction and beckoned to him to follow. James walked behind, struggling to keep up as the professor strode briskly through a series of corridors and up a flight of stairs to an imposing pair of wooden doors. Lombroso flung them open and ushered James into the room. He squinted into the gloom. The sight that met his eyes, once they had become accustomed to the darkness, was one that he would never forget.

From floor to ceiling were shelves packed with the most extraordinary artefacts. There was a selection of wax and plaster death masks propped up on a shelf as if they were ornaments, each carefully labelled with the name of the subject and the date of their execution. James peered into the empty lifeless eyes of one and wondered what the subject had been thinking as the minutes ticked away towards the inevitable. Did he know that his image would be captured and exhibited for all to see – that it would be held up as an example of the features of a born criminal? And what of its creator? How did he feel whilst smoothing plaster onto a dead man's face? Did he know of his subject's crimes? Did it matter to him or was it just another work of art? Indeed, could such a curiosity really be called art? He thought back to something his father had told him about Marie Tussaud, whose waxworks had become so popular in London. She had learned her art by modelling death masks on the corpses of the unfortunate victims of the guillotine during the French Revolution. James gave an involuntary shudder at the thought. As he did so he noticed that there was an odd smell to the place – a mixture of formaldehyde and damp mustiness – an apt combination of life and death perhaps.

Above the death masks were some jars of pickled brains and body parts which bobbed around gaily in the preserving fluid like ducks on a pond. Next to them were some samples of tattooed skin stretched onto frames.

Lombroso gestured towards them. 'Feel free to take a closer look, won't you.'

James examined the skins gingerly, running his hands over them, feeling their dryness – like parchment. He looked closely at the intricate designs, now fading. He saw angels, serpents, the sun and the moon, the names of long-lost sweethearts and even what looked to be a tarantula. For a moment so lost was he in the artistry that he quite forgot that they were pieces of human skin. Once he remembered he put them down quickly, as if touching them might infect him in some way.

Lombroso smiled and beckoned him over to a selection of books on a nearby shelf; something with which he was at least familiar – or so he thought.

'Have a look at this,' Lombroso said, handing him a compact volume. 'What do you think?'

The book had no title – just the name *Cavaglia* embossed on the front. James opened it, curious as to its contents. A slip of paper fell out. He picked it up and read it. It told him all he needed to know.

This binding is all that remains of the assassin Cavaglia who hanged himself on the hundredth day of his incarceration.

James had heard of the practice of binding of books with

human skin, although he had never seen an example before. It was lighter in colour than leather, almost translucent. As he studied it further it seemed to him that an image of a face looked back at him. He shuddered again and was about to replace it with the others when Lombroso took it from him.

'Ah yes, Cavaglia was an interesting case. A prime example of criminal man – thick dark hair, not unlike your own, and a large snub nose and jug ears. He murdered his landlord and put him in the closet, folded up like an old blanket.'

'How did he end up as binding for a book?' James asked.

'One of my colleagues arranged it as a gift for me – a tribute,' Lombroso said, as if it was the sort of thing that happened to him every day. 'Mind you,' he continued, 'the most interesting thing about Cavaglia was that his skull and brain also had all the anomalies one would expect to find in a criminal – a round, slightly asymmetrical skull, flat forehead and so on, just like his wastrel of a father, so a prime example of inherited criminality.'

James surreptitiously put his hand up to his own head. It was flat, just like his father's. What could that mean?

'Now take a look over here, Murray.'

Lombroso directed him to another part of the room where there were some weapons as well as some manacles and leg irons, shining from repeated polishing. James wondered what the poor wretches who had been held by them had suffered. He looked over to the large mantelpiece and saw some pictures, crudely drawn sketches of various crimes and executions. There were also some jugs and vases with similar illustrations, some of them obscene. He inspected each and every one of them closely, telling himself that his interest was due to scientific curiosity rather than prurience but in truth he could not be certain of his motives.

In one corner was a gigantic model of a Venus flytrap, complete with a wax facsimile of an insect crawling into its open jaws. In another was an Egyptian mummy in its case, looking as if it would step out of it at any minute and walk around the room.

James glanced over to Lombroso who was busy examining some of his own exhibits, a broad grin on his face as if he was congratulating himself on putting together such a bizarre collection. What kind of a man was he, this curator of the curious whose theories of criminality were famous throughout Europe? Some would say that he was an acknowledged and celebrated expert in evil, but although he had many supporters he also had detractors. What was evident to James, even after their brief acquaintance, was that whatever you thought of his theories, Cesare Lombroso was not the sort of person who could be ignored. And he was just the right man, James believed, to give answers to the questions that he had come all the way from Edinburgh to ask. He fervently hoped that his application would be successful and that Lombroso would agree to become both his teacher and employer. His future depended on it.

James continued to explore, touching things, smelling them, wanting to experience it all – to know everything there was to know about each and every exhibit. He tried to store each image in his memory so he could tell his sister Lucy about it all. What would she have made of it, he wondered, feeling guilty for leaving her behind. But what else could he have done? At seventeen she was too young to accompany him here, but from the expression on her face when he had told her of his plans to come to Turin it was clear that she thought he was abandoning her. What he did not – could not – tell her was that their reduced circumstances meant that there was not enough money to support them both. As a result he had been forced to leave her in the care of a not particularly sympathetic aunt back in Edinburgh whilst he pursued his studies. He resolved to write to her as soon as he could in the hope that he might persuade her to forgive him.

He became aware that Lombroso was watching him and looked up.

'Tell me, Murray, what do you make of my collection?'

It was difficult for James to find the words to express his feelings. He wanted his answer to be measured and intelligent but instead he found himself merely stating what to him was obvious. 'Fascinating, Professor, it's absolutely fascinating . . .'

Lombroso nodded and beamed at him. 'Good, good – that's really very good. We will explore them further after we have taken wine. You have only seen one room and there are five others to examine. I will give you a personal tour. Now, shall we make our way downstairs for a glass of something?'

As they went down the corridor Lombroso hesitated outside another door. He turned and looked at James, as if wondering whether or not to trust him with a confidence. 'I had hoped to show you my study but alas, it is in some disarray. We had a burglary last night.'

'Was much taken?' James asked, concerned.

Lombroso shook his head and continued towards the staircase, talking as he went. 'That was the odd thing about it. All I am missing are a few old notes. No use to anyone except me. But of course that is the thing about criminals,

Murray. As you will no doubt learn, their offences rarely make sense, not even to themselves.' Suddenly he smiled. 'I must say, your Italian is excellent. It is rare for a young man to speak a second language so fluently.'

'My late mother was from this city. She ensured that both my sister and I spoke the language at every opportunity.'

'A wise lady. Communication is paramount in science. I only wish my English was as good as your Italian. Do you have any other languages?'

'German and a little French . . .'

'*Eccellente, eccellente*. All points in your favour! Crime has no language barrier.'

Shortly after they reached the room where the experiment had taken place, Sofia arrived. She was carrying a tray on which was a decanter of wine the colour of amber and a plate of small sugared cakes. James couldn't resist staring at her again as she poured the wine into exquisite crystal glasses. She smiled at him as she handed him a glass of wine and offered him a cake, staring into his eyes so intensely that he began to feel as if he were under some kind of spell. He wasn't used to this kind of attention, particularly from a servant and it made him slightly uncomfortable. He could not imagine their maid at home being quite so forward. Lombroso looked on, his bushy eyebrows raised.

'Thank you, Sofia. You can leave us now,' he said severely. She nodded and left. The room felt strangely empty.

'I found Sofia in a prison in Pavia,' Lombroso said evenly. 'She was serving a sentence for prostitution. It was a tragic case; her father beat her mother constantly and one day he killed her and ran off, leaving Sofia to support herself in the only way she could.'

James didn't know how to greet this information. He had

been so caught up in his own misery recently that he had become accustomed to thinking that his suffering was unique. To hear of someone else's unsettled him. Lombroso went on.

'I brought her with me when I took up my position here in Turin. At first my wife refused to have her in our home. Sometimes I wonder if she was right. Women usually are, don't you find?'

James smiled. 'My sister would certainly agree with you, Professor, though perhaps she is too young to be right about everything.'

'Indeed, but in my experience it is always a mistake to tell a woman what she should be thinking, as your father has no doubt told you.'

James was silent for a moment. He hadn't expected the subject to come up so quickly and now it had, he was not sure how to respond. Eventually he found the words though they were difficult to utter. 'My father is dead . . .' He peered down at his glass, lost in its golden depths, as if he was remembering, when in fact he would sooner forget. When he looked up he saw that Lombroso was staring at him, his brows furrowed.

'Please forgive my clumsiness,' he said gently. James gave a small tight smile. It was all he could manage under the circumstances. Lombroso patted him paternally on the shoulder. 'Well, young man, I hope that if I take you on, your studies here will enlighten you and give you at least some of the answers you seek. Am I correct in thinking that you studied with Dr Joseph Bell in Edinburgh?'

'Yes, Professor, I did.'

'*Eccellente*! He is, I understand, an exacting tutor. I have read several of his monographs. He is an active supporter of the use of science in criminal investigation, is he not?'

'That is correct, Professor. I was fortunate enough to assist Dr Bell in one or two cases where he was consulted by the local constabulary. I was his clerk.'

Lombroso looked at him with fresh interest. 'Ah, I see . . . you worked and studied. That takes some fortitude.'

'My financial position demanded it,' James said, hoping that the professor would probe no further.

Lombroso smiled. 'So tell me, Murray, what did you learn from Dr Bell?'

James paused, trying to recall some of Bell's favourite phrases. It was a difficult question to answer in the space of a sentence or two but he knew that he must try. 'I learned to use all my senses in diagnosis, to deduce the facts from the evidence before me.'

Lombroso nodded. 'Ah yes, a valuable lesson in both medical and criminal matters, I am sure you will agree.'

After that they sat together in silence. It was strange but James felt somehow at home in the professor's company. It was his first opportunity to study the great man more closely. On the surface he looked avuncular and jolly and seemed as if he would be excellent company. There was, however, just a hint of a darker side to him. Perhaps it was in his eyes or his tone, James could not say exactly but it was there – a suggestion that the professor was a man whose mood could change without warning.

Lombroso held his glass up to the window and studied its amber contents in the autumn sunlight. James did not notice at first that he was being studied too, through the glass.

'There are clearly unresolved matters about your father's death. Your eyes tell me so.'

James looked at him, startled. He wondered if Lombroso could read his mind. He decided that his best strategy was to say as little as possible but he had to say something. Hopefully it would be enough to satisfy the professor and prevent further enquiry.

'My father was a doctor. He had an interest in neurology, particularly in relation to criminality. I wish to . . . to carry on his work, to find out more about criminals, Professor. I want to know what makes them the way they are.'

Lombroso stroked his beard thoughtfully. 'Such strong motives for gaining knowledge could, of course, be a good thing. It might make you a very useful assistant indeed, but it could also make you rash in your conclusions and that would not do.' He paused and sighed. James braced himself for rejection. 'Still, young man, you have managed well so far. I think that you have earned a fair chance.'

James sighed with relief and allowed himself to smile. The fact that he had been less than frank about his motives became a mere detail.

'Welcome to Turin, Dr Murray. And you have arrived at the right time. Our annual symposium on Criminal Anthropology starts in a few days – I think you will learn much from it. Many distinguished speakers will be present and –' here Lombroso raised his eyes heavenwards, as if in prayer '– some not so distinguished, of course – but these things are sent to try us.'

James could hardly believe his luck. To be here at such an auspicious time was surely a good omen.

Lombroso warmed to his subject. 'We have scientists coming from all over Europe. I am looking forward in particular to hearing Madame Tarnovsky discuss her work with prostitutes in Prague.'

'Anna Tarnovsky?' James said eagerly. He had read some of her work and greatly admired it.

'Indeed. A delightful woman and highly intelligent — unusual for her sex.'

James thought this comment somewhat unfair but he was hardly in a position to argue. 'Will DeClichy be coming from Lyon?' he asked. He had also read of this man's work and knew that he had, in the past, been critical of some of Lombroso's views, believing environmental factors to be more of an influence on criminality than a natural inclination towards crime. James had dropped the name into the conversation in an effort to impress and was unprepared for Lombroso's reaction.

'That charlatan!' he spat. 'We are, unfortunately, to be subjected to his ridiculous outpourings. I hope you don't give his ludicrous ideas too much credence, young man. If so, our relationship will be brief.'

'Not at all, Professor,' James said quickly. 'I just wondered if he might be one of the not-so-distinguished speakers that you mentioned.'

'Quite so, young man, quite so.' He took a large gulp from his glass as if trying to rid himself of the taste of Dr DeClichy and others like him then turned to James and smiled. His good mood had returned as swiftly as it had left.

The large ornate clock that stood in the corner of the room suddenly chimed the hour. It was twelve o'clock. James had been in the museum for almost two hours, though it felt as if only minutes had passed.

Lombroso checked his pocket watch. 'Would you like to see some more of the museum? Then perhaps we could lunch later if you would care to join me? And Ottolenghi too — provided he has finished checking those skulls, that is.'

He was about to accept Lombroso's invitation when there was a knock at the door. It opened to reveal Ottolenghi and

Sofia, who ushered in a young man in a blue and red uniform. He bowed to Lombroso, who leapt to his feet.

'What is it? What has happened?' he said in a sharp tone.

It was then that James realised that the young man in uniform was an officer of the carabinieri.

'Professor Cesare Lombroso?' the young man asked hesitantly.

Lombroso nodded. 'Has there been some progress on the burglary? That was unusually quick. Indeed, I am surprised to see you at all. There was little interest expressed when I first reported it. I am gratified that it is being taken seriously.'

The officer looked confused. 'No, Professor – not a burglary . . .'

'Then what is it?' Lombroso said with alarm. 'Has something happened?'

'I am Lieutenant Giardinello, Professor. There has been . . . an incident.'

'What kind of incident? Has someone been hurt? My wife, my daughters?'

'No, no, Professor, nothing like that. Marshal Machinetti sent me.'

'Machinetti! What does that fool want?'

'I have been told to ask you to accompany me, Professor.'

'Accompany you where?' Lombroso asked.

'I cannot tell you, sir. I have been told not to give any information and that you will find out when we get there.'

'Where the devil is *there*?'

'I cannot say.'

'I am not going anywhere until I am told!'

There was a short pause as the young policeman appeared to consider exactly how much he was permitted to reveal.

'You're going there anyway, Lieutenant Giardinello. You might as well tell us,' Ottolenghi said gently. Giardinello nodded.

'There has been a murder. The body was found in the Piazza Statuto.'

Sofia gave a sharp intake of breath. 'The gates of hell . . .' she murmured. She crossed herself and looked up to the heavens, as if for guidance.

Giardinello went on, 'There is a connection with you, Professor . . . with your name . . .'

Lombroso raised his eyebrows. 'Now I am intrigued! How am I connected?'

'I am not permitted to say more, Professor.'

Lombroso snorted. 'Well, I think that you had better say something, young man. Otherwise you will find me less than cooperative.'

Giardinello's face reddened. 'I really cannot.'

'Am I a suspect?' Lombroso asked, incredulously.

There was a pause. 'I do not think so, Professor.'

Lombroso peered morosely at him. 'Your hesitation speaks volumes, Lieutenant. Machinetti will answer for this impertinence!' He pursed his lips. 'Well, just for your records –' Lombroso leaned over to Giardinello until their faces were only inches apart – 'I did not do it – whatever "it" turns out to be!'

He turned to James and Ottolenghi and shrugged his shoulders. 'I suppose I had better do as I am told. Marshal Machinetti is a typical Sicilian, a dangerous man who is proud and stupid in equal measure, so not someone to be trifled with. Would you both mind accompanying me? Other eyes and ears might be useful.'

Both readily agreed and they all left the relative warmth

and comfort of the museum for the chill autumn air. It was cooler than James had thought. Somehow the name Italy had conjured an expectation of heat and light in his mind. This had been confirmed, or so he had thought, by the sunny days which had met his arrival and indeed until now it had been mild, even at night. But now there seemed to be a change in the weather. The sun had long since disappeared behind threatening-looking clouds and he was unprepared for the cold and damp that now surrounded him. He pulled his thin coat around him as he walked. The smell of rotting leaves and wood smoke hung in the air and mingled incongruously with the underlying stench of the city.

The Piazza Statuto was in the older part of Turin, an area of the city that most respectable residents avoided. It was a harsh contrast from the broad straight roads and magnificent architecture that James had seen on his way to the museum. He took an inward breath and smelled the fetid air as they made their way along the narrow, dark streets. Then he shivered. It brought back memories of his father, memories that he would rather forget.

'Are you all right, Murray?' Ottolenghi asked.

James nodded and pointed ahead. A small crowd of onlookers was gathered around a large sculpture, surrounded by a small area of shrubs and grass and then a set of iron railings with a gate, which had evidently been opened for the purposes of accessing something within.

Ottolenghi turned to Lombroso. 'I think we are here, Professor.'

Lieutenant Giardinello pushed through the crowd and then through the gate, followed closely by Lombroso, Ottolenghi and James. There was a group of carabinieri forming a semi-circle round a body. To one side, precariously balanced on a shooting stick, perched a short round figure resplendent in a dark blue uniform with silver braid around the collar and cuffs, scarlet-trimmed edges and a large cocked hat with a black and red plume at the centre. He had an enormous bushy moustache, waxed at the ends but now slightly drooping, and an extremely self-important air. He reminded James of a walrus.

'Machinetti – it has been a while since we last met,' Lombroso said, making it clear in his tone that he did not regret that this was the case.

'Professor,' acknowledged the marshal abruptly. 'I had no choice other than to summon you. You will see why shortly.'

He nodded at the semi-circle of officers who quickly stepped aside. There were some cries of horror from the crowd who, although more than ready for a grim sight, were insufficiently prepared for what they saw. Lombroso gulped. Ottolenghi put his hand to his throat as if to quell an urgent need to vomit. James stared, hardly believing what he was seeing. Before them stood a large sculpture; at first glance it seemed to be nothing more than a mound of earth but when one examined it more closely one could see that intertwined within its base were writhing bodies of men, their faces contorted in pain and anguish. At the top of the mound stood an angel, looking down on them with an expression that was the closest to a depiction of pure evil that Murray had ever seen. As if this in itself was not horrific enough, at the foot of the statue, in full view of the angel, was a body.

A small pool of sticky blood surrounded the corpse, shining blackly. James immediately recognised the smell of death, a kind of earthy sweetness underwritten by putrefaction, a foul odour that could be nothing else. He had experienced it often enough in the course of his studies.

He looked at the corpse again and saw that there was a dark red line running along the throat. The man had clearly been garrotted. But the worst of it was the way in which the corpse had been mutilated. The ears and nose had been removed with almost surgical precision and left on the victim's chest, and a note, balanced carefully on the severed ears, was held in place by the large flat nose, acting as a kind of macabre paperweight.

They stood transfixed, staring at the body. The lips were drawn back in a silent scream and the bone and gristle where the nose used to be were clearly visible. James desperately wanted to avert his gaze but found himself quite unable to do so. Despite his initial disgust at what he had seen there was an element of excited fascination that kept welling up in him. He was ashamed of his feelings but powerless to change them.

Ottolenghi, though apparently equally appalled at what he was seeing, was more clinical in his outlook. James observed him as he looked carefully at the scene, his head moving this way and that, his brows furrowed in deep concentration. It was clear that he had immediately begun to assess what he could see: the position of the body, the mutilation, blood patterns and so on. It was as if James was back in Edinburgh, listening to lectures at medical school from Dr Bell. He too had appreciated the importance of such traces of evidence.

Lombroso's focus appeared to be on the corpse itself and he peered down at it, a look of disgust on his face. 'I have seen many things, but there is something about this . . .'

'What, Professor?' Ottolenghi asked.

'To see a corpse in this state is bad enough but it's the mutilation and the posing of the body. It is so . . .' He paused, took off his glasses and rubbed his eyes in an apparent effort to regain his composure. '. . . deliberate,' he continued. 'I have never seen anything like it. This act required a level of depravity that is almost unimaginable.' He stared into the distance, a troubled look on his face.

'It was found early this morning. We have been looking for you for some time,' Machinetti said reprovingly.

Lombroso replaced his glasses and looked at him with ill-disguised contempt. 'I have been where I am most days, at the museum.' He turned to James. 'Really, if this is the level of detection then no wonder the crime rates are high!'

Machinetti's face was as black as thunder. 'We called on you earlier and you were not there!'

'I was taking my usual morning refreshment at Al Bicerin,' Lombroso said.

'Well, you shouldn't have!'

'I do apologise, Marshal,' Lombroso replied sarcastically. 'Obviously I should have known that you would wish to speak to me and cancelled all of my appointments.'

'I would advise you not to be impertinent, Professor. You are a suspect in this case as you will see,' Machinetti said, apparently with some satisfaction.

'What do you mean?' Lombroso asked.

Machinetti snapped his fingers at Giardinello. 'The note! Quickly!'

'Wait, just one minute!'

The voice came from the edge of the crowd. Machinetti turned towards it and scowled as he saw the slight figure of a smartly dressed young man stride towards them.

'Tullio, what do you want? This is my area, not yours.'

'Inspector Tullio, if you don't mind, and that is not how it works, Machinetti, as you well know,' the young man replied, patiently. 'I have jurisdiction here.'

James studied Tullio and decided that he had not been in his position long. Everything about him gave the impression of effort from his neatly clipped beard to his posture, which had him leaning slightly forward as if he was anxious not to miss anything.

Machinetti paused, frowning apparently with the effort of thinking. 'I was here first,' he declared.

Tullio smiled thinly. 'You certainly were. Only you could contaminate the scene of a crime quite so comprehensively. I don't want your officers blundering about any more, destroying the evidence as they go.'

Machinetti stared at him with hostility. James observed their mutual dislike, wondering why they seemed to be so intent on having a dispute about territory rather than co-operating in the investigation of the crime. Ottolenghi whispered in his ear, 'Inspector Tullio is an officer from our other investigating body, the Public Security Police, the PS. Machinetti hates him almost as much as the professor, and that's saying something.'

'Why?' James asked.

'The PS is supposed to police the city but so are the carabinieri. Who does what is a matter of dispute. As for Tullio himself, he's university-educated, very bright and also a believer in scientific policing, which is not widely supported here.'

James looked at Tullio with new interest. He wondered if the young policeman had also studied under someone like Dr Bell. Word of this new approach to criminal investigation had spread beyond Edinburgh, he knew, and it was obvious that Tullio shared James's view that not only the body of the victim, but also the scene of the crime and what might have been left there by the perpetrator should be given almost as much attention as possible suspects in a case.

Lombroso, who had evidently overheard, nodded with approval. 'It has great possibilities. Machinetti, you should listen to this young man. You might learn something.'

Machinetti grunted and turned away.

Tullio smiled at them. 'Professor, Ottolenghi, it is good to see you both – and signor?' He extended a hand towards James who took it gratefully.

'Ah yes, this is my new assistant, Dr James Murray from Scotland,' Lombroso said. James felt a jolt of excitement at hearing his position confirmed.

'Welcome to Turin, *Dottore*,' Tullio said. 'Now, Professor, perhaps you and your colleagues could be of some assistance with what is left of the evidence?'

'Indeed,' Lombroso replied. 'We were just about to examine the note.'

Tullio nodded his approval. 'I agree, but first let us record the position of the body.' He turned and summoned a small dumpy man with an untidy moustache carrying some equipment. 'Please proceed.'

The man, a photographer, started to set up his tripod. Machinetti snorted with derision. 'We don't have time for this. I've already got someone to record everything, although personally I don't see the need for such a thing. The man's clearly dead. That's all we need to know, surely.' Machinetti pointed to another man standing next to the body with a pad and a pencil.

'A sketch artist? That's nowhere near as accurate!' Tullio protested.

The artist positioned himself in front of the photographer

27

who immediately picked up his tripod and moved it in front again. The artist tutted and moved once more until he was so close to the body he could almost reach out and touch it. Neither of them seemed remotely bothered by the repellent sight they had been asked to capture.

Tullio rolled his eyes impatiently.

'Why don't they just stand next to each other?' James suggested. 'Then we would have two different impressions rather than one.'

Lombroso agreed. 'A capital idea, don't you think, Marshal, Signor Tullio?'

They looked at each other and both nodded reluctantly. The photographer and the artist parted slightly and began their work. Suddenly there was a flash and a bang and everyone jumped – Machinetti almost fell off his shooting stick. The photograph had been taken. Not long after that the artist folded up his sketchbook after giving his drawing to Machinetti who folded it and thrust it into his pocket. Clearly keeping it away from Tullio was more important to him than avoiding creases.

'Now perhaps we could examine the note?' Lombroso said, a little impatiently.

'Indeed, Professor,' Tullio said, nodding at Giardinello who looked over to Machinetti for the marshal's approval. There was a long pause. Tullio sighed with irritation. Finally, Machinetti nodded to Giardinello who approached the body and removed the note, gingerly holding it between his thumb and forefinger. Lombroso nodded his assent to Ottolenghi who took it carefully, peered at it and then handed it to the professor.

James craned his neck in order to get a better view. 'Odd colour of ink,' he observed.

Lombroso took the note and looked at it. James saw him pause, just for an instant, as he read it. Then the scientist in him took over. He sniffed it, his nose twitching like an inquisitive rabbit. Finally he held it up to the light. 'That is no ink, my young friend – that is blood.'

Those at the front of the crowd gasped and there was an audible murmuring as the news was passed to the back. Lombroso beckoned to James and handed him the note. 'Now, Murray, tell us what you see. Remember, be precise.'

'It says—'

'No, not what it says. What can you *see?*' Lombroso said impatiently.

James looked at it carefully and heard the words of his teacher, Dr Bell, urging him to start with the obvious and then look behind it. 'The writing is not erratic,' he began. 'Indeed it is penned in a very neat hand.'

'Penned you say,' Lombroso said. 'Are you certain? What has been used to write it – a pen, a stick, a finger?'

There was a pause as James squinted at the writing before him. 'It looks like a pen – it's a neat hand, no smudges. There's some staining, presumably from the victim's nose but other than that it seems quite clean.'

'Any other marks?' Tullio asked.

James shook his head. 'None that I can see . . . oh no, wait a minute.' He turned the note round. 'There are some smudged prints on the back.'

'Let me have a look,' Machinetti said, snatching the note. 'Oh, they're probably mine from earlier.'

Tullio stared at him incredulously. 'You removed it from the body?'

Machinetti looked at him in surprise. 'Of course. I wanted to know what it said. It might be a clue.'

Tullio shook his head and sighed. 'I wonder that you bothered to replace it.'

Machinetti smiled smugly. 'I put it back, just as I found it.'

Tullio gave him an exasperated look. James wondered why there was such hostility between them. After all, were they not both on the same side?

'Exactly what does the note say?' Tullio asked.

Machinetti smirked and held it up. 'See for yourself.'

Tullio sighed. 'Dr Murray, would you mind?'

'Go on, go on. Let's all hear it,' Machinetti said.

James read aloud: '*A Tribute to Lombroso*.'

The crowd gasped and murmured again. Lombroso stood silently and looked down at his feet. James stared at him. What could it mean?

'It is, I am sure you will agree, not much of a tribute,' Machinetti said. His eyes betrayed his evident glee at Lombroso's discomfort.

'No, indeed,' Lombroso replied quietly, 'but I can assure you it has nothing whatsoever to do with me.'

'You are not familiar with the victim?' Machinetti asked. 'He was a thief who was well known to us – Giuseppe Soldati. Have you no memory of meeting him at any point?'

There was a long pause as Lombroso considered the name. 'I may do – I think he assisted with an experiment some time ago.'

Machinetti smiled briefly in triumph. He spoke slowly, as if relishing every moment. 'Now then, let me see. A man is dead. You knew him. He has a note in his hand, naming you. More than a little suspicious, don't you think, Professor?'

Lombroso looked up. His face wore a strained expression. 'But I had no reason to see him since our brief meeting and I certainly did not do this to the poor fellow,' he protested. 'Even you must know that I could never do such a thing.'

Machinetti pursed his lips. 'Where were you last night?'

There was a long pause. 'I was working late at the museum.'

Machinetti raised his eyebrows. 'Alone?'

Lombroso sighed. 'Yes, alone.'

Machinetti looked over towards his men. It seemed to James as if his new employer was about to be taken into custody. Then he saw Tullio stride over to Machinetti and whisper to him. Machinetti's face reddened.

'Thank you for your assistance, Professor,' Tullio said.

'But the note! There has to be some reason for it!' Machinetti protested.

Lombroso shrugged helplessly. 'I agree, but I cannot think of what it might be.'

'At the very least, you seem to be some kind of an inspiration for the killer,' said Machinetti. Lombroso's shoulders drooped. He looked tired, almost defeated. James caught Ottolenghi's eye. He nodded back, almost imperceptibly.

'Can we be of further assistance, Marshal?' Ottolenghi asked.

Machinetti paused and thought about it. He looked over to Tullio who shook his head firmly. 'Do not leave the city, Professor,' Machinetti said curtly, dismissing them with a haughty wave of the hand.

Tullio frowned at this lack of courtesy and bowed slightly towards Lombroso. 'Professor, thank you for your assistance. We may need to call on you again, with your permission.'

Lombroso nodded and started to walk away. James and Ottolenghi began to follow him. As they turned away and crossed the piazza James saw something out of the corner of his eye – a movement? He turned quickly and saw, or thought he saw, a dark figure disappear into the shadows. It was only for a split second and then it was gone. He shook his head and frowned to himself. Was he really so unaccustomed to the narrow streets that his eyes had begun to deceive him? He was sure that someone had been there and whoever it was had clearly not wanted to be seen. He turned and looked back, wondering if he should inform Machinetti or Tullio, but they were arguing loudly and clearly did not wish to be disturbed. He decided to leave them to it, thinking that he had probably imagined it anyway, and walked quickly to catch up with Lombroso who was walking quickly across the piazza towards the museum.

2

It cannot be denied that from time to time there have been
criminals who are true geniuses – creators of new forms of
crime, inventors of evil.   Lombroso, 1876, p 74

When they arrived back at the museum no one was in the
mood to eat. Lombroso declared himself in need of solitude
and Ottolenghi was required to return to his Madagascan
skulls. James took his leave, having been told to report back
the following day, and was more than glad of the opportunity
to contemplate the events of the morning. Back at his
lodgings, after he had eaten, he sat and began to write a letter
to Lucy.

As he wrote he reflected on all that he had seen: the
extraordinary exhibits in the museum, Lombroso's experiment with his complicated contraption – a dynamometer he
had called it. And then there was Sofia, who lingered in his
senses without invitation. There was something intriguing
about her. He could picture her form as clearly as if she was
standing before him at that very moment, her lustrous hair
hanging down her back, her wide mouth smiling – and all
the while she looked straight at him, almost as if she was
questioning his right to be there. He sat with his eyes shut,
breathing in the memory of her delicate earthy scent. But

then, despite his efforts to put it from his mind, a quite different aroma came to him – the cloying sour-sweet stench of what he had originally thought was death. He began to lose himself in thoughts of the terrible things he had seen, the body stiff with rigor mortis, the gaping cavity of bone and gristle of the face without the severed nose, the careful arrangement of the missing features holding down the bloody note. It was the stuff of nightmares.

He stared down at the empty page, unsure what to write. Lucy had a vivid enough imagination and was forever writing stories that would rival the most lurid sensation novel. If he told her all that he had witnessed then who knows what tales she might concoct. James grimaced to himself. He wouldn't be at all surprised if Aunt Agnes, a devout woman, fervent in her Protestantism, read Lucy's letters before she gave them to his sister. She had agreed to take care of Lucy only on the basis that her rules were strictly observed.

He knew that Lucy would be waiting anxiously for his news and that she would be more than happy to hear about the museum and all that had happened. But he was protect-ive of her. He could not help himself. She had been very young when their mother died after a long illness but at least she had time to become accustomed to the prospect of her loss. The fate of their father was a very different matter. Its sudden violent and unexpected nature had hit her very hard and James had striven to keep the terrible truth behind it from her, particularly his own part in it. He was all she had left of their closest family and, perhaps as a result, she idolised him and he did not want to alter that. He took a deep breath, picked up his pen and began.

Turin, November 1st, 1887

My dear Lucy,

I hope this letter finds you well. I arrived safely in the city on Tuesday and have settled into my lodgings which are comfortable. My main news is that I met Professor Lombroso today and he has engaged me as an assistant. I have not yet started work but I am very much looking forward to doing so. My fellow colleague is a man named Salvatore Ottolenghi, who seems a good sort. I know, of course, that were you here you would tell me that I was jumping to conclusions! Anyway, he smiles a great deal which makes me think that he and I will be friends. I am not yet sure what to make of Professor Lombroso himself. I find him a little overwhelming and his museum is full of the most bizarre exhibits, beyond anything even you could imagine.

No doubt you will scold me for not describing the appearance of my new acquaintances even though you know of old how difficult I find such an exercise. I dare say that if you were here you would ask me your usual questions — so here are my answers. If he was a member of the animal kingdom then I would say that the professor resembles a wise old owl and Ottolenghi is a taller, thinner version of him!

And Lucy, the city is so beautiful! I really cannot understand why it is not better known. It is full of baroque architecture and broad, shining streets full of grand palazzos. Everywhere I go I see fine sculptures and ornate fountains and there are museums and galleries around every corner.

Now, dear Lucy, please do not reproach me for the brevity of this letter. I assure you there is really not much else to say as little has happened but I will write again soon to tell you more of my adventures. Please give my warmest regards to our aunt.

Your devoted brother,

James

He looked again at his final sentence and grinned. Warmth and Aunt Agnes did not really go together. He could picture her now, a thin angular woman with a face that looked as if nothing resembling a smile would ever dare to cross it. The letter was short and somewhat bland but what else could he do? If he told Lucy what had really happened there was a risk that she would never get to read it. Better to receive this than nothing at all. Of course he could have mentioned Sofia, but what could he really say – that he had been attracted to a servant? Aunt Agnes would have a seizure, particularly following his rejection of Elspeth Gibson.

James cringed at the memory. Presumably in an effort to restore some stability to their circumstances, given their father's fate, Aunt Agnes had taken it upon herself to find him a wife and had engineered a number of meetings with Miss Gibson, a clergyman's daughter, who was one of the dullest young women he had ever encountered. Every other sentence from her (and there were not that many to choose from) had come from the bible or the prayer book. Lucy had taken to referring to her as 'Everlasting Elspeth' as, she said, ten minutes with her seemed like an eternity. Aunt Agnes, however, was a determined woman and, like a spectre at a feast, Elspeth was at every social event he attended and was a constant visitor to their home. His aunt made it clear that it was his duty to make 'a good marriage,' as she had put it, and he had almost believed her. Riven by guilt at his part in his father's fate and uncertain about his own future he was on the verge of doing his aunt's bidding. But when it came to the day when he was supposed to ask for Elspeth Gibson's hand he had found that he could not do it. The marriage would have made them both unhappy and what would have been the sense in that? James had inherited a romantic nature from his mother and wanted to follow her example, marrying for love not convenience, no matter what the consequences.

Aunt Agnes had been furious, not it seemed at Miss Gibson's alleged devastation, which James had somehow doubted as she had never seemed to do more than tolerate him, but at what 'people would say'. It was at this point that James knew that he had to escape, not just for the sake of his own sanity but also for Lucy's well-being. It was quite clear to him that if he was ever to forge an independent future for them, away from their father's legacy, he had to look further than Edinburgh.

As he sat in the fading light of the gloomy afternoon, James resolved to spend the rest of the day with his books. After all, he reasoned, if he was to be a worthy assistant to the professor then he should ensure that he was up to date with current thinking about criminality. He took out a selection of volumes from his travelling trunk and settled down to read.

Hours passed and the day gradually turned to night. Diligently he worked on, poring over his books, determined to be the brightest assistant Professor Lombroso had ever engaged. Suddenly the yellow flame of the gaslight flickered in the draught from the window. He looked up quickly and caught his breath. He thought for a moment that he saw a shadow of something on the wall but it was just his imagination. He sighed at his folly and all at once felt tired; the events of the day had caught up with him and all he could see in his mind's eye was the mutilated body of the victim and the malicious glare of the stone angel as it looked down upon them.

He went to bed, but sleep did not come easily. He tossed and turned in the darkness, tortured by memories of

Soldate's mutilated corpse and the feelings and recollections that it had produced in him. These thoughts were nurtured by his own night demons until, like a malignant tumour, they had almost completely infected him.

When he finally slept his dreams were punctuated by disturbing images. At first they were disjointed and made little sense. A few of the faces he had seen in photographs exhibited in Lombroso's museum floated before him. Some of them were cackling loudly as if caught up in some unknown moment of hysteria. Others hissed the words 'murderer' and 'killer' at him with an intensity so terrifying it made him want to turn and run, though his feet refused to obey him.

Then came the melody . . . the one that his sister was playing on the piano when the police arrived to tell them of what had befallen their father. It was a piece by Chopin. Again and again it played in his dream like a macabre music box. As he heard it he became aware that he was walking along a dark street. It had no ending and the buildings on either side were so tall that they seemed to lean in so that they were almost touching.

Next, he saw a body. It was lying in a pool of blood, a dark figure hunched menacingly over it. As he drew closer he saw the glint of a knife in the figure's hand. He thought, at first, that it was Lombroso but when the figure turned it had no face at all. He looked over to the corpse. It was his father, looking up at him with lifeless eyes. James tried to go to him but, almost overcome with a feeling of dread and fear, he could not. Then the faceless figure came towards him. It lifted the knife as if to strike and then looked up at him. And suddenly it had a face. It was his own.

James woke with a start, his nightshirt damp with sweat,

his heart pounding. Would he ever be able to leave his past behind? He went to the window and threw it open, taking gulps of the cool night air in an effort to calm himself. Gradually he felt better. It was only a dream after all. Given what he had seen it was hardly surprising that he had reacted to it. Indeed, Lombroso had also seemed to be badly affected by the sight. Was it possible that the professor had become unhinged by his own work? Obsession was not uncommon amongst academics, particularly scientists. He knew that much from bitter experience.

But then whoever had done this must surely be cruel and merciless and Lombroso did not seem to be either of these things. The note, of course – *A Tribute to Lombroso* – meant there had to be some connection. But James could not imagine Lombroso committing such a hideous crime. Admittedly they had only met once and so he had little of substance to assist him in assessing the professor's character. And that note was odd to say the least.

James closed the window and went over to his shabby armchair in the corner of the room. He sank down in it and closed his eyes, the better to analyse the matter. It was perfectly true that he did not want his new employer to be involved – and it was very clear that the killer had sought to implicate Lombroso, which suggested strongly that the professor was unlikely to be the murderer. What needed to be established was *why* the professor had been drawn into the crime in this way. If this could be discovered, it would surely be a simple matter to identify the culprit.

Having clarified things in his mind, he made the decision that he would offer his assistance in the matter. It was imperative that this crime was solved so Lombroso could continue with his experiments, unfettered by suspicion. Either that or be prevented from killing anyone else, whichever it turned out to be. Satisfied that he had reached a conclusion of sorts, James went back to his bed and fell soundly asleep.

3

*Impulsive crimes among animals, as among humans, are
frequently prompted by love.*   Lombroso, 1884, p 171

The next morning James made his way through the streets
of Turin to Lombroso's museum. It was a beautiful day, unseasonably warm, sunny and bright, with the snowy peaks
of the Alps clearly visible in the distance, watching over the
city like a group of guardian angels. But weather and the
scenery were wasted on James. He sat in a cab as it clattered
through the unfamiliar streets and stared into the distance.
The dream was still haunting him. He had so many questions
and only Lombroso, it seemed to him, would be able to
answer them.

He fingered his starched collar nervously. Was this whole
enterprise a foolish mistake? Should he leave the city now
before Lombroso found out his secret? And what if the
professor turned out to be a killer? Where would that leave
him? A chill travelled through his body as he realised what
was at stake.

He leaned back and clenched his fists as if he was about
to engage in hand-to-hand combat with his own fears.
Breathing deeply, he tried to steady his nerves. The smell of
the cab's interior combined unpleasantly with the odour of

the many bodies that had sat there before him. Suddenly it swerved to avoid a handcart being pulled slowly across the road by an elderly man who gesticulated angrily. He was so close that James could see his hostile glare and the spittle seeping from the corners of his snarling, toothless mouth as they drove past. The sight of it jolted him back to reality, reminding him of his purpose. It was then that he knew that he had no choice but to go on, for if he turned back now he would never be complete. It was a risk. He realised that he might not like what he discovered, but it seemed to him that not knowing was even worse.

Everything had now become further complicated by the murder. If he was innocent, James assumed that Lombroso would wish to give its investigation priority, given the use of his name on the note. It would be interesting to see him apply his theories to an actual crime and he hoped that perhaps the professor would allow him to help, even if that meant that he would have to wait a little longer to address his own problems.

James looked out of the window again in an effort to find some distraction and soon lost himself in the bustle of the city. Watching the Torinesi going about their business, he thought to himself that, at first glance, this place was not so very different from home. As in Edinburgh there were two contrasting sides to the city: both were built on old ground, one with broad, clean and straight streets and another of winding narrow lanes and alleyways. Here too street traders shouted out at passers-by in an effort to persuade them to buy their wares. The gentry strolled past, their noses high in the air as if trying to avoid the city smells that inevitably surrounded them – sewage, animal and human, sweat and filth; the stink of people, the stink of life.

In Turin, though, the odour was different from Edinburgh's. It had a slight undertone of fresh herbs, garlic and olive oil, wafting over from stalls that nestled under the walkways that lined the streets. How easy it would be for the uninitiated to see only the acceptable side of the place, the almost exotic golden glow of the piazzas and archways shining in the pale morning sunlight. One could simply brush aside the sight of the filthy beggars or the sharp-faced con men, ignore the bright-eyed thieves or the snarling pimps and their blousy prostitutes, turn away from the hidden grotesques of the city, lingering in dark corners waiting for night, all the sinister undercurrents that would sweep a man away in its filthy waters given half the chance. It was too late for him. He had already witnessed Turin's less salubrious side at first hand and knew that beneath this shining surface lay a darker underbelly of shadows and secrets. And he also knew the raw truth: that he was no different.

On the surface he was quite ordinary; a little pale perhaps, and serious, with a shock of dark hair that he habitually pushed away from his forehead. A colleague of his father's had once told him that he had a noticeable pallor, as if he had rarely seen daylight, and that his eyes had a distant and haunted quality. When he had mentioned it to Lucy she had told him that he looked 'romantic' as if he was 'a man with a past'. He had not said so but, given the burden he carried at the time, he had thought that description was apt and hardly surprising. After all, it was quite possible that his appearance was a mere reflection of the state of his soul.

Finally the cab pulled up outside the museum. As before he knocked at the huge wooden doors and was met by Sofia. Today she was brusque, ushering him in as if she was too busy to pass the time of day with him. James was disappointed. He had hoped for a smile at least. He decided to regard her silence as a challenge.

'It's a beautiful day, isn't it? Is it always like this in November?' he said as she shut the door.

'No,' replied Sofia tersely as she took his hat and cane.

James tried again. 'So then it usually rains then, does it?'

'*Sì.*'

'Heavily?'

Sofia sighed. 'Sometimes.'

'How often?' he asked following her across the hallway. 'Every day, once a week?'

'Sometimes,' she repeated.

'In Edinburgh it rains all the time.'

There was no reply.

'Does it ever snow here?'

'Follow me please,' she said firmly.

'Is there ever—'

'No, never,' she replied. It was clear that she was not in the mood to talk.

He admitted defeat and dutifully followed her as they passed through various corridors, heavy with the fragrances of beeswax and lavender and just a hint of formaldehyde. Occasionally she would pause outside a door and James would think that they had reached their destination. Then, having waited just long enough to tantalise him, she would spin on her heel and on they would go. There was something sensual about the way she moved. Her bold walk and swinging hips reminded him of the girls who used to come out of the public houses in Edinburgh's less salubrious areas, once they had closed for the night. And yet her movements had a certain elegance and grace that belied her sordid beginnings. There was something about her that both moved and disturbed him but he could not say for sure what that something might be. He decided that the only way to break the spell she had over him was to try again to engage her in conversation. Besides, there was something he needed to know.

'Excuse me,' he said, hesitantly.

Sofia stopped and turned to face him. '*Sì?*'

'I heard you say something about the gates of Hell yesterday. What did you mean?'

She looked at him intently and murmured under her breath as she had done the day before. James didn't know exactly what she said but it did not sound entirely complimentary. She turned away as if to go and James seized her by her wrist.

'Wait! Answer me!'

'No!' She shook his hand away and carried on, turning left into a corridor. James quickly followed her and was about to try to speak to her again when he noticed that they were not alone. Lining the passageway were full-length skeletons, standing like sentinels guarding the very gates of Hell that Sofia seemed so reluctant to discuss. James halted, staring at them. Then he heard a low laugh. He looked up indignantly. Sofia was leaning against the wall next to one of the skeletons, a wry smile on her face. 'They will not bite!'

James looked at the nearest one to him and pulled a face at it. 'Are you sure about that?'

'*Sì,*' she said. 'I will not let them!'

James looked at the skeletons and smiled as a thought entered his head. 'Does the professor make you dust them?'

She laughed. '*Sì,* every day.'

'And do they have much to say?'

She paused, her head on one side as if she was giving

serious consideration to his question. 'No, they are very boring . . . for criminals.'

'What sort of criminals?'

'Murderers, thieves, pimps—'

'And prostitutes?' he said without thinking.

Sofia's smile disappeared and she looked at him haughtily. 'No, only criminals. Come, signore, we must go. The professor is waiting.'

'Oh, but can you not introduce me to one of these gentlemen, before we go?' James asked, in an effort to return the conversation to its previous levity.

'I will not. For one thing they have no conversation and for another . . .' She paused.

'What?'

'For another they might lead you astray and we cannot have that!'

'Do you enjoy your work, Sofia?'

Sofia shrugged and started to walk away. 'You ask a lot of questions. No wonder the professor likes you!'

James realised that she had no intention of answering him but at least they had spoken, which was a start – but of what, he wondered. Finally Sofia paused at a doorway, knocked and ushered him into a room then left.

It was not the one he had found himself in the day before, although it too had shelves from floor to ceiling, but instead of the various artefacts that he had examined, there were what seemed like hundreds of skulls, staring down at him, each with a label attached.

In the centre of the room was a contraption that in some ways resembled the one he had assisted Professor Lombroso with the day before. This one, however, had no straps. There was a platform in the centre and some dials and metal rulers.

James had started to examine it, lifting each piece with care and trying to work out exactly what it was for, when the door opened and Lombroso bounded in. He slapped him on the back with such enthusiasm that he almost lost his footing.

'Ah, Murray, you have returned. I thought perhaps you might have changed your mind and abandoned us!'

'Not at all, Professor,' he replied truthfully. 'If anything I am even more determined to stay, if you will have me, that is. I wanted to ask you about yesterday—'

'Young man,' Lombroso interrupted, 'I am delighted that you are still wishing to assist me! Welcome to my laboratory.' He beamed at him and shook his hand energetically.

James was somewhat taken aback. It was almost as if the murder had never happened. He wondered whether to mention it again but decided against it. Clearly Lombroso did not wish to talk about it at present and he was hardly in a position to force the issue. He resolved to bring it up later, perhaps over lunch.

Lombroso guided him towards the door. 'Now, allow me to show you round properly. I will take you through each room and I hope that by the end of the tour you will have reached a full understanding of what I am trying to achieve.'

James nodded. All doubt finally left him. This was where he was meant to be; he had a purpose, and in order to achieve it he knew that he needed to be single-minded in its pursuit.

He looked over to the contraption that he had begun to examine a few moments before. 'Could I ask you first, Professor, is that machine a Benedikt craniophore?'

Lombroso smiled at him. 'It is indeed. I am delighted that you recognise it.'

'I have only seen drawings before, Professor. Do you use it often?'

'We do, Murray, we do,' Lombroso said proudly. 'In fact I would say that this is perhaps the most significant item in the museum.' He went over to it and began to stroke it, almost as if it were a family pet. 'As I expect you know, it is used for holding and orienting skulls in order to measure them. I find it rather difficult to use, like so many other instruments. That is one of the areas in which I am hoping you will be able to assist me.' He paused for a second and looked dreamily into the distance, a soft smile on his face as if he was remembering something fondly. Then all of a sudden he turned and walked away, beckoning to James to follow. 'Come, young man, let's us start our tour. There is much ground to be covered!'

The first room contained a number of oversized models of carnivorous plants and Lombroso took great delight in declaring each and every one of them a murderer. James began to laugh and then, seeing the professor's serious expression, wished he hadn't.

'You see this reprobate here, Murray? This is the drosera. When an insect lands here . . .' He indicated a small leafy disc. 'Snap! It is immediately enfolded by these tentacles. They compress the poor creature, sucking the life out of it. Lured by a sweet and honeyed promise and then digested to death – it is not a pleasant way to die. If that is not murder then I do not know what is!'

James frowned. He was not entirely convinced by Lombroso's argument. 'Don't plants eat insects in order to survive, Professor? Is that really murder?'

Lombroso peered at him. 'Survival may be the motive but the intent to kill is still there.' James looked at him doubtfully. Undeterred, Lombroso went on to describe further acts of carnage in the animal kingdom. 'Horses, bulls and deer all fight and kill for control of their group. Humans do just the same to further their ambitions. Gorillas kill any male rivals to ensure that there is only one leader – another very human criminal trait. Murder is rife among animals. Cannibalism seems to be a particular favourite.'

James was still sceptical. 'So, animals can be guilty of crime, just as humans can? But surely it is in their nature. They know nothing else.'

'Exactly, Murray, you have the point exactly! It is the same for mankind, or some members of it at any rate. Some are born to crime. They have no choice in the matter. There is no question of free will here. Did you know that in ancient and even medieval times it was common for people to convict and punish animals for their actions? It seems that they were right to do so!'

He beckoned James over to the other side of the room and pointed at a large photograph of what appeared to be a series of portraits of dark-skinned men.

'These are the faces of savages, Murray, and we must equate their crimes with those of animals. They know no better. Our own criminals are just the same. Both are examples of atavistic man at his worst.'

'What form does this connection take, Professor?' James asked.

Lombroso turned and frowned at him. 'Have you not studied the writings of Mr Darwin, young man? Really, I would have thought that you would have acquired at least a basic knowledge of such matters before coming here.'

James had, of course, despite his religious upbringing. His mother had told him that Christians had been forbidden from defending any scientific opinions that contravened the faith. Before he could protest, Lombroso began to sigh and shake his head sadly, muttering under his breath. Then he began to speak slowly and carefully as if addressing a small child.

'Our origins are in the animal kingdom. It is hardly a leap of faith to suggest that those humans of a more primitive nature might possess similar criminal tendencies.'

Try as he might James could not let that go. 'But what of free will, Professor? Surely that is where animals differ?'

'Free will! Absurd! You have much to learn!'

'Actually, I think he has a point,' declared a voice in a soft American drawl.

James turned and saw a man leaning on the doorpost, smoking a cigar. He wore an expensive-looking coat with an astrakhan collar. Everything about him exuded ostentatious wealth. Even his thick dark hair gleamed as if he had been anointed with good fortune. It was brushed back revealing a broad forehead, strangely unlined, almost like that of a child. He looked over to them and smiled, sardonically, as if he despised them. He had sharp teeth and even sharper features, giving him an almost lupine quality. His nose was prominent, almost beak-like, but it was his eyes that James really noticed. They were steely grey, cold, almost lifeless, as if he did not, could not, care about anything or anyone and yet, despite this or perhaps because of it, James could not help but look into them.

Lombroso pursed his lips as the man sauntered into the room and handed James a card. It said,

WALTER B. HORTON
ALIENIST
SAN FRANCISCO

'Dr Horton is from America,' said Lombroso in a tone that suggested this explained everything. 'I thought you were arriving tomorrow, Horton. The debate is not until then.'

'On the contrary, Professor. I have been sampling the "delights" that Turin has to offer for some weeks now.'

'Debate?' James enquired.

'The professor is crossing swords with DeClichy tomorrow evening, to open the symposium. The motion is "Criminals are born not made." It's a sell-out, I understand. Should be a good show!'

'It is a debate, not a circus,' Lombroso said icily.

Horton grinned. 'I could say something about clowns but I won't.'

'Dr Horton enjoys arguing for its own sake,' Lombroso said dismissively.

Horton laughed. 'What he means is he doesn't like it when someone dares to disagree with him.'

'I am more than happy to discuss my theories with equals, Signor Horton, but I do not consider you as such.'

'What about DeClichy? What do you think about him?'

'I think he is wrong, as you will find out tomorrow,' Lombroso said, 'assuming, that is, that you can keep your own views to yourself long enough to hear those of others.'

'Well, you know, Professor, I have as much right to an opinion as the next man.'

'You have bought that right, not earned it.'

'Maybe so, but you don't have a monopoly on knowledge. Anyone with a brain can read a book!'

Lombroso sighed impatiently. 'How can I help you, Dr Horton? I am rather busy showing my new assistant round the museum this morning.'

'I was just being sociable, paying my respects and all. Don't mind if I follow you around, do you?'

Lombroso gave a look that made it absolutely clear that he minded very much but Horton had already set off to the next room. The professor sighed with resignation and went after him, again beckoning at James to follow.

'What have we here?' Horton asked, giving a low whistle.

'These are examples of criminal pictography,' Lombroso replied.

'He means drawings by criminals – quite common, or so I've heard,' Horton said. James thought that the American had a way of expressing himself that made him sound as if he always knew better.

Lombroso went on as if Horton had not spoken.

'As you can see, we have examples on paper, clothing and pottery. It is interesting to see the way in which criminals express themselves through art. Many of them seem to have a strange compulsion to do so. They're probably frustrated by their inability to express themselves through the use of language alone, although it is true that I have also seen literate criminals use illustration in this way.'

James looked curiously at the examples before him. Some of them were fairly primitive in their use of images but others were quite sophisticated. One in particular got his attention. It portrayed the bloody murder of an entire family including a number of small children. A man stood, surrounded by bodies, wielding a pickaxe in one hand and a club in the other. His expression was terrifying – not because it was particularly realistic but because of its lack of any emotion other than sheer determination. James peered at it and shivered slightly.

'Here we have another similarity between the criminal and the savage,' Lombroso announced with a note of triumph.

'Well, maybe,' Horton added.

Lombroso continued, ignoring him again. He picked up a framed piece of skin, once bright with tattoos but now faded.

'The criminal often uses his own skin as a canvas. They are often rather ingenious. Look at this!' Lombroso picked up another frame. This contained a photograph and James drew nearer to see it closely. It was of a tattooed arm, in the crook of which was the figure of a naked woman, her legs splayed. 'As the arm moves, the lady, though I doubt that we can describe her as such, masturbates!'

Horton laughed loudly. 'Well, would you look at that?'

The room also contained photographs of documents written by criminals, proving, according to Lombroso, that handwriting could reveal criminal character. Horton moved around the room, examining the exhibits as Lombroso told James about an experiment using hypnosis that he had conducted in order to confirm, as he put it, the atavistic nature of the handwriting of criminals.

'Having mesmerised him, I suggested to a young man of honest habits that he was in fact the brigand La Gala. His handwriting, normally so civilised and cultivated as to be almost feminine, became rough and malformed, resembling that of some very well-known criminals. Boggia, for instance, and Francesconi, both cross their *t*s with flourishes, you know. I was astounded. The young man even kept some of the brigand's characteristics when told that he was now an infant.'

Horton, who had been listening with interest, suddenly interjected, much to Lombroso's evident irritation, 'Maybe it was the effect of the hypnosis. He was in a trance, after all. That can't do much for your handwriting!'

Lombroso breathed heavily through his nose and went on, 'Then I returned him to the status of the brigand and, lo, the script was as rough as ever but had a certain childish roundness about it. Fascinating!'

'Will you be writing that up for the new edition of *L'uomo delinquente*, Professor?' asked James. 'I heard you were working on one.'

'I wonder why it hasn't been translated into English?' Horton said, his eyes glinting mischievously.

Lombroso grunted. It was clearly a sore point.

'I'm sure it will be before long, Professor,' James said.

Lombroso turned and beamed at him. 'We understand each other, young man. That is a good thing.' He patted his stomach and took out his pocket watch. 'Now I think it is time for some lunch. I will take you somewhere special. We should mark the beginning of our work together, I think.'

Lombroso nodded at Horton, as if to dismiss him, and then turned on his heel and walked quickly out of the room. James didn't know what to say. He thought that Horton would have been offended but he merely shrugged and bid him good day.

'Don't worry, I'm used to it,' Horton said in a reassuring tone, as he ostentatiously pulled out a silver cigar case and casually offered one to James. 'By the way, has he asked you to one of his famous salons yet?'

James shook his head.

'Don't worry, he will. They're quite something. Anyone who's anyone turns up there at one time or another. See you there!'

With that he gave a short bow and left. James followed

him out and hurried to catch up with Lombroso who had set a challenging pace, perhaps in an effort to shake off Horton. They paused only to collect their hats and canes then on they went, striding through the streets of Turin together. There was little opportunity to take in the fine baroque architecture, such was the punishing speed at which Lombroso was travelling. Occasionally he would slow down in order to greet a colleague or a friend but, for the most part, they swept along in silence, through the stone arcades that lined the streets and across piazzas, passing fountains and fine palazzos shining in the thin autumn sunlight.

James began to speculate as to what might be awaiting them. He was looking forward to trying some of the local cuisine for his landlady was that rarest of beings, an Italian who could not cook. She served up stodgy English food, presumably in the vague hope that it would make him feel at home, and he was hoping that at last he would taste something more appetising than boiled sausages and suet pudding. Still, at least she had not heard of Scottish cuisine, which was something, he supposed.

On they travelled, walking through the Porta Palazzo market, a Torinese institution. The sights and smells of fresh garlic, wild mushrooms and other produce almost overwhelmed him. Pyramids of gigantic yellow peaches were balanced precariously next to ripe strawberries, the last of the season, sent up from the South – not so much an offering but more a brash boast of the superiority of the climate and its fruits. Everywhere fearsome-looking women pushed and pulled at the produce, checking the ripeness and readiness for their planned dishes. Small, ragged boys ran round shouting cheekily at the stallholders and their customers who shouted back and shook fists in the air in a futile gesture towards discipline.

Soon they were in another section where the smell of the sea was unmistakable. James peered at the gleaming mounds of fish, their mouths hanging open sullenly as if sulking at their predicament. Then it was game, rabbits and hares hung upside down from butchers' hooks, blank eyes staring into nothingness. Brightly coloured birds swung beside them as if still in flight. Nearby, haunches of unidentifiable animals marbled with yellow fat glistened in the sunlight as butchers' muscled arms swung their cleavers into the yielding flesh. On the outskirts cheeses of all varieties were piled high on rickety tables, some oozing invitingly, others enclosed within white velvety rind waiting to be cut into to reveal the creamy white delights beneath. He longed to pause and take it all in, but on Lombroso strode, a man of purpose – and being Italian, that purpose was his lunch.

4

Criminals are generally very illogical and always imprudent.

Lombroso, 1876 p 72

When they arrived at their destination James's first thought was that his definition of special was rather different from that of the professor. Their lunch venue was a trattoria in the older section of the city, near the river. It looked dilapidated to say the least. Its whitewashed walls were decidedly grey and the sign hung precariously by broken hinges. Inside it was dark and cool and the tables, benches and chairs that were scattered around the room were basic and uninviting. It occurred to him that this was more like a working-man's eatery rather than the fine restaurant he had been expecting. James wondered how the food would compare, but it seemed that he was not to be disappointed for the aroma that greeted them was an appetising one of herbs and frying meat. And there, sitting at a table, evidently waiting for them, was Otto-lenghi.

Lombroso held up a hand in acknowledgement and they made their way over to him. The table was tucked into a corner next to the kitchen and was rather small for three. Once seated, they were forced to hunch together as if keeping warm, elbows touching in an intimacy that James found unfamiliar. He noticed how Ottolenghi looked as if he had almost folded himself in two in an effort to get his long limbs into such a limited space. Every now and then the door swung open, giving an unedifying view of a fat, sweaty chef toiling over an open stove. The proprietor, a man greeted as Paolo by Lombroso, would run into the kitchen and hurl some colourful abuse at the chef who responded loudly in kind. James fervently hoped that the food was more refined than its creator.

Eventually Paolo came over to their table and spoke at length to Lombroso, who was clearly an old friend. They chattered away in what James assumed was Piedmontese, the local dialect, for he could only make out odd words and phrases. Lombroso gestured towards him and Paolo looked at him curiously and bowed. James stood up to shake his hand and found himself being embraced. Once released, he sat down again, confused. Such intimacy between men was virtually unknown in Scotland and he was unprepared for it. He looked around for menus but it seemed that the choice was to be made for them.

'I will bring you what is good,' Paolo said slowly in Italian, presumably for James's benefit, and backed away to the kitchen, staring at James as if he was some kind of exhibit.

Lombroso sat contentedly viewing the grimy room. There were several other occupied tables and most of their fellow diners looked somewhat down at heel. James caught the eye of a man at the next table who smiled broadly at him, revealing a set of rotting teeth. An elderly woman eyed him suspiciously from a corner, gathering her basket to her as if James was about to rob her. On the other side of the room two other men were arguing vociferously about something, presumably a number of gold watches revealed in the coat of one of them as he held it open for viewing. A larger group of men sat at a round table in the centre of the room. Raucous and rough, they threw their heads back as they laughed and slapped their hands on the table when someone told a dirty joke. Lombroso was evidently enjoying the spectacle as he was watching intently and occasionally nodding vigorously, presumably at something he had seen or overheard. James was about to ask him why he had chosen the place when Paolo arrived through the kitchen doors like a recently fired cannon ball and placed before them plates of small fish, glistening invitingly in a bright green sauce, and a basket of crusty bread. Glasses of cool white wine were brought and Lombroso nodded in satisfaction. James looked at the food with interest and realised that not only did he not know exactly what it was, but that he had no idea how to go about eating it. What was the correct etiquette? Did one need cutlery? He thought back to when his mother was alive. Somewhere in his mind existed the tiniest spark of a memory. He was sure she had told him of a similar dish but he could not remember it in detail.

Ottolenghi, sensing his discomfort, smiled amiably at him. 'Anchovies in a herb sauce, a local delicacy.' With that he took some of the bread and dipped it in the sauce, scooping up some of the anchovies as he did so. Relieved, James did likewise as Lombroso looked on, beaming at them as if he had cooked and produced the food himself.

'You will not find food as good as this anywhere in Turin,' he stated proudly.

James was surprised. 'Surely there are better places? After all, there are so many restaurants and hotels in the city.'

Ottolenghi shook his head. 'Many of them serve French

cuisine. This is authentic Piedmontese fare, not as fancy, but the flavours are far superior.'

Lombroso nodded in agreement. 'This is real food eaten by real people. There is a place for French cuisine, of course. They always serve it at official dinners and it can be quite delicious. But we like to come here and experience proper cooking, basic but honest.'

As James tucked into the fish and enjoyed its piquant flavours, he had to admit that his dining companions were right about the food, if not the ambience. One thing puzzled him though. Neither of them had mentioned the murder. He had expected it to be discussed at some length, given the apparent connection to Lombroso, but it had not been spoken of once. Perhaps, he thought, they were waiting for him to raise it. He cleared his throat in preparation.

'Professor,' he began, 'I wondered what you thought about what happened yesterday?'

Ottolenghi frowned at him and shook his head.

Lombroso looked irritated. 'Please, Murray, let us not speak of such unsavoury matters whilst we are eating. There is a time and place for these things and it is not here and now.'

'Of course, Professor,' James said, beginning to wonder when and where *would* be suitable. Could there be some other reason for the professor to be reluctant to discuss it? He glanced over to Ottolenghi and decided to raise it with him when they were on their own. Perhaps he could shed some light on this mystery.

Once they had finished the anchovies their plates were scooped up and bowls of steaming brown stew were placed unceremoniously in front of them. Paolo then produced a plate of yellow glistening slabs of something he did not recognise. A carafe of red wine was also brought with three dingy glasses that, in company with everything and everyone else in the place, looked as if they had seen better days.

'Tuck in, my boy, tuck in!' urged Lombroso.

James gingerly put a piece of what looked like meat in his mouth and began to chew. It was surprisingly good, tender and flavoursome. It seemed that he had misjudged Paolo and his fat swearing chef.

'Have some polenta with your *finanziera*, it's very good!' Ottolenghi handed him the plate of yellow slabs and he took one. He bit carefully into the ochre crust and tasted the creamy combination of cheese and butter in its centre.

'What is in the *finanziera*?' he asked.

Ottolenghi smiled. 'Are you sure you want to know?'

James nodded enthusiastically.

'Chicken organs and offal.'

James stopped chewing momentarily. Then, as the taste and the texture of the food had its effect, he grinned and continued to eat with relish. Lombroso slapped him on the back with such enthusiasm that his face almost ended up in his meal. 'Good man, good man! And the wine, you must try some. It's Barolo from Paolo's cousin who has a small vine-yard outside the city.'

Ottolenghi poured the wine into the glasses. It was soft and ruby red. Finally James began to relax a little but he still wondered why Lombroso had chosen this particular location even though the food was so good. Surely there were more refined places with similar culinary standards. Lombroso seemed to have an uncanny knack of knowing what he was thinking.

'We are here as scientists, to observe,' he murmured quietly. 'Watch, you may learn something.'

Ottolenghi grinned and nodded towards the other tables encouragingly. James gave him a sceptical look and then noticed Lombroso frowning. 'Murray does not yet understand. Ottolenghi, tell us who we have here.'

'Over there are two *ricettatori* or "fences", as I think you would say in English,' Ottolenghi said, pointing at the two men arguing over watches. 'Their trade is in stolen goods.' James nodded. He had seen their like in some of the inns he had frequented as a student and the Italian version did not seem to differ much from their Scottish counterparts.

'The men in the middle are a band of robbers. They originated in Sicily but have come here for richer pickings,' Ottolenghi went on.

Lombroso nodded. 'Look at their faces, Murray, and tell me what you see.'

James opened his mouth, about to speak, but Lombroso lifted a restraining hand. 'Take your time. These things cannot be rushed.'

James observed the subjects carefully as he ate. This was an opportunity to make an impression and he did not want to squander it. Eventually he spoke. 'The fences have facial hair, but it's quite scanty and they look rather shifty. They both have quite sharp features.'

Lombroso nodded enthusiastically. 'Anything else?'

'Yes, they are both thin with rounded shoulders.'

'Capital, Murray, capital! You are a natural anthropologist! And what of our friends on the centre table?'

'They have thick, dark hair. Two of them have prominent ears and the one on the left looks like a monkey!' declared James. He was so caught up in his description that he failed to notice that he had been overheard. The men looked at them hard with threat in their eyes.

'Time to go, I think,' said Ottolenghi briskly. With that he threw some money on the table, took up his hat and made his way towards the door. Lombroso followed behind him but James found his path of exit blocked by the man he had just compared to a monkey. The man leaned towards him and grimaced as if he was about to hit him. James did not want to get into an unseemly brawl in front of Lombroso but for a minute it seemed almost unavoidable. He began to square up to his foe but Paolo saw what was happening and he approached the man and whispered something in his ear. The supposed villain stood aside, a smile of mockery on his swarthy face, and James sidestepped him and made for the door. One of the men rose as if to follow but Ottolenghi casually went over to him and slipped some notes into his hand. He nodded appreciatively and sat down again. As they left and made their way outside, the men's loud laughter followed them along the passage.

They walked towards the river at a brisk pace. As Lombroso put it, pursuit was unlikely but with the volatile mind of the criminal one can never be sure. He was smiling as he said this, so James was not sure how seriously to take the threat but thought it safer to accept it at face value.

When they arrived at the river bank Lombroso suggested that they could now afford to slow down a little and they strolled along it in a companionable silence, each lost in his own thoughts. The events of the previous day seemed a long time ago.

Being November, the sun was already setting, casting a rosy glow over the water. As they walked through the Parco Valentino towards the Piazza, the Via Po and the university, James thought to himself that he felt happier and more fulfilled than he had for a long time. His initial reason for going to Turin had almost been forgotten and he began to wonder whether he could finally put the past behind him and begin afresh.

Suddenly Lombroso shivered slightly. It might have been the cold air. After all, the sun had almost set and dusk was nearly upon them, but James wondered if, despite his best efforts to put it from his mind, the murder of Giuseppe Soldati had returned to haunt the professor. Again the tiniest of doubt about Lombroso intruded into his own mind but he put it aside, preferring for the moment to enjoy the experiences his new life was providing.

Lombroso turned to Ottolenghi. 'I must go back to the university now. There is some work I must finish. Why don't you take Murray for a tour of the city? Then perhaps you could go for some refreshment in one of our fine cafés and tell him of our current projects? I will see you both later at the house – if it is convenient for you, Murray, of course.'

James nodded, happy to be included. They watched Lombroso hurry off through the park into the distance.

Ottolenghi smiled at him. 'He must like you. It took me two months to get an invitation to one of his salons and you've only been here two days!'

James's eyes widened. 'I didn't realise that was what he meant.'

Ottolenghi laughed. 'How do you feel – nervous?'

'Should I be?'

'A little, perhaps, it is a kind of initiation, I suppose, in the professor's eyes.'

James grinned. 'I'd better pass then!'

Ottolenghi patted him on the back. 'Don't worry; I'm sure you will. Anyway I'll be there to help, if you need me and I'm sure that you won't. I think perhaps we will need to discuss your strategy, though.'

James looked up to the skies in mock despair. 'Ach, you think I need a strategy – that will need a drink!'

'Well, maybe strategy isn't quite the right word! But tour first, drink later,' laughed Ottolenghi, 'and not too much. You'll need to have your wits about you at the salon.'

They wandered out of the park and towards the Via Po where they hired a cab. Ottolenghi was an excellent guide and they drove through the streets, pausing every now and again for him to point out this building or that landmark – museums, galleries, palazzos and piazzas – until James was almost intoxicated by the sight of them all. Then they took a turn out of the centre of the city and drove through some of the less prosperous areas. The people stared at them listlessly as they drove past, as if want had drained the life from them. James could smell the poverty as it drifted in through the windows. No olive oil or herbs here, just filth and decay. He recalled smelling the same odour as he walked through the streets from the asylum on his way back from visiting his father. The thought of it made him feel nauseous. Once or twice James looked over to his companion. His face was kind and artless, trustworthy somehow. Like Lombroso his eyes darted about, taking everything in, and occasionally he would mutter something as if he was making a mental note. Eventually he rapped on the window with his cane and the driver nodded, having been told of their final destination before they set out. They had arrived at the Piazza Solferino.

Ottolenghi indicated a café on the corner. As they went in, James looked in wonder at the décor, which was heavy with gilt and mirrors, like a Parisian palace. In the centre of the room was a pyramid of delicacies, perched precariously on one another, little toasts loaded with salami and ham, quails' eggs, roasted peppers and tomatoes, olives, small balls of rice that had been deep fried until golden, tiny white cheeses and sandwiches cut so small that they looked as if they belonged in a doll's house. Ottolenghi smiled at James's expression.

'Caffè Norman is famous for its *stuzzichini*. We will be offered a plate of them with our drinks.'

He nodded in satisfaction. Despite the glories of their lunch, the walk and the tour had given him an appetite; or perhaps it was the sight of hunger in the eyes of the poor. James felt guilty that he could enjoy all of this when those they had seen earlier would be grateful for even a morsel of what they were about to eat. But of course it didn't last. He reasoned that depriving himself would not help anyone so there was little point in worrying. As they walked through the café, marvelling at the food on display, the sights he had seen less than an hour ago quickly began to leave his memory and by the time they sat down had quite gone.

They settled in a corner and Ottolenghi ordered some wine. This was smoother and lighter than Paolo's though it still had a fruity taste.

'Chianti, from Firenze,' Ottolenghi informed him.

'It's good,' James said as he sipped at it gratefully. It was particularly welcome, as the autumn sunshine had given way to a distinctly chilly evening. 'What do you make of last night?' he asked, longing to talk about the murder.

Ottolenghi looked at him thoughtfully. 'It's difficult to say. It was clearly pre-meditated. Odd about the note too, and written in blood. A strange business.'

'I wanted to ask the professor about it but—'

'He obviously doesn't wish to discuss the matter,' Otto-lenghi interrupted.

'But surely we should investigate; after all it is hanging over him, and if the university hears of it then . . .' He tailed off, not quite knowing what the consequences might be.

'I suppose you're right. They might stop the symposium and that would be a great blow. It might also give some ammunition to his enemies. Still, the professor must know that and I wouldn't like to act against his wishes. He can be very stubborn.'

'Who are these enemies?' James asked, thinking it strange that someone of Lombroso's professional stature could be under threat.

Ottolenghi counted them off on his fingers. 'Fellow academics, the university authorities, the judiciary, politicians, the police, the Church; he's upset all of them at some point or another. If he gives any of them the slightest opportunity to bring him down they're bound to take it.'

James was shocked. 'Surely that's all the more reason to at least try solving this murder, even if we have to work with Machinetti.'

Ottolenghi shook his head. 'Ah, Machinetti. There's a story in that. There's no love lost between him and the professor.'

'Could they not put that to one side – just for this?'

'I doubt it. I think it runs pretty deep. All I know is that they worked together on a case once and it didn't go well. Ever since then they've been at loggerheads and the professor flatly refuses to have anything to do with him.'

'Perhaps we could make one or two informal enquiries,' James suggested. 'He couldn't object to that, surely?'

Ottolenghi sipped his drink as he considered this. 'Well, I imagine it couldn't do any harm to revisit the scene of the crime. But that will have to wait until tomorrow. You have to get through your initiation first and we should concentrate on that for now.'

James agreed. 'Who is likely to be there?'

'Well, you've met Horton already I hear, so you know him.'

'Yes, although I can't say I warmed to the man. There was something odd about him but I can't quite place it.'

'Then there is Borelli, if he can get back from Paris in time.'

'Who's he?'

'He's a lawyer, a professor at the university and a close friend of our professor's. They have worked together on several projects over the last few years.'

'Anyone else?'

'Madame Tarnovsky will be there.'

'Yes, the professor mentioned that. I'd really like to meet her. I've read several of her monographs on the female offender. I'm actually looking forward to this evening now!' James paused. 'And of course, with all of these experts on crime in one place it would be a wonderful opportunity to consult them about the murder.'

Ottolenghi poured some more Chianti. 'So tell me, Murray, how long have you been qualified?'

'Not long.'

James wondered if the somewhat abrupt change of subject was intentional. Ottolenghi seemed almost as reluctant as the professor to get involved in the investigation of Soldati's death.

'And what brought you to medicine?'

'My father was a doctor. He specialised in diseases of the mind.' James paused, recognising, not for the first time, the irony of such a statement.

'Are you in private practice? They tell me that is where the money is.'

James laughed ruefully. 'Not in Edinburgh. There are too many doctors and not enough wealthy patients to go round for that to be true. No. I was working with my father until . . . recently. I haven't practised on my own account yet. I don't know if could now.'

'Oh, I see,' replied Ottolenghi, who evidently didn't.

James looked at his new friend's puzzled expression and wondered whether or not he should confide in him. He decided against it. They had not known each other long enough. Perhaps one day he would tell him everything but not yet. 'And you, Ottolenghi, are you a medical doctor?' he asked.

Ottolenghi smiled and nodded. 'I am indeed, though it seems a long time since I have tried to heal anyone. These days my patients are either already dead or perfectly healthy.'

'How long have you worked for the professor?'

'A while now. He is such a great mentor and I have learned a great deal from him.'

'Do you agree with all of his theories?' James asked, curious to see if Ottolenghi shared some of his own misgivings.

There was a pause. 'Well, not all. The professor is a great man but he is sometimes—'

James grinned. 'A little hasty in some of his conclusions, perhaps?'

Ottolenghi smiled back. 'I think I had better leave it there before I get myself into trouble!'

A waiter brought over their *stuzzichini*, a welcome diversion that allowed James to change the subject back to the evening to come.

'Will Madame Tarnovsky be giving a paper at the salon?'

'No, it's more informal than that. It's a forum for discussion really. I think the professor has a soft spot for the lady, though, so make sure you are attentive to her views.'

'That won't be difficult. She has done some fascinating work in Prague. I hope she'll discuss it.'

'I daresay she will if she can get a word in but there is competition. Oskar Reiner from Berlin will be there and he has done some very interesting work on eroticism in crime with a special interest in vampirism, I believe.'

'Vampirism! That sounds interesting,' James said, wondering what connection there could be between such supernatural tales and crime.

'It is. You should read his paper,' Ottolenghi said matter-of-factly, as if it was a natural subject for academic discussion. 'And of course some of our homegrown experts will be there too. They will all, no doubt, have plenty to say, and there's DeClichy, of course.'

'I got the impression that the professor doesn't have much time for him. Why would he be invited?'

'Something you should know about the professor, he thrives on conflict; that's why having so many enemies doesn't bother him. He considers DeClichy to be so wrong that it makes him look right. That's why he's agreed to debate with him at the symposium. He is very fixed in his ideas about things. Once he has made a decision then nothing will change it.'

'Certainty in science has got to be a good thing, surely.'

'Up to a point, although I have heard it argued that uncertainty is even more valuable. At any rate, certain or not, I sometimes wonder if the professor goes too far. No one is infallible after all, not even him. There are quite a few people in the city who would enjoy proving just that.'

Ottolenghi stared thoughtfully out of the window, his brows furrowed. His silence made it clear that he did not wish to discuss the topic further so James resolved to take a leaf out of his book and change the subject.

'Is there anything I should know for this evening?'

'Mmmm,' replied Ottolenghi. 'I don't think so. If in doubt ask a question. They all love to talk about their work and it will make you look interested.'

'I am interested.' James laughed. 'It's why I'm here after all – to learn.'

'Is it?' asked Ottolenghi. 'If you don't mind me saying so, you look like a man with quite another purpose.'

James stared at him. 'What do you mean?'

'Nothing, my friend, nothing. It's just that you seem to me to be here for a particular reason – as well as learning, I mean.'

James paused. He looked at Ottolenghi's open features and saw a man he could trust. 'There is something. But I don't think I can talk of it now . . . I will, I promise you, but not until I am ready.'

Ottolenghi nodded and smiled. 'Of course, of course.' He looked at his pocket watch. James recognised that Ottolenghi was trying to spare him any embarrassment and he warmed to him. He would be a good friend. 'It is almost six o'clock,' Ottolenghi said. 'I think we should make our way to the professor's house. We don't want to be late.'

James grinned. 'Indeed not. I wouldn't wish to miss anything.'

They left the café and made their way through the evening gloom towards Lombroso's residence. The gaslights were being ignited and the city was going through its daily meta-morphosis from the clarity of daylight to a dimly lit world of shadows, whisperings, and ambiguities. As they walked James was vaguely aware of a figure behind them, following them stealthily as they passed through the streets. There seemed to be a sound of faint rustling every now and then and sometimes he thought that he could hear breathing. As he inhaled, it seemed to him that there was a suggestion of a familiar sour smell in the air. He turned his head slightly once or twice but could see nothing. He had to be discreet as he did not want to alarm Ottolenghi unnecessarily but it was difficult. The further they travelled the more convinced James became that they were not alone. There were no foot-steps as such and yet he could hear something – a soft tread, as if someone was walking in James's own footprints. This time he stopped suddenly and spun round.

Ottolenghi started. 'What is it?'

James squinted into the distance. He thought he had seen a figure disappear into an alleyway, a few yards back. He held up his hand to quiet Ottolenghi and crept forward to where the alley began. He looked down the passage. It was barely lit and he could see nothing of significance. And yet he was certain that someone had been there. He turned back towards Ottolenghi.

'I thought I saw something . . .'

Ottolenghi looked down the passage himself and shook his head. 'Whoever it was has long gone, it would seem.'

'Perhaps I imagined it.'

'Perhaps,' Ottolenghi said, 'but perhaps not. Either way there is little we can do now. We should get going. We don't want to be late.'

'Should we not investigate further?'

Ottolenghi shrugged. 'If you want to, then be my guest. but I warn you, the professor is very keen on punctuality.'

'But if someone is following us . . .'

'Then it might be safer to leave them alone, don't you think?'

James weighed up the situation. Upsetting his new employer so soon was obviously not a good idea. But if someone was following him then, given what had happened to Soldati, Ottolenghi could be right. The whole thing made him feel distinctly uncomfortable. He had hoped to start afresh but it seemed as if the vague sense of unease that had blighted his life in the last year or so would not be lifting any time soon. If anything, it had deepened to something more like a feeling of being in danger somehow, although from what exactly was as yet unclear.

He looked at Ottolenghi and nodded. 'You're right. Let's go. We don't have time to waste chasing shadows tonight.'

The two young men turned and carried on with their journey. Once they reached the broad Corso Vittorio Emanuele II, not far from their destination, James looked back again but still there was nothing there. Was it really just his mind playing tricks on him? With what had happened so far in his short time in Turin, it would hardly be surprising. But it left him with more than merely a feeling of being on edge and he found that he could not shake it off. The closer they got to Lombroso's home, the more acutely James experienced an overwhelming sensation of threat.

5

It is pleasing to note that few criminals come from the world of science.   Lombroso, 1876, p 74

Before long, James and Ottolenghi arrived at Lombroso's home in the Via Legnano. It was, as James had anticipated, a large and imposing building with huge wooden doors at the front, not unlike those at the university. There was an enormous brass knocker in the shape of a man's face and James peered at it, then smiled to himself. It bore more than a passing resemblance to Lombroso himself, as if he wanted to prepare his visitors to meet the great man in the flesh.

They were welcomed in by a rather nervous young woman who ushered them upstairs as reverently as if they were royalty. She showed them into what looked like a cross between an exhibits room and a library and then scurried off like a startled mouse retreating into its hole. James felt a pang of regret that Sofia was not there.

He looked around him. The room was lined with books but every other available space was filled with artefacts that would not have looked out of place at Lombroso's museum at the university. In one corner there was a large, yellowing phrenology head which nestled next to a monkey's skull. In another were various jars containing what looked like animal organs. In pride of place on the mantelpiece was a fearsome-looking shrunken head, its teeth bared menacingly at them. James stared at it. Presumably it had once belonged to a living, breathing human being. How, he wondered, had it come to be in this state? A clock ticked monotonously as they stood in silence and waited for the great man to arrive. As the seconds passed James became increasingly excited at the prospect of meeting Lombroso's guests.

In a moment or two, though it seemed longer, they were joined by Lombroso, who greeted both of them effusively. He motioned to them to sit by the fire where there were some well-worn armchairs and sofas, arranged in a semi-circle.

'So, Murray, what are your first impressions?' asked Lombroso as he poured wine for them, more of Paolo's Barolo.

James considered the events of the day: the museum, the market, Paolo's trattoria. Despite all of it the only thing that he could think about at that moment was the mutilated corpse of Giuseppe Soldati. He had encountered violent death when working for Dr Bell, but nothing he had seen then could compare with this murder. The deliberate cruelty of the killer in the use of the knife was something completely new to him. And the leaving of the note . . . it was all so planned, premeditated. How could someone do such a thing and, more importantly, why? Try as he might, James simply could not stop himself. The words propelled themselves from his mouth like bullets from a gun.

'Who could have killed him, Professor?'

Ottolenghi shook his head at him but he was too late.

Lombroso frowned. 'You are referring to Soldati, no doubt.'

James nodded. Lombroso replied briskly, 'I do not wish to discuss it – not now or at any other time.'

'But, Professor, should we not at least look into it a little? After all, the note seemed to suggest that—'

'Suggest what? That I am involved? You are beginning to sound like that fool Machinetti!'

They sat in silence. James didn't know what to say. Lombroso was clearly annoyed but he did not know the professor well enough to find out why. Finally Lombroso seemed to take pity on him.

'Please, Murray, let us leave it there. We will not discuss it again. I assure you that I have my reasons.' He paused and sipped some wine. 'Now, about the museum – what did you think of the exhibits?'

Before anyone could answer there was a knock at the door and Sofia entered, showing in the first of Lombroso's guests. When he saw her, James felt his heartbeat quicken. She was wearing a dark blue dress, this time worn with a starched white apron, but as before, even shrouded in this drab uniform, she had a kind of effortless grace. He couldn't say what it was about her that made him catch his breath as he watched her. Her features were by no means perfect. Her lips were just a little too full and her nose was slightly too large for her face. In fact, there was something altogether uneven about her. But yes, it was this lack of perfection that made her somehow so captivating. At first he thought that she had not noticed him but as she turned to leave he caught her eye. Blinking slowly at him like a cat she gave him her half smile. He wondered if she was laughing at him. Then in a moment she was gone and he felt her absence almost immediately.

Only once Sofia had left the room did James notice that Horton was one of the party that had just arrived. He nodded at James and gave him a mock salute. James saw a broad grin cross Lombroso's face. He was surprised at Lombroso's evident pleasure, given his obvious dislike of the man. Then he realised that it was not directed at Horton but at the tall elegant woman who was standing next to him. Lombroso held out his hands to her in greeting.

'Madame Tarnovsky, it is always a pleasure!'

Lombroso kissed her hand and she smiled at him. James caught Ottolenghi's glance and saw him wink almost imperceptibly. There was something about Madame Tarnovsky that made one feel instantly at ease in her company. She was attractive, with shining chestnut hair and sparkling eyes, but it was clear that there was more to her than that. She had a certain stillness that most people do not possess. James realised that it was the self-assurance that one only finds in the truly intelligent.

'Professor, it is wonderful to see you again. I don't think that we have met since the Rome Congress.'

A slight balding man with a scant beard gave a small discreet cough. He was wearing a suit that was at least two sizes too big for him. It made him look vulnerable, as if he was a small child forced to wear cast off clothes. He smiled uncertainly.

'We also met in Rome, Professor.'

'Did we? I regret I do not recall seeing you there,' replied Lombroso coldly.

'Sure you do, Professor. It's DeClichy from Lyon,' Horton said, a mischievous glint in his eye. 'I thought you'd enjoy an opportunity to catch up before the debate.'

Lombroso peered at him haughtily and opened his mouth as if he was about to say something.

Madame Tarnovsky hastily intervened. 'May I also present Dr Reiner from Vienna?' She looked towards an immaculately dressed man with a small, neat moustache. His hair was a very pale blond, so pale in fact that it seemed almost translucent and his eyes just about achieved blueness. He looked as if he had been out in the rain and washed almost completely clean of any colour. As if to compensate, he sported a fancy brocade waistcoat in bright colours that James immediately coveted.

Reiner gave a short bow. 'We have definitely met before, Herr Professor, at a symposium on psychiatry in Salzburg. We had a most stimulating discussion on the subject of phrenology.'

'Ah yes, the science of head bumps!' Horton said, sarcastically, making his way over to a sofa where he stretched himself out like a lizard basking in the sunshine.

Lombroso ignored him. 'Yes, I remember. We had witnessed a demonstration by a gentleman from America. He was less than persuasive, I think.'

'Indeed so, although I had heard that you had become more sympathetic to these ideas,' Reiner said, sitting next to Horton, whose outstretched legs he moved with little more than a glance.

Lombroso frowned. 'Well, I don't know who told you that, one of my many critics, no doubt. They never seem to let facts interfere with a good story.'

'I thought you were a keen examiner of skulls, Professor,' Horton said with mock puzzlement.

Lombroso pursed his lips. 'As you well know, Horton, phrenology has been largely discredited. My interest is entirely different. I find physiological investigations – anthropometry, for example – to be much better indicators of behavioural characteristics. As I have said many times before, it is a pity that Bertillon's methods are not widely used in this country. Machinetti might actually catch some criminals!' He

78

turned to James. 'You are no doubt aware, Murray, that Monsieur Bertillon advocates the measurement of body parts as the most accurate method of criminal identification.'

James nodded. 'I have heard of his idea, though I've not seen its application.'

Horton snorted. 'It seems ridiculous to me. How can you catch a criminal just by knowing the size of his ears?'

DeClichy cleared his throat politely. 'Anthropometry has known some success in Paris, I understand. Bertillon has been responsible for the apprehension of a number of known criminals.'

'There we have it,' Lombroso said in delight. 'Scientific policing in action! What do you think, Murray?'

James paused. He recalled Dr Bell's rather forthright views on the subject of phrenology. 'Pseudo science' was what he had called it. And although he had been more positive about Bertillon's techniques, he had still been somewhat sceptical.

'I have heard that it is not without its problems,' James said diplomatically. 'It is a costly system and only really works if you have a proper set of records with which to compare the apprehended criminal's measurements.'

'There is that, of course,' Lombroso said quickly. 'But we should not be too quick to dismiss it. All scientific policing methods are of potential interest.'

James wondered again why Lombroso was so reluctant to get involved in the Soldati case. He was obviously interested in the application of science to the investigation of crime and this would have been an ideal opportunity to find out more.

Lombroso went on, 'You should also know, Murray, that many of my opponents claim that I am a supporter of phrenology in order to make me seem . . .' He hesitated, looking for the right words.

Horton readily butted in: 'Old-fashioned? Hopelessly behind the times?'

'One could never accuse Cesare Lombroso of that!' protested a voice from the doorway. James turned and saw the latest of Lombroso's guests to arrive, a dark-haired man with a long black beard and a florid complexion, every inch the 'hail fellow well met' type. He was thickset with a build not dissimilar to that of Lombroso. In fact, he could almost have been the professor's younger, slightly more easygoing brother, if the broad grin on his face was anything to go by. James peered behind him to see if Sofia had returned but only the maid from earlier was there, bearing a tray of drinks that she distributed carefully before scuttling away.

'Cesare, Cesare – how are you, my friend!' the man boomed as he strode over to Lombroso and embraced him warmly.

'Well, if it isn't Borelli, "the best lawyer in Turin" – is that not what your clients call you?' Lombroso said, beaming at him.

'You're too kind, Cesare!' Borelli laughed.

'How your clients must miss you when you are on your travels!' Lombroso said, teasing him.

'Absence makes the heart grow fonder, or that's what I'm hoping!' Borelli said before sitting himself down next to Lombroso. James looked over at them, perched next to each other. It was almost as if they were posing for a family photograph.

Madame Tarnovsky smiled at Borelli warmly and then looked towards Lombroso. 'I hear, Cesare, that Father Vincenzo has continued his protests against your work. The Church was particularly troublesome in Rome. I do hope we will not be disturbed by such interference again.'

'Who is Father Vincenzo?' James asked. His question was met with a brief silence and he wondered if he should have kept quiet. Then he remembered that Lombroso had not formally introduced him.

Madame Tarnovsky smiled at him. 'It is Dr Murray, is it not? Cesare told me he was hoping to have a new assistant.'

Before James could reply Lombroso butted in. 'Please forgive me, Madame. Where are my manners?' James noticed that his forgiveness was not sought, but then, as he was beginning to learn, that was just the way Lombroso was.

'This is indeed my new assistant, Dr James Murray from Edinburgh, Scotland.'

'Welcome to Turin,' Madame Tarnovsky said, smiling at James sympathetically. 'Now, Cesare, I think you should answer his question.'

Lombroso sighed. 'Ah yes, Father Vincenzo . . . he and others like him are a particularly irritating band of fools and charlatans.'

'As you are no doubt aware, Dr Murray, the Catholic church is very influential in Italy,' said Madame Tarnovsky.

'Hardly surprising, you may think,' added Borelli, 'but it goes beyond religion.'

'Father Vincenzo believes that we are under threat from the Devil,' Madame Tarnovsky said.

'Preposterous!' said Lombroso disdainfully.

Madame Tarnovsky nodded.

'Father Vincenzo is very outspoken on the matter,' Ottolenghi said. 'He is known locally as Father Hell.'

Lombroso snorted. 'After that Viennese charlatan! How apt!'

'Does he pose a threat?' James asked.

'He would like to think so,' replied Lombroso with disgust.

Ottolenghi tried to clarify. 'He has some extremely influential friends amongst the aristocracy and even at the university itself.'

'And the real Father Hell?' enquired James.

'Maximilian Hell, an astronomer from the last century renowned for his forgery of scientific data,' added Reiner helpfully, as he flicked an imaginary crumb away from his waistcoat.

'I've heard that he has been misjudged,' murmured De-Clichy, shifting uncomfortably in a rather rickety chair next to the sofa where Horton was lounging. James looked at him. His suit was ill-fitting and looked shabby enough to be second-hand. James was sympathetic. He knew how it felt to be short of funds, and he himself was wearing one of his only two suits.

'Well, *our* Father Hell is just a nuisance who should be ignored,' declared Madame Tarnovsky, firmly.

'What is his interest in criminal anthropology?' James asked.

'Professor, you should explain to Dr Murray. He is new to all of this,' Madame Tarnovsky said.

Lombroso sighed. 'Yes, I suppose you should know of them, Murray, in case they disrupt us again. This city has a large and rather excitable population of religious maniacs, all of whom seem to think that I have something against God. Father Vincenzo, for example, believes that the city is under threat from Beelzebub himself and that, through my work, I am personally assisting him to open the gates of Hell.'

'Which are reputed to be located here,' added Ottolenghi. 'Indeed, Turin is said to be the city of the Devil.'

James raised his eyebrows. This was an unexpected piece of information, although it did explain, to some extent, Sofia's comment. 'But what has this to do with the professor's work?' he asked.

'The Church disapproves of science and scientists,' Borelli said, 'and the professor here seems to particularly upset them.'

'Well, if we're all born bad, what's the point of the Devil, or God for that matter?' laughed Horton, offering Borelli a cigar. James watched Horton select one for himself from his silver case and discard the red and gold band of paper round its base, carelessly throwing it aside as if he was in his own home.

Lombroso looked to the heavens again. 'As I have told you many times, Horton, only some are born criminals.'

Horton waved a hand, languorously. 'Save it for the debate, Professor. No doubt DeClichy here will give you a run for your money. Maybe Father Vincenzo and his friends will turn up and you can let them know in person.'

'Do you think he will be there?' Madame Tarnovsky asked.

Lombroso nodded morosely. 'The university insisted that it was open to all who wished to buy a ticket. It's not inconceivable that he'll turn up at both the debate and the reception too. I know that the Marchesa will have invited him.' He turned to James. 'I have not yet informed you, Murray . . . the debate is followed by an evening reception hosted by the Marchesa Vittoria di Carignano. You are invited as my guest.'

'Ah yes, how is the Marchesa?' Madame Tarnovsky asked.

'She is very well, as far as I know,' Lombroso replied.

'I hear she only has eyes for Father Vincenzo these days,' Horton said, with a hint of mischief – or was it malevolence, James wondered.

Madame Tarnovsky tutted. 'Really, Dr Horton, I'm sure she is intelligent enough to see through him.'

'No, Horton is right,' Lombroso said ruefully. 'The priest always seems to be at her side these days and she has little time left for science.'

'Still, if she has agreed to host the reception, she must still care a little,' Borelli said. 'We must make every effort to rekindle her interest. After all, she's the most influential woman in Piedmont, is she not? To lose her patronage would be a disaster.'

Lombroso nodded. 'Indeed it would.'

'You're very quiet, Herr Dr DeClichy. Any views on Father Vincenzo?' Reiner asked.

DeClichy shifted about on his chair again. 'I remember the priest from the Congress in Rome, of course. He was difficult to forget, as were the exhibits you so helpfully provided, Professor.'

'Ah yes, the exhibits,' Madame Tarnovsky said. She turned to James. 'They were deemed to be so disturbing in nature that women and children were not admitted. I thought for a while that I was going to have to be smuggled in disguised as one of Cesare's assistants!'

'Such things do not apply to scientists, whatever their sex,' Lombroso said.

Madame Tarnovsky smiled and patted his hand. 'Not all would agree, but I am grateful for your view.'

'There were all manner of curiosities,' Reiner recalled. 'I still remember those skulls . . . oh yes, and Giona La Gala. His presence remained with me for many months.'

'I have not heard of him. Which university does he come from?' asked James. Everyone laughed and he coloured slightly.

Lombroso smiled at him. 'Giona La Gala was a particularly murderous brigand. His remains were displayed by doctors from the prison in Genoa.'

'Everything from his death mask to his brain, tattoos and gallstones were there!' exclaimed Borelli. He turned to Lombroso. 'Still, it was your skulls and photographs that stole the show, Cesare, much to the disdain of your critics!'

'So tell us, DeClichy, how is your research progressing these days? What new discoveries have you made about crime in Lyon this year?' Lombroso asked in mocking tones. 'Do men become thieves because their mothers were cruel to them? Are murderers merely reacting to their lack of education? Do rapists commit their crimes because they are hungry?'

His lips curled in disdain as he spoke. Some of the ideas he proposed sounded entirely plausible to James but he didn't like to say so with Lombroso in his current mood. He was learning more of his character by the minute and, although he was clearly impatient with those who did not share his views, James still admired him. Such certainty in one's own opinions seemed to him to be a quality worth emulating.

DeClichy pursed his fleshy lips before answering. 'It is perhaps more likely as a theory than being born to crime as one is born to be musical.'

Madame Tarnovsky interceded. 'Well now, Dr DeClichy, if I may say so, you are being a little hasty. If musical genius can be innate, then why cannot criminality?'

Lombroso beamed at Madame Tarnovsky. 'Exactly so, I could not have put it better myself.'

Horton yawned openly. Lombroso looked at him severely. 'I do apologise if we are boring you, Dr Horton.'

'You're not, Professor, although I've heard it all before. I was merely hoping for something a little more original this year.'

James started to wonder what it was exactly that Horton did believe in as he seemed to be so disdainful about everything.

'Dr Horton, remember you are a guest!' Madame Tarnovsky said.

'Don't worry, I am used to such ignorance,' Lombroso said. 'I am more interested by what Horton means by original.'

Horton stopped laughing and stared at him. 'Well, for example, I've have not heard anyone say a thing about what we should do with these born criminals once we've identified them. Are we just to allow them to continue to breed and spread their criminal genes, as if their existence didn't matter?'

'Dr Horton! I thought that you agreed with me that there is no such thing as the born criminal!' piped up DeClichy, his rickety chair rocking dangerously as he moved.

'Perhaps, but I'm just playing devil's advocate – oh, no sorry – that's the professor's role. How's the family, by the way, Professor?' Horton grinned archly. 'Will they be joining us this evening?'

Lombroso glowered at him. 'They left for the country this morning, as it happens.'

'That's a shame. Still, it's probably for the best, given the circumstances,' declared Horton, winking at Lombroso who gave him a withering look in return.

'What circumstances?' asked Borelli. 'Has something happened, Cesare?'

Lombroso shook his head, briskly. 'It's nothing. I just needed solitude while the symposium is taking place.'

Horton looked at him slyly. 'Come, come now, it's more than that. What about the murder?'

86

Lombroso stared at him with ill-disguised dislike. 'It has nothing whatsoever to do with that!'

'Murder, what murder? You must tell us, Cesare!' Borelli said, apparently concerned.

Ottolenghi interceded in an effort to control the conversation. 'A former subject of the professor's was unfortunate enough to be the victim of a killer, that's all. He was a criminal. What happened was hardly surprising, given the company he no doubt kept.'

Horton shook his head. 'My sources tell me Lombroso's involvement is rather more than that.'

'You seem remarkably well informed, Herr Doctor,' Reiner commented.

Horton tapped the side of his nose conspiratorially.

'Come on, Horton, you can't leave it there. What are you insinuating?' Borelli said.

Horton smirked. 'I notice that the good professor hasn't mentioned the bloody note.'

'A bloody note? Oh, do tell us more, Cesare! It sounds intriguing!' Madame Tarnovsky said eagerly.

'What was on the note? How does it connect to you?' Borelli asked.

There was a pause. Lombroso wore a thunderous expression. He clearly didn't want to talk about it and yet here he was being forced to discuss it at his own gathering.

Horton interrupted. James noticed that his eyes were glinting with spite. '*A Tribute to Lombroso*, that's what was written on it. Someone obviously wants to impress you!'

'I really do not wish to discuss it. Let us talk of other matters! Madame Tarnovsky, how is Prague?'

Madame Tarnovsky, apparently sensitive to her host's discomfort, then proceeded to tell the assembled company of her recent experiments on the city's prostitutes and female thieves. The way she explained it made it seem entirely natural as a process and her audience was enthralled by what she had to say.

James sensed that Lombroso was relieved that the conversation had moved away from Soldati's death. Eventually some more of Lombroso's associates arrived and the party began to separate into small groups. James was asked to go downstairs to the kitchen and tell Sofia to bring more food and wine. Evidently his role as assistant to the professor extended to the domestic. He didn't really mind. After all, it gave him an ideal excuse to see Sofia again.

When he found Sofia she was baking bread and he looked on from the doorway, entranced, as she expertly kneaded the dough, her body moving sensuously as she did so. She looked up without warning and caught him looking at her. He held her stare and she looked away, smiling as if she was laughing at him.

'The professor is asking for some more food and wine.'

Sofia nodded. 'I must finish this first or we will have no bread for the morning.'

'Then I will wait,' James said, taking a seat without looking away. Her directness fascinated him.

Sofia smiled at him. 'You wish to escape? All those fine people in one room – it can be a little overwhelming, perhaps.'

'Perhaps . . .' James returned her smile. 'How long have you been with the professor?'

'Five years. He saved me. Without him . . .'

She paused in her work and looked into the distance. There was a haunted expression on her face as if she was reliving a part of her past that she would rather forget. James was angry with himself for asking such a crass question.

Suddenly Sofia leaned forwards and grasped his hand. He felt a slight tingle at her touch, as if it was a caress. She looked intently into his eyes. 'He is good man. You must help him. He needs you.'

'But I barely know him!'

'The murder – it hit him hard. I think he is worried that there may be another.'

Just feeling her hand on his had left him almost breathless. He instinctively responded but she pulled away as if he had pricked her with a needle. She looked at him with a steady gaze and went back to her kneading.

'Another? Why should there be?'

She shrugged. 'You should ask him.'

'I want to help him but he won't talk about it,' he said.

Sofia looked at him intently as if assessing his worth. 'You must do what you can. He has enemies. They will use this against him if they can.'

'You know a lot about his work?'

'I have eyes and ears. That is enough.' She wiped her hands on her apron and put a tea towel over the dough. 'I will fetch some more food from the larder.'

'I'll help you.'

Sofia inclined her head slightly in acknowledgement and he followed her through the large wooden door in the corner. She began to load plates and bowls onto a tray. He stood behind her and she turned around suddenly so that they stood face to face. They were so close that he could feel the light touch of her breath on his face. Their eyes met and she gave him that slow half smile as she had done on the first day he saw her. He felt almost overwhelmed by the urge to kiss her.

He knew in his heart that it was wrong. Sofia was his new

employer's servant, which was bad enough. But there was also her background. From what Lombroso had said, she had done only what she had to in order to survive, but still . . . prostitution. He could hardly bear to think of what she must have gone through just to keep body and soul together. Sofia was forbidden to him in so many ways. How could he even begin think of her like that? And yet standing so close to her meant that any self-control he might have had was completely lost. He could not resist her, try as he might. He put his hand up to touch her cheek. She put her hand over his, all the time looking into his eyes and he was lost.

'Not here . . . not now . . . There are things I must tell you—'

Suddenly she stopped. Someone had come into the kitchen.

'Sofia?' It was the maid.

She drew away from him and placed her finger on his lips. 'Wait,' she breathed. She lifted a tray of food and made her way past him out of the larder.

'Would you take this upstairs, Gisella? I will follow with some more wine.'

James peeped round the door and saw the girl leave. Sofia turned and looked intensely at him. 'Another time . . . soon.' She picked up a tray of glasses and a carafe of wine and went upstairs.

James leaned against the larder door for a moment, his eyes closed, not wanting to release the memory of her touch.

When he returned upstairs Ottolenghi came over and pulled him to one side. 'You've been a long time,' he whispered. 'What were you doing?'

James looked at him and shrugged as if he did not know

what he meant. Ottolenghi shook his head at him. 'Take care, Murray, take care.'

Before James could say anything Horton sauntered over to them. 'You're both coming to the debate?'

'Wouldn't dream of missing it,' replied Ottolenghi. 'Tell me, Horton, do you really believe that the professor is wrong about the criminal type?'

Horton chomped noisily on his cigar, occasionally baring his sharp little teeth. 'Well, put it like this . . . No one's right all of the time, are they?'

'What does that mean?' James asked.

Horton smirked. 'You'll just have to wait and see, won't you. One thing I can assure you of – the debate won't be dull!' He moved away, still smirking.

Ottolenghi looked concerned.

'What's the matter?'

'I don't know. There's just something about that man. He's not to be trusted. I wonder what he's got up his sleeve. Whatever it is, the professor won't like it. We'd better be ready for him. One false move and the academic vultures will descend!'

James looked over to Lombroso. He was holding forth to a small crowd of admirers. Borelli stood behind him, a faint smile on his face. Horton stood beside him looking bored. Ottolenghi grinned. 'He's telling his skull story again.'

'What's that?'

'He'll tell you himself soon enough, probably more than once. It is rather a favourite of the professor's. It's an account of how he was inspired to develop his theory of the born criminal being a throwback to primitive man.'

James looked over again with fresh interest, listening to the performance.

'As I looked at this scoundrel's skull I could see the explanation for the enormous jaws, high cheekbones, prominent superciliary arches, solitary lines in the palms, extreme size of the orbits, handle-shaped ears found in criminals, savages and apes –' Lombroso used his hands to illustrate his words like an old-fashioned actor miming a performance – insensibility to pain, extremely acute sight, tattooing, excessive idleness, love of orgies, and the irresponsible craving of evil for its own sake, the desire not only to extinguish life in the victim, but to mutilate the corpse, tear its flesh and drink its own blood.'

Then Lombroso stopped and paused, evidently waiting for a reaction. There was a ripple of polite applause led by Madame Tarnovsky and he acknowledged it graciously, although James could see from his expression that he had been hoping for something more. Horton gave one of his audible yawns and Lombroso turned to glare at him. Madame Tarnovsky hastily asked a question and others followed her example and the moment had passed.

James wandered over to Reiner who had been listening to Lombroso's story from a distance, a wry smile on his face. 'Have you heard the story before?' he asked.

Reiner smiled. 'He may have mentioned it when we last met . . . and the time before . . . and . . .'

'The time before that?'

'Indeed, but it bears repetition nonetheless.'

'Ottolenghi mentioned that you had done some work on criminal vampirism. It sounds intriguing.'

Reiner's pale eyes lit up. 'Oh it is, it is. Have you read my monograph on the subject?'

'No, but I would very much like to.'

'Then I will send you the details, Herr Dr Murray.'

'What led you to explore that subject?'

'Ah, so many things. I was examining *lustmord.*'

'Lust murder?'

'Yes, that's correct. I have been examining the connections between sexual sadism and murder. I came across a number of cases, particularly in Eastern Europe, that featured certain activities involving the corpse after death.'

'You mean like mutilation, for example?'

'Yes, up to a point. Some of the activities could be so described.'

'Fascinating! What kind of mutilations, if I may ask?'

'Bloody ones, Herr Dr Murray.'

'Were organs or body parts removed?'

Reiner smiled at him again, though James thought that this time he seemed less sincere. 'A curious question . . . I fear that you will have to read my paper. I don't wish to give too much away. Excuse me.'

With that he gave a short bow and moved towards Lombroso who was still holding forth, though to a smaller group.

Borelli came over. 'Interesting man, Reiner.'

James nodded. 'I found him so.'

'Did I hear you mention mutilations?'

'We were discussing his paper on vampirism.'

'I see,' Borelli said, stroking his beard thoughtfully, just as Lombroso did. 'I really must get hold of a copy. It might come in useful,' he added, almost as an afterthought, before he too drifted towards Lombroso.

James stared after him. What an eclectic group these men were. They all had the same central interest but came to it from so many angles that one could never become bored in their company. According to Ottolenghi, both Reiner and

Borelli were medically trained as well as being experts in the law – just as Lombroso was. He looked again at Reiner and wondered about his interest in post-mortem mutilation. If one encountered that in any other arena it would lead to immediate arrest, but here it was almost run-of-the-mill . . . and yet . . .

It was getting late and after a while people started to leave. Horton made a tremendous fuss because he had mislaid his cigar case. He made a great show of looking for it, insisting loudly that a search was carried out. He had to be placated by Reiner who eventually persuaded him to give up and escorted him out into the night. James suspected that Horton just liked to make a dramatic exit.

Once the last guest had gone, James and Ottolenghi joined Lombroso who sat by the fire, staring into it, deep in repose. They sat opposite him but their presence was barely acknowledged. There was a perfunctory nod but that was all. They sat together in silence for what seemed like hours. This was a different side to Lombroso and James was not entirely sure how to deal with it.

Eventually the tension was broken by Sofia who came in with some coffee. As she served it she looked at James sternly as if willing him to provide some comfort for Lombroso. He wanted to but found it difficult to know how to broach the subject. Recently he had found it difficult enough dealing with his own emotions, let alone those of others.

Suddenly Sofia spoke. Her voice was soft and low. She said little but it was enough. 'You should talk. It will help.'

'You are right, Sofia, as always,' said Lombroso and smiled at her. She gave a dignified little bow and left them. 'That young woman never fails to surprise me,' he murmured softly. 'It is as if she knows exactly what I am thinking.'

'And what are you thinking, Professor?' enquired Otto-lenghi quickly, taking the opportunity offered to start a conversation.

'You are anxious, Salvatore. You have no need to be. I am just a little melancholy. A man is dead and apparently he was brought to that state in my name.'

'But you are not responsible,' James protested. 'No one could attach blame to you for this!'

'I knew him,' said Lombroso sadly. 'He had been a subject in one of my experiments. We measured him, we even laughed at him. Do you remember, Salvatore? He was so intent on pretending that this was an everyday thing for him, to have his body measured and recorded.'

'Some might say that he was just a thief. There won't be many who will miss him, surely,' James said.

Lombroso shook his head vehemently. 'How can you say such a thing? He may have had a family – children, grand-children, a wife. He had a heart and a soul just like you and me. And someone ripped away his life and said it was done in my name!' Lombroso looked down at the floor. For a split second James thought that he was weeping and was relieved to see him look up dry-eyed, shaking his head. 'I fully admit that I do not know how to respond to this. I am at a loss. I have seen and heard much to disturb me in my life; my work has seen to that. But nothing could prepare me for this.'

'Then we must find whoever did this and ensure that he is brought to justice,' Ottolenghi said firmly.

Lombroso looked almost alarmed at this prospect. 'No, no! We must leave it to the authorities. They will find the person responsible and deal with him appropriately.'

'But Machinetti is a fool. You said as much yourself!' Ottolenghi exclaimed.

'I did say that and it is true but I'll warrant that Tullio is not and neither is young Giardinello. Machinetti may think he is the chief investigator but his underlings do most of the work. They will solve this crime . . . eventually.'

'But eventually may be too late!' James replied.

'What do you mean?' asked Ottolenghi.

'What if this criminal strikes again? It is not uncommon for one person to commit a series of crimes. I have read many accounts of such men. There was a Dr Palmer in England – the Rugeley poisoner – he killed again and again. And there are others. What of Gilles de Rais – he murdered hundreds!'

Lombroso tutted at James. 'I do not think that this is such a case. Really, Murray, you have an eye for melodrama. Perhaps you should write a "penny dreadful"! That is what the English call works of sensational fiction, is it not?'

'I just do not want him to get away with his crime, whoever he is,' James said, subdued by Lombroso's scornful reaction.

'And neither do I, Murray. But we should leave it to the authorities. Nothing will be served by you and me interfering in matters that we do not fully comprehend.'

'But we are studying crime and criminals, surely we could help at least?' James implored.

Lombroso sighed and looked morosely into the dying embers of the fire. 'I can see that you will not allow the matter to rest until I explain in full. I suppose that shows a certain tenacity which may be an advantage in the study of crime.'

There was a long pause. Lombroso stroked his beard thoughtfully, gave a deep sigh, and began. 'There was a case, some time ago, in which Machinetti and I were profession-ally involved. It was before he was promoted to the position of marshal. He was eager for advancement and obviously viewed it as an opportunity to make a name for himself.'

'What kind of case?' James asked.

'A particularly hideous offence. A young woman, the daughter of a count, a very rich and influential man, had been reported missing. It was hardly surprising that the authorities were anxious that she be found. For some reason Machinetti was chosen to head the investigation and he decided to consult me. He wanted to know what kind of man he was looking for and where we might find him . . . and the girl.'

There was another pause.

'What happened?' asked Ottolenghi.

'I told him that on no account should he allow publicity. The man we were seeking was not the sort of person who could be found in that way and, anyway, the publicity itself might provoke him into violence. He did not listen to me. He arranged for posters to be put up everywhere and for broadsheets to cover the story in detail.'

'The man was not caught?'

Lombroso shook his head vigorously.

'Machinetti decided to insult the man by describing him as weak and unintelligent. He thought this might encourage him to make a mistake.'

'Did it work?' James asked.

'No, it did not,' replied Lombroso bluntly.

'Was she found?'

'Unfortunately she was – but not alive. She had been strangled and it was obvious that she had also been violated in a most obscene manner. There were some hints in the press and from the authorities that *I* was to blame for the girl's tragic end.'

Ottolenghi shook his head in disbelief. 'But surely it was clear that it was not your fault. You gave Machinetti advice and he did not act upon it. In fact, he chose to ignore it.'

Lombroso's expression was steely with anger. 'That is not the account that Machinetti gave, but even then he had to wait many more years for a promotion that he would otherwise have got in months. The perpetrator was never caught. Fortunately, some of Machinetti's superiors took my side in the matter but he somehow persuaded himself that I alone was responsible. He still believes it now and I doubt he will ever come to terms with the fact that I was right and he was wrong. Machinetti simply cannot be trusted with the truth. The man even lies to himself when it suits him.'

James peered down at his hands. He did not know where else to look. No wonder the professor had been so reluctant to become involved with the investigation.

'So you see, Murray, I prefer to have as little to do with Machinetti as possible – and now that this murder has occurred I fear that he will take the opportunity to avenge himself for what he perceives to be the wrong that I did him.'

'Surely you could reason with him, or perhaps I could on your behalf?' James suggested, outraged.

'You are very kind, Murray, but I fear that nothing anyone could say will change Machinetti's mind. If it is at all possible he will ensure that I am blamed for this killing. I only hope that Giardinello or Tullio are bright enough to see through Machinetti and have sufficient strength of character to defy him.'

'But surely we cannot take that risk? Both are inexperienced. There is no guarantee . . .' His voice tailed off, seeing the expression on Lombroso's face.

'For the last time, my answer is no.' Lombroso's voice was

stern and it was evident that he would brook no further argument. 'But you are right about one thing. We are studying crime and perhaps we should stop wasting our precious time and get on with it.' He looked at his pocket watch and frowned. 'It is late, gentlemen. We will speak no more of this.'

He dismissed them with a perfunctory wave of the hand and picked up a book.

Having collected their coats they agreed to walk together for a while as they did not live far from one another. The evening was cold and the fog swirled round them as if it was trying to swallow them whole. James was glad of the company. The streets were deserted and quiet apart from their footfall.

'What do you know about Reiner?' James asked, eager to break the silence.

Ottolenghi shrugged. 'Not a great deal on a personal level. He is a psychiatrist, very well respected in his field.'

'I just wondered. He has an unusual manner.'

'There are few of us in this field who are not guilty of that!' Ottolenghi said laughing.

'True,' James said. 'Take the professor, for example. I still can't see why a man of his experience would allow someone like Machinetti to dictate what he involves himself in.'

'Well, at least we tried,' Ottolenghi said. 'There is little else we can do.'

'Perhaps the professor will change his mind . . . if things get really bad, I mean.' James spoke hesitantly, unconvinced by his own argument.

'I doubt it,' Ottolenghi replied. 'It is quite clear the professor does not want to investigate this murder himself.'

'Maybe not,' replied James thoughtfully, 'but there is no

reason why we cannot look into it on his behalf. If we find anything we can tell Tullio.'

Ottolenghi nodded. 'Yes, I am sure that he could be relied upon to be discreet.'

'And if the professor finds out?' James asked.

'Then we will just have to hope he understands that we did it for him. But James, you should take care. The professor demands complete attention and if he thinks you have allowed this or . . . or *other* matters to divert you from your studies he will dismiss you. He is quite ruthless where that is concerned.'

James looked at Ottolenghi's face. His expression was concerned rather than hostile. He smiled sheepishly. Perhaps Ottolenghi was right. Sofia was beautiful and James was sorely tempted to see her again but he had other things to think about. They must take precedence. Ottolenghi patted him on the shoulder, obviously satisfied that he had made his point and they continued their journey in silence.

Despite this James was still unable to banish Sofia from his mind. The memory of her face, the softness of her skin as he had stroked her cheek would not leave him. It was strange. Her words to Lombroso had almost been those of a daughter rather than a servant. He couldn't work out their relationship and there was a familiarity between them that did not seem quite right.

Soon they came to the parting of the ways. They arranged to meet at the scene of the murder in the Piazza Statuto the following morning to do a little preliminary investigation before the debate. They bade each other good night and James watched Ottolenghi walk off in one direction as he turned to the other.

Before long he had to turn off the broad thoroughfare into

the labyrinth of winding, largely unlit, narrow streets that led to his lodgings. There was not a soul around, leaving him to navigate his way through the swirling mists and the darkness, hoping that he was remembering the directions Ottolenghi had given him earlier.

As he walked, James began to turn the events of that evening over in his mind. If this was the Devil's city then where exactly might the gates of hell be? He looked about him as he walked, increasingly unsettled by the oppressive, almost unnatural silence that weighed down on him. Was he imagining it or could he detect a hint of sulphur in the air? It was almost as if the Devil was leaving him a trail. As he carried on down the cobbled street his imagination began to jostle with his usual rationality. Occasionally he would pass a window where a gas lamp flickered and he almost thought that he could sense the presence of a demon squatting behind it, waiting to beckon him into hell. He began to walk faster, yearning for the safety and security of his rooms but at the same time forcing himself to think rational, more solid thoughts as he went.

He wondered why Turin had such a significant reputation for Satanism. Was there anything in it or was it just super-stition? He smiled to himself briefly as he imagined telling Lucy of the legend. She would no doubt take it at face value and write a story about it, complete with some lurid illustra-tions. He chided himself for being so ridiculous. If there was a hell, it was more than likely man-made. He had seen plenty of evidence of that in last year or so.

But as he walked on, he slowly became aware yet again of a sensation of being followed. He thought that he could hear light footsteps behind him. When he stopped, so did they. He tensed himself and grasped his cane firmly. The silence of the night bore down, crushing him like a huge burden and he felt almost unable to breathe. As he looked round he heard a slight noise coming from an alleyway nearby. This time it seemed more persistent. His heart began to beat so quickly he thought that it would leap from his body. Was he about to be robbed or worse? Would he end up like Soldati, strangled and mutilated in a lonely piazza, his blood mingling with the dirt of the city? A figure emerged. Again James held his breath and prepared to defend himself.

6

Hitherto policing was conducted much as wars used to be waged: randomly and on the basis of hunches. Successful investigations depended on the astuteness and dedication of a few individuals. What we need now is to apply the scientific method to the identification of criminals.

Lombroso, 1896 p 331

A hand came out of the gloom and rested on James's wrist.

'*Signor,*' breathed the figure into his ear. It was shrouded in a hooded cloak giving it an other-worldly air, though its touch was all too human. James gave a sigh of relief as he realised that it was Sofia.

She looked up into his eyes. 'Come, come with me now.'

'Sofia, what is it?'

She shook her head at him impatiently. 'Just follow me. I will explain.'

His head was advising caution – after all, what did he really know about Sofia? But his heart – that was a different matter entirely. It wasn't just the way she looked that attracted him. There was something intriguing about her – a hint that behind those dark eyes lay a wealth of secrets. Everything that Ottolenghi had said only moments ago became a distant memory. He went with her only too willingly as she took him by the hand and led him through the cold night. If she wanted him, then he was hers.

But there was to be no tryst that night. Instead they ended up at a tavern not far from the Piazza Statuto where Soldati's body had been found. James did not notice much about the place itself, except that it was dingy and smelt unpleasant. But that did not matter. The only thing that occupied his mind was Sofia. He noticed that her hair was no longer neatly braided but was held back loosely with combs. She looked to James as if she had just stepped out from a renaissance painting.

She sat him down in a corner and returned shortly afterwards with a small bottle of clear liquid and two glasses. James did not know what the drink was and sniffed cautiously at it when she poured him a glass and swirled it round, watching the slightly viscous liquid cling to the sides. He was about to take a sip when he saw Sofia looking at him with her customary amused expression so he took a gulp instead. It was certainly powerful and not a little rough. He coughed and spluttered as its harshness coated his throat. It was like drinking fire.

He looked up to see Sofia laughing at him. 'My poor signor! You are not used to our *grappa*.'

Annoyed with himself he took another, less generous mouthful. This time he allowed it to coast its way down his throat. He felt it warm him and it gave him a kind of courage, which, for some reason, he felt he needed.

'Nice place,' he said, looking about him at the Spartan furniture and dirty floor.

Sofia smiled. 'You are used to better?'

'Not really,' he replied, thinking wryly of some of the

places he had frequented as a student. Then it was the cheapness of the ale that mattered, rather than the décor.

'Sofia . . .' He looked at her sitting before him, bathed in the warm glow of the candlelight. It might have been the *grappa* on top of the wine he had consumed at the salon but it seemed to him that she shimmered somehow, as if she was from a different world. In fact this city and all that had happened there in the last few days had a surreal quality to it.

Sofia leaned forward and put her hand on his. 'Signor,' she whispered. 'I need to talk to you.'

'Talk away.'

'As I told you, the professor has enemies. He needs someone to protect him from them. They will use this murder to destroy him. Trust me, I know them.'

James was curious. 'Why do you care so much? He's just an employer – or is there something else between you?' He felt as if a cold hand was squeezing his heart as he uttered those words.

She shook her head violently. 'No, no! How could you think that? He is like a father to me. I owe him everything.'

James sighed inwardly with relief. 'I am a fool. I don't know why I even suggested it.'

She looked away as if she could not meet his eye. 'I have only ever sold myself when there has been no other choice.'

James felt ashamed. He of all people should have known that the past could be slow to relinquish its hold. 'I am sorry. Please forgive me.'

But even as he spoke a vestige of doubt remained in his mind.

'Who are these enemies? What kind of threat do they pose?'

'You are going to the debate and the Marchesa's reception, are you not?'

He nodded.

'Then you will find out soon enough.'

'What about Ottolenghi? Couldn't he help you?'

'He is a good man, but he has his own interests. You, I think, are different, and . . .' She paused and looked at him, almost coquettishly. 'He is not so handsome.'

James could not help but smile at her. 'I will do what I can.'

'You promise?'

'I promise.'

'And signor—'

'James, call me James.'

'James . . . you know that this must be our secret, don't you? If the professor found out that you and I . . .' Sofia clutched his hands tightly in hers.

'That you and I?'

Sofia laughed softly. 'We'll see,' she said. 'We'll see . . .'

They sat and talked a little more about this and that, acquainting themselves cautiously with one another as if they were engaged in a formal dance, keeping their distance, not giving too much away. Later, he watched as she left, negotiating her way through the tables. She turned to look at him just before she went through the door. There was something in her expression. James did not know for sure what it was but he hoped that it was an invitation for the future, and the not too distant kind at that.

He awoke in his room some hours later and stretched and yawned, the memory of last night still lingering. He wondered if he was being naïve, expecting anything from Sofia.

But for the first time in a long time something had awoken within him and she was the cause of it. He felt alive – as if he was regaining some sense of the self that he had lost in last year or so. How could he resist her?

Refreshed, James looked at his watch and realised that he was running late for his meeting with Ottolenghi. He picked up his jacket and left, slamming the door firmly behind him. It was time to think of more unpleasant matters.

He found the Piazza Statuto easily enough. It was off a narrow cobbled street near the Porta Palazzo market, in an area earmarked for potential slum clearance. The smell of rotting vegetables hung in the air and the statue where the body had been found seemed very different in the sunlight, now that its gruesome sideshow had been removed.

He knew the importance of examining the scene of the crime. Before his first encounter with Dr Bell during his medical training he had known little about the 'art of detection'. Indeed, most of his information had come from reading novels – *The Moonstone* by Wilkie Collins and Poe's *The Murders in the Rue Morgue* were two of his particular favourites. They made it seem a simple matter to identify and track down a criminal. Ratiocination was all that was required, a satisfactory conclusion to a mystery, reached by logical reasoning.

However, he had subsequently learned that it was a far more complex matter when real people were involved. According to Dr Bell it was not enough to apply a set investigative formula. One had to be a little more inventive and adapt to the circumstances as they presented themselves. He had proved to be proficient at this in Edinburgh, but only time would tell if he could bring his skills to bear in Turin. This would be an excellent test for him.

Ottolenghi was already at the scene when James arrived and he was not alone. Tullio was with him. They were both bending over the site of the body, peering at the now blood-stained cobbles where it had lain.

'Good morning, Ottolenghi, Inspector Tullio. Have you found anything of interest?' James enquired.

'Not yet,' Ottolenghi said glumly.

Tullio looked at both of them suspiciously. 'Does Professor Lombroso know that you're here?'

Ottolenghi cleared his throat in an effort to hide his embarrassment. 'No, he doesn't. For some reason he prefers to leave the investigation to the police. And Tullio, I assume that you have told Marshal Machinetti of your intention to re-examine the scene?'

Now it was Tullio's turn to be embarrassed. 'I may have forgotten to let him know. My superiors have told me to cooperate with him but I'm finding that rather difficult.' He sighed. 'Machinetti is still convinced that the professor is implicated. It is the only reason he is bothering with this case at all. He doesn't usually trouble himself if the victim is a criminal.'

Ottolenghi frowned. 'Just because the victim was a thief doesn't mean his death should be ignored, particularly given the circumstances.'

Tullio nodded. 'Quite so. Machinetti's interest may prove troublesome. I should warn you that he is intent on proving the professor's involvement. I, however, have my own ideas.'

Ottolenghi smiled with relief. 'I am glad to hear it. As the professor himself pointed out, I hardly think that he would be so intent on his own destruction that he would kill a man and then leave a note implicating himself.'

'I agree it doesn't seem at all likely. That is why I am here.'

James watched the two of them eye each other cautiously. It was clear that they wanted to trust each other but didn't know if they could.

'Perhaps then, together we might make some sense of this?' he suggested.

Tullio thought for a while. Eventually he replied.

'Three heads would seem better than one. Since I am forced to investigate without the assistance of the carabinieri, I can't see that your involvement would do any harm. Do either of you have any practical experience in this area?'

James considered what to say. As well as a foray into literature he had also read of many real cases and had studied the work of Lombroso and others. His work as Dr Bell's clerk had introduced him to investigation. James had even accompanied his tutor to the scenes of one or two crimes when the doctor was working as a consultant to the police. As a result he had picked up a good deal of information but did not have much direct experience. He decided that honesty was the best policy.

'A little . . .'

'The same applies to me,' Ottolenghi admitted.

'And to me,' Tullio said frankly. 'I am only recently appointed. Still, perhaps between us we might make some progress. It will be good to have someone to talk to at any rate.'

'What about your colleagues?' James asked.

Tullio paused for a moment. 'Let's just say we don't really see eye to eye,' he said, a little ruefully. 'I don't think that they fully appreciate the possibilities of scientific policing. If we could make some headway in this case then perhaps . . .'

He tailed off and looked into the distance with a smile on his face, as if imagining parading the killer in front of his fellow officers.

'Well let's get on with it then,' James said firmly. He knelt down and started to examine the stained cobbles more closely. Tullio and Ottolenghi joined him.

'You can tell from the stain that there was quite a lot of blood, which is strange,' James said, remembering the dark sticky pool that had been there not long ago.

'Why?' Tullio asked. 'Surely the mutilation would have produced bleeding.'

'Yes, but as you know, bleeding stops after death, when the heart ceases to beat,' James replied.

'You're right,' Tullio said thoughtfully, 'but there would still have been some bleeding if the mutilation was carried out immediately. I asked the pathologist about this. I wanted to know if the body could have been killed elsewhere and then left here. If we can work out exactly how this was done, and where, then it might lead us to the killer.'

'What did the pathologist say?' James asked.

'He said that the blood would still flow quite freely for a minute or two.'

'So he was garrotted and then mutilated post-mortem but quickly enough to produce the blood we see here,' Otto-lenghi said thoughtfully.

James looked up. 'There is another possibility, of course.'

'What's that?' Tullio asked.

'He could have still been alive when the mutilations were carried out. The garrotte could have just immobilised him long enough.'

'So Soldati would have bled to death. What a way to die!' Ottolenghi exclaimed.

James nodded. 'The killer must have some level of expertise to move that quickly, one presumes.'

'A butcher, perhaps, or a hunter?' Tullio said.

'Or perhaps a surgeon?' James suggested. 'I noticed that the flesh of the nose was removed rather than the whole. It would have required precision and a practised hand.'

'Yes, but it would have been easier than slicing through the bone,' Ottolenghi added.

'Was he definitely killed here? After all, it's quite open. The killer might have been seen. He took quite a risk,' James said.

Ottolenghi looked at Tullio. 'Murray's right. There might be a witness or perhaps the body was moved, after all.'

James frowned. 'That would have taken some strength. Soldati wasn't a small man.' He walked around the monument, looking at the ground. 'There is no sign of marks indicating that the body had been dragged anywhere.'

They joined him as he stood back a little from the scene, all three of them trying their best to come to some conclusion.

'Wait a minute,' James said, glancing behind him at the wrought iron fence that ran around the monument. 'The corpse was propped up behind these railings, as I recall.'

'That's right,' Tullio said.

James climbed elegantly over the fence and began looking around. 'At medical school in Edinburgh I was always taught to examine a patient thoroughly, not just by looking at them physically but also asking for their history. I don't see why it should be any different here. We have already looked at the body so now we need to examine the surrounding area.'

'I don't believe anyone searched behind the monument,'

Ottolenghi said. 'We were all focused on the body, at the front.'

'Exactly!' James said, walking round the statue to its rear. 'Had Machinetti thought to look further afield he might have found clues as to the killer's identity.'

Tullio looked at him with interest. 'Have you found something?'

James held up the stub of a cigar. 'It's probably nothing – after all, it could have been left at any time and by anyone.'

'Let me see,' Tullio said.

James handed it over and the three men examined it carefully.

'It looks relatively fresh,' Ottolenghi said, sniffing at it gingerly.

'Perhaps it belonged to the killer,' James suggested.

'It's a possibility,' Tullio said hesitantly. He wrapped it carefully in his handkerchief and put in his pocket

'There's something else.' James bent down to look closer. 'In the bushes here – more blood.'

'Perhaps the killer did his mutilation there to give him some cover,' Ottolenghi suggested.

'It looks like it,' James said, wiping the soil from his hands.

'Any footprints?' Tullio asked.

'Yes, but they're smudged. I don't think we could take a cast of them,' James replied. 'And I can't be sure but it looks as if there may be at least two different prints.'

'Really! I don't know how Machinetti managed to miss all of this,' Ottolenghi said indignantly.

'We *all* missed it,' Tullio said. 'Anyway the prints could have been made at any time – by a gardener, perhaps. None of it really takes us anywhere.'

'But all together the three things might be significant,' James added, trying to be optimistic.

'We need to ask the professor,' Tullio said. 'He would surely be able to shed some light on this. He's the expert in crime and criminals, after all. Any idea why he wants to leave this to Machinetti?'

Ottolenghi shrugged. 'There's bad blood between them. That's why he's reluctant to get involved. He doesn't usually investigate. Since his last case with Machinetti he prefers to advise as to likely guilt after someone has been apprehended.'

'I can't say I blame him. Still, it's a pity,' Tullio said, scratching his head. 'I'm not sure where to go from here, to tell you the truth.'

'Have you questioned anyone?' James asked, curious to know what the procedure would be here and the extent to which it would differ from that used in Edinburgh.

Tullio shook his head. 'Machinetti found out that Soldati had no family in the city and so decided that there was no one to question. I have talked to his neighbour, though, and he said that it was likely that Soldati was at his local tavern the night it happened – La Capra. Apparently it was like a second home to him.'

'Perhaps we should go there and ask a few questions?' James suggested. 'He might have been followed from there. Someone could have seen something.'

Tullio nodded eagerly and together they set off to La Capra. James hoped that they could find something, no matter how small, that would take them a little closer to solving the mystery. Physical evidence was all very well but on its own it would not solve the crime. They needed to find out more about the victim, in the hope that it might give them something more to go on.

La Capra was located in the oldest part of Turin. In this area, as Tullio informed them, the slums were still in existence despite the efforts of the city authorities to wipe them away. James could smell the poverty – the stench of waste and want, decay and desperation. There was less of a bustle here than in other parts of the city. Although the streets were full of people, they moved more slowly somehow, as if they had no real purpose.

'Signore, signore – spare us a few lire,' an elderly man cried from a doorway. James paused as if to give him something but Ottolenghi stopped him, shaking his head.

The street was narrow, the cobbles were dirty and the sun was virtually obliterated by the height of the buildings which seemed so close to each other that it was almost as if they met in an arch above, just as James had seen in his dream.

They turned down an alleyway leading to a small square. An old sign with a picture of a goat's head hung above a small wooden door. It swung in the breeze, creaking as it did so. There was something familiar about the sound. James paused and shivered. He suddenly felt a sense of foreboding that he couldn't explain. Both Ottolenghi and Tullio, however, were apparently unmoved. Neither of them hesitated but went ahead and pushed their way through the door into the dark interior.

They all blinked as their eyes became accustomed to the gloom. It seemed to James that the smell inside was not much better than the one outside. He looked around the dingy interior and tried to imagine it full of drinkers but at first he couldn't conjure up the picture in his head. Who in their right mind would want to come to a place like this? Then he realised. It was the same tavern that Sofia had brought him to the previous night. He did not know whether it was because he had been a little drunk or simply bewitched by his companion, but it had all seemed a lot more inviting then. However, there was no mistaking it. Sofia had brought him to the same tavern that the victim frequented. Did that mean she knew him? If so, why had she not mentioned it?

A fat middle-aged man in a stained apron stood behind the bar, pointlessly polishing glasses with a dirty cloth. His raddled complexion with its broken veins and wrinkled features told their own story. He was obviously a man who liked to sample his own wares a little more than was good for him. Tullio drew his official badge from his pocket with a flourish and the man scowled. Police did not seem to be a welcome sight at La Capra. No doubt it usually indicated that someone's fortunes were about to change for the worse.

'We're not open yet.'

'We haven't come to drink,' Tullio said brusquely, 'but we do have some questions. Are you the owner?'

The innkeeper nodded. 'The name's Gambro. What do you want to know?' he asked guardedly.

'Do you know Giuseppe Soldati?'

Gambro hesitated. The look on his face betrayed the struggle that was going on inside his head. Should he talk and risk being seen as an informant or refuse and annoy the authorities? Would his desire for a quiet life overcome any scruples he might have? There was only one old man in the place to see him talk and he was slumped in a corner, presumably recovering from last night. Indeed, James had a hazy memory of seeing him in exactly the same position then.

Gambro's inner struggle apparently complete, he evidently decided to take the path of least resistance. 'What, old monkey man? Yes, I knew him. He drank in here regularly.'

'Why "monkey man"?' Ottolenghi asked.

'Why do you think? He looked like one with his big ears, flat nose and hairy arms. He was an ugly bastard.'

'You use the past tense. Why?' James asked, thinking that he might catch him out.

'He's dead, isn't he? Everyone knows that. Don't you read the papers?' He pointed at a news-sheet on the grimy bar.

Tullio grimaced. Neither his superior or Machinetti would be pleased that the news of the murder had spread. He picked up the paper and looked at its contents.

'What do you know?' James asked, keen to find out whether Lombroso's connection was public knowledge.

'Not much,' Gambro said, 'just that he had his nose and ears cut off.'

James looked at Tullio who nodded at him, confirming that this was all the information given and motioned to Gambro to join them at a table. They sat down, having chosen the one furthest from the slumbering old man.

'So, how well did you know Soldati?' Ottolenghi asked.

'I served him drink and passed the time of day with him. Sometimes I threw him out if he'd had too much. That's it.'

'Was he popular?'

Gambro laughed. 'Is anyone?' He leaned back in his seat. Time for some of his home spun philosophy with which he no doubt entertained his customers whenever they would listen. 'In this place, and dare I say it, in this world, if you can buy a few drinks you can be the most popular man in the room. But as soon as the money runs out and the drink stops flowing,' he clicked his fingers, 'you disappear from view.' Gambro paused and started to pick his nose thoughtfully. 'The thing about Soldati is that he was a mean bastard. He liked to scrounge but not to share. He won't be missed much.'

James's brows were furrowed with concentration. His Italian was good but his grasp of Piedmontese, was much more limited. He thought it best to allow Tullio and Ottolenghi to ask the questions and rose to explore the tavern, leaving the other two to continue. He could still listen while he looked round the place and they could tell him what was said in more detail later. He was aware of Gambro's eyes following him suspiciously.

'Did he have enemies?'

'Well, no one liked him. But no one hated him either. Not enough to chop him up anyway.' Gambro shuddered and shook his head. 'Who would do something like that?'

'Who else was here the night he was killed?' asked Ottolenghi.

'Usual crowd – Vilella, he's always here; Fat Maria, her mother Rosa, and Maria's daughter. Oh yes, and Carlo, Luigi the Fish, a few others – old Pietro, of course.' He nodded towards the sleeping man in the corner. 'The others will be in later, I shouldn't wonder, if you want a word.'

Tullio nodded. 'Yes, perhaps. Were there any strangers that you noticed?'

Gambro stroked his chin thoughtfully as he struggled to remember. 'Trouble is, one night in here is pretty much like another. But I think there was someone . . . a man that I hadn't seen before. He ordered a glass of our best Chianti and he sat in the corner. Oh yes, I remember now, we laughed because he sat in Pietro's place. He wasn't happy. We had to move him in the end.'

Tullio edged forwards in his seat. This could be significant. 'Do you remember what he looked like?'

'No, sorry. They all blur into one after a while. He wore a cloak, though, I do remember that, with a gold clasp. I noticed it because it shone. Not much shines in here, not even money. It caused quite a stir, not that it seemed to bother him. He looked as if he was in a world of his own.'

Suddenly there was a small commotion in the corner. Pietro had finally come out of his self-inflicted coma. 'Drink, I want a drink!'

Gambro gave a wry smile and went over to the bar to comply with his customer's demand.

Tullio and Ottolenghi got up to leave and James rejoined them. He had found little of interest. The place had several rooms, all of a similar size and there were no doors as such, just huge stone archways, roughly hewn. Most of the white-wash on the walls had seen better days and was peeling off in flakes like dead skin. You could see the entire tavern from the bar but not in detail. It was full of dark corners, perfect hiding places for those who did not want their business overheard. James thought to himself that it was just like any other place that sold cheap alcohol: dirty and smelly and, more likely than not, when open, full of rogues and whores. Then he remembered Sofia. Perhaps he should be less judg-mental. After all they were still people, as the professor had said, with friends and family and feelings like anyone else. Still, the place itself did not seem out of the ordinary – except for one thing that had intrigued him.

At the end of the furthest room there was a locked door with a table and a single chair in front of it. The back of the chair was in the shape of a goat's head and carved on the door behind it was another depiction of a horned creature, again presumably a goat after the tavern's name, but this time with human features. Beneath this was a crude carving of an upside-down cross. Did Devil worshippers meet here per-haps? Was this the gate to Hell? He smiled to himself. You'd certainly need a stiff drink if you were about to be on nodding terms with Old Nick.

'We'll be back later to talk to the others,' Tullio said.

'Thanks for the warning,' Gambro grunted as he turned his attention to filling Pietro's glass and taking his money.

As they retraced their steps along the narrow street Tullio explained the gist of the conversation to James.

'So we may have a suspect!' Ottolenghi said excitedly. 'The man in the cloak!'

'Well, perhaps.' Tullio was more guarded. 'It is little use having a suspect if we cannot identify him. I will return this evening and see if anyone remembers him and, more importantly, knows who he might be.'

'Will you bring some men to assist you?' James asked.

Tullio shook his head. 'I don't want anything to get back to Machinetti and I prefer to work on my own for now. I have not been here long and I confess I do not know exactly who to trust.'

'We will join you if we may,' Ottolenghi said, having got James's assent with a nod.

Tullio agreed and James thought he looked rather relieved. Tackling Gambro was one thing but questioning a whole host of ne'er-do-wells on their home ground was doubtless much more daunting. Tullio was of slight build with a neat though wispy little beard and small round glasses, not unlike Ottolenghi's. There was something old about him despite his youth, a kind of wizened quality. He didn't look as if he could stand up in a strong wind, let alone hold his own in a place like La Capra.

Solemnly they all shook hands and were about to part when a small figure emerged out of the shadows and gripped Ottolenghi's elbow. It was an elderly woman, short and shrivelled, with thin dirty grey hair and one lone tooth in the centre of her mouth, visible as she grimaced at them. It was only much later that James realised it was meant to be a smile.

The woman looked surreptitiously from side to side as if worried that she would be overheard. 'I hear you're looking for information.'

Tullio looked at her suspiciously as if he thought that it was unlikely that she knew anything of use. He addressed her in her native dialect and Ottolenghi whispered a quick translation for James's benefit.

'Tell us what you know, Grandma, and be quick about it.'

Her eyes narrowed and she rubbed the fingers of one hand together in front of Tullio's face.

'It'll cost you. Nothing is for free.'

Tullio raised his eyes to the heavens. 'I might have known that money would come into it.' He reached into his pocket and pulled out a few lire. He waved it in front of the woman's face.

'What do you know?'

She leaned forwards as if she was about to whisper something. Then her expression suddenly changed and fear leapt into her eyes.

'Later, in La Capra . . . ask for Rosa, Rosa Bruno,' she hissed. Snatching the money and taking to her heels she ran, faster than one might have thought she could manage. They turned simultaneously to try to see what had terrified her. James saw a figure wearing a large hat disappearing into the murky back streets. He thought that he caught a glimpse of a beard but it was hard to say for sure.

He exchanged glances with the other two and then, as one, they took off in pursuit. On they went, down one dark street after another, Tullio leading, then James and finally Otto-lenghi dutifully trying to keep up. There had been a recent heavy shower and the cobbles were greasy with a covering of mud and filth. James slipped and slid his way along in his thin-soled 'gentlemen's' shoes, inwardly cursing his decision to wear them rather than his stouter walking boots. Passers-by looked on curiously as they flew past; some had to jump out of the way, others tried to do so but were less successful and once or twice James and Ottolenghi almost ended up in a heap on the ground with an angry soul or two. As they approached a large square James thought that the game was up but the figure dashed across it into a large, imposing-looking building, complete with Doric columns and what seemed at first to be stone lions but turned out to be a pair of sphinx at either side of a flight of steps. A sign at the front identified it as the Museo Egizio, which held the largest and most comprehensive collection of Egyptian artefacts in Europe. James had intended to visit it whilst he was in the city, although he had anticipated a more leisurely journey through its exhibits. As it was he tore across the piazza as if he was pursued by the Devil himself, even though the only person on his heels was Ottolenghi who was clearly out of breath. When they got to the door they slowed to a stately fast walk as they were subjected to the stare of a portly guard. They stood in the foyer, turning this way and that but Tullio and the figure were nowhere to be seen. As they recovered their breath and took stock, James peered at the contents of a large glass case in the middle of the entrance hall. It was a mummified figure covered in leathery skin, its knees hunched up in a foetal position as if it was protecting itself.

Suddenly they heard a shout from above. They looked up and saw the figure run across a balcony with Tullio on its trail. They ran up the broad stone staircase onto the next floor and began their pursuit afresh, all the while dodging sarcophagi and eerie stone statues who seemed to follow their efforts with empty lifeless eyes. James and Ottolenghi turned a corner only to see Tullio go down a narrow staircase at the back of the building. They followed him through a small door but their efforts were to no avail. As they emerged from the relative darkness they found themselves in the brightness and grandeur of Piazza Carlo Alberto. Tullio held his hands up in despair as the figure melted into a crowd of onlookers gathered at what looked like a political rally. It was impossible to see where he had gone and they stopped to catch their breath. Ottolenghi doubled up for a moment or two. He grinned ruefully as he recovered himself and James gave him a comradely slap on the back.

'It seems that we're on to something,' Tullio pondered, 'or why else would he run?'

'I agree. Perhaps the old woman will be able to tell us more this evening,' Ottolenghi said, still breathing heavily.

'Indeed. Let us hope so. In any event I had better go before I am missed.'

Ottolenghi nodded. 'We should go as well. The professor will be wondering where we've got to.'

Reluctantly they parted, having arranged to meet at La Capra that evening. As James wandered back to the museum he thought how comforting it was not to be alone in this. Between the three of them maybe they really would hunt the killer down. Then perhaps his real Turin adventure could truly begin.

7

*I would not dream of detaining for life anyone with ab-
normal features until he is accused and convicted by the
courts . . . To claim that criminal anthropology threatens
individual liberty is as absurd as concluding that when you
add two numbers, the result is a lesser rather than greater
sum.*   Lombroso, 1889 p 235

Later that afternoon James arrived at the university's Great
Hall ready to experience the opening of the symposium.
Ottolenghi had told him who would be speaking over the
next few days and it was an impressive list. His father had
introduced him to the works of many of them and they had
discussed some of their theories in detail.

James had inherited from his father a fascination with the
workings of the human mind, particularly in relation to
criminality. He remembered sitting with him in his study,
happy and excited as they talked about his work. His father
would tell him about the different areas of the brain and what
damage to them might mean. James had been particularly
fascinated by the story of Phineas Gage, a man who had
miraculously survived an horrific accident whilst working
on the railways in America. A large iron crowbar was driven
completely through his head, destroying the area at the front

of his brain known as the left frontal lobe. This was the first recorded case where the personality had changed and the man was transformed from being a shrewd and energetic person into a capricious, almost childlike character with an impulsive streak and a tendency to swear. According to the attending physician Gage had vomited and half a teacupful of his brain fell onto the floor.

James remembered the relish with which this story and others were told. 'What secrets might we find in a criminal brain?' his father had said. 'If we can find and unlock them, then who knows what we can achieve!'

'How can we do that?' James had asked.

'By looking at the brains themselves. There's a man who has done just that.' Then he had told him about Moriz Benedikt who dissected the brains of executed criminals to see if they differed from those of law-abiding men. He had found this idea at once both fascinating and repellent, even more so when his father's obsession with the subject had led to tragedy and so turned James's interest into a personal crusade. But for now, he was still a student, looking forward to seeing in the flesh those whom he had, up till now, only admired from a distance.

James entered the hall with some trepidation and immediately began to wish that he had arranged to meet Ottolenghi outside. The room was enormous, wood panelled and hung with portraits of bewigged luminaries from centuries gone by, none of whom he recognised. They stared at him sternly from the confines of their gilt frames as if challenging his right to be in their august presence.

There was a platform at one end, clearly set out for the debate, with rows of seating in front of it. The room was full of serious-looking men, soberly dressed for the most part, with the odd splash of colour from a fancy waistcoat or a cravat, sported, no doubt, to mark the wearer out as an eccentric. They stood about in groups talking earnestly. There was much gesticulation and even some raised voices, perhaps a result of the glasses of what looked like sherry being respectfully distributed by uniformed waiters. James could see Lombroso standing near the platform listening intently to Oskar Reiner whose words were illustrated by small precise hand movements as if was dissecting a body. Borelli stood with them. He saw a flash of bright colour in the distance; Anna Tarnovsky, looking resplendent in a fine purple gown. Her work was renowned and she was surrounded by a group of male admirers who were hanging on her every word. He considered going over to join them but thought the better of it as it meant pushing past the crowds. He felt a tap on his shoulder and turned to see Ottolenghi grinning at him.

'What do you think?'

'I wonder how much of the conversation is about criminal anthropology.'

'Well, not all of it, I think you'll find.'

'I'm not surprised,' James said as looked at the throng. 'Dr Bell was always complaining about his colleagues gossiping. It used to drive him mad.'

'Ah, well it's no different here,' Ottolenghi replied. 'Come with me and you'll soon see what I mean.'

As James followed him slowly through the crowds towards the row of seats in front of the platform he could hear snatches of conversations.

'He's nothing more than a bully. I told him straight – you don't intimidate me, Professor.'

'They spend far too much time together. It's not good for the faculty.'

'He only got the position because he knows the Duke.'

'Have you heard about Danillo – he claimed he had written the whole thing, when I know for a fact he only contributed a couple of lines!'

'That man is intellectually dishonest! He cannot prove a single thing he has written using the proper scientific method, so he falls back on anecdotes and flimflam.'

'I've told him a thousand times – your sample has to be pure. Yet he just ignores me as if I don't know what I'm talking about. It's too much, it really is.'

Eventually they reached the first row of the seating and Ottolenghi turned to him triumphantly. 'There! We're guaranteed decent seats now.'

James laughed. 'It's interesting, isn't it? Here are some of the finest minds in Europe all gathered together and all they do is gossip.'

Ottolenghi grinned at him wryly. 'They may have fine minds but they're academics. Gossip is their life blood – and the professor is no different.'

He indicated behind him to Lombroso who was listening intently as someone whispered in his ear. A smile spread its way over his face and he looked over towards DeClichy with narrowed eyes. No one, it seemed, was immune. Suddenly Ottolenghi nudged him and pointed at a small, rotund-looking man with a carefully waxed moustache who was making his way towards the stage.

'That's Professor Arturo Gemelli, dean of the faculty. He's going to introduce the debate.'

James looked at Gemelli's surly expression. 'He doesn't look particularly pleased about it.'

'Well, he wouldn't be. He envies the professor's success and has been trying to halt his work ever since he took over.

126

He thinks it's frivolous at best and, at worst, positively blasphemous.'

'That's interesting,' James said. 'I can understand if people are sceptical, that is part of any scientific endeavour. But blasphemous? That's going too far, surely.'

Ottolenghi grinned at his reaction. 'Gemelli is a Catholic – his cousin is a cardinal who is well known for his opposition to criminal anthropology. Welcome to the new kingdom of Italy, my friend! Here the Church is everything – or thinks it is at least.'

James was going to ask him to expand when the crowd started to fall silent and people made their way to the seating area. Ottolenghi motioned towards him to sit. The debate was about to begin. He saw Lombroso and DeClichy walk onto the stage and take their places and felt as nervous as if he was about to speak himself. He could feel the tension coming from Lombroso who looked pale and strained.

'Is the professor all right?' he asked Ottolenghi.

Ottolenghi nodded. 'Don't worry. He's usually like this before he starts speaking. He's used to it. He always plays to packed houses.'

'Aren't some of his critics in the audience, though?'

'Yes, but that won't trouble him. The professor is famous for his showmanship, so a little heckling won't faze him.'

'Heckling?'

'Passions run high here. We've even had one or two fist fights among the younger crowd.'

James thought back to Dr Bell's lectures and considered the similarities between the two men. Both, it seemed to him, had a sense of drama, although proceedings were more subdued at home. No fist fights there, just a few raised voices. He looked around him. The sense of eager anticipation was palpable. The audience continued to murmur and whisper among themselves until finally Professor Gemelli held up his hands to quieten them.

'Gentlemen, honoured guests – welcome to Turin. This afternoon we are to hear from Professor Lombroso and Dr DeClichy on the subject of the born criminal.' Gemelli paused and frowned. There was some urgent sounding coughing coming from behind a velvet curtain at the side of the platform. Lombroso got up and whispered in Gemelli's ear. Gemelli scowled back at him. 'Apparently the debate is to be chaired by a special delegate.' He spat out the last two words as if they were morsels of food that disagreed with him. His face was a study of resentment as he turned and flounced off the stage. The murmuring began again. Suddenly a tall, imposing figure with an untidy dark beard and intense dark eyes emerged from behind the curtain. Ottolenghi looked surprised and leant over to whisper in James ear. 'Borelli didn't say that he would be chairing.'

James looked at Borelli with renewed interest. He wondered why he had not mentioned his participation.

'Gentlemen – and Madame,' Borelli began, nodding briefly at Madame Tarnovsky, the only woman in the room, 'let us begin the debate. The motion is a simple one: "Criminals are born not made." To speak in favour of the motion we will hear from the distinguished gentleman on my right, Professor Cesare Lombroso, and to speak against, an equally distinguished delegate, Dr DeClichy.'

Lombroso rose and bowed slightly before going over to a lectern in the centre of the platform. 'The first thing I must tell you is that I cannot speak in favour of this motion.' This was met with a stunned silence. James looked at Ottolenghi who had put his hand over his lower face. Horton, sitting near them, was frowning.

Lombroso smiled slowly. 'Well, not entirely . . .'

'About time,' shouted a voice from the back of the room. 'Hear, hear! What about poverty?' said another. James saw DeClichy nodding vigorously. Ottolenghi nudged him. 'What did I tell you?'

Lombroso stood and stared at them, stroking his beard and nodding, as if contemplating what they had said. 'Of course one cannot rule out such matters but to my mind they are not as potent as heredity.'

Some chattering began from the floor. It seemed as if Lombroso had lost his audience. James looked around him and noticed Horton beaming. Then Borelli got up and held up his arms to hush them. The room became quiet as if he had cast a spell over it.

'Gentlemen, gentlemen – this is a serious debate, not a fairground.'

Lombroso began to speak again.

'It is always interesting to hear critiques even when they are . . . well, let us just say: misguided. However, they cannot be ignored. And that is why I have altered my view slightly . . . *very* slightly.'

There was muted laughter from the audience and some people began to clap. Ottolenghi removed his hand. He was grinning behind it and had been all along. Presumably he had been forewarned.

Lombroso held up his hand and the audience fell silent again. 'Allow me to explain. Had the motion said *some* criminals are born not made then I could agree most heartily.' This was greeted by murmurings of comprehension. Lombroso continued, 'Therefore, for the purposes of this afternoon, and in order to give Dr DeClichy something to shout about, I will assume that the motion says just that.' DeClichy smiled thinly. James could see that he had been taken by surprise and was less than happy.

'It is quite true that, when I began my researches into the nature of the criminal, I firmly believed *all* were born that way and could be detected by physical abnormalities or anomalies. But what kind of scientist would I be if my mind could not be changed by the evidence of my own eyes?'

There were noises of approval coming from the audience. The one or two voices of dissent were immediately hushed. Lombroso seemed to have everyone in the palm of his hand.

'My adversaries, and there are many, usually from elsewhere,' he looked sternly towards DeClichy, 'often complain that the rates of anomalies vary too much to advance a claim that all criminals are born so.' He paused for effect. 'And may I say that I quite agree. But we must remember that real life, in all of its glorious confusion, has a habit of producing complex data which, in turn, directly reflects the multiformity of nature.'

Lombroso looked round at them all sitting there, faces turned up towards him, bathing in the glow of his knowledge. Any strain had disappeared. This, James realised, was the real Lombroso: crafty, and manipulative, but inspiring and brilliant too. He was tricking his audience with his apparent humility and they were completely taken in by him.

'Critics also object that no criminal is a complete throwback to early man. But I do not claim that they are. According to Signor Darwin it is rare to find an anomaly that is completely isolated. Any anomaly may be associated with others, but total atavistic regression is impossible. But still when one considers the indications of the criminal type –

asymmetry of the face, large ears, eye defects, fleshy lips, cheek pouches, abundant wrinkles, excessive arm length and so on, at least some of these are visible in the born criminal. The evidence is clear from my own work.'

On Lombroso went, tackling each and every complaint about his theories and in the process sounding every inch the rational and reasonable man he wanted them all to believe him to be. He gave the audience anecdotes to illustrate and entertain them; he smiled, laughed and cajoled until each and every one of them, including the hecklers, with the exception perhaps of Walter B. Horton, was completely under his spell. Even DeClichy was listening intently though he flinched occasionally whenever heredity or atavism were mentioned. It all sounded so convincing, James thought. That is, until you started to analyse Lombroso's words more closely. Then he was not so sure. He looked at the stage. Lombroso was building to his climax, working the audience like a true showman.

'Gentlemen, we are privileged to live in these times when science can take us to places that a few years ago were beyond our wildest dreams. Let us not then deny possibilities by scorn or derision; let us not turn away from the purity of scientific knowledge and replace it with limp social theories. We are at the dawn of a new age of discovery – let us embrace it as scientists and bring a new world where logic rather than emotion is paramount. Once we have identified a criminal we will be harsh, not cruel. We will no longer treat the guilty with anger and disdain but with understanding. All of this can be achieved – but only if we rely on science.'

The response was immediate. Each and every member of the audience rose to his feet and applauded. There were cheers and whistles and cries of bravo. Some people even stamped their feet. Lombroso stood before them smiling beatifically as if they were all his children and he was their teacher. James thought about what the professor had said and he was puzzled. It didn't appear to make complete sense. His arguments seemed to have strayed far from the motion he was meant to be supporting. But then he thought back to that moment when he was as captivated by Lombroso as everyone else in the room – and he understood. It didn't really matter what the man said to them. They wanted to believe him because at that moment they loved him, no matter what. That was his power, not his experiments or his theories, but his *personality*. And it held them all in his thrall. James could also see then why he might have enemies. Envy can produce hatred like no other emotion, except perhaps revenge.

DeClichy had grown paler as Lombroso's speech went on, his lips narrowing until they were barely visible. James almost felt sorry for him. How could he possibly follow this? The doctor stood and moved over to the lectern. The room fell silent but for a few bouts of coughing and throat clearing. There was some shuffling as people began to leave.

Borelli stood up and looked sternly at them but to no avail. In a moment the room seemed no more than half full. 'Dr DeClichy will now speak against the motion,' he said.

DeClichy took a deep breath and began.

'I would like to thank Professor Lombroso for his con-cessions, although I am bound to say they do not go far enough.' His voice was quiet and faltering, a complete contrast to Lombroso's booming oratory.

The audience began to mumble and whisper. DeClichy cleared his throat. 'I may not be able to speak with the eloquence of our previous speaker but I still have plenty to say.'

'Well say it then!' cried a voice from the floor.

'Yes, get on with it!' said another.

DeClichy stared at them and drew himself up to his full height. 'It may be comforting to believe that criminals are different from you and I, that they are atavistic throwbacks to more primitive times and that they have differing physical characteristics. But I am afraid that they are not. The sad truth is that they are *just* like us.'

'Speak for yourself, DeClichy!'

'Oh I do, Monsieur, I do. I came from a poor background but my parents saw to it that I was educated. Others I grew up with were not so lucky. My best friend when I was a child is now languishing in prison – a thief and a murderer brought to crime by circumstances, not biology.'

The audience was attentive now as DeClichy went on explaining his case, with quiet dignity. As James listened he felt torn. On the one hand Lombroso was so sure of his theories and such a compelling speaker that it was hard to disagree. And yet on the other, DeClichy also spoke eloquently, albeit in a different style. The stories he was telling about his upbringing were moving and had an authenticity that Lombroso could not match, even with his tales of criminals he had examined over the years.

Finally the speech came to a close with a dignified summary of his ideas and how they differed from those of Lombroso. He sat down and Borelli got to his feet, presumably to ask Lombroso if he wished to reply. Before he could speak Horton rose and turned to face the audience.

Ottolenghi looked at James, a puzzled expression on his face. No one had expected this. Was Horton going to speak in support of Lombroso or DeClichy? It occurred to James that despite his conversations with the man he had no idea what, if anything, Horton actually believed in. James looked over to DeClichy who was leaning forward intently, almost as if he was urging Horton on.

Borelli looked irritated. 'Dr Horton, the speakers have a right to reply before we hear from the floor!'

Lombroso got up. 'I don't mind, if DeClichy doesn't.'

DeClichy nodded his agreement, as did Borelli.

'Very well, Dr Horton?'

Horton smiled slyly. 'Professor Lombroso is not the only one who wishes to depart from the motion. You see, I believe that criminals are indeed born not made. When we know this as certainly as the professor has us believe, then surely it is our duty to act on this knowledge – this pure, scientific, sure knowledge.'

Horton seemed to be spitting out the words with such venom it was hard to know if he was sincere or simply being sarcastic. DeClichy was frowning, apparently as confused as the rest of them.

'Our duty then is to catch these born criminals, lock them up and throw away the key. That or to execute them, publicly and in all kinds of unpleasant ways in order to deter their brothers.' Horton paused and smiled as if savouring the possibility. 'Alternatively, the incarcerated can still be useful. Medical science always needs subjects, after all. Even we surgeons need practice. They could be experimented on for the furtherance of science. But they must all be exterminated eventually, let us make no mistake about that. We must purify ourselves by extinguishing the impure. For, after all, that is what the criminal race is – is it not? Impure, dirty, filthy even. Something we need to expunge from our ranks.' He paused for effect. The room was completely silent.

'Humanity needs to be cleansed,' he went on. 'Then we can truly engage with free will, for those who remain will be rational and able to consider the disadvantages of criminal behaviour, with the sure knowledge that any such act will be dealt with severely. Social factors are not the reason for the depravity of crime. It is heredity, race, atavism. Criminals are savages. We know this thanks to Professor Lombroso.' Horton looked over to Lombroso who stared back, as if startled, as many others seemed to be, by what he was hearing.

'His painstaking experiments have shown us the way. Not only that but now, due entirely to Professor Lombroso and his . . . admirable work . . . we know who to target. We know who is the criminal and who is not. We know then exactly, certainly, surely, scientifically, who we need to eliminate. We know who must die.'

Horton looked around, smiling his empty smile. James had felt a slight shiver go down his spine as he listened to him speak. The words seemed horribly familiar, for James had heard something similar uttered before, by his father in an unguarded moment and, indeed, by others in the scientific community. He was as appalled now as he had been then and it seemed that he was not alone. A sea of bemused faces looked up at Horton whose eyes glinted with satisfaction. James waited for him to laugh, to say it was all a joke and that it was the only way to get attention after Lombroso's virtuoso performance. But Horton said nothing, and then James remembered his comment at the salon. He said it would not be dull and so it had proved. On and on the silence went. It felt as if it might go on forever for no one knew how to break it.

At last Borelli stood up and went over to the lectern. 'Very interesting, Dr Horton. You have given me, given all of us who are engaged in scientific research, a salutary reminder of what our theories might persuade others to do in our name. We should be grateful for your words and never forget them.' He glanced towards Lombroso who nodded sagely.

Borelli looked over to Lombroso. 'You have the right of reply, Professor. I'm sure you wish to exercise it – and you, Dr DeClichy, of course.' De Clichy shook his head. 'I see,' Borelli said. 'So, Professor, it is for you to comment.'

Lombroso nodded. 'I will address my comments to Dr Horton's ideas as you all know my view on those of Dr DeClichy.'

There was a murmur of approval from the audience. James looked over to DeClichy who looked somewhat crestfallen. He had spoken so eloquently and yet Lombroso had managed to dismiss his ideas in a sentence. It seemed unnecessarily unpleasant, somehow, like kicking a sick dog.

Lombroso rose to general applause. 'I must admit that Dr Horton's address has given me food for thought. It is of course important for us to consider not only the nature of criminals but what our conclusions mean for criminal justice and society generally. It has long been my view that for most offenders it is better to keep them out of our prisons.'

There were some mutterings of agreement. Lombroso raised his hand to quieten them and continued.

'But for the atavistic born criminal, who, by his very nature, is completely resistant to reform, I can only suggest permanent incarceration. The natural result of that would be to reduce, albeit gradually, the not inconsiderable proportion of criminality that stems from heredity factors.'

A smattering of applause greeted this, although James

found himself unable to join in. Lombroso inclined his head graciously to acknowledge it and then went on.

'I did however find some of the good doctor's points somewhat hard to swallow. I believe that he went too far with his apparent suggestions of wholesale extermination of the criminal classes. I was even a little shocked.'

Someone laughed inappropriately, perhaps overcome by the air of tension that was in the room. Lombroso looked puzzled for a moment, shook his head slightly and continued.

'But Professor Borelli, as we have come to expect of him, has seen more clearly what the doctor has been trying to do for us. The good Dr Horton has made the most affecting and significant speech that I think I have ever heard in all my years of practice. For he has issued us with a warning that, as Borelli so rightly says, we must never forget. As scientists we work diligently on our theories trying to prove that such and such is the case and sometimes we become obsessive. It is true that I am as guilty of that as any of you here today. This can lead us to forget ourselves, our families and friends. But most disturbingly it can lead us to forget one thing that we should never, ever forget.'

He paused and looked round at all of them as if he was familiar with each and every one of his audience individually. Perhaps, thought James, he was. After all, his celebrity was such that everyone wanted to know him even if the feeling was not always reciprocated. He went on.

'The one thing that we must not allow to become buried beneath our theories is this. Science has consequences and they are our responsibility. May I therefore thank Dr Horton on the behalf of all scientists everywhere. You have shown us where our work might lead and for that we will be forever in your debt.'

Then the applause began. Horton grinned joylessly and began to laugh as if he hadn't meant anything that he had said to be taken at face value. James saw DeClichy staring at Horton, not with dislike but some other emotion – alarm perhaps? It wasn't surprising, thought James. Horton would worry anyone. He fought his way through the crowd to DeClichy.

'Doctor?'

DeClichy turned and looked at him in surprise. 'It's Dr Murray, is it not?' he said in perfect English. It seemed strange to James to hear his native tongue spoken in this alien environment but it was welcome.

'I just wanted to say how much I enjoyed your arguments. They were very well put.'

DeClichy bowed slightly in acknowledgement. 'Thank you. It is much appreciated. But I think you may be in somewhat of a minority.' He smiled wryly.

'Dr Horton should not have upstaged you like that. It was badly done!'

'You are kind, Dr Murray, but it is my own fault. I should not have allowed his interruption to go on for so long. Now if you'll excuse me, I must go. There is something I must attend to. Perhaps I will see you later at the reception?'

James nodded and watched him push through the crowds almost unnoticed, almost as if he had never spoken at all. A decent man, he thought, self-effacing, the kind of person one could trust.

The applause had died away and people began to assemble in groups to chatter about what they had just heard. Lombroso came down from the platform and made his way over to James and Ottolenghi. It took him a while for it seemed that everybody in the hall wished to speak to him, offering words of encouragement and congratulation. Eventually he reached them.

'So, Murray, what did you think of that?' he asked.

'I thought it was . . .' He paused trying to think of what to say. '. . . extraordinary, Professor.'

Lombroso stared at him for a moment, as if wondering how to take this. Then he smiled. 'Thank you, thank you – but more importantly, dear boy, did you learn something from it?'

James nodded. 'I think so but I still am unsure about one thing.'

'What's that?'

'Was Dr Horton sincere in what he said or was he really teaching us all a lesson?'

Lombroso looked over to Horton who was standing on the other side of the room with Borelli. Most were giving them a wide berth, presumably because they had the same question in their minds as James. A few did seem to be approaching him, although whether or not that was because they agreed with his views was difficult to work out. Between them Borelli and Lombroso had ensured that no one knew exactly what it was that Horton really stood for.

Lombroso sighed. 'That is a question only Dr Horton can answer but I hope that Borelli was right and he was merely playing games. Now I must go over and rescue Borelli from Horton's clutches. I will see you both at the reception later.' With that he started to make his way over towards them, again being complimented and congratulated at every turn.

Ottolenghi grinned at James. 'That was quite a show!'

James smiled to himself, remembering that that was

139

exactly how Horton had described it during their first encounter at the museum. 'Yes,' he replied, 'but it was not entirely fair, was it? It was supposed to be a debate between the professor and DeClichy. Horton completely took it over!'

'True,' Ottolenghi said, 'but Horton was far more interesting, don't you think? And the professor's reply was so very clever!'

James shrugged. 'If you say so, but still . . .'

People were starting to leave. He saw Borelli and Reiner escorting Madame Tarnovsky from the room, chatting animatedly. Suddenly Borelli turned and looked over towards Lombroso and Horton. The expression on Borelli's face as he stared at them was not what James expected. It seemed somehow out of character; it wasn't exactly malevolent but there was something cold about it, as if he was willing something unpleasant to happen to one of them. James assumed that he was angry with Horton. Suddenly he caught Borelli's eye. Borelli gave him a beaming although strangely soulless smile before leaving.

Ottolenghi yawned. 'I don't know about you but all this has made me tired. I wouldn't mind a bit of a rest before we meet Tullio.'

James readily agreed. It had been a long day and it was far from over yet.

8

Nearly all criminals have jug ears, thick hair, thin beards, pronounced sinuses, protruding chins and broad cheekbones.

Lombroso, 1876 p 53

It was dark by the time James arrived at La Capra. A thick fog had descended upon the city and he could only just see the figure of Ottolenghi through the gloom. He could smell drains and a slight whiff of sulphur as if they were about to wander into hell itself.

As they pushed their way through the door James noted that the smell coming from within had not improved since that morning. In fact, it was worse. Now, as well as stale beer and tobacco, there was an overwhelming stink of sweaty bodies. This was unsurprising, given that the place heaved with a mass of drinkers. Quite why it should be such a popular venue, he simply couldn't work out. He would not have come here by choice, that was for sure.

Grotesque-looking women with brightly rouged cheeks sat around the rickety old tables with their various male companions, cackling raucously at jokes and calling out to one another. The old man, Pietro, was still in his place in the corner, a half-full tankard before him, sitting staring into the distance, muttering to himself.

The crowd fell silent as they made their way to the counter, where Tullio was waiting. James looked around and saw hostile glares everywhere. It was clear that they were not welcome. He had some sympathy. This was not their territory and the regular patrons would not have known the reason for their presence. It probably looked as though they were looking for a thrill or two by visiting insalubrious areas of the city to view its inhabitants as if they were exhibits in a zoo. He'd done it himself, as a student back in Edinburgh, and he wasn't proud of it. At the time he had told himself that it was in order to broaden his horizons. But the truth was he was just curious to see how others lived.

Tullio looked James and Ottolenghi up and down. They were both dressed formally as they had to go on directly to the reception.

'I see you've done your best to blend in,' he said dryly. 'It's just as well we're not working undercover.' Ottolenghi looked at James and shrugged. James personally thought that Tullio was being a little unfair. He hardly blended in himself with his starched collar and carefully shined boots. He looked every inch what he was, indeed what they all were – young men out of their depth. Suddenly he smiled at them and James thought that he detected a look of relief. 'Still, I am glad to see you.'

Ottolenghi nodded. 'Has the old woman shown up?'

'Not yet. The barman, Gambro, was surprised she wasn't here. Normally she's here every night without fail. Maybe she'll turn up later. I've asked him to point out who was here on the night of the murder. He thinks that man over there would be worth talking to. His name's Vilella.'

Tullio indicated a white-haired man with hooded eyes, who was having an animated, if one-sided, conversation with old Pietro. His skin was wrinkled and leathery but his expression was alert, as if he was waiting for someone to leap out and attack him.

'Shall we?' Tullio suggested.

Ottolenghi looked at him thoughtfully. 'That name's familiar. I'm sure the professor has mentioned it.'

'Could be relevant, I suppose,' replied Tullio. 'Let's talk to him.'

'Are you sure that's a good idea?' James asked nervously.

'I'm a policeman. I have authority,' declared Tullio in a voice that did not sound as if he entirely believed it.

They went over to the pair and sat down next to them. James almost retched as a curious, sour smell from Vilella assaulted his nostrils. He caught Ottolenghi's eye as he moved away slightly, hoping that a couple of inches might provide olfactory relief.

Vilella glared at them. 'What do you want? You're not from round here. Bugger off!'

Pietro whispered in his ear and his eyes narrowed to hostile slits as he scowled at them malevolently.

'Police! I might have guessed. Well, you can get lost. I'm no snitch. I've nothing to say to you.'

'We have something to say to you. Some questions,' Tullio said firmly.

Pietro whispered into Vilella's ear once more. He nodded.

'Soldati . . . well, I don't know anything. He was a dirty scrounger who no one really liked. He obviously pissed off somebody. That's all I can say. I didn't see anything.'

'Do you know Professor Lombroso from the university?' asked Ottolenghi.

James thought that a connection between Lombroso and

this old reprobate was unlikely and was surprised when Vilella nodded.

'That bastard used my uncle's skull in an experiment. He didn't pay my family a penny. What's he got to do with Soldati?'

Tullio ignored Vilella's questions and continued with his own. 'Tell me more about Soldati. Did he have any serious enemies?'

'I don't know. I barely spoke to the man. Still, what a way to go! Nowhere's safe these days.'

Ottolenghi gave an ironic laugh. 'Not with the likes of you on the streets, no.'

Tullio looked at him disapprovingly. He clearly didn't want his interrogation interrupted.

Vilella scowled. 'Look, I don't have to answer your questions. In fact, it'll cost you if want to ask me anything else.'

'You'll get a drink out of it but that's all,' Tullio said firmly.

Vilella nodded. Clearly it was better than nothing.

'Did you notice anyone unusual in here that night?'

Vilella thought for a while. 'Well, there was the bloke in the corner. I couldn't see his face though. Pietro would probably remember him, wouldn't you?'

He turned to Pietro who looked at them with a terrified expression on his face. He shook his head vigorously and whispered into Vilella's ear.

'He says he saw nothing.'

'Where were you when Soldati left?' Ottolenghi asked.

'I was still in here when they found the body. Carlo had had a bit of luck and was buying a few drinks. You don't leave when someone's feeling generous.'

'Why did Soldati go?'

'He never bought anyone a drink, tight-fisted bastard. Carlo didn't include him so he got the message and buggered off. Speaking of which, I want my drink now. I reckon I've earned it. I've told you all I know.'

Tullio nodded in resignation and they got up and went back to the bar.

'So we're not much further forwards,' Ottolenghi said.

'No,' agreed Tullio. 'Anyway, I don't like Vilella for this. He's a thief – as simple as that. He hasn't got it in him to kill anyone, not like that, anyway.'

They ordered more drinks, including one for Vilella, and found a quiet table. There they sat and discussed the case. Tullio suggested that they ask Lombroso to advise them on what sort of person they might be looking for.

Ottolenghi shook his head, glumly. 'We can't. Don't you remember? He doesn't want us to investigate.'

'Perhaps we could ask him again – or maybe just one of us. We're only trying to help, after all,' James suggested.

Ottolenghi looked at him. 'I'm not sure. Let's wait and see if the right opportunity arises.'

James nodded his agreement; after all, they had little choice. Neither of them wanted to lose their positions with Lombroso.

Tullio looked at his watch. 'Shouldn't you two be getting to your reception? It's almost eight.'

'You're right. We'd better go. When do you want to meet again?' asked Ottolenghi.

Tullio sighed. 'I'll contact you when there's something to investigate. We seem to have reached a dead end so far.'

James and Ottolenghi both rose to leave but Tullio stayed in his seat.

'I'll wait a while in case the old woman turns up. You never know, perhaps she'll have something useful to say.'

Bidding him a subdued goodbye they were headed for the door when Ottolenghi placed a hand on James's arm. 'Look, over there, isn't that . . . ?'

James followed his glance to the corner of the furthest of the small rooms at the back of the tavern where, in front of the door with the carving on it, the chair with the goat's head stood. In it sat Rosa Bruno, head bent towards a woman who was wearing a hooded cloak. They were in close conversation. A man stood next to them, in the shadows, his hat pulled over his eyes and a scarf around his mouth, hiding what was left of his face. James thought he caught a glimpse of colour beneath the man's large coat.

'Where did she spring from?' Ottolenghi said. 'And who's the man with them?'

'Go and tell Tullio,' James said. 'I'll make sure they don't get away.'

Ottolenghi did as he was asked and James began to make his way through the crowd towards the old woman. Unfortunately his clothes made him stand out and he was subjected to some jeering as he pushed his way through the tables.

A large woman who could only have been Fat Maria, as described by Gambro, got up and barred his way. She shook her enormous breasts at him and winked.

'Evening, your Lordship. How about it? Interested in a little tête-à-tête?'

'What about another drink, your highness? On you, of course,' Vilella said, leering at him.

'Drinks all round. The toff's paying!' cried someone and a cheer went up. Suddenly James was surrounded by sweaty bodies pressing themselves against him. Fat Maria ruffled his hair with one hand and he felt her other reach between his legs.

'Do you mind?' he said, removing her podgy fingers from his trousers.

She paid no attention, pushing her face into his. 'Come on, darling, don't be unfriendly . . .'

'Madam, signora, I have no wish to be rude!' he said in desperation, pushing her away.

'Ooh, signora, is it? That's a bit formal. You can call me Maria, sweetheart. Come on, m'lord Inglese. Show us what you're made of!'

'Actually, I'm a Scot,' James said indignantly as he pushed and pulled in an effort to get way. Eventually he succeeded, although not before Maria had planted a damp kiss on his cheek. As he got to the edge of the crowd he saw that the man and the old woman had gone, leaving their companion sitting alone. She turned towards him and he took a step back in surprise as she threw back her hood. It was Sofia. She looked at him, her expression cold. It was clear she did not welcome his presence.

'Good evening, signor,' she said.

Before James could say anything they were joined by Tullio and Ottolenghi.

'Sofia, where's the old lady?' Ottolenghi asked urgently.

Sofia shrugged.

'You were with her. She can't have just disappeared,' Tullio said.

'She left,' Sofia said sullenly. 'I do not know where she went.'

'And the man?' James asked.

'What man?'

'He was standing next to you,' James said.

Sofia shook her head. 'I don't know who you mean.'

'What were you talking about?' Ottolenghi asked.

'Nothing . . .'

'You must have been talking about something,' Tullio said. 'How do you know the old woman?'

'She is an acquaintance.'

'Oh come on, you were deep in conversation. It couldn't just have been gossip,' James said, impatiently.

'Why are you interrogating me?' Sofia asked.

'We need to find the old lady,' James said. 'It's important, Sofia.'

'I cannot help you,' she said.

He grabbed her hand and looked into her eyes. 'Please.'

She sighed. 'Rosa Bruno is a "*maga*".'

Tullio nodded his understanding. 'A sorceress or wise woman.'

'You believe in this nonsense?' James asked Sofia, surprised.

Sofia pulled away from him angrily. 'I do not believe in *stregoneria* – witchcraft – but Rosa is a healer.'

'What do you need a healer for?' James asked.

'It is not your business!' Sofia replied.

'What are you doing meeting her here anyway?' Ottolenghi asked. 'I'm not sure the professor would be happy to know you frequent places like this.'

'I work for the professor. He does not own me,' Sofia said, coldly. 'Now, may I go?'

Tullio nodded and she started to leave.

'Wait, I'll walk you home,' James said. 'It is not safe for you to be alone.' He turned to Ottolenghi. 'I'll see you at the reception. Please offer Professor Lombroso my apologies and tell him that I will be there as soon as I can.'

Ottolenghi nodded his agreement and he and Tullio

watched as James escorted Sofia to the door, amid further jeers from the crowd. Before they could reach it Vilella stood in front of them.

Tullio came over. 'On your way now, Vilella.'

Vilella scowled and suddenly grabbed Sofia by the arm and whispered something to her. She pulled away and ran to the door with James following in her wake.

Once they were outside, Sofia stalked off into the night, leaving James to scuttle after her like an errant child following its mother. After a while, though, she relented and her pace slowed, allowing him to catch up and walk with her rather than behind.

'Why are you so angry?' James asked. 'What did Vilella say?'

'I am angry with *you*, not him. You should not have followed me,' she replied.

'We didn't. It was a coincidence. I had no idea you would be there!'

Sofia stopped and turned to him, frowning. 'I have my own life. It is private.'

James looked at her as she stood there, her chin held up defiantly, her dark eyes flashing with fury and pride. He realised what a mistake it would be to underestimate such a woman. 'I know. I am sorry if we embarrassed you.'

'Rosa is my friend. We cannot afford doctors at fancy prices so she helps us all in one way or another.'

'She said that she had something to tell us. Do you know what that might have been?'

'No, I do not. Please do not ask me any more.'

'And the man?' James tried again.

'He was not with us.'

'Are you sure?'

'Stop this! I have told you. He was not with us. And Rosa was helping me. There is no more to say.'

'I had to ask you. You do understand, Sofia? Rosa might be in danger.'

Sofia sighed and held out her hand. 'Enough please, James. Now come. It's this way.' She began to lead him through the streets as she had done before. As they walked he could feel the warmth of her hand and smell her perfume, spice and a hint of citrus, like an exotic dish of ripe fruit. Before long she stopped. 'We are here,' she said, looking up at him and smiling in her usual enigmatic way. Suddenly James could wait no longer. He pulled her to him and kissed her. She tasted of cinnamon. He felt her body press against him, voluptuous and yielding and it was as if he had, for an instant, become part of her. All that had happened since they met and even before that seemed inconsequential. It was just he and Sofia in their world and everyone and everything else could wait.

'Do you want to come up, *caro*?' whispered Sofia in his ear. 'I have some wine or more *grappa*?'

James looked into her dark eyes. 'You are so beautiful . . .' he said. 'So, so beautiful . . .' Then he groaned. 'I can't, I just can't.'

'Why not? Do you not want to drink with me?'

He kissed her again. 'More than I can say, but I am supposed to be with the professor. He's expecting me at the reception and I'm late already. I could come back later.' Sofia smiled again. 'We'll see,' she said, laughing gently as she went up the rickety steps to her rooms. 'We'll see.' With that she unlocked the door and went through it without so much as a look behind her, leaving James determined to leave the reception as early as was decent and return to 'see' as Sofia had so temptingly put it.

9

Religiosity, a characteristic of criminals, is also found in epileptics, where it alternates with cynicism and serves as a pretext for impulsive acts.   Lombroso, 1889 p 252

As he arrived at the Palazzo Carignano James stood and stared at the exterior, which was unlike anything he had seen before. It was curved like a series of waves and in the light of the torches that lit the building's entrance, the terracotta walls seemed to be undulating gently, almost as if they were a living entity. He looked up at the windows. Most of them were surrounded by mouldings that were so cleverly carved they looked like folds of cloth. There were other decorative reliefs too in various shapes – flowers and plumes and other more abstract patterns. A rotunda crowned the façade and this was topped by an ornate cartouche in the form of a brass scroll. James could just make out enough of the lettering to see the words Vittorio Emanuele II, united Italy's first king. The whole effect was just a little too much, as if one had eaten a few too many sweets.

The torches gave a medieval atmosphere to the proceedings. The flames flickered in the chill autumn wind, making James feel as if he was arriving at a royal feast. His fellow guests, though, were rather less regal. As he walked through the entrance hall all he could see were academics standing around in groups and gossiping, exactly as they had been doing the last time he saw them.

The company might have been familiar but their surroundings were not. The room he walked into, once he had crossed the torchlit courtyard, was the most magnificent that James had ever entered. The floor was of exquisite marquetry with intricate geometric patterns inlaid into the different woods. Everywhere there was gold and gilt shining in the light of glittering chandeliers. There were frescoes and paintings at every turn – goddesses and cherubs dancing in woodland scenes. No space was left undecorated. Heavy brocade curtains hung from the enormous windows as if waiting for a performance to begin. Uniformed waiters moved around the room discreetly, offering glasses of champagne and canapés to the assembled guests.

Across the room James saw Ottolenghi waiting for him. 'You managed to tear yourself away from Sofia then!'

'I walked her home, as I said I would,' James said firmly. He looked around him and raised his eyebrows. 'I see you like to keep your décor understated.'

Ottolenghi grinned. 'This is an understated nation. Hadn't you realised?'

'So who's here?' James asked, looking round him at the assorted guests who were standing in groups chatting.

'Well, most are academics from the university or delegates from the symposium but there are some other guests too. Over there are some members of the judiciary and their wives.'

Ottolenghi pointed to a group standing by a statue of what appeared to be Zeus. The men were laughing between themselves. Their wives, like peacocks in their gaudy silk dresses, by contrast, looked rather bored.

'What about those two ladies sitting with Borelli?' James looked over to them. At first glance they appeared to be almost identical. They were even dressed in similar gowns in tones of russets and golds. But on closer scrutiny James noticed that one was bright and animated, holding forth with Borelli. He looked entertained enough, laughing every now and then and nodding vigorously at her comments. The second woman was much more subdued. She looked slightly lost, uncomfortable even, as if she was at the wrong party but could not think of a way of extricating herself without causing offence.

'Ah yes. They're the Delgado sisters, very influential here. They inherited a number of concerns from their father, bakeries mostly and a gelateria. They are not fond of the professor.'

'Why not?'

'I'm not sure exactly but it was something he said about epilepsy and crime. Their father and brother both suffer from the condition. The Marchesa had to smooth it over. Oh, and see over there.' He pointed to a large group. 'That's the opera singer Luisa Cetto and the man next to her is her husband who owns the Teatro Carignano. The Marchesa is an enthu-siastic supporter of the arts in the city as well as the sciences.'

'The Marchesa sounds like a very interesting woman. Do you suppose I'll get to meet her?' James asked.

'You may well do. She visits us from time to time. I think she has a soft spot for the professor. Mind you, since Father Vincenzo wormed his way into her circle her visits have tailed off a little.'

'He seems to have quite a bit of influence then, this priest.'

Ottolenghi frowned. 'Too much, if you ask me. I don't trust him.'

'You were talking about Lombroso's enemies when we were in the *caffè* the other day. From what you've said there seem to be quite a few.'

Ottolenghi sighed. 'Yes, I'm afraid so. They're everywhere. You see the balding man with the monocle in the group of judges I pointed out? The professor wrote a somewhat disparaging article about the judiciary and gave a case he presided over as an example of bad practice.'

'Ouch!' James said. 'Lombroso doesn't believe in holding back, does he!'

'You could say that,' Ottolenghi said. 'He likes to speak his mind.'

'Well, that's an admirable quality, don't you think?'

'Perhaps, but one day, as I told you before, if he's not careful, it's going to get him into trouble.'

James wondered to himself what kind of 'trouble' that might be. Both Ottolenghi and Sofia seemed to be worried about Lombroso but neither had really said what they thought might happen to him. Before he could ask though, Lombroso and Madame Tarnovsky came over to greet them.

'I see you were admiring the room. It is an extraordinary vision, is it not, Murray? A little overblown, perhaps, but still a sight to behold,' Lombroso said.

'It's certainly unusually ornate,' James said diplomatically.

'How elegantly put, Dr Murray.'

'Madame Tarnovsky.' James bowed to her and she smiled at him. She was dressed in blue and silver but still seemed to outshine the garish gold that surrounded her.

'Tell me, did you enjoy Dr Horton's little performance this afternoon?' she asked playfully.

'It was . . .' James paused to find the right words, 'interesting.'

Lombroso beamed at him. 'Exactly right, Murray.'

'Everyone is discussing it. No one is sure if he was really issuing a warning or actually meant every word,' Madame Tarnovsky said.

DeClichy, Borelli and Reiner joined them in time to hear this comment. DeClichy shook his head and tutted. 'He is certainly somewhat of an enigma. I have spent the last hour or so in the university library, Professor Lombroso. I could not find a single piece of work by Horton or indeed reference to him.'

Lombroso frowned. 'That is indeed strange.'

'But we met him in Rome. He gave a paper there, did he not?' said Reiner.

Madame Tarnovsky nodded. 'That's right, I remember it. It was an odd little speech. He talked of a new method of neurological intervention – the use of surgery to the frontal lobe of the brain to alter behaviour. No one quite knew what to make of it; a lobotomy, I believe he called it.'

'A lobotomy!' James exclaimed before he could stop himself. The mere mention of the word made him feel sick to his stomach. It brought back so many memories that he would rather forget – frightening as well as sad ones.

'Yes,' replied Madame Tarnovsky. 'Are you familiar with the technique, Mr Murray?'

James coloured slightly. The memory of his last encounter with the method was only too vivid but how could he say more without revealing his secret? 'I think I have read something of it,' he said lamely.

'Is Horton not attached to a university?' Reiner asked.

'I don't believe so,' replied Lombroso. 'He merely cites his ownership of the asylum in San Francisco.'

'Well, of course,' said Reiner, 'one does not have to be a professor to have an interest in these matters.'

'So perhaps there is no mystery after all,' Lombroso said. 'He is merely somewhat of an outsider, a maverick, as the Americans say, and we should not condemn him for that. After all, where would science be without such men?'

'Men like you, eh, Cesare?' boomed Borelli, laughing.

'Ah, but Adolfo, remember that today's maverick is tomorrow's genius!' replied Lombroso.

Everyone nodded sagely at that. The master had spoken and no one seemed inclined to disagree. James still wondered about Horton. There was something about him that he did not quite trust. He couldn't put his finger on it but he knew that he didn't like him and the mystery of his provenance was intriguing. He decided to investigate further as soon as the opportunity arose. DeClichy was not the only one with access to the library.

The conversation had turned to other matters. Lombroso was holding forth with his views about the use of science to solve crime. James looked on and hoped that one day he might have the confidence to speak so fluently on the subject. He had been in Turin for less than a week and so much had happened in that short time that he was beginning to feel quite overwhelmed by it all. There were so many people saying so many things that their words had begun to echo around his head in a jumbled mass. He tried his hardest to disentangle their ideas but he was beginning to struggle. He longed for a little time to himself to assimilate it all.

A hush suddenly descended upon the room and everyone seemed to turn at the same time. James followed their eyes and saw a magnificently dressed woman regally descending the staircase at one end of the room. Her satin gown was embroidered with pearls and diamonds that shone in the candlelight. She was tall and elegant and as she progressed down the stairs her movements were fluid, sinuous – like those of a dancer. Her silver hair was dressed in an elaborate coiffure. Everything about her suggested power, from her demeanour to her facial expression. And yet there was a slight smile playing about her lips and a mischievous glint in her eye which made James warm to her. She was escorted by a tall, gaunt man in a black robe and sash who looked round with a haughty glare, his lips curling slightly, almost as if he was laughing at them in disdain. Perhaps he was. It was difficult to tell. James thought he looked like a bird of prey; his features were certainly hawk-like, sharp and angular, the kind of face it was hard to forget.

As the pair reached the bottom of the stairs, those closest to them bowed. As they passed through the room the ripple of obsequiousness became a wave. Even Lombroso did his best, though James thought he looked decidedly unenthusiastic, as if his heart was not in it. His bow was little more than a begrudging nod. James gathered that the lady was the Marchesa herself but he wasn't sure at first who accompanied her. Ottolenghi leant towards him and whispered in his ear, 'Father Vincenzo . . .'

James was surprised. He had imagined the priest to be elderly, grey and cadaverous. This man was nothing of the kind. For a start, he was much younger and could even be described by some as handsome. He had jet-black hair and piercing eyes that seemed to bore through one's consciousness like a gimlet. He escorted the Marchesa to a large chair in the corner of the room. Once she was seated she only had to glance to one side and a small orchestra began to play . . . Mozart? wondered James. It was all done with such taste that it hardly seemed to belong to the ostentation and vulgarity surrounding them. The conversation started up once more and now and again a footman would approach people and whisper discreetly in their ear. They would then make their way over to the Marchesa and be presented to her. How had the chosen few had been selected? By the demeanour of Father Vincenzo it looked as if he had something to do with it. He stood by the Marchesa's side, glancing over at the throng and then speaking to her. It was clear that he wanted everyone to know of his influence.

James saw Ottolenghi give a hint of a frown as they were joined by Professor Gemelli, who had been upstaged so conclusively by Borelli at the debate. Gemelli's hair, what there was of it, had been carefully smoothed down and covered with Macassar oil to hold it in place. His head shone through it giving the impression of a badly knitted skullcap.

Gemelli looked at Lombroso. 'Ah, Professor, I am glad to have caught you.'

Lombroso smiled thinly at him. 'Professor Gemelli, I am glad you are here,' he said insincerely. Then with a glance in James's direction he said, 'May I present my new assistant from Scotland, *Dottor* James Murray.'

James smiled and bowed. Gemelli looked down his nose at him as if he had scraped him from the bottom of his shoe. James was rather startled and felt his own smile freeze. Gemelli gestured at him dismissively.

'I have not come here to meet new members of your entourage, Lombroso. We have graver matters to discuss.'

Lombroso looked at him angrily. 'Whatever you have on your mind, Gemelli, I am sure that it is not so important that it cannot wait until tomorrow.'

'I wish to discuss the Soldati business . . .'

Lombroso stared at Gemelli and shrugged his shoulders as if he didn't know what he was talking about.

Gemelli looked around him to see who was listening. 'The murder,' he hissed.

Madame Tarnovsky gave a small cry and started to swoon.

'Quickly! Get a chair for the lady!' barked Reiner. Ottolenghi obliged and James helped Madame Tarnovsky to sit down. She covered her face with her fan. And then she winked at him from behind it and started to moan slightly.

Gemelli stood helplessly nearby until Lombroso turned towards him and glared at him. 'Tomorrow!'

'I think you will find that there may be certain . . .' Gemelli paused and narrowed his eyes, 'consequences.'

Lombroso ignored him, leaving the dean with little choice but to walk away. He joined another two men – one tall and thin with a pronounced stoop and the other large and untidy-looking with unruly hair. All three of them were looking back at Lombroso's group and glaring malevolently. James was beginning to see what Ottolenghi had been getting at when he had talked of Lombroso's enemies.

'Who are the other two?' James asked him.

'Oh, just some of Gemelli's cronies.'

'Why are they so hostile?'

Ottolenghi shrugged. 'I suppose you could say it is a mixture of jealousy and academic difference. Gemelli has published several articles criticising Lombroso's work, dismissing criminal anthropology as pseudo-science, calling it an affront to Catholicism, that sort of thing. He gave the last edition of *Criminal Man* a terrible review. The professor was not best pleased.'

James imagined Lombroso's reaction would be rather

more extreme than Ottolenghi had described. He didn't seem to respond well to criticism at the best of times.

'My dear Professor, I don't know how you manage to keep your temper!' exclaimed Madame Tarnovsky, still sitting in her chair. Every now and again she looked over at Gemelli and stared at him reproachfully.

'Madame,' sighed Lombroso, 'it is not easy. But do you know what keeps me going?'

She looked at him eagerly. 'No, Professor, do tell us.'

He paused for effect and they all gathered round to hear his answer.

'It is the absolute certainty that I am right.' He grinned at them. 'That is what science gives us. We measure and record, observe and note until we are sure. Anything else is guesswork at best or groundless superstition at worse.'

'I do not think that God would agree,' a voice boomed over his shoulder and he turned to see Father Vincenzo towering over them.

'God will not be consulted,' replied Lombroso, firmly. 'As La Place said to Napoleon: "I have no need of that hypothesis." '

Father Vincenzo gave a supercilious smile. 'Ah, so witty, Professor, and so certain. But wrong and, oh, how wrong. And with what consequences!'

Lombroso raised his eyebrows at the priest. 'What might they be, Father? Could you enlighten us?'

'It would be my pleasure, Professor. It is simply this. The location of our city dictates that we must all take care for the fight between good and evil depends on it. We have already experienced violence in a place of darkness. I foresee further blood and despair if you do not mend your ways.'

'And how should I go about doing that, Father?' asked Lombroso in mock seriousness.

Father Vincenzo smiled but his eyes did not. 'Why, you must end your experiments or . . .'

'Or what?' asked Lombroso.

The priest shook his head and tutted. 'Blood and despair,' he repeated in a conversational tone, still smiling urbanely. 'I cannot say more . . . except that you will live to regret it if you do not take heed.'

So melodramatic were his words that, despite the priest's outwardly calm demeanour, James half expected him to laugh like a pantomime demon and disappear in a puff of green smoke. Instead he merely inclined his head and looked quizzically at Lombroso.

Lombroso sighed. 'Ah well, I will just have to take that risk.'

'As you wish, Professor, but you cannot say that you have not been warned.'

Lombroso nodded with resignation. 'Indeed not, Father, and thank you.'

They bowed at each other as if they had just completed a perfectly ordinary exchange and Father Vincenzo made his way back to the Marchesa.

'I see you have not been honoured with a presentation to the lady,' murmured Borelli.

'I have met the Marchesa on many occasions. I don't think we have anything new to say to each other.'

'Still, it is a snub, is it not?' persisted Borelli.

Lombroso shrugged. 'It is nothing. I have more pressing things to think about.'

'It looks as if you may have been premature, Adolfo,' Madame Tarnovsky said, looking in the direction of the

Marchesa. 'It seems the lady is coming to pay you a visit, Cesare.'

The Marchesa made her way elegantly towards them, through the crowd that parted instinctively as she approached. Father Vincenzo had been forced to turn round and was valiantly trying to follow her, though not without difficulty. The crowds were not quite as deferential where he was concerned.

'Professor, how delightful to see you.'

Lombroso bowed low and kissed the Marchesa's hand. 'Madame, it is always a pleasure.'

'I hear the symposium got off to a rousing start.'

'That is one way to describe it.'

'Ah yes, I understand that it was not without controversy. Still, Professor, you should be used to that!'

'Indeed, Marchesa, it does seem to follow me.'

'I rather think that *you* follow it.'

Lombroso smiled. 'Perhaps, Marchesa, perhaps.'

'And how is your work going generally? Are we to see another edition of *Criminal Man* before long? I do hope so. It was a tour de force!'

Lombroso beamed. 'I am working on the next edition, as it happens. There have been some interesting developments. I have found some marked similarities between the epileptic and the born criminal that lead me to believe that the condition could be a cause of offending.'

'Really. How fascinating,' the Marchesa said.

'Take the case of Misdea, the soldier assassin, for example,' Lombroso said, warming to his theme.

'Ah yes, didn't he murder some of his unit?'

'You're familiar with the case, Marchesa, I should have

known you would be,' Lombroso went on. 'Now let me tell you a little more . . .'

James studied the Marchesa as the professor spoke. If she was feigning her interest she was doing so very effectively. She seemed to have genuinely read Lombroso's work to the extent that she could converse freely on the subject. Father Vincenzo stood by morosely as the conversation went on.

'Well, Professor, this is fascinating. I look forward to hearing more,' the Marchesa said. 'Perhaps I will call on you in a day or two.'

'I would be honoured,' Lombroso replied.

The Marchesa left them and began to move through the room, pausing to greet the favoured as she went. Father Vincenzo followed closely behind.

'What a charming woman!' Borelli said.

'Isn't she?' said Lombroso. 'And intelligent too, despite the variable quality of the company she keeps.'

Borelli nodded. 'The priest is certainly forthright in his views.'

'What did he mean about the position of the city?' James asked.

'Ancient legend has it that the city is a pole of both black and white magic, a point on the triangle of white magic with Lyon and Prague and black magic with London and San Francisco,' replied Ottolenghi patiently.

'What nonsense!' Lombroso exclaimed. 'No wonder it is so difficult to create an atmosphere of intellectual endeavour when we are hampered by all this talk of magic and superstition put about by fantasists and fools!'

'Let us talk of more pleasant subjects,' suggested Madame Tarnovsky tactfully. 'Cesare, tell us about the symposium. What have we to look forward to?'

Lombroso smiled happily as he began to talk about the programme for the next two weeks. There was to be a visit to a prison to watch an experiment on some inmates. Lombroso would speak on the giving of evidence in criminal trials and there would be speakers from all over Europe on a variety of topics. James was both enthralled and astonished. It was almost as if the murder had never happened or at least simply did not matter. Soldati was just another ne'er-do-well who had met an untimely end. So what if the killer had mentioned Lombroso? What more was that than a criminal's cheap jibe at a man who was celebrated for his work to combat crime? But something nagged at James. He could not say exactly what it was but it was there at the back of his mind, gnawing gently at his instincts like a hungry worm. A man was dead which was of course some kind of an ending but, though he could not say exactly why, it seemed to James that it was more like a beginning.

Later that night after the reception had ended and the participants had gone their separate ways, James wandered along the dark, narrow streets towards Sofia's rooms. He was full of expectation following their earlier encounter and his thoughts were focused on what he hoped the rest of the night would bring. It was past midnight and the city was quiet as death itself, almost thick with silence. The now familiar damp fog swirled around every corner – yellowish, sulphurous, hellish. James shivered and looked nervously around him as he walked.

In an effort to calm his nerves he started to think about the reception and some of its guests. Many of them seemed to be incomplete somehow – a collection of people who were not what they seemed on the surface with a large and more sinister part of them hidden beneath: Gemelli, the faculty dean who was apparently so full of professional rivalry for Lombroso that it had spilled over into personal dislike; Father Vincenzo, a priest with apparently more regard for the Devil than God and yet another man whose resentment of Lombroso seemed to have warped his judgment; Reiner, the Austrian psychiatrist who had seemed refreshingly straightforward until he started to talk about his work based on lust murder and vampirism. There was something about him – the glint in the eyes, the touch of saliva between his lips as he described the cases he had studied. And then there was Horton, with no apparent beliefs except in a form of murderous crime control. He did not seem to have any connection to a university or indeed to any institution other than his own asylum. What then was his background? And if he didn't believe in any of the theories being expounded at the symposium, why was he here at all?

On James walked through the deserted streets. It was as if there had been an apocalypse, leaving him as the only survivor. All he could hear was his own footsteps on the damp cobbles. The quiet unnerved him and he began to whistle to himself, quietly at first and then more loudly, even though he attempted to persuade himself that he was being ridiculous. He was a grown man walking along a city street. What was there to be afraid of? Then he heard it – a whistle, similar to his own – reflecting his tune back to him as a sinister echo. He quickened his pace and changed his whistle to a hum but to no avail. The tune was returned to him until they were almost singing together in a macabre symphony. This was no light-hearted jape. James could sense a note of what could only be described as malice.

And then suddenly there was silence, smothering him with

its completeness, until he could barely breathe. He stood waiting in the darkness – for what he could not say. If he walked on, then he would be followed. If he stayed where he was then . . . what? The terror of the unknown made him yearn for the ordinary – a cup of coffee, his sister's laughter at some silly joke, even listening to his aunt lecture him about his prospects – anything would be preferable to this all-encompassing fear. And then the silence was broken again, by a steady beat like a thump on a door to gain entrance. Three knocks . . . then a pause . . . then three knocks again.

James stopped and turned quickly but he could see nothing. The knocks started again and at that moment some of his fear was replaced by anger. Somebody was playing games with him and he was tired of it. He peered through the mist. 'Is there anyone there? Show yourself, you scoundrel!'

There was no reply. He stood there and listened carefully for a breath, a whisper, anything. But there was nothing. The silence had returned yet again.

He could barely see a foot in front of him but he felt quite alone. Suddenly all that had happened to him, both recently and in the past, began to weigh like a leaden burden on his shoulders. He sighed and continued on his way. What was it about this city? All he had encountered since he arrived was darkness and shadows. Nothing seemed to be honest or straightforward and no one seemed to be telling him the complete truth about anything, not even Sofia. He had come here to seek a future but the past seemed to be as inescapable as ever. He turned the corner into the small square where Sofia lived and paused, looking up at her window. A solitary candle lit up the casement as if in welcome. What should he do? Sofia was a servant in his teacher's employ and not only that, she had been a prostitute – it was unthinkable that he should get involved with such a woman, even in secret. If they were found out both would lose their positions and he would have to return home in disgrace.

But to turn away and leave Sofia on the edge of his life was something he simply could not contemplate. This was not just a mere dalliance with a servant girl. There was something more between them. He knew it to be so because he had felt that way before. He closed his eyes for a second and remembered the woman who he had once loved and then lost. In his head he could hear the tune she used to hum as she worked on her embroidery. Kate, with her blond curls and skin like porcelain, had looked a little like one of Lucy's dolls, as different from Sofia as it was possible to be. He had met her at a university function because she was the daughter of one of its chief patrons, a lord, no less. As such she had been out of bounds for him but that did not stop her from flirting with him at every opportunity. She had nearly driven him mad with suppressed desire, captivating him to the extent where he proposed to her, notwithstanding her position. He went to see Kate's father in order to make his intentions clear. James winced as he remembered the scorn with which his visit was greeted. The man had actually laughed in his face before dismissing him out of hand as a potential suitor for his daughter. James had stormed out and tried to see Kate, fully intending to run away with her there and then. But she had refused to see him and he had finally realised the cruel game she had played with his heart.

It was a salutary lesson and since then he had been cautious in such matters, preferring to concentrate on his work. But even his feelings for Kate, and he could still remember how she had made his heart race with even the tiniest of smiles, seemed inconsequential in comparison to how he felt at this moment. He went up the rickety stairs and knocked on the door.

Sofia opened it and smiled at him. 'So you decided to pay me a visit after all.'

'I am sorry it is so late,' James said. 'It has been a long evening.'

'Oh, poor Dr Murray,' Sofia said in mocking tones. 'It must be hard to listen to all that grand conversation, not to mention the fine wines and food that goes with it.'

James grinned. 'Well, perhaps it was not such an ordeal. But still I am here now. Will you let me in?'

Sofia hesitated, looking up and down as if she was measuring him up. Finally she stood back from the door and allowed him to enter. 'Yes, I will . . . but just for a moment or two. I need my sleep.'

Her rooms were small, poky even, but he could see the efforts she had made to make them homely. A small table with two chairs was in one corner. It was covered with a cloth and had a vase of flowers in the centre. In another corner was a bookcase with a few books on it.

'Please sit.' Sofia indicated a sofa that had seen better days. He glanced over to an open door through which he could see a bed.

'Would you like some *grappa*?' she asked, closing the door firmly.

'Yes please,' he said, more in the hope of prolonging the visit than in anticipation of the drink itself.

Sofia brought a glass over to him and sat in a chair by the table, as far away from him as she could manage, given the available space.

'So how was the reception?' she asked.

'Interesting. I am beginning to see what you mean about the professor having enemies.'

'Good. I am glad that you understand.'

'What I don't understand is exactly what you want me to do about them.'

'It is simple. I want you to find out who killed Soldati. Otherwise his enemies will be able to use the murder to discredit him.'

'How could they do that?'

'The note – it implicates him.'

James frowned, trying to remember if Sofia had been present when the note had been mentioned. 'How do you know about that?'

'Everybody in Turin knows. Marshal Machinetti has seen to that.'

'Well you don't need to worry. We are already investigating the murder.'

'We?'

'Myself, Ottolenghi and Tullio.'

'And what have you found out so far?' Sofia asked impatiently.

'We know how he was killed and that he was a regular at La Capra.'

Sofia rolled her eyes. 'Is that it? *I* could have told you that.'

'If your friend Rosa Bruno would cooperate, we might find out more.'

Sofia stood up and threw her hands up. 'So that's the sum total of your fancy scientific policing – almost nothing!' She swore under her breath.

James also got to his feet. What did she expect? 'Look, it isn't as easy as you seem to think. The killer wants Lombroso to be blamed. He's not going to make it easy for us to find him.'

'Perhaps not but you are supposed to be experts in crime. You should be able to find out something.'

'How can we,' James asked, 'when nobody will tell us the truth about anything?'

'If people are lying to you then they must have a reason,' Sofia said, her voice getting louder with each word. 'You must ask the questions in a different way.'

'A different way? What does that mean? Are you saying we're incompetent?' James ran his hands through his hair in frustration. 'I don't understand you. We're trying our best.'

'Well, it does not seem to be good enough!'

James stared at Sofia who was standing with her hands on her hips, her eyes full of anger. 'What would you know anyway? You're just a—'

'A what? A servant? A whore?' Sofia shouted.

'I was going to say housekeeper! Really, it's impossible to speak sensibly to you!'

'Go, then!'

Infuriated, James walked out, slamming the door behind him.

10

Criminals' feelings are not always completely gone; some may survive while others disappear. Lombroso, 1876 p 64

The sun was about to rise over Turin. The city was experiencing unseasonably warm weather for November. Usually, by now, a mist of fog would be winding itself around every corner, covering everything in its wake with a thin, damp cloak, light as gossamer – a film of moist droplets that insinuated itself into every bodily crevice, making it impossible ever to feel dry. For the last two or three days, however, this had only arrived once the sun had set. During daylight hours the fog had been replaced by blue skies and hazy sunshine, giving the city an air of reckless abandonment to pleasure as its inhabitants made the most of the weather, sitting outside cafés and strolling around squares as if it was high summer.

For Antonio Bettoni the weather had a double benefit. Not only was his employment as a gardener in the Parco del Valentino a good deal more pleasant in the warm sunshine but it also made his journey to work a pleasure rather than a chore. The darkness was just abating as he made his way across the vast Piazza Vittoria, and then towards the Lungo Po Diaz, the road that ran alongside the river Po. He pulled his coat around him. Warmth would come with the sun but it was still cold in the early morning. He breathed in deeply as he went down the slope towards the water. He had always loved the river's smell although he had never been able to identify its exact components; a combination of pondweed and fish, he thought, but it was never the same aroma twice. He walked whistling along the bank by the *murazzi* – boat-sheds carved into the riverside. He was that most unusual of beings, a happy man, at peace with the world and everyone in it.

In the distance Antonio glimpsed a man leaning against one of the stone posts, his legs dangling over the side of the bank. His head was flung back as if he was dozing. Was he fishing? Antonio smiled to himself – so many things to appreciate: a beautiful morning, a solitary fisherman, a day of tending the gardens ahead and yes, there was his favourite sound of all – birdsong. A single blackbird trilled its simple tune, adding to the air of tranquillity. It was so perfect a scene that even Antonio the optimist felt that it could not last.

He was right. As he approached the fisherman the sun went behind a cloud, the bird stopped singing and Antonio saw something that he would never forget. For the man was no angler – there was no rod, no wriggling bait, no catch – just a corpse, its head flung back at an odd angle, eyes staring sightlessly up into the sky.

Antonio moved in and looked more closely. What he saw made him gasp with horror and stumble backwards. He turned to one side and vomited. There were no eyes to stare, just empty sockets. Dried black blood congealed around a neck wound and the mouth hung open loosely as if the jaw was dislocated. He could see a set of rotting teeth, which seemed to be broken and jagged as if they had been hit with something. As if this wasn't enough, something was missing. There was no tongue. Antonio looked down and saw the man's hands, cupped in front of him as if waiting to receive a gift. In one, rammed precariously between the fingers, was a piece of bloodstained paper with red writing on it and in the other was the missing tongue and two eyes.

The unmistakable sound of a pistol being fired reverberated around the panelled walls of Lombroso's laboratory. James stood, the gun drooping from his hand, shocked at the loudness of the report.

'Ah, now, that was particularly interesting,' announced Lombroso from behind a screen. 'There was a definite change in the pressure – well, good enough to note anyway. Would you record that, Ottolenghi?'

Ottolenghi was standing to one side, well away from James. He was in his shirtsleeves, holding a clipboard, his glasses perched on the end of his nose, looking like a shopkeeper doing some stocktaking. His subject, a heavily tattooed man with a receding forehead, was seated with his left arm connected to one piece of machinery and his right arm to another.

Ottolenghi looked up. 'Yes, Professor – I think the machine might need to be readjusted, though.'

'Which one – the hydrosphygmograph or the Ruhmkorff?'

'The Ruhmkorff. One of the terminals has come loose so I can't be sure we got the correct effect.'

James looked with interest at the machines in question. The Ruhmkorff was an induction coil made up of a large black cylinder surrounded by brass knobs and dials which Ottolenghi was busy adjusting. The hydrosphygmograph or 'pulse writer', like many of the machines favoured by Lombroso for his experiments, looked more like an instrument of torture than a piece of scientific equipment. It was a thin metal machine that was strapped to the subject's wrist. It put James in mind of a thumbscrew.

'Oh, never mind,' Lombroso called out. 'I'm sure it made no difference. Write it down regardless. We can't keep firing a pistol all morning. Murray will soon tire of it, not to mention our subject!'

James was actually rather enjoying himself but didn't like to say so. It was not every day that one got the opportunity to fire a pistol without fear of consequences.

The subject, Ausano, a local pickpocket, also looked happy enough. It probably made a nice change, earning money legitimately just for sitting down. According to Ottolenghi, some years before Lombroso had conducted some experiments using the same equipment in order to measure the difference in responses indicated by blood pressure readings to various stimuli, both pleasurable and unpleasant. Today he had decided to repeat the experiment. In part this was in order to clarify the results, as the previous recording left something to be desired. But James suspected there was also an ulterior motive. He hoped that Lombroso had been impressed by his dedication but it seemed that he wanted to test him, to see if he could manage such experiments, juggling complex and delicate equipment whilst dealing with subjects who were not always as compliant as they might be. Once the purpose had been explained and the financial aspect agreed, Ausano had been more than content to allow matters to take their course. He was still, however, much given to grumbling, which was proving to be test enough.

James looked out of the window. A small, agitated crowd had gathered and he could see the plume of Machinetti's hat bobbing at its centre.

'Professor, I think there may be trouble.'

'Let us try another form of stimulus,' suggested Lombroso, ignoring James's comment. 'Murray, you take over from Ottolenghi.'

Ottolenghi grinned at him as he showed him the equipment and James started to adjust the terminal.

'Is he properly connected now?' asked Lombroso, impatiently.

'One minute . . . yes, now I am sure,' James replied, hoping that he had got it right.

'So I hear you had an encounter with Judge Robertini,' Lombroso asked their subject casually.

Ausano furrowed his distinctly receding brows.

'That bastard! I'll slit his throat if I ever meet him again! Three years' hard labour for a cloth purse with a few *lire* in it and a snuffbox that wasn't even real silver. There's no justice!'

Lombroso raised his eyebrows at Ottolenghi who stifled a laugh. Ausano scowled at him.

'Any change registered?' Lombroso called out to James.

'None.'

'Try looking at this.'

Lombroso handed Ausano a picture of a naked woman.

'Very nice, I'm sure. Looks like that woman downstairs – the housekeeper is it? A sweet piece.'

James tightened the strap round Ausano's wrist a little.

'Ow! Watch it. It's too tight!'

James bent down and pretended to loosen it. 'You're not fit to breathe the same air,' he whispered.

'Careful, young man, you'll dislodge the machine,' warned Lombroso, frowning at him.

Ottolenghi raised his eyebrows at James and shook his head.

'Did anything show on the dials?' James asked innocently.

'No,' Ottolenghi replied. He started to attend to the machine, which had indeed become dislodged.

'I don't see why I should put up with this,' complained Ausano.

'Think of the money. Is that not your usual motivation? I remember you telling us that you would sell your very soul for cash,' said Lombroso sternly. 'Now, how about a nice cigar?'

Ausano sat back in his chair, apparently placated.

'Still nothing,' announced Ottolenghi, who was watching the various dials.

'What about some wine?' Lombroso showed the thief a bottle of Paolo's Barolo and Ausano nodded vigorously.

'A slight rise – no more than eighteen pulses, though.'

Suddenly the door was thrust open and Machinetti burst in with Giardinello following close behind.

'It's gone off the scale!' James shouted excitedly, emerging from behind the screen with such vigour that he almost knocked it over.

'Giardinello – the gun!' cried Machinetti. Ottolenghi was standing in the corner still holding the pistol that he had taken from James. Giardinello, presumably overcome by events, ran over to him and instead of taking the gun from his politely outstretched hand, wrestled Ottolenghi to the ground. The gun slid across the floor, landing at the feet of Lombroso who picked it up swiftly in case the temptation proved too much for Ausano.

They made an interesting tableau. Ottolenghi was pinned to the floor by Giardinello. Ausano had got to his feet and was leaning towards Machinetti with an expression of such intense hatred on his face that it was if the Devil himself had come into the room. James stood by the fallen screen holding Ausano by the arms to restrain him. Machinetti stood in the doorway, a look of alarm etched on his face. Lombroso looked at him, a sardonic smile playing about his lips, a pistol in one hand and a bottle of wine in the other.

'Ah, Machinetti, you have arrived just in time. We were about to take some wine. Will you join us?'

Machinetti puffed himself up like a cat defending its territory. 'You should be more careful with firearms, Professor.'

Lombroso sighed. 'Everything is under control, Marshal, I assure you. Now is there anything else? We are busy, as you can see.'

Machinetti pursed his lips. 'There has been another murder. You are to come with me for questioning.'

'Another!' exclaimed Lombroso. 'What do you mean? And what has that to do with me?'

'Yes, another – and it has everything to do with you,' replied Machinetti.

'Why? Who is the victim?' Lombroso asked.

'You can tell us that.'

'I can't actually, which is why I asked you,' Lombroso said.

Machinetti paused and frowned at him. 'Your note was left, again.'

James gasped. Even though he had suspected that the Soldati murder was just the beginning, to have it proved like this was dreadful. Oddly, the horror of the situation appeared to have escaped Lombroso who seemed more intent on scoring points against Machinetti than anything else. It was as if the news hadn't quite sunk in.

'As I did not do anything, I fail to see how it can be called *my* note,' Lombroso said slowly and clearly, as if addressing a stupid child.

'We'll see about that,' Machinetti said ominously.

Lombroso looked at him with one eyebrow raised. 'Am I under arrest?'

'No. But you still have questions to answer,' Machinetti replied.

'I don't see why they cannot be asked here,' said Otto-lenghi, who had been released by a somewhat sheepish Giardinello. James was still holding Ausano, who looked as if he could not quite believe what he had just witnessed.

'Neither do I,' Lombroso said firmly. 'Come, Marshal. There is a study next door. We can discuss this matter there. Ottolenghi, perhaps you can show Signor Ausano out and tidy up a little before joining us. Murray, would you mind accompanying me? I think that I would like a witness and, of course, you might find it instructive.'

With that he left the room, leaving Machinetti staring after his retreating figure. Eventually he recovered himself and he and Giardinello followed Lombroso, with James bringing up the rear, leaving Ottolenghi and Ausano looking warily at each other.

Lombroso's study was a small room and it was with some difficulty that everyone squeezed in. Machinetti perched uncomfortably on a small stool in one corner. It was, in some ways, a miniature version of the museum. Every available inch was covered with books, papers and what could only be described as curiosities — a couple of animal skulls, a phrenology head, one or two small carnivorous plants and what appeared to be a pickled hand in a jar, which Giardi-nello could not take his eyes from. Lombroso sat on a large leather chair behind his desk. He seemed relaxed but James could tell that he was covering his real feelings. Something about the look in his eyes indicated a certain tension, which under the circumstances was hardly surprising.

'So, Machinetti, tell me about this murder. I ask again, who is the victim?' asked Lombroso.

Machinetti opened his mouth as if he was about to answer him but then remembered that it was he who was supposed to ask the questions. 'I believe you know his identity.'

'I think I have already established that I don't, but I gather we are talking about a man.'

'You do know, don't you!' Machinetti insisted.

Lombroso shook his head and looked upwards.

'Do you know a man called Pietro Mancini?' barked Machinetti.

Lombroso's brows furrowed. 'The name is familiar. Although how can you be sure that this is connected to the other death?'

Machinetti looked at him significantly but Lombroso had had enough.

'Please stop playing these ridiculous games. If I did know anything then I would be foolish to tell you, would I not?'

There was another pause as Machinetti thought about what had been said. Finally he realised that he was wasting his time. 'We have found another letter – *A Tribute to Lombroso* – just like the last one.'

'In blood?'

Machinetti nodded.

'Tell me, was anything . . . missing as before?'

'The tongue was cut out.'

Lombroso seemed unmoved by this revelation. It was, of course, easier, because he had not seen the victim. All the same, James was surprised by his lack of emotion, particularly as he was connected to this murder in the same way as he had been to the first. He wondered if Lombroso was hiding his real feelings, being reluctant to show weakness in front of his old foe.

'Ah, a severed tongue. Now that is interesting – it's the traditional punishment for an informer and, of course, a warning to others.'

'This was different. The doctor who examined the body said that in his view the amount and consistency of the blood indicated that the tongue was removed prior to death. Not only that but the jaw had been dislocated, the teeth had been broken and . . . something else.'

'What?' Lombroso asked.

'The eyes had been taken from the sockets.'

James saw just a hint of anguish cross Lombroso's features. 'That would not be easy to accomplish.'

'It seems he was stunned first by a blow to the head, then the tongue was cut out, the teeth broken, the jaw manipulated and finally the throat was cut.'

'And the eyes?' James asked.

Machinetti shrugged. 'We do not know how that was done exactly. It seems as if an implement was used to . . . to scoop them out.'

James shuddered. 'Surely the killer must be insane.'

'Perhaps,' said Lombroso thoughtfully, 'but he is also thorough, methodical even.'

Suddenly Lombroso slapped his forehead with the heel of his hand. 'Of course! Now I remember the name, Pietro Mancini. I met him in Pavia and measured his head to see if informants' crania might differ in circumference. I also took notes on some jargon he was using. He had some interesting slang words, probably unique to his particular criminal gang.

What was he doing in Turin? I thought he was serving a substantial sentence. He should still be locked up.'

Machinetti scowled. 'He escaped. Evidently he felt it was safer out than in. He was already on the run from his associates in Palermo.'

'It seems that he was wrong. But still, as I'm sure even you know, Machinetti, the removal of the tongue is a known punishment. The removal before death could merely indicate a new policy.'

'I do not recall any policy regarding eyes and teeth,' Machinetti said.

'True, I'll give you that, Marshal,' Lombroso replied. 'But it still could be related to his informing activities, things he's seen and spoken of – it could be symbolic. In my experience it is the way the criminal mind works sometimes, a literal interpretation of punishment.'

'But it still leaves the letter, which clearly implicates you,' Machinetti said. 'Where were you last night between the hours of ten yesterday evening and six o'clock this morning?'

Lombroso stood and drew himself up to his full height. 'I was at the Marchesa's reception until midnight, as I am sure you know.'

'And after that?'

Lombroso sighed. 'It was late. But I came here because I wanted to do some work.'

'That is true. I dropped him off in a cab,' Ottolenghi, who had just rejoined them, confirmed.

'That, Professor, still leaves you ample time to get down to the riverside and kill Mancini!' declared Machinetti triumphantly.

Lombroso put his hands in front of him as if waiting to be handcuffed. 'Well, you had better arrest me now, had you not? Clearly, I murdered both of these poor souls and then left a letter as a tribute to myself, leading you to myself. Rather a good clue, wouldn't you say? Not much of a mystery, though. Perhaps I should have made it a tribute to you, Machinetti, and then you could have interrogated yourself and got Giardinello to arrest you!'

In any other circumstances this would have been comical but James kept thinking of the second victim. Even a criminal did not deserve such a death. Here they were, crammed into this small room with Machinetti, now such an intense shade of puce that he almost matched the purple velvet curtains that hung at the window. His eyes were bulging and he seemed to be on the verge of exploding. But there had been a second horrible murder. Surely this was not the time for either man to attempt to score points.

'If it was not you, then who killed them?' Machinetti asked.

'Machinetti,' said Lombroso patiently, 'one of us is a marshal of the carabinieri and I don't believe that it is me. Now, why don't you stop wasting your time and mine and go out there and find the answer to your question, there's a good fellow.'

Machinetti gave him a look of pure hatred. He opened his mouth as if about to speak but evidently thought the better of it. He then tried to sweep out of the room in an attempt to retain at least some dignity. Sadly, it was not to be, for when he extricated himself from his corner, there was so little room that he was forced to sidle out, squeezing past Giardinello and James and knocking over a small table as he did so. Giardinello picked it up and bowed rather sheepishly before following behind him.

Lombroso sat back down in his seat and motioned to

James to perch on the stool vacated by Machinetti. Otto-lenghi joined them and they sat in silence for a while, allowing Lombroso to collect his thoughts. Finally he spoke. 'It cannot go on,' he murmured.

'No one can seriously think that you are implicated, Professor,' Ottolenghi said quietly.

'I wish that I had your confidence, Ottolenghi, but a second murder? You know as well as I do that I have enemies and that they will take great delight in pointing the finger of suspicion at me. There will be talk at first, and then . . . well, who knows. It may even jeopardise my position here. There are many who would rejoice at my departure, were it to come to that.'

James wondered what it was about Lombroso that seemed to inspire such extremes of emotion. Did anyone really hate him so much that they would imply that he had committed these terrible crimes in order to discredit him? If so, then why?

Lombroso shook himself. 'Listen to me! How selfish I have become. What of those poor men? We should be thinking of them and their families, if they have them.'

James shook his head. 'Some might say that, as they are only criminals, they don't deserve our sympathy.'

'Murray, you don't know how it saddens me to hear that, although it does not surprise me. But some unfortunates cannot help what they become. It is their destiny and nothing less. We should not condemn them for that which they cannot change.' Lombroso slumped into his chair. He seemed very different since Machinetti's departure. 'Two men have died horribly and it seems as if it may be my fault.' He looked up at them, a look of desperation on his face. 'I don't know how to stop this!'

Ottolenghi looked Lombroso in the eye and took a deep breath. 'Professor, we need to find this killer, and soon, before he strikes again. Let us help you.'

'No, no, leave it to Machinetti. He will get there in the end. He is persistent, if nothing else.'

'Professor, please let us help,' implored James. 'In the end might be too late for some poor soul.'

Lombroso paused for a moment but then shook his head. 'No, I say again, leave it to the carabinieri. We have other matters with which to fill our time.'

James sighed. He had thought that the second murder might have persuaded Lombroso to investigate. After all, if they left it to Machinetti who knew how many others might die by the same hand? He simply could not understand why Lombroso was being so stubborn. Surely even the most ferocious of feuds could be put aside to save lives. Unless of course . . . James looked over to him. *Could* he be involved? Why else would he be so reluctant? A sense of dread filled him at the thought that the professor might be capable of such brutality. But then why on earth would he implicate himself by leaving the notes – unless it was some bizarre attempt at a kind of double bluff.

Lombroso leaned towards them. 'Gentlemen, we cannot allow ourselves to be distracted. I feel that we may be on the verge of a breakthrough. Just imagine what that might mean for the world. If we could predict who the criminals are we could prevent crime. Think of that.'

He got to his feet. 'Come, let us go back into the laboratory and write up our experiment. Ausano was an interesting subject, was he not? Almost no change in his blood pressure throughout – only the prospect of a glass of wine and an encounter with Machinetti got him going. I wonder what that could mean?'

James and Ottolenghi dutifully followed Lombroso as he left the room, exchanging glances as they did so. They both knew that the second murder had stiffened their own resolve to continue investigating. Perhaps when they had something solid to show him Lombroso might be persuaded to change his mind, James thought. Either that or something much worse – he would be forced to make a confession of his crimes.

11

Certain lawyers have deliberately misinterpreted my theories, turning them to the advantage of their least deserving clients.

Lombroso, 1889 p 231

The following day, as part of the symposium, Lombroso was to conduct a demonstration of his work at the local prison assisted by James and Ottolenghi. In the cab on the way there James watched the professor carefully to see if there was any indication of guilt. Lombroso's eyes were darting here and there as he muttered to himself. Every now and again he paused and jotted something down in an old leather-bound notebook.

James wondered how long it would be until Lombroso's fears for his future were recognised. He had been sceptical at first but now it seemed that the professor had been right to worry. Gemelli and his cronies had already been seen at the museum, like vultures circling in a search for carrion. He did not think that it would be long before they landed upon the professor and began to tear his reputation to pieces. Father Vincenzo was little better if the views he expressed at the Marchesa's reception were genuine, and there was no reason to believe that they were not. He was powerful, more so than Gemelli, and it was clear to James that trouble lay ahead. But more than this, they were faced with a killer who seemed to stop at nothing to prove some kind of a point. There had been two terrible murders but would he stop there? James doubted it. The more deaths, the more comprehensively the point, whatever it was, was driven home. It was surely a matter of urgency to find the culprit and prevent further atrocities and in doing so exonerate the professor once and for all.

But James wasn't sure how much headway he, Ottolenghi and Tullio could make on their own. Valuable time had already been lost and they could not even visit the second crime scene until that evening at the earliest. He wondered if Tullio had managed to get there before Machinetti and preserve some of the 'scientific evidence' he was so fond of. Perhaps that might give them something to go on. They could certainly do with it.

In a few moments they arrived at the prison gates, huge cast iron things that creaked ominously as they swung open. According to Ottolenghi, the prison was known as Le Nuove, but it certainly didn't look 'new'. Even though it had been built only a decade or so ago, the red brick walls seemed to have weathered already, almost as if it was aging from within. There were towers set into each corner, standing tall and looming over them like a threat. As they approached the large metal door, the temperature seemed to drop and James shivered. The smell of the interior reminded him of his father's asylum – a dank, sour smell of sweat and desperation.

They were met by the prison governor, an old friend of Lombroso's. He greeted them warmly and escorted them to the consulting rooms where they would conduct the experiments in front of a small invited audience. They walked through the dimly lit corridors lined with cells. There was a cacophony of banging and clanging, shouting and calling out of obscenities. Eventually they came to a large spiral staircase in the centre of the building. As they climbed, James looked down on the landings and saw some of the convicts being taken back to their cells. They shuffled along behind the guard. One looked up and their eyes met. He was so thin that his uniform of striped cotton seemed to hang off him. The man gave James a reproachful glare as if he was responsible for his incarceration. James turned away, unable to hold the prisoner's stare any longer. It wasn't his fault the man was there but somehow it felt as if it was.

Finally they reached the room where two of Lombroso's measuring contraptions stood in the middle of the floor, waiting to be used. James recognised the Ruhmkorff induction coil that they had used on Ausano, with another machine that measured changes in blood pressure. This time, though, it appeared to be unattached. Waiting by the equipment were two young men who were also assisting. They stood there, nervously eying the machines, presumably wondering, as James was, what their own part in the proceedings would be. Lombroso had not been particularly forthcoming on the way to the prison and he hadn't liked to interrupt his thought processes by asking him for details. James had caught Ottolenghi giving him amused glances as if he knew something James did not.

Lombroso and the governor went to greet the invited guests, leaving the young men to ensure that the equipment was in working order. Fortunately the others, particularly Ottolenghi, seemed to know what they were doing, which was more than James did, so he stood around watching as they twiddled various knobs and checked connections. A few moments later he heard the booming voice of Borelli and

Lombroso's slightly lighter tones announcing the arrival of the observers.

All of Lombroso's guests at his salon were present. Madame Tarnovsky gave James a wave as she came in and he nodded gravely at her, not wishing to appear too frivolous. He was surprised to see Horton hovering at the back of the crowd. He remembered what Ottolenghi had said about Lombroso liking to mix with those who intrigued him and he supposed that Horton was in that category. Even if the professor didn't like someone, then being interesting would still guarantee access to his inner circle.

DeClichy stood next to Madame Tarnovsky, directly opposite Horton. Every now and again he would look up at him and frown. Reiner stood next to Horton. James looked more closely at him. His stare was like an icicle and he was wearing another fancy waistcoat, similar to the one that James had coveted at the salon. James wondered if he wore them when he talked to his lust murderers. But was his interest in vampirism merely hypothetical? Not long before he had travelled to Turin, Lucy had lent James a story about a vampire who posed as an English lord and seduced the hero's sister. James imagined Reiner sucking the blood from someone. As he stared, Reiner suddenly noticed him and smiled disarmingly at him. James smiled back guiltily.

Once everyone was assembled, Lombroso rose and the room fell silent. The level of anticipation was so high that James imagined it settling on them like a great cloak. After a long pause, no doubt for dramatic effect, Lombroso, always the showman, addressed them.

'Gentlemen and Madame Tarnovsky,' he began. He looked at her directly and she smiled. This acknowledgement was no doubt made in an effort to convey respect. Women in the scientific community were few and far between and they were often ignored. As far as James was concerned it was wrong to exclude anyone from the gaining of knowledge just because of his or her sex. He knew, however, that he was in a minority and that for Anna Tarnovsky it must be a struggle she faced on an almost daily basis.

Lombroso went on. 'Today, I will be repeating an experiment that I conducted some years ago. I am doing so to demonstrate the advances that have been made in the modification of the equipment used and also, of course, our greater knowledge of criminals and their anthropology. The term "algometry" has become increasingly common in our profession since I invented it all those years ago.'

'I hate to interrupt . . .'

It was Horton speaking.

'Then don't,' murmured Borelli.

Horton ignored him. 'Hasn't someone else claimed it was their idea?'

James thought that Lombroso would be angry at Horton's intervention but Lombroso merely peered at Horton quizzically and then shook his head slowly. 'Many people have claimed many things over the years and they are nothing if not consistent.' There was another dramatic pause. 'They are always wrong!'

The audience laughed and even Horton joined in. Lombroso continued, 'Algometry is of course the measurement of sensibility to pain.'

James felt slightly uneasy. This was not really what he had hoped to hear. He held on for a second or two to the possibility that it was only prisoners who were to be examined rather than Lombroso's assistants but his hopes were soon dashed.

'We will begin by applying the electrodes of this Ruhm-korff induction coil to various parts of the body. I am ably assisted in this venture by Dr Ottolenghi and, of course, my new student Dr James Murray. They will replicate the earlier experiment previously conducted on four of my colleagues. I intend to propose this method as being suitable for the collection of evidence to be used by expert witnesses in a court of law.'

There was some murmuring from the crowd at this and Lombroso smiled. 'I know that some of you may not agree with this proposal but I am confident that once you have seen the technique demonstrated you will be as certain as I am of its efficacy in the detection of the criminal from the non-criminal.' He looked around the room as if challenging someone to disagree but even Horton did not dare to inter-vene. 'Now, in the first experiment of this type we attached the electrodes to a variety of body parts – gums, nipples, lips, eyelids, feet and, of course, the genitalia.'

James was not particularly fond of pain. He looked over to Ottolenghi, expecting him to look alarmed. He was, though, completely composed, as if to have one's private parts electro-cuted in front of an audience was an everyday occurrence. James found his friend's equanimity comforting. It couldn't be that bad, despite Lombroso's eyes glinting with what looked like fervour or possibly insanity. James hoped it was the former.

'I have chosen my subjects with great care as always. Both of these gentlemen are free of any disease and are exception-ally intelligent.' Usually James would have basked in the glow of such a remark from his new mentor, but not that day. He would have liked to have 'unvolunteer' – but then he hadn't volunteered in the first place so it would be difficult to withdraw now. He resigned himself. He supposed it would be interesting at least. James had wanted to experience new things so he could hardly complain when novelty came his way, whatever its form. Lombroso looked over to them. 'Murray, Ottolenghi – if you wouldn't mind taking a seat behind the screen?'

There was yet more murmuring from the audience until finally Madame Tarnovsky could contain herself no longer. 'Cesare, really, you cannot be serious about conducting such an experiment on these two young men, even in the name of science – it is too cruel! I will not allow it!'

Lombroso smiled politely. 'Madame, of course as you are present perhaps we will confine ourselves to fingers and feet.'

James breathed a sigh of relief. His genitals had been reprieved!

'We can dispense with the screens,' directed Lombroso. As they were removed he gave some more details of the experiment. 'After this we will conduct the same process on some inmates and compare the differences between the results. Please note that all participants are volunteers.'

James thought that Lombroso's concept of voluntary was rather different from his. He caught Ottolenghi's eye and he gave one of his characteristic wide grins. James suspected that he had been party to the whole thing all along and that there had never been any intention to extend the experiments to their more tender parts. It was merely a case of Lombroso entertaining the crowd.

The experiment began. The algometer, as Lombroso called it, was essentially an induction coil powered by a current. Once the electrodes were attached, the current was passed through each part and the strength of it was gradually increased. At first they felt a prickling sensation, eventually culminating in a sharp pain. Their thresholds of sensibility were then recorded by the two assistants. Ottolenghi turned out to be more sensitive than James and was announced to be the more intelligent as a result. James wasn't sure about the final conclusion reached but he conceded his 'defeat' gracefully enough.

Two inmates were then brought in to undergo the same procedure. One was a short, brutish-looking chap with coarse features and a dark skin. He was, they were told, a brigand from Palermo who was serving a life sentence for a string of violent robberies in the area. He sat patiently in his seat as the electrodes were attached and, much to Lombroso's evident satisfaction, hardly seemed to respond at all to the current, no matter how strong.

The second inmate was completely different. He was tall and refined-looking, or as refined as one could look in the baggy striped uniform of a convicted felon. James tried to apply some of Lombroso's typologies and decided that he was an embezzler, a businessman perhaps who, down on his luck, had decided to steal from his company. He was soon disabused of this, however, and he began to have some doubts about the work of his new employer. Perhaps Lombroso was not as infallible as he claimed to be. The inmate was not an embezzler but a killer. He had once been respectable, it was true, but for reasons that could not be fathomed, not even apparently by himself, he had gone to his work as a bookkeeper one day and then, as the clock struck noon, he had taken a machete from his desk and set about his colleagues, killing all but one young post boy, whom he spared. This final act of 'compassion', if that is what it was, the gathering was informed, had been an error of judgment, as the boy went on to become the main prosecution witness against him. The murderer responded to the experiment in a much more extreme fashion than his fellow convict, wincing at every application. This demonstrated without a shadow of a doubt, according to Lombroso, that one's pain threshold reflected intelligence, somewhat of a giant leap, to James's mind and not only his, apparently. There was some muttering going on in the audience.

Lombroso, however, seemed oblivious, announcing that before the proceedings came to a close, there was one final subject to be tested. James thought for a minute that it was to be Lombroso himself. Ottolenghi had told him that the professor never fought shy of subjecting himself to the rigours of his own experiments. James was wrong, however. The door opened and in came a woman wearing a long cloak that hid her features. She seemed familiar somehow.

Lombroso held out his hand to her and he led her to the centre of the room. 'Here we have a female subject. We will see if she reacts to the experiment in a different way to the male subjects.'

The woman stood in the centre of the room and threw back her hood. James gasped and took a step towards her. It was Sofia. She stood there, her head held up, high and proud, her long dark hair secured in a chignon. She was in a simple grey dress with a white collar – an even more demure costume than she usually wore. It made her seem more vulnerable, somehow, and her fragile beauty almost took James's breath away. She looked haughtily around the room but did not meet his bemused stare. They had not spoken since their disagreement and he could see that she had not forgiven him. He saw Ottolenghi nod to her and she responded with a slight smile. James looked at him angrily. It seemed that he had known of her participation but had not seen fit to warn him.

Lombroso announced that 'the subject' was to be tested only on her finger. James was relieved at this. He did not think that he could have borne anything more. Even then he wanted to intervene but it was clear that Sofia was doing this of her own volition. He knew that he could say or do nothing but stand there and watch as she was tested, for if he tried to stop the proceedings it would be a disaster for both of them. He wondered at Lombroso and Ottolenghi's attitude. Both seemed oblivious to the pain and discomfort of the people they experimented on. To them they were just subjects, like rats in a laboratory, barely human at all. James remembered Lombroso's rebuke when he had suggested that some thought of criminals as being unworthy of compassion but there seemed little evidence of any compassion here.

The test was done and Sofia seemed much more susceptible to pain than any of the other subjects had been, wincing at the slightest current. Each time she did so James felt like leaping to her side to procure her release and it took a supreme power of will to stay where he was. He was curious to hear how Lombroso would describe her. He waited until she had been disconnected from the equipment before addressing them.

'This subject was a criminal but is now completely rehabilitated and is currently in my employ.'

James was relieved at this. He had not wanted to hear anything about Sofia's past life under these circumstances. If she wanted to tell him, he would listen, but it had to be between them.

Lombroso went on. 'The reason for her reaction to the test is not her gender but the result of her reform. This demonstrates that some criminals can change, as I indicated in my speech at the debate.'

James glanced round as Lombroso was speaking about

Sofia. Horton was leering at her in a most ungentlemanly fashion. Really, the more he saw of that man the less he liked him! For her part Sofia stood quietly, listening attentively as Lombroso spoke and nodding now and then to confirm his words. DeClichy was staring too – but not at Sofia. He was looking intently at Horton, his eyes screwed up in concentration. He seemed to have a small piece of paper in his hand and every now and again he would refer to it and look up at Horton again. Suddenly Horton glanced over at him and DeClichy hastily returned whatever it was to his pocket. James didn't think Horton had seen as he looked away again almost immediately. Then Lombroso stopped speaking, and waited for Sofia to leave before asking for questions. The first came from Borelli.

'You say, Cesare, that this technique could be used to collect evidence for a court case. Could you say how this might work?'

'Ah yes, Adolfo, a good question to start us off. Well, the point is really that algometry, when applied to a person accused of a crime, can tell us about the sort of person they are and the likelihood that they are of a criminal type. This could assist a judge and jury in their assessment of the character of the accused. In simple terms – it could show us the dangers that atavism can pose. I have used similar techniques in several cases already and have successfully identified more than one offender as a result.'

'Most interesting,' Borelli said. 'Could you give us an example?'

'Yes, indeed,' replied Lombroso. 'There is one case which has always stayed in my mind, even though it was some years ago. It concerned a young man, I forget his name now, who was accused of the murder of his next-door neighbour, an elderly lady. She had been beaten to death in a frenzied attack with some kind of blunt instrument. I was asked to interview the suspect with a view to answering a particular question: the police wanted to know whether or not this particular young man had the capacity to kill in this way.'

He paused and stroked his beard, a faraway look in his eye.

'What happened, Cesare?' asked Madame Tarnovsky gently.

Lombroso smiled sadly. 'It was a tragic case. The young man was clearly mentally disturbed. One only had to look at his posture. He sat throughout the entire interview rocking backwards and forwards with his arms locked tightly around his body.'

'Did he say anything?' asked Borelli, leaning forward slightly.

'He spoke only one sentence,' replied Lombroso, 'though he repeated it over and over again. I will never forget it. "Nothing can harm a good man, either in life or after death."'

'Socrates!' James exclaimed.

Lombroso nodded sagely.

'Well done, Murray. Yes, it was indeed Socrates. You can imagine my surprise that a young man from humble origins should be in a position to quote such wisdom.'

'And did it change your view of him?' asked Borelli.

Lombroso shook his head. 'No, it did not.' He paused, no doubt for dramatic effect. 'I took one look at this young man and I knew his past and, more importantly, his future, if left to his own devices. There was no doubt in my mind that he was a criminal born and bred.'

'How could you tell?' Borelli asked, who appeared to be genuinely bemused at Lombroso's conclusions. 'You seemed somewhat hasty to conclude his guilt!'

This level of criticism from someone who claimed to be a supporter of Lombroso sounded a little odd to James. But then, after all, James himself was not a little troubled by the professor's certainty about things, particularly his apparent willingness to condemn people on the basis of what they looked like.

'His appearance was enough,' Lombroso said, as if he had read James's mind. 'He had a cold stare, almost glassy – in fact, his eyes appeared almost filmy. His nose was hawklike and prominent, his jaw strong, his cheekbones broad. He had an abundance of dark hair but a scanty beard and thin lips. All of these are characteristics of the habitual murderer. And that is what I told the authorities. I gave evidence in court to that effect. Later the unfortunate boy's defence lawyer told me that my testimony was so certain that he did not dare to test it!'

'What happened to the boy?' asked Madame Tarnovsky.

'He was convicted, and rightly so. His sentence was a life of penal servitude. The judge said that he had little choice, for, having heard my opinion, it was clear that the young man could never be rehabilitated.'

'So you were responsible, almost single-handedly, for his incarceration?' murmured Borelli.

Lombroso bowed slightly as if expecting applause. 'I was . . .'

'He was lucky that you do not execute murderers in this country,' said Madame Tarnovsky, shivering slightly.

Lombroso looked over to her and nodded sadly. James wondered how that would have made him feel. To be responsible for someone's death is a heavy burden and not one that he would ever wish to carry.

'Professor?' It was Horton, still standing at the back.

Everyone turned to look at him. He didn't seem troubled in the slightest by their attention.

'Yes?' Lombroso said tersely.

'Bringing us back to today's demonstration – is it not possible that what you have actually measured is merely the action of the electricity on the muscles rather than levels of pain?'

Lombroso sighed. 'I see that you have read Gemelli's critique of my work in some depth, Horton. I believe my experiments have clearly demonstrated my point. His efforts, I might add, are rather primitive in comparison.'

There were a few more questions from the audience but they did not go on for long. The governor thanked Lombroso and brought the proceedings to an end. Ottolenghi and James started to attend to the equipment as people were leaving, but Lombroso ushered them away and beckoned the two other assistants over to deal with it so James took the opportunity to slip out of the room. He was hoping to catch Sofia before she left and make things right between them.

He saw her about to leave. He was just going to call out to her when he saw Reiner, already in his hat and coat, approach her. He hung back and watched, puzzled. What could Reiner have to say to Sofia, he wondered? Reiner whispered in her ear for a moment. She nodded, said something back, and they parted. It looked as if they had made some kind of an assignation. As Reiner left, James caught sight of a flash of colour from beneath his coat. It had been Reiner with Rosa Bruno and Sofia, that evening in La Capra!

'Sofia!' James called.

She turned and saw him but was clearly going to ignore him.

'Wait, please!'

'What is it? I am in a hurry,' Sofia said abruptly.

'I just wanted to see if you were all right.'

She looked puzzled. 'Of course I am, as you can see.'

'Sofia, you really shouldn't let him use you like that!'

'Really? I thought the professor had used you as a subject or is it one rule for you and another for me?'

'That was different.'

'Why, because you are a man, not a servant girl who cannot make up her own mind?'

'No, yes . . . oh I don't know!' James ran his hand through his hair in confusion. 'What did Reiner want?'

Sofia stood before him, her arms folded. 'That is none of your business. I may be a servant but, contrary to what you may think, I am perfectly capable of making make my own mind up about what I do and who I speak to. I don't need you or anyone else to tell me. *Arrivederci*, Dr Murray.'

James grabbed her hand before she could go. 'Please, Sofia, I was just worried about you.'

She looked at down at her hand in his. Her expression softened slightly and he saw the beginnings of a smile. She muttered under her breath and shook her head. 'Oh, James, what am I to do with you?'

He grinned at her. 'You could allow me to visit you later.'

'Perhaps, *si*, but not too late. Remember, I need my sleep!'

They heard voices. It was the professor and Ottolenghi. Sofia squeezed his hand and ran out of the door before they could see her.

'Ah, Murray, there you are. I was just saying to Ottolenghi that you should both be rewarded for your endeavours. I also think that it is time to introduce Murray to the delights of Caffè Torino. What do you say, Salvatore?'

Ottolenghi nodded eagerly. James was in two minds.

Although he was keen to experience all that Turin had to offer, particularly when it meant dining with Lombroso, he was also angry with both Lombroso and Ottolenghi for including Sofia in the demonstration. As it was, though, the decision was taken out of his hands. They were just leaving Le Nuove when they were approached by a young boy who announced in trembling tones that he had an urgent message for signor the professor.

'Thank you, young man,' Lombroso said, taking the letter. Ottolenghi tipped the boy, who bowed graciously and ran off into the dusk.

Lombroso opened the letter and as he read the contents his expression became grim. 'Gentlemen, I am afraid we must change our plans. I will need you as witnesses.' He held the letter aloft and glared at them. 'This is from Gemelli. Apparently my presence is requested immediately at an urgent meeting. There is one item on the agenda – the subject under discussion is my dismissal!'

12

While most murders are caused by a motive, such as religious belief, jealousy or revenge, others have no clear cause.

Lombroso, 1884 p 180

'I am surrounded by fools! This whole is affair is utterly ridiculous. I have not killed anyone and yet I am being treated as if I have been convicted of a crime!' Lombroso threw up his hands in the air in exasperation.

'If you continue to behave in this way I will have no option but to ask you to leave,' replied Gemelli severely.

James and Ottolenghi exchanged glances. The meeting was not going well. If the professor was not careful he would play right into Gemelli's hands which would be a disaster.

'Perhaps if you could outline your views, Professor Gemelli?' Ottolenghi said carefully.

Gemelli gave a slight smirk and Lombroso glowered at him. The rest of the committee, made up of several members of the Board of Governors including Borelli, Father Vincenzo who was acting as Chair and a couple of Gemelli's cronies, looked on with interest.

'The connection is quite clear,' Gemelli said primly. 'Professor Lombroso has been linked to two of the most horrific murders this city has ever seen. If we allow him to continue to represent the faculty there is a danger that he will bring the entire university into disrepute.'

'*É ridicolo!*' shouted Lombroso. '*É assurdo*! I have never heard such nonsense! I will sue you for criminal slander, Gemelli!'

'Come, come, Professor,' Father Vincenzo said. 'There is no need for this meeting to be so ill-natured. We must remain calm.'

'Calm!' Lombroso shouted. 'How can I remain calm when I am being accused of such a crime?'

'You are not being accused directly, or so I understand it,' said Father Vincenzo. He looked over to Gemelli. 'You are not suggesting that Professor Lombroso is responsible for these events, I take it?'

Gemelli shrugged. 'We cannot know. The crime has not been solved. I am told by Marshal Machinetti—'

'That imbecile!' Lombroso interrupted.

'Professor, I will not tell you again!' responded Father Vincenzo.

Lombroso slumped in his seat and pursed his lips. James thought that if his face flushed any redder he might have a seizure.

'I do not think it is any secret that the marshal and Professor Lombroso do not always see eye-to-eye,' Borelli said.

'That may well be the case but there is still the matter of the note,' said Father Vincenzo.

'I have absolutely nothing to do with that,' protested Lombroso.

'Your name is on it!' responded Gemelli.

'But I did not write it!'

'Nonetheless, Professor, it does represent a link, I think you must agree,' said Father Vincenzo.

'Not one of his making,' interjected Borelli, quickly.

Father Vincenzo nodded thoughtfully and whispered to the other two governors for a moment. 'I think we have reached a decision, Professor Lombroso.'

With that Lombroso stood up, turned and stalked out of the room, not even waiting for them to announce their findings. Borelli watched him go and looked over to James and Ottolenghi, exasperated. It was not looking as if the professor would last much longer in his post and what would happen then, James wondered. He glanced at Gemelli, triumphant and gloating and then got to his own feet to follow Lombroso. Something had to be done.

They convened outside the meeting room and James slumped onto a hard bench by the door. It was his future as well as Lombroso's fate that was being decided, for if he was dismissed there would be no option but to return to Scotland. He had just begun to feel alive again and he could not bear the thought that the progress he had made could be lost at the whim of Gemelli and his cronies. Their only hope was Borelli. If he could persuade the other members of the board to back Lombroso then the professor might survive with his position at the university intact.

'I'll see what I can do,' Borelli, who had followed them out, said, patting James on the shoulder before turning to go back into the meeting. He seemed oddly calm, given events.

Ottolenghi sank down on the bench beside James.

'What do you think will happen?' James asked anxiously.

'The professor will probably be barred from further teaching until the crimes are solved,' replied Ottolenghi.

'Well, at least it's not a dismissal.' James was trying hard to sound positive. 'After all, where there's life and all that . . .' He tailed off.

It was clear that Ottolenghi did not share this optimism. 'Dismissal will be the next step. That much was made clear.'

At that very moment, the door opened and Borelli walked out, shutting it firmly behind him. 'Gentlemen . . .' They rose to greet him. He beckoned to them to follow him down the corridor a little way, presumably to ensure that they could not be overheard.

'I did what I could but the committee were adamant that Cesare's involvement in these murders is bringing the university into disrepute. There is just one thing that can save him now.'

The door opened again and Gemelli came out with a smug expression on his face, closely followed by his cronies. Then Father Vincenzo emerged with one or two other people that James did not recognise. Borelli waited until they had disappeared through the doors at the end of the corridor.

'What was the priest doing there?' James asked.

'That man gets everywhere,' Ottolenghi said bitterly.

'Gemelli invited him to sit on the faculty board in order to please the Marchesa. Her patronage is extremely valuable to the university. And Father Vincenzo has real influence. We must be wary of him,' cautioned Borelli. 'I only wish Cesare had been more circumspect at the reception.'

'So what can we do?' James asked.

Borelli sighed. 'The professor has been forbidden to teach – a formal letter will be delivered to him by hand within the hour – but I managed to persuade the committee that he should be allowed to carry on with his research and that the symposium should continue.'

James wondered how he had achieved that. Borelli answered his unspoken question.

'I told them that to stop Cesare's research was far too draconian when no connection to the murders has been proved. Thankfully Father Vincenzo agreed, no doubt influenced by the Marchesa, who is a great supporter of research in all its forms. As for the symposium, I suggested that to cancel it now would only cause awkward questions to be asked.'

'You did well to persuade them, Professor,' Ottolenghi said. 'Had it not been for you, I dread to think what would have happened.'

'You mentioned that there was one thing that would save the professor?' James said.

Borelli nodded. 'Indeed there is. Cesare must find out who committed the murders and why. He must use his expertise to investigate.'

'But that is exactly what we have been trying to persuade him to do,' Ottolenghi said in an exasperated tone. 'He won't budge an inch on it, no matter what we say.'

'I think you may find that he will have a change of heart,' Borelli said.

James readied himself to leave. 'No time like the present,' he said firmly. 'Let us go to him and ask.'

Borelli put a restraining hand on his arm. 'No, leave it a while. Let it sink in overnight and speak to him in the morning, when he's had a chance to absorb things. It might make a difference.'

They nodded their agreement and Borelli bade them good evening and went on his way.

'Shall we discuss strategy over dinner?' James asked Ottolenghi, keen to talk over the events of the day with him.

He shook his head. 'No, not tonight, my friend, if you don't mind. I think I need an early night. You too – so we can be fresh for the morning. If we are to persuade the professor, we will need our wits about us.'

Reluctantly James agreed and they parted company. He was about to make his way towards his lodgings when it occurred to him that this was an ideal opportunity to continue DeClichy's research on Horton as he had decided at the reception. He looked at his watch. It was almost eight o'clock but the library was opening late during the symposium so he was confident that he would be able to gain admittance.

The university library was not far from the building where the meeting had been held so a few moments later James was walking up the imposing staircase towards the main desk. Behind it sat a short, balding man with wire-framed spectacles perched on the end of his nose at such a precarious angle they looked as if they would fall off at any moment.

'May I help you, signor?'

James wondered where to start. Then it came to him. 'I am an acquaintance of a gentleman from the symposium, Dr De Clichy.'

'Ah yes, such a diligent gentleman and always so polite – unlike some others I could mention.'

'He has asked me to continue with his research,' James said. 'Could you tell me what it was he was looking at?'

The librarian stared at him, suspiciously. 'I would have thought he could have told you himself.'

'He . . . he has been taken ill.'

'Oh dear.' The librarian shook his head. 'I'm sorry to hear that. He is such a nice gentleman.'

'So what was he looking at?' James reminded him.

'Well, I suppose there's no harm in it,' the librarian muttered. 'He was looking at some of our old newspapers, an odd request in itself. He wanted to see some of the American collection from the 1860s. I don't think anyone has had those out for many a year.'

'May I look at the binders?'

The librarian paused. 'Well, I don't see why not, as long as you promise not to move them so your friend knows where to find them when he's better.'

'I won't, I promise you,' James replied.

'Mmm. Well, all right. Follow me. They are still where your friend left them. You won't be disturbed. You're the only person here now.' The librarian led him up some more stairs until they were at the very top of the building in a smallish room lined with tall shelves. In them were large leather-bound volumes, held together with brass bindings.

The librarian stopped by one of the shelves. 'Here we are.' He indicated a table in front of them with two of the binders left open. 'Well, I'll leave you to it, if I may. We are closing soon, I'm afraid, so you will not have long.'

James smiled at him. 'Thank you. You have been most helpful.'

The librarian gave a short bow and left.

James began to examine the binders. A few moments later he threw them down onto the desk in frustration. Far from providing some sort of clue, they had revealed precisely nothing. He could not understand why DeClichy would be looking at newspapers from around the time of American civil war. It made no sense.

He shivered and looked around him at the wooden panels and shelves. There were no fires because it would only take one spark and the building would be aflame. As a result, the outside chill permeated through the walls into the room. The desk in front of him was covered with scratches from the labour of hundreds of years of scholars moving their books and papers around and the silence was almost oppressive. Every now and then he heard the shelves creaking as if complaining about their heavy burden and he wondered idly if the place was haunted.

James turned his attention to the newspaper. It was a copy of the *Chicago Tribune* from a few years back. He looked through it but could find no mention of Horton. In fact, the only thing that caught his eye among the seemingly endless advertisements for various remedies for afflictions such as warts and stomach complaints, was the report of a murder in the city. He studied it, but soon dismissed it as irrelevant. The victim was a prostitute whose throat had been cut and there were other wounds to her stomach but apparently the killer had been disturbed by a witness. Unfortunately the witness was reported as having been intoxicated and so was in no fit state to say anything useful. There were no organs displayed, and no note, so there seemed to be little to connect it to the murders that had taken place in Turin. Elsewhere in the volume he noticed that some pages had been ripped out. Surely DeClichy would not have done this? It seemed completely out of character. Wouldn't he just have made notes?

James rubbed his eyes in frustration and yawned. It was time to go. He closed the volume carefully and left it on the desk for the librarian to replace. As he did so, a piece of paper fell out. Perhaps DeClichy had left something behind. He picked it up and looked at it. It was full of meaningless scribbles – diagrams and doodles – nothing of importance. He turned it round. At the top was some writing. It said *Dr Death*.

He stared at it. What could it mean? As he was considering this he heard a commotion coming from downstairs. Voices were being raised and one sounded all too familiar. He went over to the stairwell and listened.

'Do you know who I am?'

'*Sì*, Dr Horton, but it makes no difference. It is late and we are about to close. No one can be admitted to the library at this late hour.'

'Oh, come on. I just want to look at a few notes that my colleague DeClichy has left me. I won't be more than a minute or two.'

'No, Doctor. You will have to come back tomorrow.'

'Now listen to me, you jumped-up little nobody, if I want to go upstairs then no one will stop me. You'll just have to wait!'

James heard the librarian sigh loudly. 'Doctor, it is not as simple as that. Someone else is already up there looking at the material you mention. It would not be fair to disturb him. Come back tomorrow.'

There was a pause as Horton took in this information. 'Very well,' he said. 'But you'd better make sure that the material is available for me – and I mean all.'

'*Sì*, Doctor, of course,' the librarian said.

Then James heard the door slamming shut and the librarian's footsteps as he left his station, presumably to inspect the lower floors before closing.

So Horton knew that DeClichy was on to something, although exactly what remained to be seen. Whatever it was it seemed that Horton certainly had something he wanted to hide.

Suddenly he heard a sound from the corridor. It was the creaking of a loose floorboard, as if someone had just trodden on it. James froze. Silently he crept towards the sound. Was it just the librarian come to remind him that the library was about to close? If so, where was he? Hadn't he said that no one else was here?

James moved quietly along the corridor and stopped. The only sound was that of his own breath. He held it for a few seconds. There was more creaking, this time from behind him. He turned quickly and thought he saw a shadow ducking behind some shelves. He walked quickly in that direction but could find nothing. Then he heard the sound of books falling to the floor and some quiet cursing. There was definitely someone there! James caught the sight of a figure out of the corner of his eye and ran towards it. He could not see clearly in the gloom as not all the shelving was lit. Whoever it was ran between the shelves and began to push books into James's path in an effort to slow him down. He slid about and almost tripped several times until he came hurtling round a corner and straight into a footstool that had been placed right in the middle of an aisle. James went over it and came down with a clatter. He heard a figure coming from behind and turned fearfully to face it.

'Really! This isn't a playground!'

The librarian stood peering down at him. Then he put a hand out which James gratefully took. 'I thought you were different but you academics are all the same. No respect. Come along. Time to go, young man.'

As they made their way towards the stairs the librarian treated him to a number of anecdotes of previous academic misbehaviour in the library. James tried to look suitably contrite. When they got to the desk James heard the main door swing shut. Whoever it was had gone and by the time James had extricated himself and left the building, having apologised profusely to the librarian, whose help, he reasoned, he might need again, there was no one to be seen.

He started to make his way through the cold night towards Sofia's rooms. He felt restless as he walked through the city, as usual now shrouded in mist. This day, as every other day he had spent in this city, had been eventful – the prison demonstration, Sofia whispering to Reiner, the professor's suspension and now the events in the library. It was hard to make sense of them all. Perhaps Sofia might be persuaded to tell him what Reiner had wanted and perhaps more about Rosa Bruno and what she might know. He would have to tread carefully, though. He did not want to upset her again, but if she *did* have information that might help them catch the killer then he needed to know.

It was not far to Sofia's rooms but by the time he reached them anticipation had almost overwhelmed him. As he rounded the corner of the alleyway he saw the candle in the window – a sign that she was waiting for him. He smiled at the thought of her touch. But then he saw something that he had not expected. A man approached Sofia's door and rapped on it with his cane. It had a distinctive silver top that James was sure he had seen before. He strained in the murk to see the man's identity as the door opened to admit him. Was it Reiner? No – the build was wrong. Sofia stood in the hallway holding a candle. She stepped back and for a split second James caught a glimpse of the man's features as the light shone briefly upon his face. He saw heavy brows and a beard. Was it . . . could it be . . . Lombroso?

The door slammed behind Sofia's visitor, leaving James standing, still wondering about what he had seen. Could Sofia have lied to him? Was there something between her and Lombroso after all? He tormented himself by imagining them together, Lombroso enjoying Sofia's kisses as he himself had done, whispering words of love to her. He felt sick at the thought of such betrayal. How could she have deceived him so blatantly? Of course he knew of her past and that was difficult enough to deal with, but at least the anonymity of her erstwhile clients and the distance of time meant that, for him, they were just shadows that he could put aside. An affair with his employer and mentor could not be so easily forgotten. How could he look at either of them in the same way again? And if Lombroso was capable of this deception, then could he be responsible for other, even greater, lies? Why was he so reluctant to investigate murders when his connection to them via the bloody notes threatened his reputation? Could he be involved, perhaps with an accomplice, as the footprints had indicated? Did Sofia know and was she only with James to keep him quiet?

James was toying with the idea of confronting them when he heard footsteps coming down the rickety stairway. He instinctively turned into the alley and hid there. He heard the door open and a muffled exchange before it closed again. By the time he emerged all that he could see was a figure retreating into the mist. He sighed with relief. Perhaps it was an innocent meeting after all. He began to chide himself for being such a paranoid fool. Of course Lombroso was no murderer. He was a man of science. There was no conspiracy. How could he have thought such a thing, even for a moment. It was only natural for Lombroso to call on his housekeeper. He might well have had orders to issue for the following day. She had told James that they were not lovers and he had seen nothing here tonight to make him suspect that she had lied to him. He wanted to ask her about it, just to make sure of her in his own heart, but he realised that he could do no such thing. If she knew that he had been lurking outside her home, what would she think of him? She had already accused him of not trusting her and this would just prove it. No, tempting though it was to call on Sofia and demand answers to his many questions, it was safer to make his way home to his lonely lodgings and the cold supper, thoughtfully left out for him by his landlady. DeClichy, Horton and the missing newspaper pages were quite forgotten.

Ausano whistled to himself as he made his way through the old market at Porta Palazzo. It had been a good night. True, he'd spent the last of the cash he had made from helping out the professor with his crazy experiment but it had been worth it. That night, just for an hour or two, he had been king of the tavern. Everyone had laughed at his jokes and listened attentively to his anecdotes – that is until the money ran out and the drink ran dry. Still, it had been good while it lasted, Ausano thought philosophically, as he wove his way home. You have to enjoy life while you can because who knows when fate will catch up with you.

It was cold and clear but Ausano was insulated from the chill by cheap wine and *grappa*. He belched into the night air and muttered to himself, retelling one of his stories that had so entertained his drinking companions. He paused in a small piazza in order to relieve himself in a convenient alley. Leaning against a pillar for support he was doing up his fly and preparing himself for the last stretch home when he felt a blow to the back of his head – and blackness descended.

Some hours later, the proprietor of Al Bicerin, one of Turin's most famous cafés, arrived with his young assistant Benito to begin opening for the day's business. As he unlocked the door he turned and saw a figure slumped on the steps of the church opposite, known as the Consolata.

He tutted to himself. 'Another drunk,' he thought. 'If he doesn't move soon I'll have to send the boy for the carabinieri.' Later he looked out of the window and realised that the figure had not moved for at least an hour. Curious, he sent Benito over to take a look. He watched as the boy bent over the apparently slumbering form and then stepped back quickly, crossing himself as he did so.

'Signor, signor!' cried Benito. His boss hurried over, took one look and pulled the boy back.

'Call the police, now! Tell them a man is dead and that half of his face is missing!'

13

Habitual murderers have a cold, glassy stare and eyes that are sometimes bloodshot and filmy, the nose is often hawklike and always large; the jaw is strong, the cheekbones broad; and their hair is dark, abundant and crisply textured. Their beards are scanty, their canine teeth very developed, and their lips thin.

Lombroso, 1876 p 51

James arrived at the museum, ready to try his best to persuade Lombroso that he should investigate the murders. Both the victims were connected to him and had been horribly murdered. And it was at least a possibility, it seemed to James, that there would be more killings. The murderer was trying to make some kind of point and until Lombroso at least reacted by investigating then perhaps he would feel the need to drive it home yet further by killing again. Surely the professor could not put his own professional pride before someone's life? It was unthinkable.

Sofia greeted him at the door and his heart lifted at the sight of her. She was looking as beautiful as ever, wearing her hair up as she had at the prison demonstration. It gave her a look of understated elegance that moved him and made him long for her touch.

She looked at him coldly. *'Buongiorno, Dottore.'*

He realised that she had been expecting him to visit her last night.

'Sofia . . . I am sorry . . .'

She frowned at him and shook her head. He nodded, realising that she was trying to tell him that they might be overheard. 'How are you today?' he asked.

'I am well, *grazie*. And you, signor? Are you well also?' Sofia said formally. Her eyes, flashing with anger, told a different story.

'I am, thank you.' James gazed at her, entranced.

She stood back to allow him to enter. He wanted to take her in his arms, explain his absence the previous night and beg for her forgiveness – but propriety forbade it. She closed the heavy door and, turning, swept past him. Her hand brushed his. He felt a frisson of desire pass through his body.

'The professor is in the laboratory. Follow me.'

He did as she asked and, as they walked along a dark corridor, he seized his chance and pulled her into an alcove with a large plinth in the centre of it. On top was a glass dome over an ape's head.

She looked at him in alarm. 'James, if we are caught!'

'I don't care,' he murmured and kissed her. For a few seconds she tried to resist but then she yielded to him and he felt her tongue fluttering gently in his mouth. Suddenly a door opened further up the corridor and she pulled away. James pulled her back. She was about to protest when he put his fingers on her lips. Footsteps were coming towards them. James breathed in Sofia's scent as she pressed herself against him and closed her eyes, like a child playing hide-and-seek. Suddenly the footsteps stopped and whoever it was opened a door and went into a room. They were safe.

Sofia opened her eyes and kissed his finger, still resting on her wide luscious lips. Then she nipped it playfully.

'Ouch! What was that for?'

'Where were you last night?'

'Something came up. I'll explain later.'

They embraced again, then she smoothed down her dress and walked on. James followed her, grinning from ear to ear, until they reached the laboratory.

Before she knocked on the door she whispered in his ear. 'Come to me later. I have something to tell you.'

She opened the door and ushered him in. 'Dr Murray is here, Professor.'

'Thank you, Sofia,' Lombroso replied. He was standing by the window, looking mournfully down to the bustling street below. Tullio and Ottolenghi were perched on a couple of laboratory stools as if they were about to begin an experiment.

Lombroso turned and smiled wanly at James. 'So, Murray, I see you too are here to witness my reputation crashing about my ears.'

'Surely it has not come to that quite yet, Professor?' James said, thinking that perhaps he was overstating the position a little – after all, he did have a penchant for drama.

Lombroso looked at him sadly. 'Yesterday, I might have agreed with you.' He sighed heavily. 'But today . . . today is a different matter. Everything has changed.'

'There has been another murder,' Tullio said, 'and I am afraid that this time the victim was known to you all, Murray.'

'Ausano,' murmured Lombroso, 'and I killed him.'

Ausano! James could not take it in. He had only seen him two days ago and now he was dead.

'You did not kill him, Professor,' Tullio said, 'but the murderer wants to lay the blame at your door, it seems.'

Lombroso shook his head. 'I *am* to blame. If he had not worked for me then he would be alive now.'

'We cannot be certain of that,' Ottolenghi said. 'It could just be coincidence.'

'Good of you to say so, Salvatore, but I think that is stretching credulity somewhat,' replied Lombroso.

'I'm afraid that the professor is right,' Tullio said, grimly. 'He knew all three victims and a tribute note naming him was left with each corpse. He does seem to be the connection.'

'A note again!' Ottolenghi exclaimed.

'I'm afraid so,' Tullio said.

'In the same hand?' James asked.

Tullio nodded.

'Was the body mutilated as with the other two?'

'I am afraid the mutilation seems to be escalating,' Tullio said.

'What form did it take this time?'

Lombroso held up his hand. 'Rather than you tell us, Tullio, perhaps we had better visit the scene for ourselves. Is the body still in situ?'

'Yes, Professor. It is not far, though we will have to be quick if we are to view it before Machinetti has it removed.'

'Indeed,' Lombroso agreed. 'Then we need to go now.'

They left immediately. Tullio was right. The scene of the murder was only five minutes from the museum and soon they were standing in a small square with an elegant church on one side and a café on the other.

Tullio pushed his way through the crowd that had gathered in front of the church. Lombroso followed in his wake and people started to whisper to each other, presumably remarking upon the presence of the great scientist and expert in crime.

Machinetti stood by the body, his lips pursed as he saw Lombroso approach.

'What do you want? Your presence is hardly appropriate, under the circumstances,' he declared. There was some muttering in the crowd.

'I asked the professor to attend,' Tullio said crisply.

'Interesting that the body should be found here, don't you think, Lombroso?' Machinetti said with a sneer on his face. 'After all, this is where you take your morning refreshment, is it not?'

Lombroso's face reddened slightly but he did not reply though it looked to James as if it was a supreme effort of will for him not to speak.

'Have you removed the note?' Tullio asked.

Machinetti nodded. 'Of course. I did not want certain persons to get their hands on it – which should come as no surprise to you.'

Tullio stared at him. 'I would advise you to keep your opinions to yourself. If you wish to be useful you might get your men to clear this crowd so that we can observe the scene properly. Oh and return the note to give the professor here an opportunity to examine it.'

Machinetti scowled. 'I will take this matter higher, you can be sure of that.'

'*I* have already done so,' Tullio replied grandly. Machinetti looked at him, his mouth open in surprise. Tullio went on, 'I have been assured that I may proceed with my enquiries and that you will assist. So, I would advise you to follow my instructions and clear the scene . . . and then stand away from us, if you don't mind. We have work to do and you are obstructing it.'

Machinetti glowered at him. 'Very well, Tullio, but you have not heard the last of this.' He reluctantly followed Tullio's instructions and, having handed over the note, stood watching them morosely.

'Have you really taken over?' James whispered.

'Not exactly,' Tullio replied quietly. 'I was told that we should work together, but by the time Machinetti works that out we should have what we need.'

Lombroso went over to the body and began to examine it. James and Ottolenghi stood beside him, ready to assist if required. The weather was warm and James thought how incongruous it seemed to be shading one's eyes from the sunshine whilst looking down on a corpse.

The sight was almost more than James could bear, notwithstanding his medical training. Tullio had been right about the escalation of the mutilation. There was no question but that the killer was becoming more and more violent. The skin had been almost completely removed from one half of Ausano's face. It reminded James of a model that used to be in his father's office which had shown a head with half of the skin removed to display the muscles, sinews, etc, that lay beneath. As he looked down at the body, James tried to remember what Ausano had looked like but found that he could not. All he could see were the veins, some red and some blue, standing out and glistening in the pale sunshine. Splinters of bone were mixed in with the sheen of the blood and a few flies buzzed around half-heartedly before landing in the eyes and lips – or what was left of them. James shook his head as if to dislodge them from his own features. As with Soldati, there was a small pool of dark red blood by the body.

'The poor man was both skinned and scalped,' Lombroso replied grimly.

'Scalped?'

'His hair and face have been removed on one side. The jaw and cheekbones are completely smashed, and the lips and the flesh of the cheeks has been carved away.'

There was a sombre silence as the horror of this sank in. James tried to put his feelings aside and be more objective. He had seen bodies before when he clerked for Dr Bell but none of them had incurred injuries like this. A man without half of his face was an obscenity but the rest of the mutilation was so barbaric as to be almost beyond belief. He shook his head slowly, trying to come to terms with the horror of what he saw. 'This is surely the work of a lunatic.'

Lombroso stood back from the body and frowned thoughtfully. 'It depends what you mean by lunatic.'

'Tell me more, Professor,' Tullio said. 'In fact, perhaps you could do a report for me.'

Lombroso walked away, shaking his head violently. 'No, no, no! You and Machinetti can deal with it. You do not need me.'

Ottolenghi and James looked at one another – so much for giving Lombroso an opportunity for reflection. It seemed that he was entrenched as ever.

Tullio, however, decided on another approach. He sidled up to Lombroso and spoke quietly. Machinetti craned his neck in an unsuccessful effort to hear.

'Professor, I am afraid to say that if we leave it to certain persons, justice may be elusive. His investigatory techniques are rather . . .' he paused, apparently searching for the most tactful description, 'haphazard.'

'Besides, would it not be rather a coup to solve the murders?' James added.

'Indeed!' Tullio declared. 'Your reputation would be enhanced, Professor, and it would be a chance to demonstrate the applicability of your theories.'

Ottolenghi nodded enthusiastically. 'Indeed, Professor, it would enable you to demonstrate your brilliance and confound your critics in one fell swoop. Think of the reaction of your rivals – Lacassagne in Lyon, for example!'

Lombroso stroked his beard thoughtfully and Ottolenghi went on. 'He would be furious – after all, he likes to think of himself as the only criminal anthropologist able to solve crimes.'

'And naturally Professor Gemelli will have no option but to reinstate you,' James added.

Lombroso grinned. 'With a full and public apology, of course.'

'Of course, Professor,' Ottolenghi said.

Lombroso turned to the corpse again and peered at it, evidently pondering the pros and cons of the situation.

'But if you do not think that you can do it, Professor, I would quite understand,' Tullio said. James wondered if this somewhat blatant appeal to the professor's vanity would achieve their aim.

There was a slight pause and then Lombroso turned and stared at Tullio. 'Of course I can do it! My theories are beyond question.' He threw his arms up as if conducting an orchestra. 'Gentlemen, we will start directly! Murray, what should our next step be?'

James knew the answer but he was not sure if it was what the professor wanted to hear. Ottolenghi nodded to him discreetly so he decided to take a chance. 'Examine the scene for evidence?' he suggested.

Lombroso paused and looked at him in surprise. 'I was going to suggest we considered motive and then applied it to my criminal type.' He pondered the matter for a moment or two. 'But perhaps you're right, if we are to be truly scientific.'

With that James, Ottolenghi and Tullio began to search the surrounding area, much to Machinetti's apparent amusement. 'What are you doing? Looking for coins left by the crowd?' he mocked.

'They are doing your job for you, Marshal,' Lombroso said tersely. 'Perhaps you should lend a hand.'

Machinetti frowned and stalked off into the café Al Bicerin.

James could hardly contain his excitement. For a second time he was able to use the skills he had learned from Dr Bell, only this time it was even better. He actually had an opportunity to demonstrate the method of deduction in front of the professor, and with his approval. It felt like a breakthrough. He walked the area as he had been taught, scanning the ground for any trace of matter that might have been left by the killer.

'Have you found anything of interest?' asked Lombroso, after a few moments.

'There's some cigar ash over here,' James said, pointing at a minuscule mound of grey power by the steps.

'And more blood in this doorway,' added Ottolenghi.

'Looks like the mutilation was carried out there, out of plain sight as before,' James said, without thinking.

'As before?' Lombroso said.

There was an awkward pause before Tullio came to the rescue.

'We examined the scene of Soldati's murder,' he said matter-of-factly. 'It seemed the right thing to do.'

Lombroso's eyebrows rose slightly. 'I see, and did you find anything significant.'

'Just a cigar butt and some footprints, that's all,' James said.

'My dear young man, there is no "just" about it. This is scientific policing and you, Ottolenghi, know how long I have advocated its use.' Ottolenghi nodded meekly as Lombroso continued, almost like a man possessed. 'If we add together photography, telegraphy and above all our knowledge of criminal man, then we can extinguish crime!'

James wondered exactly how Lombroso's criminal type would help in this but he didn't dare to interrupt the professor's flow.

'So, you found evidence of a cigar at both scenes. These things could lead us to the killer, if we can identify the make of cigar. I am sure I have read a monograph on the subject but I cannot for the life of me remember the name of the author. The footmarks might also be of interest. Do we still have the cigar butt? I would like to see it, if it can be arranged.'

Tullio shook his head. 'I am afraid that won't be possible, Professor.'

'I thought you kept it,' James said.

'I tried to. It was disposed of by Machinetti.'

'Typical!' Lombroso said. 'And the footmarks?'

'Too smudged to tell us much, but there were definitely two sets,' James said.

'I see . . . well that's something at any rate,' Lombroso said. 'Now, have we completed our search?'

'Almost,' James said. 'I think I'll take a sample of that ash, just in case.'

Lombroso nodded distractedly. 'If you wish, Murray, though I am afraid there is little we can do with it. It is the butt we really need.'

James shrugged and scooped some of the ash into a piece of paper from Tullio's notebook and put in his pocket. He thought that it could be more of a clue than Lombroso thought. All he needed to do was send it away to an expert and, as luck would have it, he knew someone at home in Scotland who might just fit the bill.

'Now, are we ready?' Lombroso asked. They all nodded. 'Good, well since that has revealed little of interest perhaps we can follow my initial suggestion and consider other aspects. Let us leave the scene to Machinetti and discuss the matter in comfort.'

Moments later they were back at the museum and Lombroso was briskly issuing orders like a general at the start of a battle.

'Murray, bring that blackboard over here. Ottolenghi – if you go to my study you will find a bundle of papers on the floor by the hat stand – would you bring it in? Oh and ask Sofia to bring us coffee and *grappa* – it will help us to think.'

They bustled about doing Lombroso's bidding, relieved that he had finally agreed to help them. Eventually they were ready to begin. Lombroso sat in an armchair with the three of them gathered round him like students before a teacher.

He gestured towards the blackboard. 'I thought it might help to see our thoughts on display, as it were, away from prying eyes.

'So gentlemen,' he continued, 'what do we have so far?'

'Three victims, all male.'

Lombroso nodded and threw a piece of chalk in James's

direction, which, not being very good at cricket, he promptly dropped.

'Would you mind, Murray?'

Not at all,' James said as he scooped the chalk off the floor.

'How were the bodies found, Tullio?' asked Lombroso.

'All were mutilated: Soldati had his nose and ears removed, Mancini's tongue was cut out and his jaw dislocated, teeth smashed and eyes removed. Ausano . . .'

Tullio paused as Sofia entered with the coffee and *grappa*.

'Go on, young man. We must speak plainly if we are to catch a killer,' said Lombroso, impatiently. 'Don't mind Sofia.'

James looked over to her as she put the tray down on a side table. She arranged each cup and saucer slowly and precisely. She wasn't usually so careful and it seemed to him that she was listening carefully to what was being said.

'Ausano had his face and hair removed.'

'Cause of death?'

'Soldati was garrotted. Mancini had his throat cut and Ausano was hit over the head several times with a blunt instrument.'

'It is interesting that different methods are used for each crime. Other repeat killers seem to keep to the same one,' James said.

'Examples?' Lombroso asked.

'I read of a case in America where a number of servant girls were killed with an axe. In England, Dr Palmer of Rugeley used poison,' James replied.

'You are right, Murray,' Lombroso agreed. 'And of course Eusebius Pieydagnelle from Milan – he killed at least six people with the same method.'

'Was he not obsessed with the smell of blood?' Ottolenghi said. 'I seem to remember Oskar Reiner dealing with the case in a paper on lust murder. He suggested that white males commit most such crimes.'

'Indeed,' Lombroso said. 'That is interesting but these can hardly be described as lust killings. Now, Tullio, have you had an opportunity to view the bodies close up?'

'No, only Machinetti and Dr Gallini, the pathologist have examined them in detail,' he replied.

'Gallini, that drunken fool,' Lombroso groaned. 'Do you think you can get us access, Tullio, without the marshal finding out?'

'I will try,' he replied. 'By this afternoon they will all be in the city morgue. Machinetti has not released them for burial yet.'

Lombroso nodded his approval. 'Good. I will examine them myself. I need to look at them all in more detail and we must find out if there are any connections other than the letters and the fact that they were all known to me.'

'These are both clear links, Professor,' Ottolenghi said. 'But why should anyone claim these killings as a tribute – and why to you?'

'Naturally, I have thought very carefully about that. There are only two possible answers, to my mind. Either this person has some kind of twisted admiration for me or they are trying to discredit me.'

'Love or hate . . .' James murmured.

'Indeed, Murray, well put. The trouble is that I cannot think of anyone who loves or hates me to such a degree that they would kill in order to get my attention.'

'You have no enemies or admirers?' Tullio asked incredulously.

'I have both but they are not the kind of people who would go to such extremes, I can assure you.'

'What if it is someone who is insane?' James asked. 'You may not even know them but in their fevered mind they wish you ill.'

'Or they admire you and want to demonstrate their allegiance,' Ottolenghi added.

Lombroso furrowed his bushy brows and nodded thoughtfully. 'There are, of course, many kinds of insanity. But I think you may be right in a general sense. These are not the actions of someone in sound mind. The fact that the note is written in blood, for example, indicates a need for attention, common in the insane.'

'Are the notes written in the victim's blood or the killer's?' Tullio asked.

'If only we could know for sure,' Lombroso replied, 'but I think it is more likely to be the victim's. There is an ample supply, after all. However, it depends on what kind of a person we are dealing with. If he takes pleasure in being hurt or abused as well as inflicting such tortures then I suppose it could be his own blood.'

'The note left with Soldati was in a neat hand. It did not look as if it had been written at the scene,' Ottolenghi said.

'Well, there we are. That indicates he probably used his own blood so it seems we are looking for a person who enjoys both giving and receiving pain,' Lombroso said. 'Let me see the latest note, Tullio.'

Tullio fished it out of his pocket and handed it to Lombroso who looked at it briefly before handing it to James. 'Tell me, Murray, what would Dr Bell make of this?'

James looked at the note with care. 'It looks almost identical to the first one. It is neatly written. Indeed, the handwriting is almost too neat – uniform, even.'

'What does that tell you, Murray?' Lombroso asked.

'I think it is at least possible that it may have been disguised.'

Lombroso nodded enthusiastically. 'Ah, so this is an organised killer, the kind of person who plans crimes with great care. This is a special kind of lunacy, mercifully rare.'

'A killer with some kind of mission, perhaps,' James suggested.

'Indeed, Murray, and we need to find out the nature of that mission.'

'A strange sort of man to be looking for,' James remarked.

Lombroso paused and stroked his beard, as he always did when thinking.

'What makes you so sure it is a man? Women kill too. We should not jump to any hasty conclusions.'

'Would a woman have the necessary strength to commit these crimes?' Tullio asked.

'Ah, an excellent question! What do you think, Murray?'

'I think it is unlikely, Professor. A woman would not possess the physical strength, in my view.'

Lombroso looked at him. 'I agree that it would be unusual but we must consider the possibility.'

'Well,' James said slowly, 'a garrotte has the element of surprise and Soldati was not a young man. I suppose if the woman was tall enough and had sufficient muscular development in her upper arms, she might be able to manage it. The mutilation though . . . I would argue that it does not seem to me to be the work of a woman. It would take a lot of physical strength.'

'Again I agree, Murray, but it is not impossible and we must examine the unexpected as well as the likely, if only to exclude it, as no doubt Dr Bell taught you. What about the other killings?'

'The second victim had his throat cut, and was then mutilated, possibly before death,' Tullio said.

'Well, that is uncertain,' Ottolenghi said. 'It could have been just after. Presumably we only have the word of Dr Gallini that it was otherwise and he is hardly reliable. He'll say anything to impress Machinetti.'

'Hmm, I do not think we should pay much attention to the view of anyone who thinks it is necessary to impress the marshal,' Lombroso commented cuttingly.

Tullio ignored this and went on. 'Assuming he was bludgeoned first or that again there was an element of surprise, then a woman could have killed Mancini.'

'And Ausano too – so again we cannot rule out the hand of a woman,' Ottolenghi said, 'though she would have to have been unusually strong.'

'There are plenty of women with that kind of strength. Serving girls, washerwomen and the like,' Tullio said. 'You have only to wander round the Porta Palazzo market to see that.'

Lombroso nodded. 'So you see, gentlemen, we should not be too hasty to exclude the possibility of a female killer, however disturbing we may find the idea.'

'But what kind of a person, male or female, would do such a thing?' James asked.

Lombroso had got up by now and was pacing around the room. He studied the blackboard that James had been dutifully filling with the information they had discussed. He started to mutter to himself. The three young men looked at each other and Ottolenghi shrugged. It looked as if genius was at work and none of them felt ready to interrupt. Eventually Lombroso stopped and turned to them.

'We have already discussed the idea that the perpetrator of

these crimes must be insane but I do not think we are looking for a drooling madman here. There are, throughout history, men and women who commit violent crimes without a hint of remorse. Such people when questioned are often quite amazed to discover that other people have feelings.'

'So is this the sort of person we are looking for, Professor?' Tullio asked.

'Well, that is difficult to say. The evidence suggests that the killings are very much pre-meditated. These do not seem to be chance encounters and the victims all have underworld connections, which is interesting.'

'And of course they are all connected to you, Professor,' James said.

'Indeed, that is so, which indicates a high level of organisation, does it not?'

They all nodded.

'This killer is not a born criminal, it seems to me,' Lombroso said. 'Quite the contrary, in fact. His madness has grown from some event that has happened to him in the past.'

'How will we know this killer? What physical characteristics might he possess?' Tullio asked eagerly.

'If this is an habitual killer, then the eyes would be cold and perhaps bloodshot, the nose will be aquiline or at least large, the jaw strong and the lips thin with well-developed canine teeth. The hair will be abundant and, if it is a man, the beard will be scanty,' Lombroso replied.

James stared at him in wonder. How could he possibly know what the killer looked like? It was almost as if he knew who it was.

'Is this definitely a case of one killer committing all of these crimes?' Ottolenghi asked.

'I would say so,' Lombroso agreed. 'They seem too similar

to suggest otherwise and I gather that Machinetti has kept all mention of the note out of the newspapers which would indicate that this is not a case of someone copying the killer.'

Tullio confirmed this and went on, 'One of the questions that we need to explore is this. Why does he choose these particular victims?'

This had been puzzling James and he waited with interest for Lombroso's comments.

There was an awkward pause. The answer hung in the air, a truth that no one wanted to acknowledge. Lombroso sighed, his words filling the uncomfortable silence.

'As I said earlier, I believe that they died because of their connection to me,' he said sadly. 'I can think of no other reason.'

'We also need to know how the murderer knew of the connection,' James added.

'Yes indeed,' Lombroso agreed.

'How do you select your subjects, Professor?' Tullio asked.

'They are mostly chosen for me by whoever is in charge of the institution in which they are incarcerated,' he replied.

'And if they are not incarcerated?' Tullio asked.

'They usually approach me.'

Ottolenghi nodded. 'It is well known amongst the criminal classes that the professor requires subjects for his experiments and that he pays well. Also . . .' Ottolenghi paused and looked at James.

'Go on,' Tullio urged.

Ottolenghi continued. 'Also, Sofia has certain contacts.'

James looked at him and wondered why he had mentioned her. Did he think that Sofia could be involved in some way? He thought back to the evening that they had found her in

La Capra. Could it really be no more than a coincidence? And what of her connections to Rosa Bruno and Reiner?

Lombroso took off his glasses and rubbed his eyes, wearily. 'I do feel responsible. The killer wants my attention. We need to find out why.'

'Perhaps the bodies will tell us more,' Ottolenghi said.

'Indeed. When can I see them, Tullio, do you suppose?' Lombroso asked briskly.

'Machinetti has a meeting with the mayor this afternoon, so he will not be an obstacle,' he replied.

'*Eccellente*,' Lombroso beamed, having shaken off his melancholy. 'Let us meet then. Now, though, I will take my leave of you, gentlemen. I am a little tired. Tullio, we will see you later.'

They all went their separate ways; Lombroso to his study in order to think and doze a little, Tullio to the security police headquarters and Ottolenghi and James to an upstairs laboratory to measure the Madagascan skulls. All of them, though, had little else on their minds other than the murders. James was excited, although he felt slightly guilty for feeling so. At last the real hunt for the killer was underway. But at the back of his mind he was also fearful. He had come to Turin on a quest for certainty but all he had experienced to date was the direct opposite. No one was as they had first appeared and secrets were everywhere. Not for the first time in his life he felt that there was no one that he could really trust. There was a killer at large and it could be almost anyone.

14

Religion, which tends to preserve ancient habits and customs, certainly perpetuates the practice of tattooing.

Lombroso, 1876 p 60

A few hours later they entered the city's morgue, a suitably dark and forbidding building attached to the university's pathology department. All the bodies had been assembled in the high-ceilinged room. As James looked up at the two tiny windows which let in a small amount of light, he thought that they looked like eyes peering down at the poor unfortunates who lay on the slabs before them. Lombroso approached the nearest of these and pulled back the sheet that covered the corpse. It was that of Giuseppe Soldati. The professor began to examine the body, pulling it this way and that, prodding and peering at it through his little wire glasses. At first Ottolenghi and James kept their distance, not wishing to get in the way. Tullio stood at the door, keeping a lookout.

Lombroso beckoned them over impatiently. 'Come, come, gentlemen. This is no time to be squeamish.'

They went over to the corpse and looked on. After a few minutes of various muted but interested noises Lombroso stood back and sighed.

'Have you found anything, Professor?' James whispered.

235

'Perhaps, but you must be patient. Rome was not built in a day! Now, Tullio, show me the next one, if you please.'

Tullio complied, lifting the sheet that covered Pietro Mancini. Lombroso was quicker with the second body, as if he knew now exactly what he was looking for. It was the same with the remains of Ausano. Once the sheet was lifted he made a perfunctory examination and then paused before looking at it more carefully. When he had found what he sought he spoke to Tullio.

'Has Dr Gallini said anything of note to Machinetti about the bodies?'

'Not as far as I am aware,' Tullio replied. 'He merely informed him of the cause of death and approximate times. There was nothing else. His examination was somewhat perfunctory, the cause of death being obvious, according to him. Why, Professor? Have you found something?'

Lombroso stroked his beard. 'Perhaps. I will give it some thought and we can discuss it later.'

With that he left abruptly, without revealing his findings. It seemed to James that this was not so much because of a need for the professor to collect his thoughts but more a case of creating a dramatic tension. Lombroso's theatricality was all very well in a lecture, he thought, but here it just seemed self-indulgent.

Dutifully Tullio began to replace the sheets over the corpses. James turned before leaving the room, looking at the forms lying there on the cold mortuary slabs beneath their final covering before burial. He shivered, not from the cold air but from the thought of death and its randomness. Even if the killer, as seemed likely from the evidence, had chosen these victims, was it merely because they happened to be in the wrong place at the wrong time? Did they just attract his attention because they laughed a little too loudly or brushed past him in the street, or were they simply associated with the wrong person – in this case, Lombroso? He shivered again, this time through fear. Then he steeled himself. The priority was to find this murderer and everything must be focused on that, for until he – or she – was in custody, no one in Turin was safe.

That evening they all reassembled in the same room as before. There was an atmosphere of expectancy. Lombroso looked excited. His cheeks were slightly pink and he moved around the room touching things, picking them up and putting them down again in a slightly distracted manner. Every now and again he would give what looked like a little jump as if he could hardly contain himself. Eventually, once he was satisfied that there was the correct amount of tension for the revelation of his findings, he began.

'Gentlemen, we were searching for connections between the victims other than the bloody notes and their association with me. I can tell you now that I believe that I have found such a connection.'

Lombroso paused and looked around the room as if he was addressing a large audience rather than just the three of them. The suspense had built to such a crescendo that it was almost audible. He threw his arms out as if declaiming.

'The bodies are marked,' he boomed.

There was an awkward silence as they all tried to work out if that was all that was to be said. James noticed that Tullio did not seem as surprised as the rest of them. He had a slight smile on his face as if he knew more than he was saying. Eventually Ottolenghi intervened.

'In what way were they marked, Professor?'

Lombroso took a deep breath in order to make his announcement.

'*Il segno del diavolo*!' Tullio exclaimed.

Lombroso looked rather irritated at the theft of his limelight. 'How did you know that?' he asked.

Tullio shrugged. 'I saw it when you were examining the last body.'

Lombroso narrowed his eyes as if trying to decide how to react. He chose to be generous. 'Young man, you have guessed correctly. The inverted cross, the sign of the Devil, was carved into the left shoulder of each victim.'

'Isn't the inverted cross also a sign of St Peter? What could it mean?' James asked. He knew that he had seen such a cross somewhere recently but he couldn't for the life of him remember where.

'At the moment I confess that I do not know the answer to your question,' replied Lombroso. 'However, I doubt that its use by the killer indicates an allegiance to Christianity.' He turned to Tullio. 'Do you know any active covens or sects, Devil worshippers and so on, who use the symbol?'

'It is hard to believe that such things could go on here,' James commented. 'Turin seems to be such a civilised and modern city.'

Ottolenghi grinned. 'James, you've met Father Vincenzo, and he's the respectable side. He just *believes* in the Devil rather than worshipping him. This city has been known for its attachment to Satanism for centuries.'

Lombroso nodded. 'For all our knowledge and science we still seem to possess an unhealthy interest in the supernatural in general and the black arts in particular. Such nonsense!'

Tullio nodded. 'Professor, I am afraid that the answer to your question is that most such organisations, and there are plenty that are currently active, have used that symbol at one time or another.'

'But what does it signify?' James asked.

Lombroso and Tullio both paused and then, seemingly in perfect unison, gave their answer.

'Evil.'

'I thought that you said it was nonsense, Professor,' James protested, somewhat confused.

'It is exactly that, but those who use this symbol believe in the supremacy of the Devil. They follow their master in everything and that includes a propensity to murder.'

'So the murderer is likely to be some kind of Satanist, then?' James asked.

'Looks like it,' Tullio said.

Lombroso did not agree. 'Not necessarily. We should not be too hasty in our conclusion.'

'It is worth following up though, Professor?' Tullio said.

'Indeed it is,' agreed Lombroso. 'But I am not sure you will find out much without the advice of an expert and it is not without risk. These people are deranged and almost certainly dangerous.'

'Then what do you suggest?'

'Leave it to me. I think I know someone who can help us,' Lombroso said.

Tullio gave a short bow. 'Of course. I will return to headquarters and see if I can find out anything from my colleagues. I'll see myself out.' As he left, James wished that he had waited for Sofia to escort him to the front door. Even a glimpse would be something.

Lombroso looked at them, thoughtfully. 'I think we have achieved much today. But now, is there anything else we should consider?' He pulled out a carafe of ruby red port from a cupboard and proceeded to pour three generous glasses.

There was a silence as they considered the events of the last week. So much had happened and at such a speed that it was something of a relief to just sit and think about it quietly. It was Ottolenghi who eventually broke the silence.

'We have not discussed the mutilations,' he said. 'They must mean something.'

Lombroso nodded thoughtfully. 'A message of some sort? Yes, I think that is more than likely, Ottolenghi.'

'But what could they signify?' James asked. 'The body parts are all different.'

'Perhaps that is the point,' replied Lombroso. 'It could be part of the message. So what do we have?'

'Nose and ears for Soldati, the tongue, teeth and eyes for Mancini and the half face and hair for Ausano,' Ottolenghi said slowly, looking down at the floor as if the body parts were laid out before him.

'Did they use them to commit their crimes?' James asked. 'Wasn't Mancini an informer?'

Ottolenghi looked excited. 'Of course! What do you think, Professor?'

Lombroso shook his head. 'No, I don't see how that fits. Soldati was a thief. He didn't use his nose and ears for that. And Ausano was a pickpocket. I do not see how his face and hair came into that.'

'Surely the body parts must mean something though?' Ottolenghi said. 'Otherwise why perform the mutilations in the first place. You said yourself that they were done with care.'

Lombroso frowned. 'Did I? I don't remember saying so,

although, having seen the bodies, I do agree. There must be a reason,' he murmured, frowning with concentration.

James was thinking through the list of mutilations. They were clearly done in a very deliberate way and listening to them recited by Ottolenghi had jogged something in his memory. Suddenly it came to him.

'Professor, do you have a copy of your book, *Criminal Man*, to hand?'

Lombroso looked at him curiously. 'Ottolenghi, could you go into my study and fetch the first edition of *L'Uomo Delinquente*? You know where it is.'

Ottolenghi nodded and left to do Lombroso's bidding. The professor strode around the room, excitedly, muttering to himself under his breath. After what seemed an age, Ottolenghi returned with the book.

Lombroso handed it to James who started to flick through it. He found a particular passage, smiled to himself with satisfaction and handed it back to Lombroso, indicating the place with his finger. Lombroso almost snatched it from him and began to study it, muttering all the while.

'Yes, yes, I see now . . . that's right . . . of course, it could be nothing else . . . naturally, naturally . . . ears, nose . . . yes . . . correct . . . and now . . . the tongue . . . but of course! I should have seen it straight away . . . and the last piece in the puzzle . . . aaahhh!' He sighed and flopped down onto an armchair, as if a great weight had been lifted from his shoulders. Then he looked up. 'Well done, Murray!'

'What is it?' Ottolenghi asked.

'Gentlemen, it is always imperative to know one's enemy.' Lombroso looked at their faces intently, his eyes bright and sharp, like a wild creature seeking its quarry. 'But I believe that through Dr Murray's careful scientific deduction I now know something of the motivation of our perpetrator.'

They stared at him in anticipation. The large clock in the corner of the room ticked loudly. The tension was almost unbearable.

Suddenly there was a soft knock at the door and Sofia entered, bearing a small silver salver with a card on it. She went over to Lombroso who scowled at her for stealing his moment of glory. Sofia raised her eyebrows slightly and pushed the salver under his nose. He tutted and took the card, looking imperiously down his glasses at it. Sofia stepped back until she was standing next to James. She brushed his hand slightly and gave him a slow smile. He had to force himself not to acknowledge her. Ottolenghi noticed and shook his head slightly in disapproval.

'Really, this is too much!' shouted Lombroso. James looked round at him in alarm, thinking for a second that he had seen Sofia touch him.

'DeClichy, that wretched man! Sofia, tell him I am too busy for fools and charlatans today!'

Sofia hesitated.

'What is it?' Lombroso said irritably.

'He was most agitated . . .' she said.

'Agitated! I am not surprised. His intellectual folly is probably weighing him down! I do not care. Tell him to leave me alone!'

Sofia nodded and left, giving James a sideways glance as she did so. Lombroso turned and glared at them. 'DeClichy, of all people. I can't think what he wants but whatever it is, it can wait. Now where was I?'

It was obvious that there was nothing he disliked more

than having a dramatic moment of his engineering broken so comprehensively.

'You were about to tell us of the murderer's motivation,' James said, helpfully.

'Ah yes. Thank you, Murray,' Lombroso said. 'But first, why don't you tell us about your deduction?'

James nodded. 'It is quite simple really. If we examine the passage here –' he indicated the page to Ottolenghi '– we can see that there is a list of a criminal type and physical characteristics.'

'Go on, Murray. Read it out. I want to hear my genius again,' Lombroso said as he leant back in his chair again, this time closing his eyes.

' "The abnormal characteristics that predominate among born criminals, especially murderers, are the absence of an ethnic type, a large jaw, a scanty beard, enlarged sinus cavities, a shifty gaze, thick hair and jug ears. Secondarily we find, in descending order, asymmetry, femininity, sloping foreheads and prognathism." '

Ottolenghi's eyes widened as he realised the connection. 'Of course! They reflect the mutilations.'

Lombroso took a sip from his drink and leant back in his armchair. 'The killer has taken the words I myself have written and applied them quite literally to his own work,' he said slowly. 'There, do you see? That's the key to all of this. It is clear to me that the killer's main motive is to demonstrate his allegiance to me by imitation.'

'And he is doing that by mimicking the characteristics of the born criminal,' James said.

'Correct, Murray. He is showing his appreciation of my work. In his own, admittedly somewhat twisted way, he is telling me that he supports my theories.'

James looked again at the passage the professor had marked and frowned. There was a mention of jug ears – and certainly Soldati had those, until that is, they were removed. But there was no mention of tongues, or a flat nose like Soldati's. Lombroso sighed impatiently. 'Oh, I know he is has not been exact in his "tribute" but he is a killer, almost certainly insane, so of course one expects a little variation. But nonetheless it is clear to me that he is an enthusiast. In that at least he has shown some sense.'

James looked at the book again. 'Well, let's see. You write of a jaw and the killer smashed Mancini's teeth. You speak of a shifty gaze, which would account for the removal of the eyes. Then there is asymmetry – so that would be why half of poor Ausano's face was removed.'

'*Eccellente*!' Lombroso boomed. 'There we have it!'

James paused and took a deep breath. He did not want to contradict Lombroso, particularly as it had been his own ideas that had started this train of thought, but he felt that he had to inject a note of caution into the proceedings. 'I agree with you, Professor. I think that he is mimicking you in a way. But this passage does not mention a tongue or a nose.'

Lombroso smiled and looked pityingly at him as if he was mentally deficient. 'You should learn to think laterally, Murray. I wonder that Dr Bell did not tell you so. If you do not, then I see your future here as being limited. Diagnosis, whether it be medical or criminogenic, is a matter of logical deduction.'

'Murray could not know of this, Professor. It was before he arrived,' Ottolenghi said, defending him.

'What was? I don't understand,' James asked.

'It was some work the professor and I were doing a

few months ago. We were comparing the characteristics of epileptics and criminals. They share a number of anomalies including—'

'Overly acute eyesight, dullness of hearing, taste and smell,' Lombroso interrupted. 'Yes of course, that's what I was thinking of, naturally. Still, clever of you to make the connection.'

'The point is,' Ottolenghi said patiently, 'that we made a much fuller list of anomalies for a new edition of the book.'

'So?' James thought he knew what was coming.

'The list includes all of the mutilations we have seen so far – the tongue and nose included – taste and smell.'

'So this could be a real tribute, then,' James said.

'Well, it could be except . . .' Ottolenghi looked at him, frowning. 'We had not publicised our findings so how could the killer know what mutilations to conduct?'

'You are forgetting something,' Lombroso said. 'The burglary.'

'I thought not much was taken,' James said and then he realised. 'Except some notes. And the list was among them, I suppose.'

There was a brief silence and then Lombroso stood up and went over to the blackboard. He picked up a cloth, rubbed out some of the scribblings and, taking up the chalk, began to write. When he had finished he turned towards them. 'This is our true motive. I knew it in my heart but I didn't want to acknowledge it. Now I think I must.'

He stood aside so that they could read the board. He had written the words,

TRIBUTE - TEST

'This monster is no admirer of mine and his handiwork is not any kind of tribute. He is using the term ironically. His true motivation is to present me with a challenge.' Lombroso paused again but this time it did not seem as if it was for mere dramatic effect. 'This challenge is one I must meet head on or who knows how many more he will kill.'

'What exactly is the challenge?' James asked.

'Why, to catch him, of course,' Lombroso said. 'Our killer wishes me to use my skills to track him down.' He turned towards them. 'Gentlemen, it is time for the science of Criminal Anthropology to come into its own. Lombroso must act as a detective and hunt this beast down. My theories are to be put to the test.'

15

The seeds of moral insanity and criminality are found in man's early life.   Lombroso, 1884 p 188

That evening James left the museum feeling distinctly unsettled. He still could not quite believe in Lombroso's theory of what was motivating the killer. Why should anyone wish to test him in such a violent way? He simply could not begin to imagine the thought processes of such a person.

He was on his way to see Sofia. It was only a day since he witnessed Lombroso leaving her rooms and there was still some doubt in his mind as to the nature of their relationship. She did not seem to have even a vestige of servility towards her employer. She did as he asked, but in such a way that made it plain it was what she would have done anyway. She was more like a dutiful daughter than a maid or a house-keeper . . . or a wife.

James sighed. He wanted to know more about her rela-tionship with Lombroso – in fact, he *needed* to know. He also wanted to ask about Rosa Bruno and Reiner. But it was plain to him that to confront Sofia would be a mistake. They were not close enough for him to start making demands even though he felt in his heart that he had known her forever. He smiled at his arrogance. As if a woman like Sofia would ever listen to demands. She had a kind of inner strength that he found both enticing and unsettling. He got the feeling that she would always do whatever she thought was best. It seemed to have worked for her up to now, so why should she change?

He walked happily through Turin, smiling at those who passed him on their *passeggiata*, the Italian evening stroll. It was raining, as James had been told it often did in the city, but its baroque architects had thought of that. They had designed magnificent covered walkways and it was possible to walk for miles without getting the slightest bit wet. He thought what a pity it was that Edinburgh did not have the same amenity, given the frequency of rain there. It was dark but the lights from the shops and cafés lit up the way and it seemed almost festive, though Christmas was more than a month away. He felt a pang of guilt. He knew that he really had no right to be so happy when his mentor was in such difficulties, but he couldn't help himself.

Soon he arrived at Sofia's rooms and this time he was the only visitor. She smiled her slow, half smile as she greeted him with a candle in her hand and led him up the stairs. Her hair was pulled loosely back from her face and as she turned to look at him for the first time he saw just a hint of fragility in her eyes. But then he remembered what he had seen the night before. Sofia put the candle down and enfolded him in a passionate embrace. Suddenly he felt almost overwhelmed and he found himself drawing back from her. All that was going through his mind was whether the professor had been given the same reception when he visited her.

She broke away and looked at him with a puzzled expression. 'Your desire has been quick to cool.'

James shook his head but found that he could not meet her gaze.

'So – now you think you have me and already you are bored. How typical of a man.' Sofia sighed and turned away from him. He noticed how she emphasised the word 'think'.

He could see that she had gone to a considerable effort to prepare a meal. There was a white cloth placed carefully over her rickety little table. Cutlery gleamed in the candlelight. He suspected that she had borrowed that from Lombroso's kitchen for he doubted that she earned enough to own silver such as this. There was a ham and some cheese and a freshly baked loaf. A bowl of figs stood in the middle and there was a carafe of wine, no doubt from Lombroso's cellar. She had taken such risks just to please him. How could he reproach her for something that might not even have happened?

James went over to her and pulled her to him. She was stiff and unresponsive at first but slowly she relented and allowed him to kiss her. 'Forgive me. It has been a difficult day.'

'You are not tired of me?' she asked, raising her eyebrows.

'Never! How could any man become so with a woman such as you?' he murmured.

They kissed again but then James pushed her gently away and held her at arm's length. He wanted her, it was true, but not like this. She was better than that.

'*Caro*, what is it?' she asked.

'There is no rush,' he replied. 'We have the whole night. Why don't we talk a little? You said you had something to tell me?'

She frowned. 'Is that the only reason you are here?'

'No, no,' he said hastily. 'You can tell me whatever it is later. I just want to get to know you better. I don't even know your full name.'

'My last name is Esposito. It means abandoned. There is nothing more to know.'

James looked at her standing before him, proud and strong, but he knew that behind this façade was a kind of vulnerability that drew him to her. Sofia Esposito . . . even her name sang to him and the sadness of its meaning made it even more poignant. But he could see that she did not understand. He thought that he had gone too far and wondered whether he should pursue this. It occurred to him that she might not be used to love. After all, what did he really know of her past?

He put his arms around her. 'Forgive me, Sofia Esposito. As I said, it has been a long day and I am tired. That is all there is to it, I promise.'

Sofia smiled at him. 'I see the professor is working you too hard. I will have to talk to him about that.' She led him over to the table. 'Let us eat, have some wine.'

'Yes, but on one condition,' James said, pulling her to him.

'And what is that?'

'You tell me something – just one memory – from your childhood.'

She shook her head slowly. 'I have nothing I wish to remember.'

'Then tell me of something or someone you prefer to forget.'

There was a long pause. Then she looked at him, her eyes half closed as if she was trying to reach a memory. 'It is difficult,' she said sadly.

'I will go first then.' James was determined to find out more about her past even if it meant probing some of his own dark memories. He wanted to know all that there was to know about Sofia. There seemed to be a bond of sorts between them but they needed to know more about each other – their likes and dislikes, their past memories, good and bad. Their backgrounds were so different, and yet James sensed that they shared something, although he could not say what that was. It seemed to him that exchanging bad experiences could tie them together even more effectively than talking of their better moments. He led her over to the old green sofa that squatted in the corner of the room. They sat side by side. James took her hands and held them gently as he began to talk.

'For as long as I can remember, I wanted to be like my father. He was a hospital doctor and as a child I used to watch him set off for work with his big leather bag. I longed to go with him and work at his side.'

'You were lucky to have someone like that,' sighed Sofia. 'How I wish . . .' She stopped and stroked his hand. 'Go on, caro.'

'He encouraged my interest in medicine. Sometimes, when I was a little older, I was allowed to accompany him on his rounds at the hospital. It was then I learned that he was employed in a mental asylum rather than an ordinary general hospital.'

Sofia shuddered. 'I have heard of these from the professor. They are terrible places!'

'Yes. The insane are treated as outcasts and are often housed in filth and squalor. I thought that my father was attempting to change that in some small way because he seemed really to care for his patients. Unlike the other doctors, he would take time to talk to them. At home he would pore over books about their conditions. I remember looking at pictures in them when he had left them open in his study. I could not have been more than about ten years old but I was not afraid. I can see them now – pictures of brains sliced in two and diagrams picking out different sections – like the professor's phrenology heads.'

'I do not like to go near those. They look as if they are watching me!' said Sofia, shuddering again.

'I found his work fascinating and I decided that I wanted to follow in his footsteps. That is why I studied medicine.'

'You must miss him very much.'

James looked into her beautiful dark eyes and wondered how much more he could tell her. Should he leave her with the impression that he was a loving son, tragically parted from his idolised parent or could he expose her to the terrible truth about what had happened on that dreadful day?

'I do miss him, of course, but it is more complicated than that . . .' He paused, unable, for a moment, to continue.

He heard Sofia sigh as if he had given her his own burden to bear. 'I understand, *caro*. There is more to tell but you are not ready . . .'

James took her in his arms and held her. He felt understood, somehow, and he knew then that he would be able to tell her everything. The relief was almost overwhelming. He had found it easier to talk of than he had thought. Whether it was because he loved Sofia but did not know her well or because she was part of a different world to the one he had come from, he did not know. But he felt liberated and he wanted more than anything to give Sofia the opportunity to feel the same way.

'You are right, my love,' he murmured. 'But now it is your turn to tell me something of *your* past.' He felt her stiffen in his arms and then she moved away from him a little as if being close to him might cloud her thoughts. Then she began to speak.

'No doubt the professor has told you something of my story

already,' she said, in bitter tones. 'He loves to do that. Sometimes he forgets that I am not an exhibit in his museum.'

James remembered Lombroso telling him of Sofia's father who had beaten her mother to death. Sofia was right. Lombroso *had* seemed oddly dispassionate, as if she was merely a patient. 'He told me about your father and what he did. That must have been so hard for you. Did you ever hear from him again?' James asked.

Sofia narrowed her eyes suspiciously. 'You ask a lot of questions. I am not one of your case studies.'

'I know!'

'Since you ask, I despise my father more as each day passes. He was a drunkard and a thief. The bastard stole my mother from me. She was the only person who ever cared whether I lived or died.'

'Until now,' he said gently.

'Perhaps . . .'

He felt her relax slightly as she fell silent and they sat together quietly, holding tightly on to one another as if doing so would put up a protective barrier against their past lives. James did not know what to say to her but he could sense that something had changed between them. He felt somehow that they were closer, as he had hoped they would be, although he had not expected such extremes of emotion from her. But then it was hardly surprising that she found it difficult to trust people after such a betrayal.

'Sofia,' he said softly.

'You wish to tell me more?'

James nodded. 'I feel ready, if you are willing to listen.'

Sofia raised her head to him. 'I am here.'

He looked into her eyes, took a deep breath and began again.

'Just after I qualified as a doctor I worked with my father for a time at an asylum in Edinburgh. It meant so much to me, being able to follow in his footsteps, and I wanted to specialise in brain diseases and mental conditions, as he did. It was the most wonderful time of my life, or so I thought.' He paused.

'Go on James,' Sofia said gently.

'Then I discovered that he had started to conduct experiments on some of his patients. But these were . . . were not always necessary . . .'

'Are you sure?' Sofia asked. 'Could it not have been that your judgment differed? He was more experienced than you, was he not?'

'For a while that is what I told myself but then something happened that made me change my mind. There was a young man called Richard who was brought in by a relative. He had begun to attack members of his family for no apparent reason and they were no longer able to control him. Most of the time he just seemed sad, unless, that is, he was painting. He used to create the most beautiful illustrations of what he called his fantasy world. I think he may have been a genius of a kind.'

'Ah yes, I have known someone like this, a man who did violent things but was gentle and clever too,' Sofia said. 'I have heard the professor speak of such people too. He said that a recovery is possible in some cases.'

'My father did not agree. He performed a procedure on Richard's brain. He called it a lobotomy. It is a new idea, purely experimental. He had no right to use it!' James could feel his old anger returning as he remembered.

'What happened?' Sofia asked.

'Richard never uttered another word and certainly did not

paint again. He retreated into some kind of inner world. He would have been better off dead.'

For the first time in many months James allowed a dreadful memory to re-enter his mind – the first time he saw Richard after his so-called treatment. He had stared blankly into the distance, his mouth slack. James had tried to put a paintbrush in his hand but he had dropped it to the floor. And then Richard had started to laugh. James shivered as he remembered the sound, empty and uncontrolled, the sound of a madman. Sofia squeezed his hand and he continued.

'It was then I discovered that my father had performed . . . other operations. He was quite open about it and did not see anything wrong with his experiments. He was *proud* of them. He took me round the asylum showing off his handiwork, talking about each patient as if they were things not people.'

Sofia stroked his hair in an effort to comfort him.

'You have not heard the worst of it,' he said. 'We argued violently. I told him that I hated what he had become and that I would tell the authorities and put a stop to his work. I told him that I wished he was dead and, God help me, at that moment, I wanted to kill him. If he had not walked away . . .'

'But he did, James,' Sofia said.

James sighed raggedly. 'Yes, he did, but I might as well have killed him. From that moment he went into a decline. He began to drink heavily and went missing for days on end. Then one night, during one of his absences, we received a visit from the police. My father had killed someone in a drunken brawl. He ended up in his own asylum and he is still there to this day, a pathetic shell, an abomination, a perversion of the man he used to be. To all intents and purposes he is dead. He is dead and I killed him . . .'

'You did not, James,' Sofia protested.

'I wanted him dead and he knew it. He knew I would take his life's work away. He could not live without it and I knew that but I threatened it anyway. I might as well have stabbed him myself. What he has now could not be called life.' James looked into Sofia's eyes. 'My greatest fear is that I have inherited his gene for immorality and violence, that I'm a born criminal, no better than whoever has committed these terrible murders here in Turin. That's why I came here. I had to find out. I thought the professor would be able to tell me, but now . . .'

He pulled away from Sofia and sat with his head in his hands as if shielding himself from his thoughts. She knelt at his feet. 'James, *caro*.' She took his hands in hers and kissed them. 'Wanting someone dead is not the same as killing them. If it was then I would have been guilty a thousand times over.'

'But what if I have inherited his violence? The professor seems to think it entirely possible for a man to be born with such characteristics.'

Sofia shrugged. 'I am just a servant and I know nothing of science but I do know people and I know criminals – and you are not one of them, born or otherwise.'

James shook his head. 'I wish I could believe that, but, Sofia, if only you knew what is in my head sometimes.'

'But that is it, *caro*. It is in your thoughts only and not your deeds. You are a good man, James. I have known plenty who are not, so I am . . . what is it that the professor is always saying?' She stood up and puffed out her chest as Lombroso often did. 'I am an expert in crime!'

James laughed at this, despite himself. 'And what does this expert say?'

Sofia pulled him to his feet and looked into his eyes. 'I say that you are no criminal. In your heart there is only love. Your father was – is – broken but you are whole. I am sure if you were to ask the professor, he would agree.'

'I will, just to be sure, when all this is over.'

Sofia nodded. 'You do what you must do, but I know he will say the same as I have, just with fancier words.'

James held her in his arms and kissed her with a passion that came from deep within, released by his confession to her. He knew then that whatever happened in the future for the two of them, he had known love and that meant every-thing to him. It was no longer merely physical desire that they shared but a meeting of minds. Sofia may have had a turbulent and dark past but she had an inner light that shone more brightly from her than any other woman he had known.

Eventually she broke away from him, laughing. '*Caro*, you must eat. You need to keep your strength up.' She pulled him over to the table again. They did not discuss further what they had shared. It spoke for itself. Instead, they sat and ate and James told her of the day's events, leaving out Tullio's mention of her own contacts.

'So the old man thinks he is being challenged. Well, it wouldn't surprise me.'

'Why not?' James asked, sipping at the wine she had poured for him. It was good. Not as smooth as Paolo's Barolo but still tasty. It reminded him a little of bramble jelly – fruity and sweet but with a slightly acidic aftertaste.

'People either love or hate him. There is no middle way.'

'How so?'

'When he is working he does not notice people, their emotions, their lives. All he can see is the shape of their skulls, the size of their feet or whatever he happens to be measuring. Everything else is irrelevant.'

'He is a scientist. For such a man the pursuit of knowledge is all encompassing,' James responded, surprised at both her eloquence and her apparent understanding of the professor's work which revealed that she did not seem to have a great deal of respect for him.

'Perhaps, but surely such little regard for those around you would serve only to cloud a man's judgment?'

James looked into her dark eyes, shining intensely with passion. At their centre there was something harder that told the story of her past and perhaps of her present. There was something he had to know. He breathed deeply and took her hand. 'Sofia, my love, I have to ask you this . . .'

She looked at him with a puzzled expression. 'What is it, *caro*?'

'Would you ever sell yourself again?'

She snatched her hand away and stood up, her hands placed defiantly on her hips. 'What kind of a question is that to ask? I will not answer it! It is not your business. I am free to do as I choose.'

'But surely you have enough to live? You would not need to . . .' His voice tailed off as he saw Sofia's expression.

She did not reply but just stared at him. Her silence seemed to go on forever. Finally she sighed heavily. 'I have other things to pay for.' She sat down again and stared into his eyes. 'Do not ask me any more,' she said firmly.

'I have a little money. I can take care of you and whatever else it is you need to pay for.' James could not bear the thought of her with anyone but him.

She smiled and shook her head sadly. 'What if you tire of me and go away, back to *Scozia*? What then?'

'I will never leave you. I . . . I love you.'

Sofia gave an amused smile and he was immediately angry with himself. He had wanted to tell her how he felt gently in a romantic moment, not blurt it out in the middle of an argument.

'Perhaps you do, perhaps you don't. It is of little consequence.'

He could not believe what he had heard. 'Little consequence! Is that how you see me? After all we have just shared?'

She came towards him and put her hand up as if to stroke his cheek but he pushed her away.

She spoke softly, '*Caro*, you do not understand. I have to be practical. I cannot allow myself the luxury of love.'

Finally James understood what it was she was trying to tell him. He had been so consumed by his own feelings towards her that he had assumed that she would return them immediately. For Sofia, though, there were different considerations. He took her in his arms again. 'Then you will have to allow me to love for us both for now until . . .'

She nodded and whispered in his ear, 'Until . . .'

Then, as they kissed, she led him slowly into her bedroom where they made love with a passion and tenderness that all but consumed him. And whatever she might say, this was the beginning of something important for both of them. He had shared more in that one evening with her than he had ever done with anyone and he hoped with all his being that it might have been the same for her.

Some hours later he lay in bed with Sofia sleeping quietly in his arms. He looked up through her tiny window at the crescent of a new moon and allowed himself to dream of their future. He would become an eminent criminal anthropologist and Sofia would be his wife, helping him with his work and bringing her beauty and wit to his table as they entertained fellow scientists. Lucy would love her. Everyone would love her. How could they not? Except, of course, in his heart he knew that such a scene could never be played out in reality. Sofia was a servant and, in society's eyes, one with a criminal past. They had no future outside these four walls. But still, he was here with her and he would have to make do with that.

Sofia sighed and smiled in her sleep and James looked down at her, his heart full of joy, enraptured. He was the happiest he had been for a long time, since his father's death, in fact. It was if he had finally awoken from a nightmare that had played itself over and over again in his mind. But still the memory remained and he had to be sure that all vestige of his fear was gone before he could be at peace. The murders must be solved and Lombroso consulted. He started to go over the facts in his mind – three men murdered, all known to Lombroso, all mutilated in different ways, apparently reflecting his work, all left with a tribute note and a Satanic sign carved into the shoulder. James had no doubt that the professor was right about it being some kind of challenge. But the nature of that challenge and the reason for it was still a puzzle, despite what Lombroso thought, and one they needed desperately to solve before any real progress could be made in the investigation. And there was still the question of Rosa Bruno and Reiner. With all that they had shared it had not seemed appropriate to ask Sofia about them but he knew that sooner or later he would have to broach the subject with her.

Eventually he began to doze and dream a little – of bodies

and Satanists and Madagascan skulls. It seemed little more than a few moments later that he was awakened by the sun shining through the window into his eyes. Sofia was not there. He got up from the bed and went into the other room. She was making coffee in her tiny kitchen. The smell of it was glorious – rich and aromatic. Fresh pastries were on the table. She had even provided the morning's newspaper. James felt a tug at his heart. She had so little but was doing her best to look after him. He embraced her, losing himself in the sweet, slightly musky scent of her hair.

She told him to sit at the table and brought the coffee over as he opened the newspaper and saw the main headline.

WORLD EXCLUSIVE BY BALDOVINO.
LOMBROSO MURDERS: KILLER CONTACTS THE
PEOPLE'S VOICE!

Shocked, he read the article quickly. 'It's all there, everything, even the notes!' he exclaimed. 'How did the paper get hold of all of this? According to Tullio, Machinetti was supposed to be keeping the news about the notes quiet.'

'Huh! Machinetti hates the professor. He will have told the reporter on purpose!' Sofia said, angrily.

James got up from the table. 'I must go to the professor. He may not know. I need to warn him.'

'Of course,' Sofia agreed.

He kissed her goodbye reluctantly and left, grabbing the newspaper and his coat as he ran through the door and down the stairs.

16

Since we usually attribute little value to everyday phenomena, the idea that a man's handwriting can provide clues to his psychological state may seem useless and even bizarre . . . I know full well that copious data is needed to prove my argument that criminals can be diagnosed by their handwriting.

Lombroso, 1878 p III

As James made his way to the museum, everyone he saw seemed to be reading the *People's Voice*. Whether they were sitting in cafés, leaning against lamp-posts or just walking along the street it felt as if they were staring and even laughing at him, the student of the man who might be a killer.

He looked at his watch. It was half past ten. No doubt Lombroso would be on his way to Al Bicerin, his favourite place for morning refreshment. James could not see the professor being deterred despite Ausano's body having been found close by. He decided to go there in the hope that he could head him off before he walked into the crowded café and got a nasty shock. He got there just in time to see Lombroso and Ottolenghi making their way through the outdoor tables towards the door and he hailed them.

Lombroso smiled at him. 'Ah, Murray, you have caught us out in our daily vice! Come and join us. You must try our local drink. Once you have, I guarantee coffee will never taste quite the same!'

'Have you seen the paper?' James asked.

Lombroso ignored him and strode into the café, leaving James and Ottolenghi to follow him in.

The place was tiny. There must have been only four or five small marble-topped tables placed around the room in front of plush red velvet benches. Lombroso spread himself out and indicated some elegant gilt chairs. Ottolenghi went to the counter to order. James passed over his newspaper, indicating the piece in question. As he read it Lombroso started to tut and his smile was soon replaced by a frown. Ottolenghi joined them and Lombroso handed the paper over to him without a word, his lips pursed.

'I thought Machinetti had been persuaded to keep the details to himself for now?' Ottolenghi said.

Lombroso nodded wearily. 'Well, it seems that either he has changed his mind or someone else has seen fit to tell the . . .' He picked up the paper and looked at it again, his nose wrinkling in disgust. '*People's Voice*. Really, Murray, I'm surprised at you reading such an inferior publication. It's the sort of thing only servants bother with.'

Ottolenghi looked sideways at James who shifted uncomfortably in his seat. The waiter brought over their drinks on a tray; three small glasses seemingly filled with coffee and topped with cream. Both Lombroso and Ottolenghi visibly brightened at the sight.

'What should we do, Professor?' James asked anxiously.

'Do? Do about what?' Lombroso replied.

'About the paper – it mentions you by name!'

He waved it away. 'Oh, that is of no real consequence. It is an irritation, nothing more.'

James wondered how he could be so dismissive of it given his already precarious position at the university. He looked over to Ottolenghi who shrugged. It seemed that to some extent Lombroso was trying to pretend to himself that all was well. James had noticed that the professor had an ability to detach himself from reality when the occasion demanded. As he often reminded James, he regarded himself as a scientist and scientists are supposed to be objective.

'But the letter the reporter received, might that not be interesting?' Ottolenghi suggested.

Lombroso nodded thoughtfully. 'Perhaps, if it is indeed from the killer and not the product of a journalist's fevered imagination. I know Baldovino of old. He is not a keen purveyor of the truth if it might spoil a good story. Still, there might be something in it. I think it is time to pay him a visit.'

'What will the letter reveal?' James asked.

Lombroso peered at him over his glasses. 'It is not just what is in the document that is significant, but how it is written. One can tell much about a man from his script. It is a significant area for study but few have given it the attention it deserves.'

This was a new idea to James but it sounded interesting.

'We need to see the original document,' Lombroso said.

'Might it be useful to take Tullio with us?' suggested Ottolenghi. 'It would give us more authority.'

Lombroso looked at him imperiously, as if he considered himself to have all the authority that would be needed. But then he nodded reluctantly. 'I suppose you're right. It might smooth the path. We can pick him up on the way, if he's free.'

James started to get to his feet but Lombroso placed a

restraining hand on his arm. 'There is no rush, Murray. We will finish our drinks first. *Bicerin* cannot be hurried. It must be savoured. Try it and you'll see what I mean.'

James sat down again, picked up his glass and sipped the hot liquid through the cold cream. Lombroso was right. It was both delicious and surprising, for through the rich dry note of the coffee was a sweeter one – chocolate. He could see why this had become a habit for both Lombroso and Ottolenghi. As he enjoyed the enticing mixture of flavours he decided that he would make every effort to join them in future. This was something not to be missed. The café was beginning to fill up with people of the same view and James noticed that some of them were staring at Lombroso. It could have been due to his existing status, of course. He had noticed a similar effect wherever they went with him, such was his reputation, but today he thought that he detected a difference, something more prurient and less admiring than he had seen before. Lombroso, however, seemed oblivious to it and appeared to be concentrating on his *bicerin*.

He finished drinking and spooned up what remained of the chocolate in his glass. This was clearly an acceptable practice as James noticed several other people doing the same. Lombroso wiped his beard fastidiously and got up to leave. 'Come, gentlemen, Signor Baldovino and the *People's Voice* await.'

They followed obediently. As they bustled through the city James noticed people looking at them. Some whispered to their companions behind their hands. There was no doubt in James's mind. The connection between Lombroso and the murders had been made in the minds of the public. The repercussions from this would no doubt follow swiftly and yet Lombroso seemed either unaware or simply unconcerned.

James shivered slightly – perhaps due to the anticipation of what might be coming or perhaps it was simply the cold air. It was a chilly, bright day and the city's buildings were at their best, shining in the pale sunlight. It was hard to believe that such terrible events had happened not far from here. They called in at the headquarters of the Public Security Police, a grand building nestling next to the carabinieri offices situated in a large piazza in the heart of the city. Luckily Tullio was there and Lombroso's celebrity meant that they could see him without a problem. It seemed that neither Tullio nor his superiors had read that morning's *People's Voice*. Ottolenghi explained the situation and showed Tullio the article.

Lombroso looked at him steadily. 'I am sure that a man of your calibre can understand why I need to see the letter.'

Tullio nodded. 'Graphology, the art of handwriting analysis . . .'

Lombroso beamed at him. 'Ah, I see I was right. You are that rare thing, a policeman who is also a man of science.'

Tullio smiled back. 'I have an open mind about most things, Professor. Any new techniques we can find to help us catch criminals have to be explored.'

'If only others in your profession were as enlightened,' said Lombroso. 'So you will accompany us?'

'I will, but I need to explain it to my superior first.'

He disappeared for a few minutes but soon returned. With him was the familiar form of Lieutenant Giardinello.

Tullio explained. 'My superiors are eager to encourage co-operation between the security police and the carabinieri. Besides, it may be that Signor Baldovino will require persuasion.'

Lieutenant Giardinello grinned amiably and Lombroso acknowledged him with a nod. 'Shall we go, then?'

With that they set off on the short walk to the offices of the *People's Voice*. Before long they reached a small square and Lombroso pointed at an uninspiring-looking building in the corner. James was surprised. He had been expecting something bigger and finer. As they entered what looked like a front office he saw that the ceilings were low, giving the room a poky, claustrophobic feel. Lombroso rapped on the counter with his cane but no one came. He rolled his eyes impatiently and strode through to the next room with the others following in his wake.

He paused at a desk where a boy was sorting through post and asked him for Baldovino. The boy pointed over to the corner of the room where a small, sharp-featured man was seated.

James thought that if he were to describe him to Lucy he would say he resembled a weasel. Baldovino's small eyes were looking into the mid distance as he thoughtfully probed his ear with a pencil. He had thin, sandy-coloured hair, slicked back revealing a pronounced widow's peak. His complexion was sallow, with a kind of waxy sheen, not unlike that of a corpse, and his expression suggested that he was a man who always thought the worst of people. He was lounging at his desk, his feet balanced on it, and his chair tilted and wobbled precariously with each new aural probe. One of his colleagues helpfully kicked at it, almost causing Baldovino to fall. There were one or two sniggers as he tried to recover himself.

He scowled but then his eyes grew wide with surprise at the sight of Lombroso. He leapt to his feet and bowed slightly. 'Professor, I am so pleased to meet you!' He held out a hand towards Lombroso who looked down at it with disdain. Baldovino smirked and shook his head. James thought it might prove a mistake for Lombroso to make his dislike so obvious. After all, the fellow might be repellent but he did have the power of the press behind him.

A chair was brought for Lombroso who sat down gracefully on it and leaned on his silver-topped cane.

'I have come to see the letter.'

Baldovino thought for a few seconds and then smiled broadly, no doubt as he realised that there might be a possibility of making some money.

'What letter?' he said, adopting what he probably thought was an innocent expression.

Giardinello placed his hand on Baldovino's shoulder and bent down to his recently explored ear. 'You know what letter. Hand it over.'

'Why should I?'

'Because if you don't I will take you out to the back of this building and explore the reasons for your refusal to cooperate with the carabinieri in much more detail,' Giardinello replied threateningly.

Suddenly Baldovino's beady little eyes lit up. 'Wait a minute, why is it the professor here who wants to see it and not Marshal Machinetti? And why does he want to see it at all?' He looked directly at Lombroso then. It was clear that he sensed a story in the making. 'Can you tell us who the killer is, Professor? Is that it?'

There was a pause. Everyone looked away, not wishing to catch Baldovino's eye. He warmed to his theme.

'Don't you think the people have a right to know? A killer in their very midst but the high and mighty scientist won't reveal his identity. Now that *is* a good story, don't you think?'

Lombroso pursed his lips at Baldovino, who smiled and nodded with the certainty of a man who realised that he had the upper hand. 'Machinetti doesn't know that you're here, does he, Professor? Now, why might that be? Let me guess: is it that he wouldn't let you near this letter or any other evidence because you're a suspect? Is that why you won't tell us who did it, Professor? Was it you? I can see the headlines – "Lombroso the killer". That's what Machinetti thinks, isn't it?'

'That is ridiculous,' Lombroso said angrily. 'I am not a suspect.'

Baldovino shook his head. 'Is it ridiculous? After all, he hates you, Professor, doesn't he? I remember that case, the young girl who died. Now that was a real tragedy. Machinetti swore he wouldn't work with you again.'

Still no one spoke. Baldovino was speaking the truth. Machinetti was already convinced of Lombroso's involvement. He certainly would not want Lombroso anywhere near the letter and if he found out that he had been here he would no doubt jump to the worst conclusion.

Baldovino hesitated for a moment. 'You can see the letter but it'll cost you.' Lombroso rolled his eyes in irritation. Tullio pulled out his wallet and took out a note. Baldovino tried to take it from him but he snatched it away. 'Letter first, money later.'

Baldovino put his thin hand into his shirt and pulled out a piece of paper. Giardinello took it from him and, holding it at arm's length, his nose wrinkled in disgust, handed it to Lombroso, who examined it carefully and began to write in a small leather-bound notebook that he had taken from his pocket. Suddenly there was some shouting from down the stairs. Giardinello's eyes widened in alarm as he recognised the hectoring tones of Machinetti. Tullio sighed.

'Baldovino! Where the devil is he, the devious little

bastard!' Machinetti came striding round the corner, a couple of Giardinello's hapless colleagues in tow.

'Ah, there you are. Hand it over now and I won't arrest you for obstruction, perjury and theft!' He came to a sudden halt, having caught sight of Lombroso still examining the item he was seeking.

'Lombroso! Why is it that everywhere I go, you are there first?'

'Because I am quicker than you in all respects, Machinetti,' Lombroso replied in a withering tone, handing the letter to James, who was standing next to him.

Machinetti pursed his lips. 'Tullio, I have spoken to the questor. He confirmed that *I* am investigating this crime.'

'Really?' Lombroso said. 'You seem to have precious little to show for it.'

'Actually, I think you will find we are both investigating it,' Tullio said firmly.

Machinetti glowered at him. 'Give me the letter,' he ordered, glaring at James.

'Well now, Marshal,' Lombroso said in a conversational tone, 'I do not believe that it is addressed to you.'

'It is for the people,' Baldovino added self-righteously.

'Indeed,' Lombroso said. 'Well then, Marshal, why don't you read it in the paper like a man of the people should?'

Machinetti stared at him. 'If you do not hand it over I will have you taken into custody right now for tampering with evidence.'

Lombroso raised his eyebrows. Out of the corner of his eye James could see the two carabinieri that Machinetti had brought with him, standing tensely by as if readying themselves for what would no doubt be a difficult arrest.

'Give the letter to me now!' Machinetti barked. 'It is evidence.'

'Tssk tssk, Machinetti. You remind me of one of my children.' Lombroso wagged his finger and shook his head like a nanny admonishing one of her charges.

Machinetti paused as if he was weighing up the situation. 'This is not helping your case, Lombroso,' he said in a quieter but more threatening tone.

'What case?' Lombroso asked brusquely.

'Why murder, of course,' Machinetti replied. 'The evidence against you is mounting. The notes name you and now you appear to be anxious to get to this letter. What's the matter? Are you afraid it might name you as an accomplice?'

Lombroso stood up, took the letter from James and held it up as if to give it to him. 'Here, have it. I have seen enough.'

Machinetti walked slowly over to him, a sly smile on his face. 'You will be hearing from us soon, Professor, I promise you that. Now give me the letter. It is police property.'

'Indeed it is,' Tullio said firmly as he took the letter from Lombroso. 'As such, I will take it.'

Machinetti went towards him as if he was about to snatch it back. James wondered for a second if there was to be an unseemly brawl but at the last moment Machinetti appeared to change his mind and smirked at Tullio instead.

'I expect it is just a hoax, anyway,' he said dismissively.

Lombroso's expression darkened and he looked at Machinetti. 'Perhaps, perhaps not. But as you should know by now, Marshal, assumptions are dangerous things.'

With that he swept out, rather magnificently, leaving Machinetti standing open-mouthed and Baldovino looking as if he was making mental notes for his next story.

James went to leave but turned back and studied the

marshal for a few seconds from the doorway. Machinetti seemed intent on thwarting their investigation at every turn. Evidence was far from safe in his hands. Could it really be nothing more than a feud that made him behave in such an obstructive fashion?

Machinetti scowled at him. 'Hurry along, Dr Murray. Your master is waiting for you.'

James spun on his heel contemptuously and walked out of the building into the street, breathing the fresh air gratefully. Machinetti hated Lombroso, that much was clear. But was it enough to make him a killer? James thought of the hatred in the policeman's eyes and concluded that it was entirely possible it was.

17

'Gentlemen, I believe we have a clue!'

Lombroso sat back in his chair, clutching a copy of the *People's Voice*, and looked at them with an expression of satisfaction etched upon his face. Having left Baldovino and Machinetti, Lombroso had promptly invited everyone to lunch at the museum, in order to discuss the murders and the significance of the letter that Tullio had handed back to him as soon as they had left the newspaper's offices. He turned the front page towards them and they all looked at the headline.

'What does the letter say?' Ottolenghi asked.

Lombroso cleared his throat and began to read.

'*To whom it may concern. My work is inspired by men of science. I will not stop until the gates of Hell have truly opened. I am but a lone voice crying in the wilderness.* It is signed, *Pilgrim.*'

'Not much of a clue,' Ottolenghi declared.

'I thought it might help us establish an identity or a motive,' Tullio agreed, 'but it's just a vague reference.'

Lombroso threw his hands up in despair.

'Really, you should all know better! It is not a clue in the established sense. But if this letter *is* from the killer it will help us to understand what sort of a person he – or she – is. Murray, what would Dr Bell suggest we ask?'

James had only to think for an instant before his tutor's voice came into his head. 'Why would he or she write such a letter in the first place? Do they want to be found and if so why? Are they seeking attention? Again, if that is so, then why? What kind of language is employed? How have they expressed themselves? What paper and ink was used? Is this someone who has access to good quality writing materials? If not, then are they poor or pretending to be poor?'

'Well done, Murray,' Lombroso said. 'And I would add this question. Are they a savage or refined, or something in between?'

Tullio looked even gloomier than before. 'Questions, so many questions – but no answers. Sometimes I feel as if we will never get to the bottom of this and the murders will just go on and on.'

'Questions that once they are answered will tell us more about our killer,' Lombroso said patiently. 'He, or she, will be caught.'

'Of course, what is interesting is the name he gives himself,' James said thoughtfully.

Lombroso stroked his beard. 'Mmm, yes. What is the significance of the name "Pilgrim", I wonder?'

'It clearly has some religious connection,' James said.

'Yes, a religious devotee of some sort, perhaps,' Lombroso said. 'The quote is from the bible, as I recall.'

'Or it could mean that the writer is on some kind of quest,' James said, thinking of Bunyan's *The Pilgrim's Progress*, a book he had been made to read at school, much to his

274

displeasure at the time. Now, of course he wished that he had paid more attention.

'Mmm, but a quest for what?' Lombroso said.

'How certain can we be that the letter is genuine?' Tullio asked.

'We cannot be certain at all. That is why I needed to see the original,' Lombroso explained. 'I need to ascertain if the handwriting is the same as in the Tribute notes found with the victims. I will need to see all of them together, with the letter.'

'They are held by Machinetti but I may be able to get hold of them, with or without permission,' Tullio said.

There was a tentative knock at the door. It opened softly as if the person did not wish to disturb him.

'*Mi scusi, Professore?*' Sofia came into the room. James looked at her and an image of her, a sweet golden memory from the previous night's lovemaking, flashed before his eyes, making him catch his breath.

'Sofia, what is it?' Lombroso sat up straight, his eyes wide and alert. 'Has there been another murder?'

'No, Professor,' Sofia replied quietly. 'This letter was left at the front door a few moments ago.'

She handed it to Lombroso who held it up for all to see. The envelope was written in red and addressed as *A Tribute to Lombroso*. There seemed something faintly theatrical about the whole thing, as if it had been rehearsed. James wondered if Lombroso had asked Sofia to bring it in like that, to play up the element of drama. Would the professor really go to such lengths just for that, or was there another reason?

'Did you see who delivered it?' James asked, a trifle sharply.

'I'm afraid not.' Sofia left quietly, giving him a barely perceptible nod of acknowledgement before she did so.

Ottolenghi raised his eyebrows at him and James had to admit to himself that he was enjoying the subterfuge involved with his and Sofia's relationship. It added a certain thrill to the affair. But ever since he had seen Lombroso leaving her rooms the possibility that she was somehow playing with him, was perhaps in league with the professor, was still in his head, like a tiny worm burrowing away at his faith in both of them.

Lombroso did not even seem to notice that Sofia had gone. He studied the envelope closely. 'It looks the same as the others. The handwriting seems to be identical.'

'What does it say?' James asked.

'Wait, young man, wait. We must not be impatient. The killer has apparently seen fit to communicate directly with us. The least we can do is to treat such a message with respect.'

'I'm not sure I hold with the idea of respecting a common criminal,' Tullio said.

'A criminal he certainly is but common he is not. It is only by recognising that fact that we will catch him.' Lombroso held the letter up to the light and examined it carefully. 'Mmm, reasonably good quality notepaper, expensive but not prohibitively so.'

'What about the handwriting?' Ottolenghi asked.

Lombroso leaned back in his chair, with a smug look on his face.

'It so happens that I have considered the subject of criminals' handwriting before, and though I say it myself there were some very instructive findings. On studying them it became clear that the signatures of known murderers shared a number of characteristics. There were no flourishes in their vertical extensions and the letters were all slightly distant from each other and rather squashed and rounded. Many of them were young but showed evidence of a trembling hand. This however does not fit in. There is a very clear cross of the "t" – see, it is elongated – that signifies a certain energy. There are also a number of distinct flourishes, can you see?'

Lombroso showed them the envelope and pointed to some of the letters which were elaborately curled.

'Look at this. It is extraordinary, is it not? See the way he has included curlicues and arabesques. It is almost—'

'Artistic!' Tullio exclaimed.

'Perhaps, but more importantly it is familiar. It puts me in mind of the kind of signature that is common to killers, more precisely vicious and ferocious murderers. And yet . . .'

Lombroso looked at them and paused dramatically.

'I do not think that this is in the same hand as the letter to Baldovino!'

'Are you sure?' Tullio asked.

'No, not really,' Lombroso admitted. 'This is not a precise art and I did not have sight of the first letter long enough for a thorough examination. I was able to make a few notes but that is all. I can only make an educated guess but there are sufficient differences in the writing to suggest that they are in a different hand.'

'Or perhaps it *is* the same hand,' James suggested tentatively. 'Maybe we are meant to *think* they are from two different people. Should we not look inside and see?'

'Be patient. In a moment I will open the letter but first . . .' Lombroso brought the letter to his nose and began to sniff at it. His nose wrinkled as if he had smelt something unpleasant.

'What is it?' Tullio asked.

Lombroso frowned slightly. 'I do not know. All I can tell

you is that, whatever it is, I have smelt it before, and recently.'

Lombroso handed the letter to Ottolenghi who also sniffed at it. He shook his head. 'I cannot smell anything, just ink.'

He handed it to James. There was a slightly sour smell to it, like milk or cream on the turn. He was going to say so but something made him keep it to himself.

Lombroso shrugged, took the letter back and began to open it. 'See how it is folded in three.'

'What does that signify?' Ottolenghi asked.

A few seconds passed.

'Nothing,' Lombroso replied. 'The skill is to identify what is relevant but also what is not. Really, one can place too much emphasis on these things!'

He shook out the letter and began to read it. His eyebrows shot up with such ferocity that for a moment he looked like a startled rabbit looking into the barrel of a poacher's shotgun.

'What does it say?' Tullio asked.

'*Behold each tribute that is made; for my work is your work. We will both be at the gates of Hell before long,*' read Lombroso

'Has he signed it?'

'Yes, but interestingly not as "Pilgrim" but as "P".'

'That implies a certain intimacy, does it not?' James suggested.

Lombroso nodded. 'Perhaps he is feeling more secure. That would be excellent.'

'How so?' Tullio asked.

'If this is from the killer then it signifies that he is starting to make mistakes. For example, he has also included the same symbol that was found on the bodies. That was not on the first note to Baldovino.'

'Ah, the inverted cross. So it *must* be the killer. There can be no question. If the same symbol appears on his letter as seen on the bodies of the victims . . .' James said.

'Your reasoning is sound, of course, Murray, but you have forgotten something that we have already considered.'

They all looked at him, as confused as each other but it was Tullio who dared to ask the question. 'But, Professor, what other conclusion could there be? The killer and the writer of this second letter must be the same person.'

'Or two people!' Ottolenghi added. 'Remember we thought there were two sets of footprints at the scene of Soldati's murder.'

'Indeed! If there are two people involved then the writer need not be the killer. But,' Lombroso shook his head, 'this seems like the work of one person to me. There are no variations in method. Everything is very precise. No, I think we have one killer, perhaps with a dual personality, but one person all the same. The reference to the gates of Hell is interesting. It appears in both.'

'So does the signature, Pilgrim in the first and P in the second,' Ottolenghi said.

'Did you see that the word Hell was given a capital letter in both letters? Could that be significant?' James asked. 'That would indicate that they were from the same hand or from two people intimately connected, perhaps by the murders, to the extent that they have picked up one another's habits – a killer and his apprentice.'

'Or the first letter is a hoax and the second is not,' Ottolenghi said.

'Or the second is a hoax and the writer read about the gates of Hell in the *People's Voice* and decided to put in the phrase, complete with capital "H", to make it sound more authentic,' Tullio added.

They sat in silence for a few moments. It seemed that the more evidence was gathered or emerged, the greater the puzzle.

'Should I inform Machinetti about the second letter?' Tullio asked.

'No,' Lombroso replied firmly. 'He will only want to retain it as evidence and I think it should remain here – for now, anyway. It is my property, is it not? We do not want it to fall into the wrong hands. Machinetti is a fool. Who knows what skewed conclusion he might reach?'

For a second James again considered the possibility of the professor being involved. He looked at Lombroso as he sat forwards in his chair peering at the letter in his hand. He seemed genuinely puzzled by the case. Either that or his theatrical skills were even more developed than James had thought.

'What can we do now, Professor?' James wondered if they were any nearer to finding out the truth.

'I fear that there is very little we can do on a practical level, Murray. I know for certain that there is something missing, perhaps more than one thing, but alas that is all I know. The answer is lurking at the back of my mind somewhere. It will come to me I am sure but in the meantime I think that we should carry on with our work and hope that this Pilgrim is not moved to kill again.'

'We still have no real suspects,' Tullio said glumly.

'Not yet, but give it time,' Lombroso said. 'Now let us go in to lunch. I'm sure it is ready by now. We can discuss the matter further as we eat.'

Was Lombroso still unwilling to investigate? It was almost

as if he had given up. This was counter-intuitive to James. He had always been taught that if there was some mystery to be solved, whether medical or criminal, you should keep digging away at the evidence until you came up with something. That, he decided to himself, was exactly what he would do, with or without Lombroso.

Luncheon was prepared and served by Sofia. A table was laid up in the laboratory and James thought how curious it was to dine in the company of the dead. The skulls that surrounded them stared rudely at them throughout, almost as if they resented their presence, but the food was delicious. There were some tender veal cutlets, sautéed with lemon and fragrant rosemary, served with the creamiest saffron risotto James had ever tasted. It was the colour of daffodils and glistened in the sunlight that poured in to the room. Soon Sofia came back with a carafe of cool white wine and a note for Lombroso.

'Not another letter!' He opened it and groaned at the contents. 'That man DeClichy! He is so persistent! He wants to meet me. As if I have time for that.'

'Will he be at the theatre tonight?' Ottolenghi said. 'Perhaps he could see you then?'

'Theatre?' James asked.

Lombroso looked over to him. 'Ah yes, Murray. We are invited to the opera this evening at the Teatro Carignano with some of the other delegates from the symposium. With all this fuss I forgot to say. We are to be guests of the Marchesa. There will be drinks beforehand at the Hotel Inghilterra and dinner afterwards.'

James gave a half-hearted smile. He had a particular dislike of opera. His sister Lucy loved it and dragged him to performances whenever she could but he had never really enjoyed them. They always seemed so overblown – like someone screeching at a deaf person.

'I am sure you will find it a welcome diversion from recent events,' Lombroso said. 'We are to see a new opera by Verdi, *Otello*. It premiered in Milan earlier this year.'

Ottolenghi nodded enthusiastically. 'It is to be conducted by Arturo Toscanini who caused something of a sensation here last year, so I hear. I'm looking forward to seeing him.'

Tullio laughed. 'You are all welcome to it. I will be spending the evening somewhere less salubrious.'

'La Capra?' James asked.

He nodded. 'I will be observing the comings and goings. Perhaps Rosa Bruno will turn up and I can finally find out what she knows, if anything.'

'Do you think La Capra is the key to this puzzle then?' Lombroso asked.

He, of course, had not been told about their previous enquiries there.

'It is the last place where Soldati was seen and a well-known underworld haunt. It could be important,' Tullio said.

'And this Bruno woman?' Lombroso asked.

'A possible informant. She claims to know something about Soldati's murder but has yet to divulge it.'

The professor nodded vigorously. 'Well, keep us up to date, Tullio, won't you.'

'I wonder what DeClichy is so anxious to talk to you about. It's the second time he's tried to see you,' Ottolenghi said.

'I can't imagine,' replied Lombroso. 'Still, I doubt I'll have time this evening. He'll just have to wait.'

18

A few tenacious passions dominate criminals in place of their
absent or unstable social and family feelings. First among these
is pride or rather an excessive sense of self-worth, which seems
to grow in inverse proportion to merit.   Lombroso, 1876 p 65

The Hotel Inghilterra was as full of gilt and red velvet as the
Marchesa's palazzo had been but this time they were in a
smaller room to accommodate the more select nature of the
gathering. Beneath the large window framed by ornate
brocade wall hangings sat the Marchesa with Father Vincenzo by her side as if he was her consort. She wore a gown in
emerald green with gold embroidery embellishing the sleeves
and bodice. James thought that she looked every inch the
renaissance monarch, regal and powerful. Father Vincenzo
whispered to her every now and then, just as he had at the
reception. His eyes were glinting malevolently as if he was
Iago pouring a toxic potion into Othello's ear. Eventually
they both rose and began to process majestically around the
room with Father Vincenzo presenting each gaggle of guests
to the Marchesa. James looked for the sanctuary of familiar
faces and before long he saw Madame Tarnovsky and De-
Clichy, who were standing with Borelli. They seemed to be
deep in conversation and he was reluctant to interrupt them.

Madame Tarnovsky, wearing a gown the colour of red wine with a delicate black lace trim, was dressed almost as magnificently as the Marchesa. There were other women there, wives of academics mostly, and the Delgado sisters who were in matching outfits of a rather drab brown, like two harvest mice. But none could match the Marchesa or Madame Tarnovsky. It was not just the opulence of their gowns, although that attracted the eye, but the way they carried themselves, with an inner confidence, he supposed. He thought of Sofia and her ability to transform the dullest of costumes. He tried to imagine her in a gown that would really do her justice but he couldn't and he realised that Sofia's beauty was a rare thing in that it was entirely natural and needed no such embellishment.

The only other person he recognised was Horton who was huddled in what looked to be a conspiratorial group with Gemelli and some of his supporters. Every now and then he turned and James saw a flash of purple silk from the lining in his evening coat. Only a man without any thought or care for the views of others could carry that off, James thought to himself, as he wondered again exactly where the man came from.

Eventually he found the professor and Ottolenghi skulking behind a large flower arrangement. He waved at them and Lombroso beckoned him over.

'Ah, good evening, Murray.'

He wondered why they were hiding. It seemed to him to be most uncharacteristic. Lombroso was usually only too happy to draw attention to himself, the better to put forward his theories.

'We are observing the natives, a fascinating pastime, I think you'll agree. Look over there at Gemelli, holding court

284

like a primitive tribal chief, instructing his subjects.' He gesticulated towards the group who were all listening attentively as Gemelli held forth, with the exception of Horton who just looked bored and stifled a yawn as if to emphasise it.

'And we're avoiding DeClichy,' Ottolenghi replied with a grin. 'He won't leave the professor alone.'

Lombroso nodded ruefully. 'I'm afraid Ottolenghi is right. DeClichy has been following me round like a lapdog. It is most infuriating.'

'Still, it must be something important,' James suggested. He felt rather sorry for DeClichy. He had seemed to be a good man with some interesting ideas but Lombroso continually brushed him away as if he was an irritating insect.

'I do not wish to listen to him pontificate on the rightness of his theories and the wrongness of mine,' Lombroso said tetchily. 'I have heard his nonsensical views too many times already, not least at the debate.'

'Oh come now, Cesare. If we do not listen to others how are we to learn?' Borelli had joined them in their corner. It was beginning to get a little crowded.

Lombroso looked at him and scowled. 'If you must know, it is Gemelli I am avoiding. I do not wish to give him an opportunity to gloat.'

'Professor, what are you doing? Anyone would think that you were hiding from us!'

It was the Marchesa with Father Vincenzo behind her.

'I am merely taking stock, Marchesa,' Lombroso replied.

'Still, it is not like you to avoid the limelight,' Father Vincenzo added with barely disguised glee. 'Even given the circumstances.'

285

The Marchesa frowned. 'Ah yes, I have heard of your troubles, Professor. We must see what can be done.'

James watched as the priest's face fell slightly before he recovered himself.

'It is just a misunderstanding, Marchesa,' Lombroso said graciously.

'Nonetheless, it needs to be attended to,' she said, with a slight frown. 'I shall visit soon to discuss it.'

'We will be honoured, Marchesa,' Lombroso replied with a deep bow. The Marchesa smiled and swept away.

Father Vincenzo also smiled but his was laced with poison. 'I would not hold out too much hope, if I were you, Professor,' he said, as he turned to follow in the Marchesa's wake. 'The lady has not visited you yet.'

Before anyone could comment a small gong was sounded. It was evidently time for them to make their way to the theatre. The performance was about to begin, or rather, James thought wryly, a second act, for Lombroso had a talent for drama that was hard to ignore.

A few moments later they were in their seats, having successfully avoided both Gemelli and DeClichy, much to Lombroso's evident pleasure. They had been given the honour of a box adjacent to that of the Marchesa who sat next to Father Vincenzo, still murmuring in her ear. Gemelli and his colleagues had been relegated to the stalls. Lombroso leaned over and waved regally at them and was rewarded with a scowl from Gemelli. Horton, however, who was sitting with them, smiled and nodded. In the box directly opposite sat a sombre DeClichy and Reiner, deep in conversation. The latter sported a waistcoat of dark pinks and purples which made his pale hair and eyes even more noticeable.

With them was Madame Tarnovsky. James was rather

sorry to have been denied the pleasure of her company, for it was always stimulating. Ottolenghi nudged him and whispered, 'Look at DeClichy.'

James peered over at him and saw that he was still obviously agitated. He was constantly fidgeting and kept looking down at Gemelli and frowning.

James whispered back to Ottolenghi. 'Perhaps DeClichy will be joining us at dinner. Then he can discuss with Lombroso whatever it is that's causing him such anxiety.'

Ottolenghi shrugged but before he could add anything the room was filled with the sound of rapturous applause as the young conductor Toscanini entered and the evening's entertainment began. To his surprise, James enjoyed it. There was something carefree about the performance despite its tragic subject matter. Even the atmosphere in the theatre itself seemed to radiate a certain *joie de vivre* which seemed a million miles away from anything he had experienced in Edinburgh. It was more colourful, more heartfelt somehow. He wondered if it was the fact that he was not at home that merely created the impression of difference. Whatever the reason, he came away feeling that he had witnessed something quite out of the ordinary and he couldn't wait to put an account of it down on paper for Lucy. She would be quite envious, he was sure, and at least this was something he could tell her about with impunity. Even Aunt Agnes couldn't object to opera and Shakespeare!

There had been a short interval. Champagne was served and while Lombroso was discussing some abstruse point with Borelli, Ottolenghi and James took the opportunity to further observe DeClichy. He spent the entire time staring at Gemelli and his party as earlier. It was most peculiar. He had shown little interest in the man before and they could not deduce why he would have suddenly become so fascinated now, yet his eyes were on him for the entire interval.

'Perhaps he suspects Gemelli of the murders,' Ottolenghi suggested.

'I think that is doubtful,' Lombroso said dolefully, having unexpectedly overheard them. 'Gemelli is occasionally unpleasant, sometimes he is even foolish, but I do not think he possesses the capacity for murder.'

'Still, he has an excellent motive. He commits the murders and then implicates you. A plan worthy of Machiavelli himself,' Borelli interjected, a sarcastic note in his voice. 'I do not think you should dismiss the possibility quite so readily, Cesare.'

Lombroso shrugged his shoulders and peered down at Gemelli and Horton who appeared to have run out of conversation and were sitting in silence, their heads turned away from each other. 'I know he dislikes me but I cannot think that he would take it so far as to take the lives of others, just to get back at me.'

Borelli shook his head. 'Ah, Cesare, you know as well as I that one can never be certain about the motives of men.'

Lombroso waved his hand dismissively. 'I hardly think that any academic would commit multiple murders just to discredit another.'

Borelli smiled to himself as Lombroso turned pointedly towards the stage and the performance that was about to start again. It was clear he did not wish to discuss the matter further and they settled down in their seats for the remainder of *Otello*. It was somehow fitting that they were watching a story of jealousy and its potentially murderous consequences unfold before them. Could Gemelli have become so resentful of Lombroso's success that it had driven him to discredit the man through murder? It seemed unlikely, and yet so much about this affair was perplexing that James could not completely rule it out as a possibility.

After the performance drew to a close they made their way to the Palazzo Carignano for a late supper. They were served champagne as they waited to go in. The conversation was mostly centred on the city of Turin and its history; a subject which seemed to fascinate Horton in particular. When Lombroso started to describe the tunnels that ran under the city and their part in the siege of Turin he became particularly animated, asking a number of questions about the network and where they began and ended. Even Borelli's eyes widened slightly as Lombroso told them of the tunnels that were reputed to run between the palazzos of the various dukes of Savoy, which were wide enough to take a carriage. It was when Lombroso mentioned the presence of Satanists in the city, however, that everyone became truly attentive. He wove his stories well and related them in a theatrical style that was particularly entertaining. It was clear that he was enjoying himself immensely.

'Do you know,' Lombroso said, with a touch of what sounded like glee in his voice, 'that once, not that long ago, there were monks in an abbey outside the city who were actually excommunicated for the corruption of young girls in the name of the Devil! And to this day there are those who insist that . . .' he paused for the maximum dramatic effect and a sideways glance at Father Vincenzo, 'the spirits of the girls can be seen dancing with the Devil on All Hallows' Eve and the ancient Celtic feast of Beltane, an excellent time to summon demons, I believe.'

Father Vincenzo nodded. 'I know that you are teasing me,

Professor, but you make a point in God's favour without even realising it.'

'How so, Father? Do enlighten us,' Lombroso said, sarcastically.

Father Vincenzo gave him the faintest of smiles. 'You see, Professor, how God punishes those who transgress. We must not sup with the Devil for we will suffer the consequences.'

'And that is what I am doing, is it, Father? Supping with the Devil?' Lombroso asked, a slight sneer playing about his lips.

'You and your brethren.'

James wondered if he meant scientists or Lombroso's Jewish kinsmen. Were anti-Semitic sympathies as rife here as they were at home?

'Do go on, Father. Tell us more,' Lombroso said. There was a harshness to his tone that James had not heard before.

'Your work is nothing more than a dangerous game and I fear that we have already seen the results, for your activities do not bring misfortune to you alone. Have we not already suffered a great shaking of the earth to signify God's divine displeasure?'

Lombroso laughed. 'The earthquake in March! I really do not think that even I can be blamed for that!'

Father Vincenzo shook his head sadly and put an avuncular hand onto Lombroso's shoulder. 'But, Professor, can you not see what is so clear?' His voice became hushed and all gathered round to listen. 'If you do the Devil's work we are all at risk from the vengeance of God. Who knows how many more shall die as the result of your sacrilege and blasphemy?'

There was a brief silence as Lombroso seemed to be considering his reply. James wondered exactly how the professor would greet the priest's accusation. As luck would have it he was interrupted by a footman summoning them into dinner. James thought he saw just a hint of relief in Lombroso's eyes.

'Never underestimate the power of the Church in Italy, my friend!' Ottolenghi said quietly.

'So I see,' James replied as they went into the dining room. He looked at the large table, covered in crisp white linen. On it were crystal glasses sparkling in the candlelight like raindrops on a spider's web. All was opulence and grandeur, a far cry from Sofia's table, but despite the promise of the fancy cuisine to come, James knew where he would rather be.

As James made his way over to his place, he was accosted by Horton, who grabbed his upper arm and pulled him to one side.

'I understand that you have been making enquiries about me?'

James looked at him. 'I don't know who told you that, but you are mistaken. I have absolutely no interest in you.'

Horton gave him a thin smile. 'That's good to hear, Murray. I don't take kindly to snoopers.'

'What are you saying?' James asked.

Horton smiled again. 'Nothing, my dear Murray, I am merely voicing my concern. Snooping can be a dangerous occupation. We wouldn't want anything untoward to happen to you now, would we?'

With that he walked away to take his place as if their conversation had been the most natural thing in the world. James pushed his hand through his hair nervously. He wasn't used to being threatened and it could only mean one thing: Horton had seen him in the library. But what was it that he was so anxious to keep secret?

Before he could think about the matter any further he was

waylaid by Ottolenghi who ushered him to his seat. One thing was for sure, James thought as he looked around him, the next hour or two would not be dull. He saw Gemelli pause briefly to whisper into Father Vincenzo's ear, all the while staring at Lombroso. The priest nodded and smiled. The Marchesa, seated naturally at the head, looked on, frowning slightly. Lombroso himself was apparently oblivious to all of this. He was sitting next to Madame Tarnovsky and was beaming at her as she talked. James wondered if the professor's wife would have attended, had she not left the city. What would she have made of all of this? He realised how little he knew of Lombroso's personal life. Had he really sent his family away to rid himself of the distraction during the symposium or was it because he was afraid for them after Soldati's murder and the veiled threat in the tribute note?

'You seem very pensive,' Ottolenghi, who was sitting next to him, said.

'I was just wondering about what Father Vincenzo was saying earlier, about the earthquake.'

'We had one earlier this year. We get them from time to time. The damage here was not too great although elsewhere they were not so lucky. I think it's bad form for the priest to mention it but he's a law unto himself these days, given the exalted company he's keeping.'

The meal began. DeClichy was seated at the far end of the table, a result, James suspected, of Lombroso's machinations earlier on. He had swapped places with Madame Tarnovsky in order to ensure that he would not be sitting with the Frenchman. As each splendid course followed another and the wine flowed, the conversation seemed to do likewise, almost as if it had a life of its own.

The Marchesa presided with Father Vincenzo yet again at

her side. His bright eyes were darting around the room and it was clear that he was watching everyone intently. He was a powerful man and his malign influence seemed to be all-consuming. He was clearly intent on discrediting Lombroso and his work – but how far might he go in that regard? It was hard to tell. The man was a priest but how many of them had turned to murder to achieve their ends; a fair few throughout history, he knew. But was Vincenzo likely to go that far? James simply couldn't say. He was a newcomer and was still finding his way around the intrigues and relationships of the society in which he was moving. Even Ottolenghi seemed unsure and he had been there much longer.

Lombroso was engaged in conversation with Horton as Borelli looked on. It was apparent that despite his misgivings as to Horton's character the professor still found him interesting, perhaps even intriguing. Their discussion was a little like indulging in a game of chess. Each would make a move that would then be countered by the other. They were talking about Lombroso's favourite topic, the concept of the born criminal.

'Some say that the idea of inherited criminality is somewhat far-fetched, Professor. What do you say to the argument that external factors play a part?' Horton asked. For some reason he gave the impression that he was rather on edge.

'Indeed so. I do not claim that every criminal has been born that way. However, my research has indicated that some certainly have had the misfortune to be so fated.'

'Fate!' Reiner declared, his pale eyes flicking from side to side. 'I do not believe in such a thing. One creates one's own destiny.'

The conversation seemed to have hit a nerve. Lombroso

turned to Reiner with interest, apparently surprised by his interjection.

'Perhaps, for most people, that is true, but not in every case,' he said. 'There are significant numbers of criminals who are brought into the world with criminality as their destiny, unformed and unasked for, but there nonetheless.'

'Professor, you would have us believe that these people can be identified by their physical characteristics.'

Lombroso nodded. 'Yes, Reiner, I would. I was not aware that you were so familiar with my work.'

'I have read much of it and I have found it most fascinating. What kind of characteristics would you say were the most common to be found in the criminal?'

'That depends on the crime for which they have a propensity. It can be quite marked, such as prominent ears or something more subtle, such as a cranial malformation.'

James watched his fellow guests carefully in order to gauge their reactions. Assuming he had been right to make the connection between Lombroso's observations and the mutilations of the three victims, then this could be an opportunity to catch the killer out. After all, the culprit had to be someone who was familiar with Lombroso's work and in particular the notes he and Ottolenghi had made for the new edition of *Criminal Man* that had gone missing in the burglary. Unfortunately the subject was changed and the opportunity was lost.

Borelli leaned forwards. 'Cesare, you speak of physical characteristics but what of motive? Surely that can be as telling in the identification of a criminal?'

Lombroso shook his head. 'A person who is born to crime does not need motive. If you read my work you will see that I do not dwell for long on passion or impulse crimes.'

'Why is that?' Reiner asked. 'Because I agree with Borelli. Surely it is as important to know why as much as who, in relation to criminality?'

Borelli nodded forcefully. 'A criminal's culpability, and therefore his punishment, can be measured by his motive. Take the drama we have just witnessed in *Otello*, for example. The murder of Desdemona was motivated by jealousy due to the poisonous contributions of Iago. Without them, Otello would never have killed her, so his culpability must surely be measured in relation to the circumstances.'

Lombroso frowned. 'No, no, no, gentlemen! One is not comparing like with like. We are talking here of two distinct criminal types – one with a full-blooded and nervous temperament, such as Otello, and the common criminal who is more devious and thoughtful, such as Iago. Otello displays an exaggerated sensitivity and quite excessive affections, such as those one finds in a savage. He is a wonderful example of atavism. Shakespeare clearly understood the concept when he made the central character a Moor.'

Wouldn't that mean that all men, and women for that matter, who killed out of passion were savages? James wondered.

Borelli grinned. 'I am not sure that Shakespeare was an early follower of criminal anthropology, Cesare!'

'Perhaps not, but you see the point that I am making,' said Lombroso, a note of exasperation in his voice.

'I do,' said Borelli, 'but jealousy is not the only passion. What of others such as ambition or greed?'

'Again they are different,' replied Lombroso. 'The passions that feed crimes of impulse are not gradual things that come from within over time and can be controlled. On the contrary, they are explosive in nature and unforeseen.'

'What of revenge?' asked Borelli. 'That is one of the most common motives for violence.'

'Revenge is one of the chief motives among common criminals, along with lust and alcoholic rage, ignoble and primitive passions,' replied Lombroso dismissively.

'But a crime of revenge is committed in order to achieve the righting of wrongs,' said Borelli slowly. 'How can you say that it is not noble?'

Lombroso paused and thought for a minute. He looked into the distance as if the answer to the question might lie behind one of the brocade curtains that lined the room. 'Because as a motive it is weak, like those who claim it,' he said decisively.

Borelli raised his eyebrows and James thought that he might challenge the professor but before he could do so Horton evidently saw the opportunity for some mischief and seized it.

'And what of Pilgrim, Professor? I hear you are intimately acquainted with him! What is *his* motive?' he said, archly.

'Oh yes, do tell us, Professor. What kind of person is Pilgrim?' piped up a small, bossy woman who was seated nearby.

Lombroso looked down his spectacles at her. 'I do not give public consultations, madam,' he replied rather pompously and she turned away, disappointed.

Horton laughed loudly. 'Come, come, Professor. Don't be so reticent. After all, he has been writing to you, has he not? It was in the *People's Voice*, so it must be true!'

'Do not believe everything that you read in the news-papers, Signor Horton!' replied Lombroso.

'Now in that we do agree, Professor,' Horton muttered with a sideways glance at DeClichy. James noticed that he suddenly looked uncomfortable, as if he had inadvertently let something slip.

Borelli snorted. 'I think we can put aside Signor Baldovino's musings on the subject. Did he not also say in the same article that this Pilgrim had reportedly been seen in the Piazza Statuto performing a satanic ritual? This, according to him, required dancing with eight naked virgins round a bonfire! Not what you might call a reliable source of information, by any stretch of the imagination.'

'Ah yes, the Piazza Statuto, scene of the first tribute murder. Isn't it also the centre of black magic in the city?' Horton asked.

'It is certainly said to be so, signor. I am surprised you have not yet visited it,' Borelli laughed.

'There's still time,' Horton replied, smiling. 'Why, I believe I may even go there on my way home. If I'm lucky perhaps I'll make the acquaintance of Baldovino's naked ladies!'

There was a brief hush at the rather risqué turn of the conversation. Horton, however, seemed to have no reservations and sat grinning at the assembled company as if he had made a witty comment rather than a coarse one.

Suddenly there seemed to be a small commotion coming from the top table. The Marchesa was taking her leave and leading the ladies out, given the lateness of the hour. Father Vincenzo stayed and began to hold forth to those who remained. Among them was DeClichy. He had been deserted by Madame Tarnovsky who had been obliged to withdraw with the Marchesa, and was left at the table looking distinctly uncomfortable. He shifted around on his seat as if he wanted to say something but could not screw up enough courage to do so. Then he caused something of a stir by getting up and leaving the table, knocking over his glass as he did so.

He seemed to be heading in their direction and Lombroso groaned audibly. 'Is there no escape from that wretched man! I suppose I had better speak to him.'

DeClichy, however, had other ideas. Instead of Lombroso he seemed to be making his way towards Horton who was leaning back on his chair, puffing at a cigar. Horton, suddenly noticing DeClichy approaching him, leapt to his feet and seemed to back away. DeClichy was clutching a small piece of paper in his left hand. Horton visibly paled as DeClichy waved it at him and on reaching him, clutched his shoulder and whispered something in his ear. The expression on Horton's face was a combination of both fear and fury. Before anyone could say anything he had shaken away from DeClichy's clutch and moved swiftly towards the magnificent oak doors leading to the exit. DeClichy was left staring after him with a look of incredulity. He seemed frozen in his position for a second or two as if he did not know quite what to do. Then he recovered himself and went off, apparently in pursuit of Horton. All of this had been witnessed by Lombroso, who sat back in seat and watched the scene with interest.

After both DeClichy and Horton had left he leaned over to James and Ottolenghi. 'Gentlemen, may I suggest that you follow them? I don't know why, but I feel that they may lead us to something.'

They nodded their assent and left almost as abruptly as those they were pursuing but by the time they got outside they could see only Horton who was making his way across the Piazza Carignano towards the Via Pietro Micca. DeClichy, however, seemed to have completely disappeared.

19

At first Horton seemed to be an easy mark. He moved slowly and his extravagant astrakhan-trimmed coat, together with his ornate silver-topped cane, certainly made him stand out. Ottolenghi and James pursued him through the streets. Occasionally he would come to a halt and they were forced to take cover behind one of the city's many arches or down an alleyway. After a few minutes it started to drizzle and the landscape took on a strange glow as the yellow light from the flickering gas lamps was reflected in the windows of the shops and cafés that lined the streets. It felt good to be doing something concrete at last. For so long all they had done was talk about the murders. Now perhaps they finally had a suspect in Horton, who fitted Lombroso's criminal type to some extent – but then, so did most people in one way or another.

All at once Horton's pace began to speed up and then slow down again as if he knew he was being followed and was doing his best to confound his pursuers. More than once Ottolenghi, who was slightly ahead of James, would be forced to stop suddenly in order to avoid being seen, causing a minor collision from behind in the process.

On they went through the murky night. Visibility was low thanks to the combined forces of the rain and the fog which had started to curl round their feet and then risen to their faces. It smelt bad – like rotten eggs or sulphur. Were they getting nearer to hell? James wondered. He knew that was a fanciful suggestion, conjured by nerves and fear, but the pursuit of their quarry seemed endless and James was beginning to ache with the effects of the cold and damp. On and on they went, across piazzas, round corners and through walkways until suddenly Horton disappeared.

'Where on earth did he go?' James asked.

Ottolenghi shrugged. 'Maybe it wasn't on earth at all,' he said gloomily.

James shook his head. 'You've been listening too much to the priest. Horton's here all right. He's just ducked into a building somewhere.'

'I expect you're right. There are a couple of brothels in this area and I've heard he is a frequent visitor to such places.'

'I don't know why, but that sounds just like Horton.' James shivered. 'After all this I think we deserve a large brandy. I'm frozen to the bone. Should we visit these places ourselves?'

'No, let's leave him to his pleasure,' Ottolenghi said. 'I really don't think we will accomplish anything by tracking him down. Besides, La Capra's not far from here. We could see how Tullio's been getting on.'

James nodded reluctantly. Ottolenghi was right. What would following Horton to a brothel achieve? It made sense to head for La Capra, even though he'd been thinking of somewhere a little more refined for their reviving drink: one of Turin's famous cafés, perhaps, or the bar at the Hotel Inghilterra.

Instead they made their way through the narrow streets until the sign of the goat's head came into view, swinging in the wind, its hollow eyes staring eerily at them. As they pushed their way in through the door James could smell the same odour as he had last time they were there – sour milk, combined with stale sweat and tobacco. He thought to himself that he must have been mad to agree to go there rather than to the gilt splendour of Caffè Norman.

Their ears were met with a cacophony of raucous laughter and shouting as one group of drinkers tried to make themselves heard over another. James saw Tullio sitting at the bar looking miserable and pointed him out to Ottolenghi. They made their way over to him, and his eyes lit up as he saw them.

'I am glad to see you,' he said.

'Has the old woman shown up?' Ottolenghi asked.

Tullio shook his head glumly then suddenly his expression changed. 'Look, over there in the corner, by that door at the back! It's the man we were following the other day.'

It was hard to see in any detail as there was so much shadow but James could make out a cloaked figure sitting in front of the door that had the carving on it, a carafe of wine before him. Could Tullio be right? Swiftly, he got Gambro's attention and the barman confirmed that the man had drunk in La Capra before.

Not wishing to alert him, they agreed to approach cautiously. They made their way towards him, as if they were merely looking for a free table. Every now and again James looked over in an effort to see the man more clearly. But it was hopeless. Not only was he shrouded in shadow but he also wore a hat pulled down over his face. He was certainly not eager to be identified.

They were about halfway to his table when a commotion erupted in front of them. Someone's drink had been spilt and an argument began. There was much pushing and shoving. Insults were exchanged and then punches. Before long everyone seemed to be involved. Even old Pietro had got to his feet and was waving his tankard and shouting abuse at no one in particular. Two women were rolling on the floor screaming at each other and pulling out each other's hair.

It was a traditional drunken brawl – little more than a free-for-all – and James's party were not left out, their formal dress making them into targets with Tullio joined by association. An elderly man leapt onto Tullio's back and started to hit him. He threw him off and picked up a nearby stool, waving it at the man who thought the better of continuing his assault. Ottolenghi was punched in the eye and pushed to the ground. Tullio, having rid himself of another assailant, rescued James from the fray. Beer and wine was everywhere. The place was in chaos.

Gambro waded in and began to pull people apart, then, with the help of one or two others, ejected the worst brawlers from the bar. Unfortunately, Ottolenghi, James and Tullio became part of this mass eviction and found themselves thrown into the mud in the street outside. Tullio's nose was bleeding copiously. James could see from his expression that he was furious, and not a little embarrassed at having been caught up in something like this. He looked as if he might call for reinforcements and start arresting people.

'We might as well go back in,' he said.

'Won't we get thrown out again?' James asked nervously. He was doing his best to clean himself with his handkerchief but was making little headway.

Ottolenghi grinned. 'Don't worry, at least now we'll blend in!'

James looked down at himself – a man in a dirty dress suit – and grinned doubtfully.

'Anyway,' Ottolenghi continued, 'I don't think Gambro meant to get rid of us. We were just in the wrong place at the wrong time. It was accidental.'

'It had better have been!' Tullio replied. 'If he or his friends try it again they'll find themselves sharing a cell. Come on. I want to find out if that man was the same one we followed.'

By the time they were inside again things had calmed down somewhat. One or two people limped out assisted by their companions but most that remained, including the dark-haired man who had started the whole thing, had taken their seats again and were drinking happily as if nothing had happened. They all looked over to the corner where the shadowy figure had sat. The seat was empty.

'Where could he have gone? I didn't see him come past us,' James wondered aloud.

Tullio shook his head. 'We were somewhat preoccupied. He might have got past us, either of his own volition or propelled by Gambro. Let's ask him if he saw anything.'

'He certainly didn't get past me,' replied Gambro to their question. 'Last I saw him was in the corner where he was sitting.'

They ordered drinks, by now sorely needed, and made their way over to the table where the mystery man had been sitting. Where had he got to? Had he managed to get past them in the confusion? As James placed his drink on the table he noticed something. Carved into its top was the same symbol as that on the door behind them. He pointed it out to Tullio and Ottolenghi.

'I meant to mention the inverted cross on the door earlier, but I wasn't sure that it was significant as it's apparently so common.'

'The inverted cross,' said Tullio, 'just as the professor found on the bodies.' He breathed in sharply and crossed himself, which startled James a little. It was a sign of superstition that seemed out of place given Tullio's interest in scientific policing. Ottolenghi frowned with concentration as he examined both carvings carefully. When he had finished they sat in silence for a moment as if digesting the possible significance of the symbol. Tullio looked worried and puzzled at the same time. It was as if none of them knew quite what to do at that point.

Suddenly Tullio's eyes lit up. He seemed to have had an idea. He turned to the door behind them. It was not locked and opened easily. He beckoned to Gambro to come over.

'Where does this door lead?' he asked, urgently.

'Just to the cellar – I wouldn't go down there if I were you. It's damp as hell and smells worse than in here,' Gambro counselled.

'Is there any other way out of here or the cellar?' Tullio asked.

'No, not really – well, not unless you count the tunnels.'

'Of course, I should have realised!' He turned to his companions. 'Did you know that there's a network of them running under the city?' They nodded, having heard of them just hours earlier. 'It never occurred to me that there might be an opening here.'

'Well, there's only one thing for it. If that man has gone down there then we'll have to follow him,' Ottolenghi said firmly.

Gambro shook his head. 'It's not safe. There have been quite a few collapses recently.'

'I'll be careful,' Tullio replied.

'"I"?' James protested. 'Don't you mean, "we"?'

Tullio shook his head. 'There's no sense in all of us putting ourselves at risk. I'm paid for this. You are not.'

Ottolenghi shook his head. 'If you go, we go,' he said firmly.

A few moments later they were all making their way down some decidedly rickety stairs, armed only with three lanterns Gambro had given them and Tullio's truncheon. As they went down into the depths James shivered and looked longingly back up towards the light. He couldn't help thinking that it was as though they were descending into hell itself. James could have sworn that he caught a whiff of sulphur as if, with every step, they were drawing closer to the Devil.

One thing was certain. There was no going back now and James was apprehensive. What if they found the killer? James had conjured up in his mind a shadowy image, half human, half demon, with glowing eyes and . . . well, he wasn't sure what else he envisaged.

Of course, the terrible truth of it was that this murderer was no supernatural being, but a man. That was a far more frightening thought than anything that James could imagine and none of Lombroso's theories, or indeed those of anyone else concerned in the study of crime, dealt with the reasons for this level of depravity.

He shivered in the chill atmosphere. 'It's so cold down here,' he complained.

'It is said that the tunnels are haunted by the spirits of dead soldiers,' whispered Tullio. 'Perhaps that is why.'

'Who built them?' James asked. Conversation made him feel less nervous, whatever its content.

'Soldiers, I think,' replied Tullio. 'The tunnels are named after Pietro Micca, a soldier who died in 1706 while defending the city during the siege of Turin. He detonated a mine down here, somewhere.'

Their lanterns flickered in the gloom as they made their way through the archways and brick-lined passages. There was no sign of anyone, although once or twice James thought he saw a figure in the distance. Tullio told them that it was just his own shadow on the walls ahead but James was not so sure.

And then they heard it, a soft rhythmic drumbeat from what sounded like a few hundred yards away. They stopped to listen for a few seconds and then decided to follow the sound. Could this really be some kind of ghost? For a moment or two it seemed as if they were all seriously considering the possibility. The tunnels were dark and atmospheric and seemed an ideal habitat for a spirit.

They began running for the sound seemed to be moving away from them. Then suddenly there was an unearthly scream, shrill and terrifying, which stopped them in their tracks. There was a clatter and then more darkness. James came to a halt, his fear so acute that he could barely move.

Ottolenghi had dropped his lantern. Now the light was so dim that they could hardly see anything. James looked down at his own. It was dangerously close to going out. He had never encountered anything like this before. He felt as if his whole body was clenched with the tension. On went the drumming – it seemed to be getting louder but also was moving away more quickly until it was difficult for them to keep up. It was not helped by the fact that they would occasionally get to a dead end and have to retrace their steps and make a turn. The drumbeat seemed to change direction as if it was taunting them. On and on they went, through tunnel after tunnel for what seemed like hours. Then Tullio came to an abrupt halt and put his finger to his lips.

'Sssh – listen . . .' he whispered.

The drumbeat had stopped as quickly as it had begun. There was what sounded like laughter, the sound of footsteps running and then silence.

Tullio looked around him. They had been so intent in their pursuit that it seemed he was no longer sure of their exact location. James looked at his face and his heart sank.

'We're lost, aren't we?'

'Not exactly,' Tullio said. 'The tunnels run all over the city and there are entrances and exits everywhere. It's just a matter of finding one.'

James shivered. What if they couldn't find their way out? It had to be a possibility at least. He could hear scrabbling noises that sounded alarmingly like rats and the smell of sulphur he had noticed earlier seemed to be getting stronger. He felt panic rising in him.

Ottolenghi looked absolutely terrified. Then, in the gloom, they heard footsteps again. He could hear his own heart, hammering away in his chest. Tullio beckoned to them to follow him and they did so although James was not at all sure that he wanted to meet whoever they were pursuing. The footsteps gradually increased in speed until they were running. Then, as they rounded a corner, Ottolenghi fell to the ground in a heap and scrabbled in the darkness in an effort to get to his feet. James offered him a hand to get up and when he took it he could feel that it was wet. Ottolenghi's face was filled with horror as he looked down. James thought that he had tripped over a dead animal of some kind, a dog or a cat. It was neither.

Tullio brought his lantern lower and they could see that Ottolenghi's hands were covered in blood. He was sitting next to a corpse. Once he had been helped to his feet they began to examine what they had found. They stared down, transfixed by the sight before them. The body lay in a large pool of blood, dark and sticky in the fading light, like a slick of oil. Tullio started to move his lantern slowly downwards and they saw her face, her eyes staring up at them as if she was pleading for help. Her mouth was opened in a grimace – almost a snarl. Then something on her chest shone in the flickering light of the lantern. They looked at it more closely. It looked like a piece of a liver. James looked at Ottolenghi. He had his hand over his face as if trying to protect himself from breathing in the horror.

It was the body of Rosa Bruno.

Tullio moved his lantern down further to reveal yet more.

Rosa's skirts were up around her waist. The skin of her stomach had been sliced open and her intestines pulled out and arranged on her thighs. Somehow, James thought, it looked slightly surreal, as if someone had drawn it.

'My God. Who . . . who could do such a thing?' he said. He was about to look away when something caught his eye. 'What's that in her hand?' he asked. As Tullio lifted her left arm they could see that she was clutching a note.

'Let me see,' Ottolenghi said, sufficiently recovered to apply his scientific policing methods. He looked at it carefully. 'Another tribute note to Lombroso.'

'What do we do now?' James asked. 'We can hardly leave her down here.'

'I'll go back to the surface and alert the authorities,' said

Tullio, decisively. 'Assuming I can find my way out of here, that is. The entrance can't be far away. The killer would have had to get the victim down here to perform the mutilation.'

James looked at the pool of blood. 'She was still alive when he did this.'

Tullio nodded grimly. 'It certainly looks that way but even if she wasn't the killer would not want to go far from the exit.'

'He must have done this at least an hour or two ago, from the state of the blood,' James said.

'You're right,' Ottolenghi said.

'In which case . . .' James said, his eyes widening in fear.

'What?' Tullio said urgently.

'Who screamed?'

They stood in silence and the darkness seemed to close in on them, as if the walls were moving ever closer.

Tullio lifted his lantern. 'I must go. This must be reported in the proper way and besides, I want to let the professor know first in case he wants to examine the body. You two stay here and keep guard. Don't worry, I won't be long.'

'What if the killer comes back? Presumably those were his footsteps,' Ottolenghi said, nervously.

'The killer was obviously leading us here. He wanted us to find the body,' Tullio said. 'I don't think he'll be back.'

James looked over to Ottolenghi who nodded at him with a confidence that he really did not share.

They watched Tullio as he made his way along a passage. Soon the light of his lantern had disappeared into nothing, leaving them with the dim flicker that was all that was left of James's. All they could do now was wait and hope that Tullio knew what he was doing. As they sat, James heard more scrabbling, and he saw some movement out of the corner of his eye. Soon the rats began to join them. Presumably they could smell the blood. There was plenty of it, after all. The men kicked out at them but made little impression. James could still hear them scratching and squeaking and it made his skin crawl. They sat in silence for a while, alone with their thoughts. Then Ottolenghi spoke.

'So what is it that really brings you here?'

James wondered why he had raised this now. Was the fact that they were currently guarding a corpse significant? He hesitated. How much did Ottolenghi know? Could he really be trusted? James realised that it was unlikely that he knew anything. They were stuck here, possibly with a killer nearby, and nothing to do but talk so perhaps, he thought wryly, it was as good a time as any to ask.

'I came to learn, just like you,' James replied cautiously.

'But there's more to it than that, isn't there. You said as much in the café, before the salon.'

'Do you think that someone can really be born to crime?' James asked, ignoring Ottolenghi's comment.

'Yes, I do,' he replied. 'But as Lombroso says, others are brought to it for different reasons. Why do you ask? Don't you have faith in the professor's theories?'

'I am not sure that faith is the right word. Scientists are supposed to ask questions, aren't they? I just wondered . . . well, how does one tell a born criminal from an ordinary person? Is it really just a case of physical characteristics? And . . .' he paused for a moment before continuing, 'is criminality hereditary?'

'Well, I suppose the answer is yes and no.'

'Ach! Why am I not surprised? Is nothing straightforward?'

Ottolenghi went on, with, James detected, just a note of impatience in his voice. 'The professor's theory is that one can see criminality in physical characteristics and that these can be passed on through family members, and of course he may well be right. But *I* can't help feeling that there is more to it than that.'

'Such as?'

'There are so many other reasons for the committing of crimes, particularly those of violence. How can we be sure that it is merely a question of birth? Some may be sorely provoked to commit their deed, for example, or it may be a question of genuine need or desperation.'

'Or insanity?' James suggested.

'Well, perhaps, although that would be rather more difficult to justify. People could claim insanity as an excuse even though they had a propensity to violence all along.'

James paused. 'But what if the criminal is genuinely out of his mind?'

'I would say that depends on the crime.'

'Murder, for example?'

Before Ottolenghi could give his answer a rustling sound came from a side tunnel, then they heard footsteps coming slowly towards them. They shot to their feet and stood on either side of Rosa Bruno's bloody corpse, ready to defend it and, presumably, themselves. James could hear Ottolenghi breathing rather shakily. He held up his lantern. He could just about see that a few yards away there was a figure moving slowly along the passage away from them.

'Stop there! Identify yourself!' shouted Ottolenghi.

The figure seemed to half turn as if it was about to obey. Then it started to move quickly away from them. Without a thought James and Ottolenghi began to follow it through one tunnel after the next, twisting and turning as much as before until it was no longer clear whether they were following a real figure or mere shadows cast by their lantern. Eventually they came to a halt, too breathless to continue. Then their lantern gave a last defiant flicker and went out, plunging them into darkness. Instinctively James put out his hand but could feel nothing. Then he heard more rustling as if someone or something was moving closer, brushing against the wall. He wanted to call out but when he opened his mouth no sound came out. Something touched his face, something soft, as if it was fluttering past him. Blindly he tried to brush it away and suddenly a hand grabbed his wrist. Desperately James tried to pull free of its grip.

'It's me!' Ottolenghi's voice rang out in the blackness.

'Let's just stop for a moment,' James said with relief. Once they had recovered a little they stood quietly but there was only silence. Not the rich, velvet kind of silence when one is safe and secure in one's own bed but a heavy, oppressive silence full of threat and what seemed to James to be nothing less than pure evil. Then they heard breathing.

'Murray?' Ottolenghi hissed. 'Is that you?'

'No, I don't think so.' So terrified was he that he could, in truth, no longer tell.

The breathing seemed to get closer and closer to them. James sniffed at the air. There was a familiar stench surrounding them – something between sour milk and decay. He almost gagged at it. And then the breathing began to fade and they heard the someone – or something – moving away from them at speed. This time they did not follow.

'Murray?' Ottolenghi said again, his voice thin and small with fear.

'I'm here.'

'I can feel some cooler air.'

James concentrated and then he felt it too, just a hint of a breeze. 'Let's go towards it.'

James clutched Ottolenghi's arm. He did not want to be parted from him down here in the darkness, not even for a second. They made their way slowly towards the air and then they saw a faint orange glow in the distance.

James started to think again of the Devil. Had they reached the opening to Hell? Were the legends right? 'Should we go on? We don't know what we'll find,' he asked nervously.

'We have no choice. We'll never get out if we don't,' Ottolenghi replied.

Hesitantly they made their way towards the light. As they did so they heard murmuring in the distance and the sound of yet more footsteps and some dragging noises. James's imagination got the better of him for a moment as he saw in his mind demons with cloven hooves and heavy reptilian tails trailing in the dust of the tunnel. Terrified, they turned a corner and stared at the sight before them.

There was a fire, or rather the remains of one. The orange glow had come from its dying embers. Surrounding it were some markings in the dust. Ottolenghi walked over to examine it further and suddenly turned away in disgust.

'What is it?'

Ottolenghi held his lantern near to a bundle on the ground. 'It looks like organs of some kind.'

'Human organs?' James said in alarm.

Ottolenghi looked at it more closely. 'No, they are too small . . . unless . . .'

'Not a child!'

'No, no, they're definitely not human. A pig, I think.'

'Thank God!'

That having been established James started instinctively to

look around him at the markings. 'These look like some kind of pentagrams, so there may be a link to black magic after all.'

'Ssh.' Ottolenghi held up his hand. Someone was approaching. They looked at each other fearfully. It was too late to run. They would have to face whoever or whatever was coming towards them.

Terrified, they peered into the shadows and suddenly they saw them – Lombroso and Borelli coming towards them, both carrying lanterns. Borelli had a stout silver-topped cane, similar to Lombroso's, and was brandishing it threateningly. Lombroso was wielding a sword stick. The pair put their weapons down when they saw Ottolenghi and Murray.

'Good evening, gentlemen,' Lombroso said, as if nothing untoward was happening.

Borelli bowed slightly to them. 'We thought you might need assistance.'

James looked at Lombroso's swordstick.

'Just a precaution,' he said crisply. 'One never knows who one might encounter in a place like this.'

'Rosa Bruno wasn't so lucky,' Ottolenghi said.

'So we saw,' Lombroso said.

'How did you find us so quickly?' James asked him.

'Borelli here knows the tunnels like the back of his hand, luckily for you.'

Borelli nodded. 'We were in a cab on our way to the Via Legnano and we saw Tullio. He told us where you were. We dropped him off at his office and came straight here, then we heard you.'

'Heard us?' James said.

'You are only a moment or two away from the body,' Borelli said.

'We must have been going round in circles,' Ottolenghi said with a grimace.

'Follow me, gentlemen,' Lombroso said. 'I want to take a look at the victim.'

'But what about these organs and the pentagrams?' James asked, bemused at Lombroso's evident lack of interest.

'Oh, they're just the usual Satanists,' Lombroso said airily. 'I don't think there is a connection.'

'Shouldn't you at least take a look, Cesare?' Borelli suggested.

'Oh, very well,' he said tetchily, wandering over to the bloody bundle and poking it with his cane. 'As I thought, pig and chicken organs. Just some kind of sacrificial ritual. It needn't trouble us. These lunatics are everywhere.'

'Still, it is a coincidence, is it not?' Borelli said.

'Perhaps. I will consult an expert in due course, just to rule out a connection,' Lombroso replied. 'Now let us find our victim, poor soul. Borelli, you lead the way.'

They followed Borelli's lead and found that they were just round the corner from where they had been told to wait.

'Interesting that he should choose a woman this time,' Lombroso said, thoughtfully. 'It seems that our killer is diversifying. I wonder which criminal characteristics he was emulating here. Is there a note?'

'There is, but seeing it again I would say that it looks different,' Ottolenghi, said holding it up.

'Let me see that,' Borelli said sharply. He took the note from Ottolenghi and peered at it. 'You're right, it is different.'

'How?' James asked.

'The writing is all over the place. The first note was much neater,' Ottolenghi said.

'So were the others,' a voice said from the gloom. It was Tullio, accompanied by a couple of carabinieri who he sent off to search the surrounding area.

'The notes were mentioned in the newspaper, thanks to Baldovino. Could someone be trying to copy the murders?' said Ottolenghi.

Lombroso peered at the corpse in the dim light. 'That is possible. Ottolenghi, Murray, could you turn her over and pull down the collar of her blouse a little?'

They did so, allowing Lombroso to take a close look. He stood up and frowned. 'She has been strangled – prior to mutilation, I would guess. That's interesting . . . and she is not marked like the others. This would seem to support your theory, Ottolenghi.'

'And the mutilation?' Tullio asked.

'It is savage, of course, but if I am not mistaken it does not directly reflect anything that I have written. Was this woman a criminal?'

Tullio nodded. 'Indeed so. I am told that Rosa Bruno was well known as a prostitute for many years. Recently though, she had been merely finding clients for others as well as working as a maid in a brothel.'

'How enterprising!' Borelli remarked.

Lombroso seemed to be deep in thought. 'The question is, though, if this is the work of the same person, and we cannot be certain that it isn't, then why are these particular victims being sought out?'

'That is a very good question,' Borelli murmured.

'I thought that we had established they all had worked for you?' James said.

'That's right,' Lombroso replied, 'at least until now. I have not, to my certain knowledge, encountered Rosa Bruno before.'

'*We* have, though,' James said.

Lombroso looked at them thoughtfully. 'Go on.'

'I think I may be able to assist here,' Tullio said. 'We met Rosa Bruno outside La Capra. She told us that she had something to tell us but ran off before divulging it.'

'Then we saw her later,' Ottolenghi said. 'She was in La Capra with Sofia – then she disappeared again.'

James frowned. Did he have to bring Sofia into it?

'I see. And what has she said on the matter?' asked Lombroso.

'Nothing. She would not tell us why they were meeting.'

'Mmm. Well, Sofia knows many people in Turin and not all of them are particularly savoury characters,' Lombroso said. 'Still, I think we should ask her to tell us more now. You can ask her, Murray. She seems to have taken a shine to you.'

James looked at him and wondered how much he knew about his relationship with Sofia.

'It seems likely that this Rosa Bruno was murdered for what she knew, not who she was,' Lombroso said. 'But why is the note so different this time? And why mutilate the woman down here in the tunnels?'

Questions and more questions, thought James. Four people were dead and that seemed to be all they had. Except, that was, for one thing: Rosa Bruno had known something and it looked as if she might have died because of it. It was time for Sofia to speak up, whether she liked it or not.

20

The morally insane repay hatred with hatred.

Lombroso, 1884 p 215

As they were making their way out of the tunnels the sheer horror of what James had just experienced began to sink in. A woman lay dead, her corpse horribly mutilated. But was this the work of the same killer? It hardly seemed credible that there could be two such depraved beings at work in the city at one time. And yet the note was different, as were the mutilations. They were more savage, if that was possible, not so precise.

Having consigned the body to the care of the carabinieri they walked through damp and darkness in subdued silence. Soon James could see light in the distance and the passageway seemed to go into a slight incline. Eventually he could see an exit and the glint of what looked like an expanse of water. They made their way towards it and soon found themselves emerging through a stone archway and up some worn steps out into the night.

James breathed in the fresh air thankfully. It was a distinct improvement on the stale, musty atmosphere with the additional pervading smell of death that they had just left. He sank down onto a bench. Ottolenghi came over to him, leaving Tullio, Borelli and Lombroso deep in conversation.

'I'm sorry I mentioned Sofia, but you do see I had little choice, don't you?'

James nodded. 'She doesn't talk to me about that side of her life and I don't like to ask too many questions.'

'Because she used to be a prostitute?'

James paused before speaking. He badly needed to confide in someone and he now believed Ottolenghi was someone he could trust. 'I think Sofia may be hiding something – something important. I saw her discussing something with Reiner after the prison demonstration.'

Ottolenghi looked at James in shocked surprise. 'Are you sure? Why do you think that?'

'They both looked furtive somehow. I hope that I am wrong.'

'So do I. If the professor finds out that she has withheld important information he will dismiss her.'

'I will try to persuade Sofia to tell us what she knows. But she is stubborn. It is one of the reasons I . . . it is why I . . .' He paused.

Ottolenghi finished the sentence. 'You love her – or think you do.' He looked at James with concern. 'Friend, Sofia is beautiful, I know, but she is a servant. She is not for the likes of us. You must break off your liaison with her.'

'I cannot, Ottolenghi,' James said quietly. 'I *do* love her, there is no doubt in my mind, and I don't think that I can give her up, no matter who she is or what she has done.'

'What, even if she is protecting a killer? You cannot seriously think that you can continue! Murray, you must leave her, even if your suspicions are wrong. She is of a different class.'

'You do not understand,' James replied. 'I want to be with her.'

'And what does she say to this?'

He hesitated. 'We have not discussed the future. There is something I need to attend to first.'

Ottolenghi seized him by the shoulders. 'There is no future – not for you and her. You must stop this now. It will not end well, you must know this.'

James shook his head. 'Life is so brief, Ottolenghi. Can't you see that one should take any opportunity to be happy?' Ottolenghi looked at James blankly and it was obvious that he would never really understand.

'Please do not tell anyone,' James begged.

Ottolenghi sighed. 'You know that I won't, but I cannot support you.'

'I worry that she may be in danger from what she knows, particularly given her connection to the professor,' James said.

'We will make sure nothing happens to her,' Ottolenghi said.

They both looked over to Lombroso. 'He doesn't seem too shaken up by the murders, given his connection to them,' James remarked.

'Don't be deceived,' Ottolenghi said. 'I can tell that he's upset from the way he is concentrating on solving the puzzle. It is his way of dealing with it. Besides, he was an army doctor. He must have seen worse sights then.'

Lombroso, Borelli and Tullio came over to them. The professor looked tired. 'So our murderer, or should I say, *a* murderer, has presented us with another conundrum – a single female victim, dead for at least a day, by the look of things, an ex prostitute, though still working in the trade, I believe . . .' Tullio nodded and Lombroso continued. 'Strangled and mutilated by disembowelment, with her organs arranged on the bodies. A note was left but this time the body was not marked.'

'She was not known to you, as the others were, though,' Borelli reminded him. 'Although your housekeeper knew her.'

'That is no surprise,' Lombroso said. 'The prostitutes in this city, old and new, all tend to stick together.'

James saw Ottolenghi steal a look at him, pity etched onto his face.

'His killing is getting faster now it seems,' Borelli remarked.

'Indeed, if it is the same killer,' Lombroso agreed, 'and we are no further forwards with identifying him, or perhaps them, on tonight's evidence.'

'I wonder who was making those noises at the beginning?' Ottolenghi said. 'Was it the killer or an accomplice, leading us to the body?'

'Who knows? Perhaps it was a ghost, playing with you. Or a shadow,' Lombroso replied, sighing. 'Shadows seem to be all we have.'

'It might just have been some children or drunks leading us on a merry dance for their own amusement,' James said, though he knew this was as implausible as it having been a ghost, but he was trying desperately to keep a sense of perspective.

'Perhaps, although it is late in the night for that; it is past midnight, after all,' Ottolenghi said.

'So where are we?' James asked, looking around him. There were some stone arches cut into a bank, forming a kind of shelter. It was from one of these that they had just emerged.

'Don't you recognise it?' Tullio replied, pointing behind him.

He turned and immediately saw that they were by the river. 'The Po?' he asked.

Tullio nodded. 'Not only that, but this is the scene of the second murder – just there.' He indicated a stone pillar to his right where the body of Pietro Mancini had been found.

'We were led here, then,' Lombroso said thoughtfully. 'That is interesting, although I confess I am not sure how it was done. Obviously someone is trying to tell us something.'

'Or trying to make you think one thing, when something else is the case,' Borelli added.

'That too is a possibility, but at least we have some kind of a clue. It is something to think about, don't you think?' Lombroso said.

There was a long pause as they all stood round in a kind of semi-circle like a dejected witches' coven, unsure of the spell its members wished to cast. James suddenly felt exhausted.

'Whatever the truth of it, it is certain that the killer is long gone, so we might as well leave it until morning,' he said firmly.

Tullio yawned and nodded his agreement. 'What was it that you wanted to tell me, by the way?' he asked.

'Nothing that will not keep,' James replied, too tired to explain Horton's activities.

He wandered slowly home through the chilly damp streets, hunched into his coat against the cold wind. As he was passing Sofia's home, he paused, then made up his mind. He could not leave it a moment longer. He had to find out what she knew.

21

Statistics show fewer criminals among atheists than among Catholics and Protestants, perhaps because atheists in Europe tend to be highly educated. Lombroso, 1896 p 324

James hammered at Sofia's door. A moment or two later she came down the stairs and opened the door, peering at him through bleary eyes.

'It's late, James, and I am tired. Come back tomorrow.'

He shook his head and barged past her, taking the stairs two at a time in his determination to make her see him. She followed him, scowling.

'What do you want at this hour?'

They sat down on the settee and he took her hands in his.

'What is it? You are scaring me,' she asked.

'Sofia, Rosa Bruno has been murdered,' he said evenly and held her tightly in his arms as she wept.

When she stopped, she looked up at him. 'Who is doing these terrible things?'

'I don't know. I wish I did.'

Sofia seemed to almost shake herself free of him and sat up straight. 'Then we must find out,' she said with determination, wiping her tears away. 'Let us go through the suspects. Would that not help?'

James looked at her. 'Are you sure you want to do this?'

'We have no option. These crimes must be solved.' She got up and lit a candle. 'I will make some coffee. Begin! Who is on your list?'

'List? I don't really have one.'

She stood before him, her arms folded. 'Well, how else would a scientist go about solving a crime? The professor is always making lists. I find them everywhere.'

Sofia sat at the table, James opposite her, a pot of coffee between them. She nodded formally as if she was about to interview him. 'So, the first suspect?' she said.

'Oskar Reiner,' declared James firmly. He looked at her. Her face coloured slightly. 'Sofia, I have seen you with him and Rosa. It is time to tell me why.'

There was a pause. 'This is nothing to do with the murders.'

'I think that I had better be the judge of that,' James said firmly. 'Rosa is dead. There may be a connection.'

'Rosa works – worked, as a maid at Madam Giulia's.'

'That's a brothel, I take it.'

Sofia nodded. 'Yes. She looked after the girls, made sure that the clients behaved themselves, that kind of thing.'

'And Reiner was a client?' James tried to imagine him in a place like that. Somehow it did not seem likely. He was too fastidious – or that was the impression he gave.

'No, not as far as I know,' Sofia said.

'Then why were you and Rosa in La Capra with him?'

'He wanted to interview some of the girls.' Sofia smiled at him. 'It happens more often than you think. The professor has been there too, with Madame Tarnovsky.'

'Really?' James simply could not picture it.

'They were measuring them.'

'Ah, I see. But Reiner wanted to talk to them.'

'*Sì.*'

'About what?' James asked.

'About their experiences. He wanted to know about any clients who had asked them to do anything . . . strange.'

'Such as?'

'He was particularly interested in the infliction of pain, both by and on the girls.'

'And what was your part in all of this?

Sofia sighed. 'I was just in the middle, arranging a meeting, nothing else. He wanted to keep it quiet, as did Rosa, in case Madam Giulia's clients got to hear of it.'

'I think I'd better talk to Herr Reiner,' James said. He thought back to their conversation at the salon and Reiner's interest in lust murder and post-mortem mutilation.

'Don't you believe me?' Sofia asked.

He took her hand. 'Of course I do. But he might have found out something, or perhaps Rosa did.'

'And what of the other suspects?' Sofia asked.

'What about Horton?' James suggested.

'He has been to the museum several times. I do not like him at all, but why is he a suspect?'

'He disappeared from the dinner last night and there is no love lost between him and the professor.'

'*Sì, si,* and there is something else, I think.' Sofia poured the coffee.

'What's that?'

'Well, does he not match the professor's "criminal type". He has very sharp teeth and his hair is dark and bushy, like a dog.'

'That's true, and from what he said in his debate speech he

seems to hate criminals so that would give him a reason to target them as victims.'

Sofia looked thoughtful. 'I have met men like him. They cannot be trusted.'

James looked at her and wondered who these men might be and how she had met them. He did not enquire. Some things were best left alone. For the same reason he neglected to tell her about the warning, or perhaps it had been a threat, that Horton had issued at the dinner. Why would he do that unless he had something to hide?

'Who else?' he asked.

'Gemelli,' Sofia said. 'Lombroso has many enemies and Gemelli is one of the loudest.'

'Why does he dislike the professor so much?' James asked.

'He is jealous,' Sofia said simply.

'That is not enough to make him a suspect.'

'Ah, but he is obsessive. I have observed him when he has visited. The way he looks at Lombroso is strange. He stares at him with such hatred!'

'Do you know why?' James asked.

'I know a little,' Sofia said. 'According to his housekeeper, years ago when the professor first came to Turin, Gemelli was about to be promoted. The professor stole his job – or that is how Gemelli sees it.'

'Would that make him capable of killing?'

'The professor would say so. I think he calls it moral insanity, when a person seems normal on the outside but doesn't know the difference between good and evil. If you were obsessed about something, might that not make you kill?'

James looked at Sofia in a new light. She was as much of an expert on crime as any of the delegates at the symposium, perhaps even more so because she had her own experience to draw on.

'In that case we must not forget Father Vincenzo and all his talk of the Devil and demons,' he said. 'He seems to think the professor's work is evil. Who knows what lengths he might go to in order to stop it?'

Sofia nodded. '*Sì*, he is a suspect too, and he has influence in all kinds of places.'

'Yes, I'll put him on the list and we need to add DeClichy.'

'He does not seem the type to kill,' Sofia protested.

'I know, but he has been acting strangely for the last day or two. Also, he too disappeared last night. If anyone had a motive to discredit Lombroso it was him, and he had no alibi.'

In fact, James thought to himself, DeClichy was the only one without an alibi, assuming that Horton had actually gone to a brothel, which seemed more than likely, given what they knew about him. Could DeClichy's calm demeanour be a cover for something more sinister? After all, it was odd that he had been so serene in the face of Horton's upstaging of him at the debate. What normal person would react like that? He sat back and shut his eyes.

What about the people, if there was more than one, in the tunnels? What was the significance of the drawings in the dust and the animal organs? Of course there was still Lombroso himself. Could it be a double bluff – making his involvement so obvious and therefore casting doubt on his guilt? It would be a clever ruse, but then he was a clever man. But again, why? Would he really commit these savage killings just to promote his own ideas? And then it could be the work of a woman if she was strong enough – or two women – or a man and a woman – or two men. The possibilities seemed almost endless.

Sofia yawned. 'It is late. Let's go to bed, *caro*.'

James opened his eyes and allowed her to pull him to his feet and be led into her bedroom. Before long he was lying next to her, listening to her breathing steadily. She had gone to sleep almost immediately but he lay awake, his mind racing with thoughts of the murders.

Sofia moaned slightly in her sleep and he put his arm around her. He had to make the most of each precious moment with the woman he loved for who knew when and indeed how 'this', whatever 'this' was, would end.

The following day was a Sunday, although that meant little to Lombroso, being as immersed in his work as he was. He had asked Ottolenghi and James to come to the museum and complete their cataloguing and measuring of the Madagascan skulls although, given the lateness of the hour when they had left him, the professor had conceded that they could arrive mid-morning.

This meant that as it was also Sofia's day off James was able to linger with her a little, and as he lay with her in his arms, her head resting on his shoulder, he dared to imagine what it would be like if they could be together always. He thought of them sitting around the breakfast table, him reading a newspaper and drinking coffee as Sofia gazed fondly at him. Perhaps there would be children. He could see them strolling though a city park, arm in arm as the children played. The infants would be handsome like their mother, with dark hair and dark eyes and people passing would remark on their beauty.

But unless he sacrificed everything for Sofia, they could

never have a future together, and it was not a sacrifice that was his to make. His sister would be part of it and he could not do that to her. He would have to make the most of what they had now and leave the future to take care of itself.

Suddenly he was jolted out of his daydream by shouting from the street outside Sofia's rooms. He could not hear clearly what was said. There was the sound of running feet going past but it soon faded into the distance and all was peaceful again. Sofia, however, had stirred during the disturbance and she gave an almost feline stretch.

'*Che cos'è, caro?*' she murmured.

'Sshh, my love, it is nothing,' James replied. He thought about the murders.

He was wide awake now. Pulling a blanket round him, he got up quietly and went to the next room to fetch a glass of water from a jug on the table. He sat down on the settee and began to think. The door to the bedroom opened and Sofia emerged, yawning, a shawl draped around her bare shoulders. She looked like a native from a Pacific island – beautiful and exotic.

'*Che succede?*'

'Nothing, my love. Go back to bed.'

She ignored him and sat next to him in the darkness, pulling her shawl round her. He enfolded her in his arms.

'You are still thinking about the murders,' she said.

'Yes, I am – I can't help it. Four deaths and all connected in some way to the professor. There must be something that we have missed.'

Suddenly Sofia sat up. 'You know, there is something that no one has mentioned.'

'What's that?'

'Well, the killings, they started so suddenly.'

James frowned. 'That's true but what are you getting at?'

'Even the most skilled person has to practise, do they not? Whatever their art?'

James leapt to his feet. 'My God! Sofia, you are a genius!'

She smiled bashfully. 'I do not think the professor would agree.'

'In order to get the mutilations so clean, of course the killer must have practised! All we have to do is to find out how and where and then we have him.'

Barely an hour later, James was at the museum. His head was buzzing with Sofia's idea and he couldn't wait to share it with the others. Ottolenghi was already there, fully occupied with the skulls, and looked up to smile at him before getting back to his work. Lombroso was sitting at the other end of the room, reading.

'Professor?'

Lombroso looked up and smiled at him absent-mindedly. 'Ah yes, Murray. Join Ottolenghi, would you? I have something to finish.'

'Yes, but—'

'Just get on with it!'

James sighed. It seemed his thoughts would have to wait. He took off his jacket and joined Ottolenghi to attend to the skulls. He was not yet certain as to why they were doing what they were, but he hoped that, when the work was completed, as it soon would be, Lombroso would explain. It seemed that the professor was not particularly anxious to hear about the events of the previous night, or indeed anything connected to it. He decided to wait until he could talk to Ottolenghi and Tullio alone. Perhaps they would see the merit of what he had to say.

James had not been there for long before they heard the sound of the brass knocker on the great wooden door at the front of the museum, and minutes later there was a knock and a maid showed in a tall imposing figure.

Lombroso stood to greet his guest. 'Good afternoon, Father Vincenzo.' He looked past him into the hall. 'I was expecting the Marchesa.'

'She is indisposed. I think that your connection with four murders was too much, even for her.'

'Ah, I see. The news is out already. I suppose I should have expected it. Well, thank you for coming, in any event,' Lombroso said.

The priest looked self-assured as usual. 'Think nothing of it, Professor, though I confess I was surprised to be included in your invitation to the Marchesa.'

'Shall we be seated?' Lombroso wandered over to a sideboard upon which a silver tray and some fine crystal decanters sat, glinting in the gaslight.

'May I offer you some refreshment? A drink, perhaps, since it so cold outside?'

Father Vincenzo accepted a glass of sherry and the two of them sat before the fire. James looked over to Ottolenghi and shrugged. The priest had not acknowledged their presence, which seemed to James both ill-mannered and odd at the same time. Clearly he did not regard either of them as being of sufficient importance to pay them even the most fleeting courtesy. Lombroso was, of course, an entirely different matter. Further pleasantries were exchanged and then the visitor glanced over to a small table beside him.

'I see you are a chess player.'

'I am indeed. I find it helps me to think and to relax, on occasion. Do you play?'

Father Vincenzo nodded. 'I do. To my mind mastery of the game indicates an exceptional intellect.'

'Perhaps,' said Lombroso with some scepticism in his voice, 'but also a love for strategy and even a little bluff. We must have a game some time.'

'I would enjoy that very much indeed. So what can I do for you, Professor?' Father Vincenzo asked crisply. 'Is it to do with Pilgrim? I have been following the case with some interest.'

Lombroso nodded. 'I am glad to hear it. We could do with some assistance for I confess that these murders have been perplexing me, somewhat. I have only recently been in a position to theorise with any certainty as to the type of person responsible and even then I am not entirely certain.'

'I would be most interested to hear your conclusions,' Father Vincenzo said. 'But you wish to consult me about something in particular?'

Lombroso nodded. 'There is some indication that the perpetrator may be influenced by some kind of black magic or Satanism.'

'I see. What makes you say that?'

'I cannot give detail at this point in the investigation, I'm afraid.'

'So what do you want from me?' Father Vincenzo's tone had hardened slightly, James noticed. He clearly did not like to be excluded in any way. Either that or . . . could *he* be responsible? The possibility of a priest committing such atrocities was profoundly shocking. But if he had, then obviously he would want to know exactly what the professor had found out. James looked over at the two men and wondered if the same thought had occurred to Lombroso.

'Are there any cults or covens that are particularly active in the city at the moment?' the professor asked.

Father Vincenzo placed his hands together, as if in prayer. 'There are several. As you know, such people are drawn to this city as moths to a flame. Can you be more precise as to what you are looking for?'

Lombroso paused and stared at him. It seemed to James that he was reluctant to give anything away but he would have to in order to get anything meaningful from Father Vincenzo. 'Symbols, for one thing. We found something at one of the scenes – an inverted cross. I know, of course, that it is a Satanic emblem but is it one that is of special significance to any of the cults you speak of?'

Father Vincenzo raised his eyebrows. 'How interesting. Yes, there is a Solomonite sect that use that sign.'

'For what?'

'For their rituals – sacrificial mostly – attempts to summon evil spirits.'

Lombroso looked over to James and Ottolenghi. 'My two assistants found some evidence of such a rite in the tunnels. Murray, tell Father Vincenzo what you saw.'

'There was a large double circle and three pentagrams,' James said.

Father Vincenzo nodded. 'Was there a diamond marked in the centre?'

'Yes,' James replied.

'That signifies the forty-fifth parallel – black and white magic coming together for a common purpose.'

'What purpose?' Lombroso asked.

Father Vincenzo frowned. 'That is the worrying aspect. We have had a number of macabre murders and under those circumstances I would think that the aim is to conjure up something or someone to either deal with or collude with the culprit.'

'Who?' James asked, both fascinated and appalled by this information.

'Only one being could deal with evil on this level: I have no doubt that this rite was conducted in order to summon the Devil himself.'

For a moment silence descended on the room. 'Ludicrous!' Lombroso declared.

'I know you do not believe in the Devil, Professor,' Father Vincenzo said quietly. 'But many inhabitants of our city do and that in itself could be dangerous.' He turned to James and Ottolenghi. 'I imagine you found certain remains, did you not?'

'Yes,' Ottolenghi replied. 'They looked to be pig and chicken organs.'

'I see,' Father Vincenzo said. 'Well, that is something. But I should warn you that this rite may well have been a mere preparatory exercise.'

'What do you mean?' Lombroso asked.

'To summon the Devil himself the sacrifice must be human.' Father Vincenzo looked at Lombroso. 'It is surely possible that the murders were committed for this purpose – to provide human organs as a sacrifice.'

Lombroso shook his head. 'No, no. The organs are left at the scene, not removed for some ill-conceived ritual. There is no connection. The murders are the work of a person who suffers from moral insanity, albeit at a level that I have not come across before.'

'I have heard you talk of this before, have I not?' Father Vincenzo said. 'I seem to remember that you suggested that such a person could be both rational and insane – an interesting idea.'

'Indeed, that is what I said, although I am not sure of the extent to which that might apply to the killer.'

'Why must evil be considered an act of the insane?'

Lombroso looked him in the eye. 'I do not see evil as anything other than an irrational choice. Indeed, the concept is a conundrum in itself. Does it really exist at all, I wonder?'

'It is abstract, naturally, but its consequences are clearly visible, as we have all seen.'

Lombroso sipped at his drink and pondered the question carefully. He appeared to be looking around the room at his various artefacts in search of an answer. Eventually he spoke. 'If evil men had cloven hooves and horns, how simple life would be! That is what people like the members of this cult seem to think, I believe, encouraged by the Church. I do not share that view. Evil can hide in all sorts of places, minds included.'

'So your research is wrong?'

Lombroso smiled and shook his head. 'Not at all. Crime is one thing and evil is another. My work tells me that some criminals can be identified physically and are a throwback to more primitive times. Evil, however, is different and much more easily concealed than a tendency towards criminality. A man can be evil in intent but never commit an evil deed.'

'So you could not then, as an expert in such things, as a scientist, identify an evil man from his appearance?' Father Vincenzo asked, his eyes narrowed as if preparing not to accept the answer.

'I think I could, yes,' Lombroso replied with unfamiliar modesty.

'How?' Father Vincenzo asked. He seemed to be enjoying himself.

'I would look into the eyes, Father. That is where the soul lies. One can see everything, provided that is, one looks in the right way.' With that Lombroso drew closer, stared into Father Vincenzo's eyes and smiled enigmatically.

The priest laughed. 'Say for the purposes of argument that a person is evil, does it necessarily mean that evil has to amount to an irrational choice?'

Lombroso nodded thoughtfully. 'Choosing evil over good – how very interesting.'

'We have come full circle, have we not, Professor?' Father Vincenzo said, a trifle smugly, it seemed to James.

'Indeed we have,' Lombroso said. 'Back to moral insanity – and I am as uncertain as I was before.'

Before Father Vincenzo could respond, the door opened suddenly and Machinetti pushed past the maid who was attempting to prevent him from entering without being announced. He was closely followed by an embarrassed-looking Giardinello. Machinetti paused briefly to acknowledge Father Vincenzo with a deep and ostentatious bow before turning his attention to Lombroso.

'It has happened again and all roads lead to you, Professor!'

Lombroso looked severely at Machinetti. 'What has happened?' he asked in a tone of thinly veiled impatience.

'There has been another murder . . .'

There was silence as they all tried to take in this information.

'Will it ever end?' Lombroso muttered beneath his breath.

'And this time we have evidence of both your motive and opportunity so I must insist that you accompany me to be questioned.' Machinetti nodded at Giardinello who reluctantly moved towards Lombroso. James and Ottolenghi stood open-mouthed but silent in response to what was going on. Father Vincenzo looked on, a slight smirk on his face, which, James thought, was a puzzling reaction, particularly after he and Lombroso had seemed to reach some kind of an understanding. Fortunately, at that moment both Borelli and Tullio arrived.

'Marshal, what is happening here?' Tullio asked brusquely.

'I am taking the professor in for questioning,' Machinetti replied. 'Yet another body has been found with a note as before. I advise you not to interfere, Tullio. The *questore* himself has authorised this.'

Tullio frowned at him. 'On what basis are you detaining the professor? Is there evidence?'

Machinetti smiled triumphantly and looked at Lombroso. 'Oh, there is plenty, I assure you.'

Borelli stepped forward, a look of puzzlement on his face. 'Who is the victim? We know about one, found last night in the tunnels. But who is the other?'

Machinetti took a deep breath, puffing himself up until he looked like a fat turkey in a farmyard. 'There is a fifth victim and he is well known to all of you. It is Dr DeClichy.'

'DeClichy!' Ottolenghi exclaimed. 'But that cannot be. We saw him late last night and he looked to be on his way home!'

'It is true, I'm afraid,' Tullio said grimly. 'He was found early this morning, in an alley off the Via Pietro Micca.'

'He was strangled then disembowelled,' Machinetti said with apparent relish.

'That is indeed a tragedy,' Lombroso said quietly. 'That poor man. Why would anyone want to do this to him?'

'This changes things, Professor,' Tullio said. 'The victim is a respectable academic. People will be frightened.'

'They should be. Who knows where he will strike next?'
Borelli said. 'What information do you have, Tullio? Is it
definitely the same killer as before?'

'There was a note. That means it must be the same killer,'
Machinetti declared firmly. 'Not only that, but DeClichy was
known to Lombroso here, as were the other victims. We also
have a number of witnesses who have told us that there was
bad blood between them.' He turned towards Lombroso.
'Come, Professor. It's down to headquarters with you.'

Giardinello approached Lombroso who protested loudly,
in company with almost everyone else. A small scuffle broke
out as Tullio tried valiantly to prevent the arrest. Ottolenghi
and James joined in. Borelli started to shout at Machinetti.
Then suddenly a voice boomed out over them all.

'How is the faithful city become a harlot! It was full of
judgment; righteousness lodged in it; but now murderers.'

They all turned to look at Father Vincenzo who was
standing with his hands clasped before him. 'I will pray for
you, Professor.'

'Thank you, but there is no need, Father,' Lombroso said.
'I can assure you all that I have not murdered anyone – well,
not directly anyway.'

'I don't believe you,' Machinetti spluttered. 'You had
motive, opportunity and knowledge. It is my duty to arrest
you.'

Lombroso nodded patiently. 'Naturally I would expect
nothing less. However, loath though I am to disappoint you,
Marshal, I feel that I must point out the fatal flaw in your
accusation.'

'And what is that?' Machinetti asked. His lips formed a
thin line but some spittle had escaped from the one of the

corners. James watched him, mesmerised, as it trickled slowly down to his chin.

'The professor has an alibi,' Borelli said firmly. 'We left the dinner together last night then walked back here and sat and talked until Tullio summoned us to the scene of Rosa Bruno's murder.'

'It is true. We had much to discuss, given recent events,' Lombroso agreed.

Machinetti snorted. 'Why should I believe you?'

Borelli glared at him.

'Your belief or otherwise is irrelevant, Marshal,' Tullio said. 'Evidence is paramount here. What reason do you have for supposing that the professor killed DeClichy?'

'He was heard by various witnesses to have expressed a wish that the man would go away and leave him alone,' Machinetti replied smugly.

Tullio looked over at Lombroso. 'Professor?'

'I did say that on a number of occasions,' he agreed.

'But still the man persisted, did he not, and so you decided to take matters into your own hands and do away with him. Isn't that how it went?' Machinetti declared forcefully.

'Really, Marshal, this is not an interrogation!' Borelli said.

Lombroso put a restraining hand on Borelli's arm. 'No, no, Adolfo. Let him finish. I want to hear all the evidence against me. It is most fascinating. So, Marshal, there I was in a state of, well, what would you say – fury, incandescence, apoplectic anger, uncontrollable rage, slight irritation?'

Marshal Machinetti looked at Lombroso with a bemused half smile, as if unsure whether he was being mocked or hearing a confession.

'And then I ran out into the night and followed DeClichy, having paused briefly to tell Borelli of my movements and asking him to risk his entire career and reputation by giving me a false alibi. Then, having waited for an opportune moment, I smote poor DeClichy down, strangled him and disembowelled the poor fellow with – what? A knife or some such, was it – which I happened to have secreted about my person throughout an opera and a dinner, just in case I should feel the need to kill someone? Then, not content with that, I turned up at the tunnels having been alerted by Tullio here and looked at what – an earlier victim? I have been remarkably active, have I not?'

There was a pause. Everyone was staring at Machinetti whose face suddenly blanched. For a moment James felt almost sorry for him.

'It could have happened as you say,' Machinetti said, almost inaudibly.

'What was that? Speak up, Machinetti,' Tullio said, his authority growing visibly as Machinetti's shrank.

'It is plausible enough to believe . . . to believe he could have . . . he might have . . .' Machinetti spluttered desperately.

'But I didn't,' Lombroso said, almost gently.

'No indeed you did not, because you were with me as I stated earlier,' Borelli said, his hand on Lombroso's shoulder in a show of support.

'Come, Marshal, it is time we were going,' Tullio said crisply. 'We can discuss the case on the way back to your headquarters. Good afternoon.' He paused for a second and then turned. 'And, gentleman, please be careful. You are all potential victims now.'

'Tullio,' called out Lombroso. Tullio came back into the doorway and Lombroso whispered something in his ear. He nodded and left again.

There was a short pause as everyone present seemed to be taking stock of what they had witnessed in the last few moments. James was almost ashamed that he had allowed himself to become involved in what was little better than the drunken brawl of the previous night. It all seemed extraordinary and, indeed, faintly ludicrous.

Father Vincenzo, who had been watching all that had transpired with apparent interest, gave a short bow. 'I will also take my leave of you, gentlemen,' he said quietly, as if he himself had played no part in what had just passed. He turned towards Lombroso. 'Before I go I will say this. We should not forget that five people have now died in tragic circumstances.'

'Indeed, you are right to remind us, Father,' Lombroso said.

'And they all seem to be connected to you, Professor . . .' he said, striding out of the room before anyone could speak.

Lombroso sank into an armchair as if he had been deflated. He looked mournfully into the distance and despite having known him for only a short time, James still recognised the signs of the melancholy that overcame him from time to time. Clearly the priest's words had struck a chord.

Borelli went over and sat by him. Ottolenghi signalled to James to continue their work and they set about measuring the skulls. It was good to be occupied with something. The news of DeClichy's death had cast a terrible pall over their world. Before, the murders had seemed almost remote, even though the victims had been familiar to at least some of them. But this was different. This time they had lost one of their own and it had brought the horror even closer. James could see that Ottolenghi was thinking about it but they remained in silence for a good few minutes until finally Lombroso spoke.

'He is right. I did kill DeClichy.'

Startled by this admission, James looked over and wondered, though for no more than a split second, if he was about to make a bizarre confession, although the thought of such betrayal seemed unlikely.

'Nonsense, Cesare, you were with me, remember?' Borelli said.

Lombroso shook his head, violently. 'No, you don't understand. I did not strangle him or wield the knife that mutilated him but I might as well have done. If it were not for me he would still be alive.' Lombroso leaned towards his friend and placed his hand on Borelli's wrist. 'I turned DeClichy away, again and again. He wanted to tell me something. If I had let him then perhaps he would not be dead now.'

'That is not so, Cesare. Even if you had spoken to him you could not have saved him.'

Lombroso looked at him, frowning. 'I disagree. I think he was trying to tell me something and died for his trouble.'

'You think he was killed by the Pilgrim, then, as Machinetti says?' Borelli asked. 'Or was there a second killer, an accomplice perhaps?'

Lombroso looked into the distance. 'I don't know who committed the act but this much I do know: if evil acts such as these are repeated often enough then immorality becomes a habit.'

Borelli stared at Lombroso. 'A habit? Surely these murders amount to more than that.'

Lombroso gave a wry smile. 'You misunderstand me, Adolfo. The thing about habits is that they breed mistakes. And where there are mistakes there are clues.'

'Has he made an error then?' Borelli asked urgently.

Lombroso smiled enigmatically. 'That, my old friend, is what we must find out.'

22

Because the majority of criminals lack any moral sense, they
fail to understand the immorality of crime.

Lombroso, 1878 p 109

Later that afternoon, when the Madagascan skulls were finally measured and each detail carefully recorded, James and Otto-lenghi were instructed to meet Lombroso downstairs in ten minutes when, he told them, they would all be embarking upon a short journey. Borelli had long since left and so it was just the three of them moving in a carriage through the encroaching November darkness to their mystery destination.

Lombroso seemed to have cheered up a little since his earlier attack of melancholia. He looked over to them and smiled. 'I am assuming from your silence on the matter that you did not find anything of consequence by following our friend Horton last night?'

As they explained the events of the previous evening, Lombroso listened intently, nodding and grimacing according to what they told him. 'Interesting. We have not one but two slippery characters at large last night and two murders to boot. My hunch is that this is no coincidence.'

'You think only one of them is the Pilgrim?' James asked.

Lombroso peered at him through his glasses. 'Perhaps, perhaps not – well, not completely.'

James was confused but did not wish to admit it. He looked over to Ottolenghi who had a faint frown on his face. It seemed that he was not alone. He remembered something that his father had told him: that if he wanted to learn, he should never be afraid to ask questions.

'But Machinetti said that there was a note. It must be the Pilgrim who killed DeClichy, surely.'

The carriage came to a halt. 'Well, Murray,' Lombroso said, 'we may find out for certain in a few moments.'

They alighted and James saw that they were outside the city morgue. It seemed that they had come to examine poor DeClichy's corpse.

Tullio was waiting for them at the entrance. He looked tired and it occurred to James that his constant battle with Machinetti must be taking its toll.

'I have managed to obtain access to the body, Professor. It's this way.'

They followed him along a tiled corridor to a small room. James noted that even after death one's station in life was recognised. The other corpses shared their accommodation whereas DeClichy, as a gentleman, was given a room of his own, although it was far from palatial. There was little in the way of natural light and the only furniture was a table in the centre on which the body lay, discreetly covered by a sheet. An orderly stood respectfully by and, on a nod from Tullio, pulled it back to reveal DeClichy.

He looked peaceful despite the manner of his death. His glasses had been removed and James could see that the man was younger than he had at first thought. There was a certain vulnerability about him but then he had seemed, from their brief acquaintance, to be a compassionate and thoughtful man. He had cared about his work just as much as Lombroso, even if his conclusions were different. James wondered what might have been if he had survived. Perhaps he would have done great good in the world had he been permitted to continue with his work. Madame Tarnovsky had told him that DeClichy would often give money to those he studied and their families because he believed that poverty and a lack of education were the two chief causes of crime. Having seen the slums of both Turin and Edinburgh, James was inclined to think that perhaps he had a point, even if Lombroso did not agree. But the question remained: why had the Pilgrim chosen him as a victim when the others had all been criminals of one kind or another? It did not make any sense.

Lombroso had removed his coat and pushed up his sleeves. He bent over the corpse and looked more closely at DeClichy's injuries. There was a gaping hole in his middle. It looked as if he had been operated on and, indeed, it reminded James of an illustration in one of the anatomy books he had used for his medical studies.

'What happened to the stomach and so on?' asked Lombroso.

Tullio looked sheepish. 'I am afraid that by the time I arrived the body contents had been washed away on the instructions of Machinetti. He said that the cause of death was obvious and he did not want to dirty his boots on the remains.'

Ottolenghi shook his head in despair. 'I cannot believe that he would be so stupid. There are *always* clues at the scene of the crime.'

Tullio smiled ruefully. 'Machinetti does not believe in

evidence. He investigates crimes using hunches and what he likes to call his hunting instinct.'

Lombroso tutted. 'And I suppose his instinct told him not to allow the body to be photographed in situ, as with the first murder?'

Tullio shook his head. 'I am afraid so, Professor. And there are no drawings either. The sketch artist was not available until later in the morning and Machinetti did not want to wait.'

'Mmm, eager to arrest me, no doubt. And the note – do you have it?'

'No, I regret that I don't. I am informed that it was the same as the others but I cannot verify that.'

Lombroso sighed. 'Well, we will just have to concentrate on what we *do* have.' He began to examine the body, presumably to look for the carving that had been left on the other victims, when the door was flung open and Machinetti stormed in, accompanied by Giardinello and another young carabinieri officer.

'Stand back from the corpse immediately!' he barked.

Lombroso glared at him angrily but obeyed the order nonetheless.

'What is this, Marshal? We have permission to be here!' Tullio said in exasperated tones.

'You may have permission but he doesn't.' He jerked his head towards Lombroso, dismissively. 'This man is a suspect – a fact you omitted to tell the *questore*, your superior. He could be tampering with evidence.'

'What evidence?' Lombroso said impatiently. 'You and your men have destroyed it all.'

Machinetti turned slowly towards the professor. 'If you

and your friends do not leave now I will have you all arrested. Explain *that* to Professor Gemelli!'

Lombroso pursed his lips angrily and snatched his coat, politely offered to him by Giardinello. It was clear that Machinetti had won the day. Lombroso stalked out and everyone followed in his wake. James brought up the rear and just as he was leaving Machinetti grabbed him by the arm.

'Never judge a book by its cover, Murray. That's my advice. Watch your employer. He's not as innocent as he seems.'

James thought his comment was ironic as that was exactly what Machinetti seemed to do. 'What do you mean?' he said, indignantly.

A cry came from outside.

'Murray? Where are you?'

'Go on,' Machinetti said. 'He's waiting for you!'

James looked at him with disdain and left, catching up with the others at the front entrance. Tullio was explaining himself.

'I do apologise, Professor. I did get permission but Machinetti is right. I left out the fact that you knew DeClichy. We would never have been allowed in if I had not.'

'That's quite all right, Tullio. You are working in difficult circumstances, I can see that,' Lombroso said. 'I know Machinetti of old; he will do all he can to impede a proper investigation unless it ties in with his theory, and he is convinced that I am a murderer.'

'What can we do?' James asked.

Lombroso shrugged. 'We must find the real killer or killers. Only that will satisfy Machinetti. Let us go back to the museum and discuss our findings. Science is what is needed here.'

Ottolenghi nodded his agreement. 'Do you think that the symposium will be cancelled now, Professor?' he asked.

'No, it must continue,' Lombroso said vehemently. 'There is no doubt in my mind that it is what DeClichy would have wished.'

'Let us hope that Professor Gemelli agrees,' Ottolenghi murmured as Lombroso hailed a cab.

A few moments later they arrived back at the museum. Sofia was there to greet them.

'I have heard about poor Dr DeClichy, Professor,' she said. 'I thought you might need me today.'

'That is kind of you, Sofia, but isn't it your day off?' Lombroso said.

'*Sì*, but I do not mind,' she said as Lombroso patted her hand absent-mindedly. 'You have a visitor, Professor.'

Madame Tarnovsky was seated in the laboratory. As they entered, she sprang to her feet and stood looking at Lombroso. It was obvious that she had been crying.

'Cesare, you are back at last!' she said in relief.

'Madame, I am glad to see you,' replied Lombroso, a concerned expression on his face. 'How are you? Should you not be resting?'

'I had to come. I could not stand my own company a moment longer. How could I sit idle when a good man has been taken from us?'

'Indeed, Madame Tarnovsky, I quite understand. We were just about to discuss the case if you would care to join us?'

They sat around the large table, now finally cleared of the Madagascan skulls. They were silent at first, each of them in their own world but thinking of the same thing – murder. Lombroso stroked his beard thoughtfully and was the first to speak.

'It seems to me that the first question we need to answer is whether or not the murders of DeClichy and indeed Rosa Bruno were committed by the same person as the other killings.'

'The evidence suggests that they were. After all, there were identical notes left at the scene,' Ottolenghi said.

'Really, Ottolenghi, what have I told you so many times?' Lombroso said impatiently. 'You must remember to challenge all that you hear. Never take things at face value. It is the first rule of scientific policing.'

'We have not seen the last note,' James said. He knew that he should have allowed Ottolenghi to finish but he could not help himself. 'It may not be identical. We only have Machinetti's word for that and he is by no means reliable.'

Lombroso nodded approvingly. 'Indeed, Murray, that is so. Anything else?'

'We cannot be certain that there *are* two killers. It seems too much of a coincidence even though the method of despatch used was different. There did not seem to be the same care taken with the mutilation – after all, disembowelment is a messy affair and—' Suddenly he noticed Madame Tarnovsky who sat, looking pale and drawn. He had forgotten himself in his excitement.

She looked up and smiled wanly. 'Do not trouble yourself, Dr Murray. I knew of the method. I overheard some of the hotel staff gossiping about it. It is just a little hard to hear it again. One learns to detach oneself as a scientist but still, when it is someone one knows . . .'

'I am so sorry. I did not wish to upset you.'

She shook her head. 'It is of no consequence. These matters must be discussed if justice is to be done.' She turned to Lombroso. 'So, Cesare, if we really have two murderers rather than one then we must ask ourselves why anyone would wish to kill Dr DeClichy. He was such a gentle sort of person and I cannot believe that anyone would wish him dead.'

Lombroso sighed and looked down at his hands, folded in front of him on the table. 'I wish I had not been so dismissive of him.'

Madame Tarnovsky leaned forwards and put her hand on his. 'Cesare, this is not your fault.'

He shook his head. 'But if I had listened to DeClichy perhaps I could have saved him.'

'You do not know that. What was it he was going to say to you?'

Lombroso shrugged. 'I have no idea.'

'Well then,' said Madame Tarnovsky, 'it could be unconnected or perhaps it was something you could not have helped him with. Conjecture is pointless. As a scientist, you of all people should know that.'

At that, Lombroso seemed to recover himself. 'Indeed you are right, dear Madame Tarnovsky, as always. Facts are what we need. So, what do we know for certain?'

James took a deep breath. It was now or never. 'The killer is unlikely to have started with Soldati.'

Lombroso stared at him. 'What do you mean, Murray?'

'Well, the mutilations for the first three murders were clean, neat even. The killer must have practised.'

'I think it unlikely that a morally insane killer would be that organised,' Lombroso said dismissively. 'Anything else?'

James felt deflated. It had seemed like an obvious lead to him.

'We know that someone is killing people in order to test you, Professor,' Ottolenghi said.

Lombroso looked at him. 'But does that really get us anywhere?'

'I think it does, Cesare!' Madame Tarnovsky said.

'How?' he asked.

'Well, if we can work out why he feels the need to test you then we should be able to gain a better understanding of his overall motive,' she replied.

'That does not feel very scientific. Wouldn't we be better off looking at the physical evidence?' Ottolenghi suggested. 'Or perhaps taking up James's idea and looking for evidence of practice.'

Madame Tarnovsky shook her head. Even she would not support him over Lombroso, thought James. Ottolenghi looked at him and shrugged. At least he had tried.

'That cannot be ignored, of course,' she said, 'but sometimes one needs to understand the way a criminal's mind works in order to catch him. Am I not right, Cesare? After all, your work covers personality as well as physical attributes, does it not?'

Lombroso nodded slowly. 'So we should think of reasons for these tests.'

'Indeed,' Madame Tarnovsky said. 'Let us create a list of possible motives, then. Mr Murray, will you be our scribe?'

He agreed, though he did not feel particularly enthusiastic having had his suggestion dismissed so conclusively.

'Greed is one of the most common motives for murder,' Ottolenghi said.

'That doesn't apply in this case, surely?' James argued. 'None of the victims had much in the way of material possessions and there was no sign of robbery.'

'I do not think that slaughter such as this could have a motive as commonplace as greed,' Lombroso said. 'I am still of the view that this is the work of a person suffering from moral insanity.'

'Revenge is a motive that could come from a lack of moral sense and would sit well with the actions of our killer,' Madame Tarnovsky said. 'It is also fairly common in the criminal, as you have said yourself.'

'Well then,' Lombroso said, with something close to his old certainty, 'clearly we are looking for a morally insane person, hell-bent on revenge of some sort. He is using these murders to test me and the mutilations are in some way meant to reflect or symbolise my work. As the morally insane criminal almost always shares the physical characteristics of the born criminal he will resemble atavistic or primitive man and possess a large set of jaws, facial asymmetry, unequal ears and a scanty beard – assuming, as I believe we can, that the culprit is a man.'

'So surely all that is needed is to persuade Tullio and Machinetti to round up all the men in the city who have such characteristics and have some kind of connection to you,' Ottolenghi suggested. James noticed that he seemed to be wearing the expression of someone who did not quite believe in what he had just said. Frankly, he didn't blame him.

Lombroso sat back in his chair, a triumphant grin on his face. 'Indeed, there you have it – criminal anthropology in action. Once we have tracked this brute down I can use the case in the next edition of my book. I could open an institute for the study of the morally insane. That should shut Gemelli up for good. And it will wipe the smirk from my critics' faces once and for all. Ottolenghi, ring for Sofia. We need coffee. We will need our wits about us to design a trap for our monster.'

Ottolenghi and James exchanged glances of concern.

Something told James that the solution to this particular puzzle might not turn out to be as simple as Lombroso seemed to think. James supported some of the professor's ideas and his work but he had his doubts about other parts of it, particularly when it came to solving crimes. It seemed too simplistic just to give a list of physical characteristics and expect the murderer simply to emerge from his hiding place and match the description given. James had seen killers before, at the asylum. They shared no resemblance to one another.

He worried that the professor was merely wasting time. There were solid clues to follow and surely they were more likely to lead to the killer being caught than designing some convoluted trap using the criminal type theory as a basis? James made a decision. Perhaps Lombroso was right. He was experienced in criminal matters, after all. But, just in case he was wrong, there would be nothing amiss in doing some investigation of his own. What harm could it possibly do?

23

Forensic medicine should recognise that in the case of the criminal man who is in constant struggle against society, tattoos – like scars – are professional characteristics.

Lombroso, 1876 p 62

Having finally extricated himself from the museum, James was on his way to see Sofia. For once they would have a whole precious evening together. They could talk and laugh and pretend, just for a few hours, that they were a normal couple. James bought some flowers from a stall on the Via Po and when he arrived Sofia greeted him with a kiss and a cry of appreciation for his gift.

'Sit, sit,' she said, 'I have cooked something special for you: *coniglio con peperoni*, rabbit with peppers using my mother's recipe.' James grinned. He had already noticed an enticing aroma coming from a pot on her tiny stove. 'And to start I have prepared *agnolotti al sugo di arrosto*, pasta filled with veal!'

James looked at her standing before him, beaming at him proudly, and felt a surge of joy as if he had been confined in a cell and had suddenly been let out into the warmth of the sun. He walked over to Sofia and seized her in his arms, whirling her round and then kissing her.

'I love you, Sofia Esposito!'

She smiled at him but in response said only, 'Enough, let's eat before it gets cold.'

James wondered if he would ever hear her tell him that she loved him too. Looking at her expression he decided that it would be best not to pursue it. He merely nodded and did as she suggested.

The food was sublime. It was accompanied by a carafe of familiar-tasting wine. Sofia was a little coy about its origins saying only that it was a Dolcetto. James suspected it came from Paolo's vineyard via Lombroso's cellar but he did not care. The pasta parcels were fragrant with rosemary and garlic and Sofia showed him how to eat them as her mother had taught her. The steaming pasta was covered with a little of the wine and then with a fork she fished out the parcels one by one and put them in his mouth, and he did the same for her. Then she served the tender rabbit with the sweet and aromatic peppers. As they ate they sipped at their wine and talked of their early childhoods when each of them had been happy.

Later, when they were sipping *grappa* and drinking coffee, James leaned forward and took Sofia's hand. 'What I said earlier . . .'

'Let us not speak of that now, *caro*.'

'I just wanted to tell you how happy you make me.'

Sofia nodded. 'I know, *caro*, I know.'

He smiled and shook his head.

'What is it?' Sofia asked.

'It feels wrong somehow to be so happy when such terrible things are going on.'

'Perhaps, as the latest victim was a gentleman, there will be more attention paid,' Sofia said.

'Perhaps, but I cannot help but feel that we are in some way responsible. If we had taken more notice of him then maybe . . .'

She nodded. 'I understand, James, but you could not have known what would happen to him. He was just unfortunate to be in the wrong place at the wrong time.'

'Perhaps you're right but I'm sure he was trying to tell us something before he died.'

She shook her head. 'Where I come from there are only three reasons for killing someone – revenge, greed or fear.'

'So which could be applied to DeClichy?' James asked.

'Was he likely to have wronged someone?'

'I doubt it, and he didn't strike me as being wealthy.'

'So we are left with fear – someone was afraid of him.'

'I can't think why anyone should be afraid of someone so meek and mild.'

'Ah, *caro*, fear is not always rational.'

'But still, why would anyone fear him?'

'It might not be him but something he knew that frightened them. In the underworld there is only one way to deal with informers,' Sofia said, drawing a hand across her throat dramatically.

He thought for a moment and realised she was right. DeClichy had been trying to tell them something. It was too much of a coincidence to ignore. 'Yes, but I have no idea what he might have known.'

'Well then, that is where to start, is it not?' said Sofia, decisively.

James pulled her towards him and held her close. She had cut through his confusion in a moment and he felt better already. 'I don't know what I would do without you. You help me to see so clearly.'

Later, as he lay in Sofia's bed, James tossed and turned, yet again unable to sleep. His mind was haunted by images of DeClichy lying in the morgue, pale and lifeless. When he finally managed to drop off it was only fitfully. In his dreams DeClichy opened his eyes and sat up as he was examining him. So vivid was the sight, he fancied he could sense the smell of the place, the sharp aroma of disinfectant mingling with the stench of death. DeClichy clutched his wrist and looked at him, his eyes full of sadness. 'Remember the news,' he whispered and a single tear ran slowly down his face. It was the colour of fresh blood.

James woke with a start. Sofia sighed gently and turned towards him. '*Che cosa c'è?*' she murmured.

He shook his head. 'Nothing, my darling. Go back to sleep.'

He lay awake until the sun came up, DeClichy's plea echoing through his mind. Remember the news . . . what could that mean? It invoked a memory, though, something that had been driven to the back of his brain by all that had happened. He was certain that it held the key to the murders. All he had to do was remember – and that was the one thing that eluded him.

When he arrived at the museum the following morning he fully intended to tell Lombroso and Ottolenghi of his thoughts about the death of DeClichy. However, they were far too preoccupied with putting Lombroso's plan into action to be interested in anything James had to say. A meeting with Tullio at Al Bicerin had been arranged in order to persuade him to round up suspects with the correct physical characteristics. It was obvious that Lombroso was excited at the prospect of seeing his theories put into practice – and his enthusiasm was infectious. Having listened to him outline his views again, James was keen to see how it worked out, despite his doubts as to whether it would catch the killer. When they walked into the café, Borelli was there, sipping his *bicerin* and peering through his glasses at the morning newspaper. James smiled inwardly. Even though everyone was critical about the standard of Baldovino's journalism they seemed only too keen to read his work. Borelli looked up and grinned amiably.

'Good morning, gentlemen. I see the Pilgrim has been in touch with Baldovino again.'

Lombroso looked surprised. 'Really? So soon? What has he to say?'

'Not much. He is gloating over the death of DeClichy. He calls him "*ciarlatano* – the charlatan".'

'That is interesting. I see the Pilgrim has some criminological knowledge, enough to express an opinion, at any rate,' Lombroso said.

'And Baldovino, does he say anything?' Ottolenghi asked.

Borelli handed the newspaper over to him. 'See for yourself. I've read enough.' He looked to Lombroso. 'I hear you were turned away from the mortuary yesterday.'

Lombroso pursed his lips. 'Indeed, I was. How fast news travels.'

Borelli nodded. 'Especially when the source is Machinetti.'

'The professor has a plan that will shut Machinetti up once and for all,' announced Ottolenghi, gleefully.

Lombroso inclined his head with what was undoubtedly false modesty. Borelli raised his eyebrows. 'And what might that be, Cesare?'

At that moment Tullio entered and joined them at their

already overcrowded table. Once drinks were ordered Lombroso outlined the details of his plan to Tullio who listened politely, without comment. James could sense, however, from the look in his eyes, that he held similar doubts to his own. Once Lombroso had finished Tullio sat and sipped at his drink thoughtfully.

'It would not be an easy task,' he said finally.

'Indeed, but anything worth the effort seldom is,' Borelli said. 'Personally, I think it is a stroke of genius. The professor here is famous throughout Europe for his theories. Do you doubt them, Tullio? And if so, on what basis?'

Tullio looked a little worried then. Clearly he did not wish to upset Lombroso, given his influence – the professor might have had enemies, but he also had strong support from some very influential quarters in the city so Tullio was obviously in a difficult position. To put Lombroso's ideas into action would alienate Machinetti still further, assuming he could overcome his almost inevitable opposition. But not to . . . Finally he spoke.

'I will do all I can to make this happen, Professor, but—'

Lombroso slapped him on the back with some force. 'That's a good fellow. I knew we could rely on you!'

'But if it does not meet with any success I feel it is my duty to warn you that there could be quite severe consequences. It will be difficult to undertake such an exercise without attracting attention. Baldovino will no doubt wish to cover this in detail. If we fail, then all of our careers may be in jeopardy.'

'My dear fellow,' Lombroso cried, 'how can we fail? My theories are correct. It is all about the criminal type. There is absolutely no doubt in my mind and if we act on them we will catch our killer. After all, how many murderers have been incarcerated as a result of my work?'

He looked round for an answer. Borelli provided it. 'Countless numbers, no doubt, Cesare. Many men are languishing in jail as a result of your efforts.'

'Exactly! Well put, Adolfo. So you see, Tullio, there is really nothing to worry about.'

Tullio smiled thinly. James could see that he was not quite so sure and he shared that uncertainty. In his opinion they would have been better served by looking more deeply at the murder of DeClichy. Something with that whole affair did not, to his mind, sit right, though he could not say exactly what it was.

James was not sure quite how he managed it but Tullio persuaded Machinetti to follow Lombroso's instructions and arrest all known criminals with the specified physical characteristics and a connection, however tenuous, to Lombroso. In the end there were not many on the list that Lombroso thoughtfully provided, once those with an alibi had been excluded.

Tullio hinted later that he detected a glint of satisfaction in Machinetti's eye when he was asked to cooperate, as if he knew that it would only serve to tarnish Lombroso's reputation further and give his enemies even more ammunition than they already possessed. Machinetti insisted on bringing in Baldovino as an observer so that, as he claimed, the people could see that something was being done.

James, Lombroso and Ottolenghi were all present at the carabinieri headquarters when the suspects were brought in, and a motley crew they were. Unfortunately, the officers had been given the wrong instructions, no doubt also by courtesy of Machinetti's intervention, and had been trawling through the streets of Turin for days, arresting anyone who fitted the description issued, regardless of their connection or otherwise with Lombroso.

As a result the place was in chaos and Baldovino sat in a corner grinning slyly at the confusion. If Lombroso was worried, he did not show it, but one could not say the same of Tullio, whose face was a study in misery as the noise grew louder with each protesting criminal escorted through the doors. He tried his best to create some order out of the chaos by eliminating those who had an alibi or did not know Lombroso, but all of this took time and it gave an overall impression of incompetence even though none of it was Tullio's doing.

It was a peculiar spectacle and at times James thought that it resembled a cartoon from *Punch*. Each group of ne'er-do-wells seemed more grotesque than the last and the oaths and curses that emitted from their mouths were both colourful and often creative. Lombroso, and sometimes Borelli, sat at the heart of it all, leaning on their silver-topped canes and observing with, in Lombroso's case, a kind of detached interest and in Borelli's case, amusement.

This pandemonium took several days until finally the suspects were whittled down to five, all of whom had taken part in Lombroso's experiments or been turned down by him at one point or another. At long last they were ready to begin interviewing them.

The first was a fellow called Ratti. He had coarse features, including a large, uneven jaw and a flat bulbous nose. His skin was swarthy and pockmarked. His details told them that he was from Sicily originally and had come to Turin in search of work. He looked completely bemused.

Lombroso peered at him over his glasses. 'Signor Ratti – we have met before, have we not?'

Before Ratti could reply Machinetti burst in, as if he expected to find them all sitting round the table planning a crime. Tullio followed in his wake, looking sheepish.

'Machinetti, what are you doing here?' Lombroso asked tersely.

'I am here to interrogate *my* suspects,' Machinetti said pointedly. Lombroso sighed and looked imploringly at Tullio, who shrugged helplessly. Clearly it was out of his hands.

Lombroso turned again to Ratti. 'So do you know me?'

Ratti nodded feebly. 'You measured my feet.'

Lombroso nodded. 'Ah yes.' He turned to James. 'It was a preliminary study that Ottolenghi and I conducted last year. We were measuring the anomaly of prehensile feet where the first two toes had an ability to grasp objects – as a monkey does. The results were most interesting.'

'You drew them,' Ratti added in wonderment. 'Why did you do that?'

'We wanted to record the shape which indicates—'

'Enough!' Machinetti cried, impatiently. James saw Tullio flinch. 'Did you kill Giuseppe Soldati?'

Ratti looked at him and frowned in confusion. He shook his head, apparently unable to speak.

'Did you know Soldati?' Tullio asked, gently.

Ratti shook his head again.

'Then how do you know you did not kill him?' Machinetti asked triumphantly. Tullio stared at him. Ottolenghi started to snigger. Machinetti's face reddened as he realised the stupidity of his question.

'Do you drink at La Capra?' Tullio asked.

'Sometimes,' Ratti replied cautiously.

'Are you sure you do not know Soldati? He drank there regularly.'

There was a pause. 'I might do.'

'He looked like a monkey,' added Lombroso.

Ratti's eyes lit up. 'Yes, I remember – monkey man! Was that him?'

'Almost certainly. Did you like him, this monkey man?'

Ratti shrugged. 'Not much. He was stingy. He never bought a drink, except for one night. I never saw him after that.'

Lombroso leaned towards him. He instinctively sat back in his chair. 'Did I pay you for your feet?'

'Yes, you did. Most generous, sir.'

'So you hold no grudge against me then.'

'Not at all, sir. I'll work for you again if you like. I've got hands too. You can measure them.'

Lombroso grinned at him. 'That won't be necessary at the moment but I'll keep you in mind.'

'Thank you, sir, I'm sure.'

Machinetti looked at Ratti sourly. 'How do you make a living? Theft, pickpocketing, robbery?' He moved towards him and bent down until they were face to face. 'Murder?'

'I'm an honest man, as far as I can be. I never killed any-one,' Ratti protested.

'Do you know anyone who would wish to harm Soldati or the professor here?' Tullio asked.

Ratti thought for a moment and looked at Lombroso. 'There has been some talk about a man who wishes you ill, sir. But I do not know any more than that.'

Lombroso looked shaken. Tullio seized Ratti by his scruffy lapels. 'What have you heard?'

'Just rumours, nothing more, about a man who holds a grudge.'

'What kind of grudge?' Tullio asked.

'I don't know, sir. Really I don't. I've told you all I know.'

'This man – have you seen him in La Capra?' Tullio barked.

'No, sir. I mean . . . I mean I have drunk there but I don't know who this man is.'

Lombroso sighed and smiled at him wearily. 'Will you tell me if you hear anything more?'

'Indeed, sir, I will.'

'Good man. Here is something for your trouble.' Lombroso tossed a few coins onto the table. Ratti seized them gratefully and got up to leave.

'Wait a minute,' Machinetti snapped. 'Did I tell you that you could go?'

Ratti looked at him fearfully. Machinetti paused and narrowed his eyes suspiciously. 'Now you can leave and be sure to keep out of our way!'

Ratti scuttled away and James couldn't help feeling sorry for him. He seemed a million miles away from Lombroso's criminal type, in all but looks, that was. Still, there was something about his answers that did not seem quite right. When he was talking about the man with a grudge Ratti had looked terrified, particularly when La Capra was mentioned. It seemed to James that this was a man who knew more than he was saying.

Lombroso himself seemed deep in thought. He was clearly rattled by the suggestion that someone wished to harm him in some way. It made all of this seem more real somehow. Before, it had all been speculation, but now that it seemed likely that somebody really was out to get him, it changed everything.

The interviews continued but none seemed particularly helpful. Of the remaining four suspects only one appeared to hold any kind of grudge against Lombroso and that was merely because he had been turned away from one of the experiments for being drunk. All of them, though, had heard some kind of rumour about a man wishing Lombroso some kind of harm, although none of them could give any detail, even when pressed. Overall the exercise had been a complete disaster. All it had achieved was a gift of further moral superiority to Machinetti, in his eyes anyway, and a ticking off for Tullio.

Baldovino, of course, made the most of it and was busy not only painting the professor as a fool but also whipping up people's fears with graphic rehashes of the murders, giving all the most gruesome details. These were illustrated with clumsy drawings of screaming women and bodies with limbs missing. He was not the only one. All the newspapers were vying with each other as to who could produce the most sensationalist stories.

Since DeClichy's murder the atmosphere in the city had palpably changed. Before his death the victims were just criminals and people thought that they were more likely to meet a violent death, so the public did not worry. Now a respectable academic had been killed as well as a woman, and that made a big difference to how people felt. At night the streets were practically deserted. Extra carabinieri had been drafted in from rural areas and posted around the city, creating a 'visible police presence' as Machinetti was quoted as saying in Baldovino's column. Several arrests were made after well-meaning 'witnesses' had reported strange noises or behaviour from acquaintances and even strangers. Suddenly people had started to care. Until then, no one outside their small circle had known enough to connect the first three killings. But now there was a new urgency about the situation for all involved. All of this was made worse by adverse weather conditions. The warm weather had been replaced by a thick fog which had descended on the city shortly after DeClichy's murder and showed no sign of abating. This unnerved people even more. The sound of footsteps became even more of a potential threat when one couldn't see who they belonged to.

A gaggle of reporters had taken to hanging around outside Lombroso's museum, accosting everyone who went in or out. James himself had been forced to fend them off several times as they shouted out their questions in mocking tones.

'Has the professor solved it yet?' 'Is he as clueless as everyone says?' 'I've got big ears – am I the killer?'

The symposium had continued, although quite a few people had left following the bad publicity. Now only the real enthusiasts were left which, Lombroso said, meant that they could get down to some real business – whatever that meant.

James himself was worrying about a number of things, none of them to do with his work. Mostly he worried about Sofia because she was part of a world that he knew little of and he was concerned for her safety, particularly since the death of her friend Rosa.

Since the interviews with Ratti and his associates, little progress had been made and James was getting impatient. He wanted to resolve this case. Then perhaps he would be able to plan his future. He decided to follow what seemed to be the only lead they had   Ratti's remark about the man with a grudge. No one else seemed to think it important, but James had recognised raw fear when he saw it. God knows he had felt it himself more than once in the last few years, so it was hardly surprising. He decided to pay Ratti a visit using the address he had noted down after they had met at the police headquarters. He did not tell anyone in case nothing came of it.

When he got there, a filthy basement room in a building that looked as if it was on the verge of being condemned, James thought it was unoccupied. He had knocked loudly and cried out Ratti's name but there was no reply. He bent down to look through the grimy windows – they were barred, giving the impression of a cell – but he could see nothing.

'What do you think you're doing?' James looked up to see the face of an elderly man who looked and smelt as if he had last encountered soap and water a decade ago. His trousers were so filthy they were almost solid and his shirt – if that was indeed what it was – hung off him in shreds. The whole ensemble was finished with a brightly coloured shawl with large red flowers on it, the only relatively clean piece of clothing he appeared to possess.

'I'm just paying Signor Ratti a visit,' James said. 'But he doesn't seem to be at home.'

'He's there, all right. He probably thinks you're a bailiff or the police.'

'Well, can you ask him to open the door?'

'I don't know about that. Are you?'

'Am I what?'

'Are you a bailiff or the police?'

'No, I'm just a friend.'

'You say that,' the old man said doubtfully, 'but you're

foreign – you might be a murderer. There's one on the loose. It says so in the papers.'

James took a deep breath. 'I am from Scotland. I am not a bailiff. I am not a policeman and I am *not* a killer. I am, however, getting tired of waiting.'

He took a few coins out of his pocket and jangled them in his hand.

'Now why didn't you say?' the old man said lugubriously, holding out his own hand. James gave him the coins and the man went down the steps and started to unlock the door.

'He must be in. I heard a row only a few minutes ago,' he said, standing back to allow James to enter.

The room smelt almost as bad as the old man. Some of the fog began to swirl in through the door and James squinted through the gloom. There were piles of newspapers stacked precariously in every available space, looking as if they might topple over at any moment. He saw what looked like a heap of rags in the corner – and – was that blood seeping out from underneath? Steeling himself, he looked more closely. It was a body, almost certainly that of Ratti, although from the state of him it was difficult to tell. He was clutching a note in his left hand and it had the familiar bloody writing on it.

Before he could perform even a perfunctory examination he heard a noise in an adjoining room, a movement of some kind – casual, almost careless. He froze.

James looked at the old man who stood in the doorway and stared at him as if he was mad. He put his finger to his lips and walked slowly towards the noise, moving carefully through the debris so as not to alert whoever it was. Then there was the sound of a loose floorboard creaking. James stopped. It creaked again. He began to move once more. He crept slowly, like a hunter after its prey, foot after foot, his nerves making his whole body seem to tingle.

Suddenly there was a loud crash as one of the piles of papers, disturbed by movement, fell over onto another and then another and another in a domino effect. He heard a door slamming. He rushed towards the noise and saw someone climbing some steps at the back of the building. James ran out and found himself in a narrow alleyway. He looked to the left and right but could see little through the swirling fog. He thought he saw movement to his left, so he ran towards it but he could barely see ahead of him, so thick was the murky cloud. Then he thought he heard the sound of footsteps running so he followed that. There were openings into all kinds of backyards and buildings – it was a veritable labyrinth with possible hiding places everywhere he looked – but they were deserted. Then he came to a dead end. Whoever he had pursued had escaped. He slapped the wall in frustration. It was the killer. He was sure of it. Slowly he trudged back to Ratti's place.

When he got back he found two carabinieri officers kneeling by Ratti's body, as if worshipping at a shrine. One was middle-aged with a jutting chin and a defiant expression. The other was very young, little more than a boy really. His ears were large and stuck out from his head almost at right angles.

'He's had it,' said the older one with an air of fascination. He looked up at James. 'Who are you?'

'I found the body. Will you send for Inspector Tullio and Professor Lombroso?'

'What about Marshal Machinetti?'

James sighed. 'Him too.'

The officer nodded and the younger boy scrambled to his

feet and left the room, still looking over his shoulder at the body as if he could not bear to shift his gaze.

Once he had left, James began to search the scene. The carabinieri stood guard by the body so he could not examine Ratti further. He knew that if he waited for Machinetti and reinforcements to come there was every possibility that they would tramp all over the area and obscure any trace of evidence that might have been left. As he moved through the room he could hear Dr Bell's mantra in his head, words from *A Manual of Medical Jurisprudence*.

'The first duty of a medical jurist is to cultivate a faculty of minute observation . . . A medical man, when he sees a dead body, should notice everything.'

Carefully he looked about him, gently pushing the debris from the fallen piles of papers aside to make sure that nothing of significance lay beneath. At first the officer watched his every move but he soon got bored. Before long he was leaning against the wall, his eyelids drooping as James conducted his search.

Initially he thought that there was simply nothing to find and then he saw it, not far from Ratti's broken body. It lay next to an overturned glass, almost as if it was mocking him: a small but distinctive red and gold band made of cardboard. At first he didn't think it was necessarily significant but then it hit him. He had seen something similar before.

24

We can conclude that abnormalities of moral character, which in an adult would constitute criminality, appear in greater proportions in the child. Lombroso, 1884 p 196

An hour or so later a crowd of people had gathered and there were some reporters too. James was standing outside at a distance from them with Lombroso and Ottolenghi. He had told them about his pursuit of the killer but not about the piece of cardboard. He needed to work out where he had seen it before. He was certain it was important but he didn't yet know why. Besides, there was some further information he was waiting for, something that might make all the difference to their investigation. But he wanted to wait until all the strands were complete before he presented them to Lombroso.

Machinetti and Tullio had disappeared inside the building. A few moments later Machinetti came out. Uncharacteristically he said nothing but merely nodded at Lombroso as a familiar figure carrying a notebook ran towards him from the crowd. Machinetti looked with distaste at his thin face with its sharp features. It was Baldovino, no doubt seeking another scoop for the *People's Voice*.

'Marshal, this is the sixth murder in a short period of time

– our readers are beginning to wonder why you haven't caught the brute.'

Machinetti's face began to redden but he still was silent. He tried to move away but the reporter danced around him, preventing him from escaping.

'Is it carabinieri incompetence? Is it true your position is under review?'

'Giardinello!' Machinetti bellowed.

As Giardinello approached, the reporter raised his hands in mock capitulation.

'Just informing our readers, Marshal. Six murders . . .' He held up his fingers in Machinetti's face.

'Get lost, Baldovino. I have nothing to say. Giardinello!' Machinetti bellowed again.

'Nothing to say to the *People's Voice*! Now how's that going to look, Marshal? The people have a right to know.'

Machinetti scowled at Baldovino. He looked as if he wanted to say a great deal but was making every effort to keep quiet. Fortunately, at that moment Giardinello arrived and escorted Baldovino away, to Machinetti's evident relief.

'I take it the victim is definitely Ratti?' Ottolenghi said.

'Looks like it,' replied Machinetti curtly. 'Giovanni Ratti, army deserter and recidivist. One of your interviewees . . .' he added malevolently.

Lombroso seemed momentarily crestfallen.

'May I examine the body?' he asked in an unusually polite manner.

Machinetti paused, as if wondering whether or not to be difficult. He apparently decided that he couldn't be bothered and nodded. Baldovino's words seemed to have shaken him. According to Tullio, Machinetti had been trying his best to keep any hint of police incompetence out of the press by encouraging them to focus on stories involving Lombroso. Until DeClichy's murder he had mostly succeeded. But now the public were frightened, just as Baldovino wanted them to be, and Machinetti looked to be distinctly unsettled by the prospect of further press attention, particularly as it was likely to be negative. He had been subjected to it before when the girl was kidnapped and murdered and it had cost him a promotion. Now he was hoping for a political career, he could not afford a repeat. But Baldovino was reputed to be almost as aggressive and ambitious as Machinetti was.

It seemed to James that if the reporter smelt a story he would pursue it like a terrier until he got what he wanted – and the way things were going that was likely to be Machinetti's head on the mayor's block. Ottolenghi had often spoken of Machinetti's ambition to be mayor himself one day and the power that the position would give him.

Lombroso, Ottolenghi and James went into the building, escorted by Tullio who handed Lombroso the note.

'Mmm. That's interesting,' he said, passing it to James. 'What do you think, Murray?'

'It isn't like the others, though it still looks to be written in blood. There is just one word: *FINITO.*'

'The end? The end of what?' Tullio wondered.

'The murders, perhaps,' Lombroso said, looking mournfully down at the body. 'Who knows?'

The face had been bashed in and it looked as if some effort had been made to carve away the chin. As if this wasn't bad enough, a piece of skin had been carved from Ratti's chest and was draped over his neck. On it was written, in the form of a rudimentary tattoo, 'I will come to a miserable end.'

'He got that right, well enough,' Tullio said.

Lombroso winced as he looked closely at the carnage

before him. 'The murderer carved that into Ratti's chest himself. The worst of it is that I cannot say for sure that he was already dead. There is quite a lot of blood so I fear that he was mutilated whilst still alive, though I doubt he was conscious. I'm guessing that he would have died from blood loss soon after.'

'Did you know him well before the interview?' asked James.

Lombroso stood up and said, sadly, 'Not really. I spoke to him briefly while he was in military prison and he showed me his tattoo. See, here on his arm?'

James peered at the body and saw the figure of a naked woman etched on Ratti's arm, with *Mother* written at the base.

'He was so proud of it. I remember us laughing at the inscription. He was trying to be ironic, I think. Then I invited him to take part in our foot measurement experiment.' He sighed and took off his glasses in order to rub his eyes. James thought that he was looking tired.

'Are you certain that it was blood loss that killed him?' Tullio asked. 'How did the murderer keep him still enough?'

Lombroso examined the body more closely. 'Yes, I am certain. Prior to the mutilation I think he may have been given some kind of a sedative – chloral hydrate would do the trick. And look at his left hand.'

The man was clutching an empty hip flask.

Lombroso went on, 'It looks to me as if he was offered some drink laced with the drug. Once it took effect he was at the mercy of the killer. It would have had an almost total paralytic effect.' He continued to examine the body, paying particular attention to the left shoulder. He stood up and looked at them significantly. 'It is exactly as I thought.'

James started. He could swear that he had a seen a faint movement from the body. There it was – nothing more than a slight twitch of a finger, but it was unmistakable.

'The man's still alive!' he exclaimed. He knelt by the body, lifting the hand to feel for a sign of life. 'Yes, there is a faint pulse. Get this man to an infirmary now!'

Suddenly there was a roar of pain and the 'body' tried to sit up. Ratti tried to speak and James put his ear to the man's lips.

'What are you trying to tell me?' he asked gently.

At that moment Machinetti arrived with Tullio close behind him. 'That is enough! Come away from the body,' he barked as if they had been trespassing.

'Firstly, this man is not a body. He is alive!' Lombroso beckoned to James, who left Ottolenghi to tend to Ratti, groaning more loudly now with the pain of his dreadful injuries.

Machinetti looked on in shock as two carabinieri approached and began to lift the man onto a makeshift stretcher ready to be taken to the infirmary.

'Did he speak? What did he say?' Machinetti asked James, completely ignoring Lombroso.

'He said "Do not trust him".'

'Who did he mean?' Machinetti said.

James shrugged. 'He did not say anything else.'

'Are you sure? Did you listen carefully?'

'Of course I'm sure,' James replied indignantly.

He watched as Machinetti tried to speak to Ratti as he was being taken away but the man had lapsed into unconsciousness. James wondered if Ratti would say anything more. It didn't seem likely, given the amount of blood he had lost and his rather cryptic comment merely served to deepen the mystery further. Who should he or they not trust?

Lombroso paused, as if taking stock. 'Now, it's back to the museum, gentlemen. There is much to discuss.'

They followed him as he strode away from the scene. James put his hand into his pocket and felt the piece of cardboard there. If he was right, it could provide the answer to this dreadful puzzle. But if he was wrong, then they would have to rely on Ratti. He shivered. The fog was even thicker now and glowed a ghastly yellow colour. This was certainly a devilish city in so many ways. Still, they had a surviving victim and a clue. Perhaps they were nearer to a solution now than they had ever been.

Back at the museum, Ottolenghi, Tullio and James sat in the laboratory, deep in their own thoughts. A message from the infirmary had been delivered. Ratti was deep in a coma from which he was not expected to wake. Having heard this, Lombroso had gone to his study 'to think'.

James took this opportunity to update Tullio on his thoughts that the killer might have practised his horrific skills before attempting the 'tribute' killings.

Tullio frowned. 'That's an interesting theory. You think that there may have been attacks prior to Soldati's murder.'

'It has to be possible at least, given the way everything seems to have been planned,' James said. 'Could it be checked?'

'I don't see why not.'

'I hope you're right, James. Without it, unless Ratti wakes up, we are no nearer to tracking the killer down than we were at the beginning,' Ottolenghi said.

James was about to contradict him – they did have some leads to work on – but he was interrupted.

'Don't be so sure of that,' announced Lombroso, who was standing in the doorway. His usual certainty seemed to have returned. He wore a strange expression – not quite triumphant but certainly there was an air of smugness about him as if he had just won an argument. James wondered how much of their conversation he had overheard.

'Has the killer left some other trace behind that we can use?' asked Ottolenghi eagerly.

Lombroso shook his head. 'No, he is too intelligent for that, I'm afraid.'

James almost contradicted him but thought the better of it. He wanted to be sure of his ground before he said anything.

Tullio got to his feet. 'So what have you deduced, Professor?'

'I believe that we are looking for a new kind of criminal type!'

'And what are the characteristics?' Tullio asked.

James felt more than a little disappointed. It seemed to him that they had been here before.

'Let us examine the evidence,' Lombroso said as he strode into the room towards the blackboard.

He went through each criminal type from morally insane to mattoid – detailing again each characteristic both in body and mind. James thought that Lombroso kept restating his theories because they were comforting in their familiarity. They were his only constant and he returned to them with a sort of desperation in an effort to explain the terrible events that threatened to bring a premature end to his career. But James was struggling to find any relevance in the application of Lombroso's ideas to the matter in hand. The criminal they were seeking seemed to not only defy description but also any classification as a type. He wanted to focus on real tangible clues, not just theoretical concepts.

'I believe that we are on the threshold of a new discovery,' Lombroso announced dramatically. 'I have not encountered a criminal before who is so artful, so creative in his activities. He must be a fully functioning member of society to have avoided detection for so long and yet his crimes are so hideous that they must be motivated by something extremely potent, such as intense hatred. This person is two-faced in that he is, to all intents and purposes a fully functioning and probably rather charming individual. However, he has a dark side that allows him to commit his crimes without compunction. Gentlemen, may I introduce you to the schizoid criminal.'

At this point Lombroso actually stood aside as if he was revealing a person who was present in the room with them. They sat in silence for a moment, taking in what he had said. James did not think these conclusions were particularly new. That the killer hated Lombroso had become only too clear over the last few weeks – but could it be more complex than that?

'Is it just hatred we are seeing here?' he suggested.

Lombroso looked at him, nodding. 'You are right, Murray. He may well love or hate me, perhaps even both, given his apparent obsession with me. But the important factor to understand is that he has learned to hide his true feelings.'

'That would be quite an achievement if the emotions are as intense as they seem,' James said.

Lombroso looked over his glasses at him. 'It is as if he is two people, Murray. The world sees one person and yet his inner life reveals another; hence the term "schizoid", from the Greek meaning separate or apart.'

379

James suddenly remembered hearing something about this kind of condition before. 'Hasn't Oskar Reiner written a paper on something similar?'

Lombroso nodded. 'Indeed. I believe Reiner identifies it as a disease of the brain. He discusses the condition in relation to sexual proclivities. Here, of course, it has led to criminality without a sexual motive. The cunning and ingenuity displayed by our killer is typical of the morally insane but it is combined in this case with the savagery of the primitive or atavistic offender. He will appear to the outside world as a perfectly normal person but this hides an inner turmoil that is manifesting itself in these crimes.'

'Then how are we ever to catch him?' Ottolenghi said in despair.

Lombroso went over to him and placed a hand on his shoulder. 'His hatred will get the better of him before long. I am sure of it.'

Tullio stood suddenly. 'I have an idea. It's not exactly scientific policing, but it could work.'

'Go on,' Lombroso said.

'Based on this new criminal type of yours it seems that we can conclude that this man loves or hates you to the level of obsession, Professor. Is that right?' Tullio asked.

Lombroso sighed. 'So it would seem.'

'Then his obsession will drive him. He will want to show you his work either by murdering in your presence if he loves you or—'

'Making you his last victim,' Ottolenghi said.

'*Finito*,' Lombroso murmured quietly. 'Hence the question mark.'

'So if we were to put you in harm's way, Professor, then . . .' Tullio said.

James frowned. 'Isn't that a rather risky strategy?'

'Sometimes one has to take risks in the name of discovery, Murray,' Lombroso said, thoughtfully. 'This is scientific policing, Tullio, but based on criminal anthropology, not mere investigatory techniques!'

'I cannot guarantee your safety, Professor,' Tullio warned.

Lombroso smiled. 'Of course I am hoping that he will be caught before that happens. I will merely be the bait, the fly to catch the spider, as it were.'

And so after some discussion a plan was hatched. Wherever the professor went, one of the others would follow. Sooner or later, or so it was hoped, the criminal would reveal himself and the case could be solved. James was happy enough to assist but he could not help thinking that Lombroso's faith in his own theories might be somewhat misplaced. He decided that he would continue on his own path as well. Hopefully he might then be in a position to identify the killer before Lombroso put his own life in danger. Then, perhaps, the gates of Hell could be firmly and finally closed.

25

We believe that those individuals least responsible for their behaviour are most to be feared.   Lombroso, 1896 p 336

It was the final day of the symposium. They had gathered to hear a talk by Borelli on the use of criminal anthropology in criminal courts. Lombroso was then to close the proceedings with a short speech in reply. James could see Madame Tarnovsky dressed in black but still somehow managing to shine out like a precious stone in a sea of grey. Horton was there too, sitting with Gemelli and his two cronies. He looked smug, somehow, as if he knew something that the rest of the party did not. He waved a greeting but the look on his face was insincere. He was a strange man. James wondered again where he had disappeared to on the night of DeClichy's murder. Was he really in one of the local brothels? And what was it that he had been so worried about James finding out about his past?

On the other side of the room sat Father Vincenzo. James was surprised to see him. He did not think that this was a subject about which the priest had much interest. He looked engaged enough however, as he looked around him like a hawk seeking it out its next victim. James remembered the curious warnings he had uttered to Lombroso. Perhaps his fear for the consequences of the professor's work was genuine but still something told James that Father 'Hell' was a man to be wary of. His allegiance was to the Church and to himself and that made him a man who could not be trusted.

Tullio was also present, keeping a watchful eye on the professor. He beckoned James over. 'I've asked Giardinello to find records of violent assaults for the last six months. I haven't been able to check them yet but you're welcome to take a look yourself.'

James nodded. 'I'll do that.'

'I've left them at my office. Just ask and Giardinello will show them to you,' Tullio said.

James thanked him and went to find a seat. Part of him wanted to go to Tullio's office immediately but he forced himself to stay. He was still a student and Lombroso might not take kindly to his absence. The atmosphere was more subdued than at the previous talks but the level of interest was high as Borelli rose to his feet to speak.

'Ladies and gentlemen, I have come here today to discuss the application of criminal anthropology to criminal proceedings. It is my view that we should be wary of its use as, although it has much to commend it, mistakes are still all too easy to make.'

'Why don't you ask Lombroso about mistakes? He's becoming somewhat of an expert!' called out Horton in his American drawl. There was some muted laughter. Everyone knew of the events at the police station and it would take some time for Lombroso to live them down amongst his peers.

Borelli gave a mock bow in Horton's direction. 'Thank you, Dr Horton, for your comments, which are as helpful as ever.' More laughter followed and Borelli lifted his hands to quell the disturbance.

'If mistakes are made when testimony is given then the results can be catastrophic for all those concerned. Such errors can result in miscarriages of justice and the consequences that can follow on from them are truly tragic. Our work is still in its infancy and we should beware of intellectual arrogance and complacency that can infect us like a disease if we are not careful.'

James looked round at people's faces. He could see that they were not convinced.

Borelli continued, undeterred by an undercurrent of hostile muttering in the audience. 'When we give evidence in a trial we must always ask ourselves this question: are we sure of our ground? And if we are not, we should say so, loud and clear for all to hear. We should never present guesswork as fact, for to do so can bring about some terrible changes to innocent lives.'

There was some fidgeting. Perhaps, thought James, some of them were discomfited by the prospect that they could ever be anything less than certain.

Borelli went on for some time. Trained in the law as well as medicine, he knew his subject well. He gave various examples of where evidence had been wrong and how it had ruined the lives of those involved. It was a moving speech and a fitting end to the proceedings. Finally he came to an end and after the plentiful applause had died down, Lombroso got to his feet to reply and bring the symposium to a close.

'Fellow scientists,' he began. There was applause at this, for that was exactly how his audience wished others to see them.

'I thank Professor Borelli for his timely and interesting

speech. However, although I agree that we should be careful not to be intellectually arrogant, I would still like to remind us all of how useful our work can be in the maintaining of an orderly and just society.'

Lombroso looked around him at his audience. He had a way of looking which made each person feel as if he was addressing them directly.

'Knowing one's enemy is paramount in any battle and the war against crime which blights so many lives is no exception. If we can point at a man and say he is a criminal then we can rid society of this blight upon it. Some are unfortunate enough to be born to crime and our work means that we know who these people are. Because of this they can be removed from our society. But there must be a trial. They have to be given an opportunity to state their case. We are there at such occasions to ensure that justice is done and that the guilty are not able to confuse or lie to a jury. Our evidence is scientific and should not be doubted.'

Lombroso looked over to his old friend. 'Unlike Borelli here, I believe that errors are unlikely. I believe in science. I apply scientific methods in my work and this brings me certainty. Without certainty then we have only emotion and that is of little use in such matters. I am confident that I can use my science and know when a man is a murderer. '

The attention of the crowd was palpable. Everyone knew of the events that had cast a shadow over the symposium and there had been all kinds of speculation as to the possible outcome.

Lombroso went on, 'You all have heard about the tragedies of the past weeks. I can assure you as a scientist that the killer will be found. He will give himself away by his own characteristics – what he looks like, his background, his personality – all of these will bring him to justice and when he is found I will examine him and I will be able to say with complete scientific certainty that he is the one and that he must be punished.'

The audience rose as one and cheered and clapped and stamped their feet. Here he was again, Lombroso the showman. He was playing to his audience and they loved it. James looked round at their jubilant faces and wondered how many of them really believed in the certainty of criminal anthropology. Even Horton was on his feet, although James thought that his cheers were nearer to jeers. Only Father Vincenzo was silent. He shook his head slowly then turned and left the room. Presumably he felt that God and the Devil were more likely to be both their salvation and reason for crime and that science had little to do with anything. Perhaps, thought James, Lombroso, with his words of defiance, was merely tempting fate.

Eventually the audience drifted away to their respective hotels to ready themselves to leave. James wondered if the killer was one of their number.

Ottolenghi had been deep in conversation with Madame Tarnovsky but he came over once she made to leave. James waved at her but she did not see him. He was sorry not to have said goodbye. The last few days had been so hectic that he had not had the opportunity to attend much of the symposium.

'So it is all over for another year or so,' he said with a note of regret.

Ottolenghi nodded. 'Yes, but we still have this evening to look forward to.'

'This evening?'

'The professor asked me to tell you. He has decided to

hold one of his salons. Most people are not leaving Turin until tomorrow so he thought it would be pleasant for a select few to meet for one more time – as a kind of tribute to DeClichy. Oh, and there's something else.'

'What?' James asked, intrigued.

'The professor did say that there is to be a mystery guest, brought by Horton, apparently.'

'Interesting,' James said. 'Who on earth could it be?'

'Perhaps he's going to reveal the identity of the killer?' Ottolenghi suggested.

James thought that it was just the kind of dramatic stunt the professor might attempt to pull off. 'Sounds as if it could be an eventful evening.'

'Yes, perhaps.' Ottolenghi pulled out his pocket watch. 'Good. I think there is just time to go home and change. I'll see you later.'

'What about the professor?' James asked.

Ottolenghi looked over to Lombroso and James followed his gaze. Tullio was sitting not far from him, discreetly pretending to read a pamphlet. As Lombroso moved towards the entrance, Tullio followed at some distance behind like a guardian angel.

'I think he'll be safe enough,' Ottolenghi said.

As he walked to Tullio's office, James thought over the events since his arrival in Turin. There he had been, a young man on the threshold of something bright, new and honest – a future, a vocation. Then the first murder had happened and everything had changed. Each new death was more savage than the last and a solution still eluded them. The biggest conundrum of all was the murder of DeClichy. How did that fit in? He was no criminal. There was no mark on him, which had to be significant, and his disembowelment did not correspond to the other methods of dispatch and mutilation. And why was Rosa Bruno killed? She was a prostitute so she fitted the class of criminal but again the method was different and its execution less precise than the other murders. Was her death connected to something she knew? She had wanted to tell them something and they still had not worked out what. Could it be in relation to Oskar Reiner and his interviews at the brothel? It would be worth talking to Reiner directly about that. Hopefully an opportunity would present itself at the salon that evening.

James stopped in the Piazza San Carlo for a moment, looking in admiration at the elegant buildings, at the cafés beneath the porticoes where so much of Italy's history, both political and cultural, had been forged. How had Ottolenghi described it during their tour – the city's drawing room? That conversation had taken place only a few days ago and yet somehow it seemed as if months had passed. He had come to learn about criminal anthropology and, he hoped, about himself. Instead he had been plunged into an alien world of intrigue, murder and mutilation and was feeling increasingly disillusioned. Could Lombroso's criminal types really be of any practical application in a criminal investigation? Otto-lenghi seemed to think so and he was an ardent supporter of scientific policing. But still, he had been Lombroso's assistant for a while now and perhaps loyalty had clouded his judg-ment.

James sighed dejectedly as he crossed the square and reached Tullio's office which was in a smaller, less grandiose piazza. He had expected some difficulty in getting access to the papers but fortunately Giardinello was in the front office when he arrived and took him directly to them.

Tullio's office was in the basement, in a dark and musty corner. Giardinello opened the door and ushered him in. James looked around in astonishment. He had expected a dingy, windowless cell. Instead the room was large with a high window that, whilst narrow, ran right round three sides and let in a reasonable amount of light. There was a rug on the floor and pictures on the walls and in the corner was a sizeable bookcase. A large, leather-topped old desk stood in the centre. He sat behind it and picked up a photograph in an elaborate gilt frame. Tullio was standing looking proudly down at a young woman who was balancing a baby on her knee. At her side was a small boy with a mischievous grin. Tullio had never mentioned his family once, presumably wanting to keep his personal life separate from his work. James thought to himself how little he really knew about the people he had encountered in Turin over the past weeks. A tiny niggle started at the back of his mind. Ratti's last words before he lapsed into unconsciousness – 'do not trust him . . .'

He looked again at the photograph and imagined a similar picture of him and Sofia with their own children and felt a pang of jealousy. But no . . . it was no good dreaming of things that could never happen. He had to be realistic.

Putting the photograph firmly down, James turned to the matter at hand and began to look through the papers. It was a rather sorry catalogue, mostly gang-related attacks, or so it seemed. There was nothing to suggest any connection with the horrible mutilations that they had encountered.

He yawned and rubbed his eyes. He looked up at the window. It was almost dark. He would have to go soon if he wanted to get to the salon on time. He sighed and turned back to the pile of reports. He picked up the next piece of paper and then casually glanced down at what was underneath. Then he looked again. There was a paragraph of writing but at the bottom was a drawing of a torso with a mark carved into the upper left shoulder. The mark was in the shape of an inverted cross.

26

Madmen with pellagra, epilepsy and alcoholism often manifest homicidal and suicidal tendencies at the faintest provocation.

Lombroso, 1889 p 276

The salon was in full swing when James arrived, although the atmosphere was more subdued than last time. Ottolenghi came over immediately, wearing his usual amiable expression.

'*Buonasera*, James. I was beginning to think you weren't coming.'

'I was looking at those papers that Tullio found for me.'

Ottolenghi looked surprised. 'I didn't realise you were following that up. I assume you didn't find anything.'

James paused. Then, 'No,' he replied, 'nothing.' He heard those words again – 'Do not trust him . . .'

Ottolenghi shrugged. 'Well, it's hardly surprising. As if a killer would need practice. A man like that is of a particular type, as the professor has described. He is born to kill. Scientific policing is all very well, but it needs theoretical input to produce results. I'm beginning to see that now.'

James didn't agree with Ottolenghi but there was no point in arguing about it now. It merely stiffened his resolve to investigate in his own way. He looked around the room. 'Where's Horton?' he asked.

'No doubt he's hoping to make an entrance with his mystery companion.'

James grinned. Ottolenghi was right. Horton had a similar quality to Lombroso in that he enjoyed a certain amount of theatricality. He looked round at his fellow guests and their interaction – which was worthy of an anthropological study of its own. As ever, Lombroso was the centre of attention. He was holding forth on his latest ideas about Pilgrim and his likely characteristics, particularly in relation to his latest 'discovery', the schizoid criminal.

James was not sure of the wisdom of providing such a picture. Lombroso had, after all, been wrong before. Despite this he spoke with such authority and confidence that his ideas sounded compelling even though they didn't necessarily bear close examination. Those that surrounded Lombroso seemed to be agreeing with every word he uttered. The only exception was Borelli, who was at least asking him some questions. Even this gave the impression of a kind of comedic double act except, of course, that jokes were few and far between. Everything Borelli asked was met with an 'I'm glad you asked me that' or 'Ah yes, an excellent question, thank you,' as if it had all been set up in advance. Had it not been for Borelli's somewhat exasperated expression he might even have thought that it had.

James looked over towards the door and saw Sofia approaching. She smiled at him discreetly. She was carrying a platter of *stuzzichini* just like those he had tasted at the Caffè Norman. There were tiny ham rolls, mini toasts decorated with glistening olives and delicate crustless sandwiches. As she caught his eye she gave him a barely perceptible wink. James smiled and looked around to see if anyone had noticed but they were all too involved with their own conversations.

He wondered idly what would have happened if he had gone over to her, thrown the platter aside and taken her in his arms. Nothing good, he imagined.

'I see Gemelli's here with his chums,' he observed to Ottolenghi.

They looked over to the academics as they stood in a little huddle in the corner of the room, staring at Lombroso as he spoke. Every now and again Lombroso would glance over in his assistants' direction and nod cordially at them, leaving them little choice but to acknowledge him. Gemelli gave him a curt nod but the expression on his face was unmistakably hostile.

'I confess I'm not sure of the wisdom of inviting them,' Ottolenghi remarked.

'The professor's playing some sort of game with them, isn't he?' James replied. 'He's teasing them with the invitation. He must have known that they would be quite unable to resist it.'

'Perhaps, but it's a risky strategy,' Ottolenghi said. 'Let's not forget that Gemelli has already suspended Lombroso. He would not need much in the way of further ammunition to deprive the professor of his position on a permanent basis.'

'True enough, particularly given the press coverage so helpfully provided by Baldovino with the malevolent encouragement of our friend Machinetti.'

'That man's a fool!' Ottolenghi exclaimed.

'But a fool with influential friends,' said a voice behind them. It was Tullio, and they greeted him warmly. James looked at him differently. Seeing that photograph had given him an intimate glance into his life and as a result he felt he knew him better.

'Are you on duty?' he asked.

Tullio shrugged. 'Yes and no. I was invited as a guest but I'll be keeping my eyes open for anything unusual.'

'Surely the Pilgrim would not dare to strike here, in front of so many witnesses?' James said.

'It's unlikely, I grant you. But, from what the professor has said, he seems to know a good deal about his work.'

'So we may actually be in the company of a killer!' Ottolenghi exclaimed.

'It's possible, that's all I'll say. We can't be too careful.'

James looked round again at the assembled guests. Could one of them be a multiple murderer? It seemed incredible and yet so did much else about this whole affair. He wondered if he should mention the report he had found to Tullio. They were his papers, after all. But something made him pause.

As he observed the various guests in their various cabals he saw Oskar Reiner who beckoned James over. 'Herr Murray, I am glad to speak to you before I leave.' His hair and eyes seemed paler than ever.

'What can I do for you, Reiner?'

Reiner pulled him roughly though discreetly to one side, as if he was being arrested. 'Come with me. I don't want anyone to hear.'

James, curious to hear what he had to say, did not resist, though he wondered if such force was entirely necessary. He followed Reiner out of the door into the hallway where they skulked by a large aspidistra.

'I realise that you may think that I am overreacting by talking to you here,' Reiner said, 'but it could be a danger to you if we were overheard. At least one person, possibly two may have already lost their lives.'

James looked at him, startled by this revelation. 'So what is it?'

'It's about Horton . . .'

'Go on.'

'I was conducting some interviews with some prostitutes introduced to me by a woman named Rosa Bruno, the woman who was murdered.'

Remembering what Sofia had told him, James nodded and Reiner continued, 'I was asking them about the sexual proclivities of their clients, particularly involving violence. Both she and they told me about a particular client who had an overwhelming need to inflict pain.' He paused. 'Murray, I have heard many shocking things in my career, but what they told me . . . *Mein Gott*! Nothing could have prepared me for this individual's depravity!'

'And this individual was . . .'

'Horton, yes.'

'And have you told anyone else?'

Reiner looked down at the floor for a moment. When he looked up James was alarmed to see that his pale eyes were brimming with tears. 'That night at the opera . . . I had to . . . you must understand. I needed to speak to someone and I knew he had an interest.' He paused again as if he was willing himself to say the words.

'I told DeClichy – and now he is dead!'

Suddenly James remembered the expression on DeClichy's face as Reiner had whispered into his ear. No wonder he had looked so shocked. He took Reiner by the shoulders.

'Now listen. There is nothing to say that either you or even Horton has caused harm to either Rosa Bruno or DeClichy.'

'But if I had not told DeClichy—'

'You had to tell someone and he was investigating Horton, as you, as we *all* knew.'

Reiner nodded miserably.

'Reiner, I would have done the same in your place. There is nothing to reproach yourself about. Just leave it with me and I will tell the authorities as soon as I can.'

'Thank you, Murray,' Reiner said, shaking him by the hand. 'You will let me know what happens, will you not? Whether or not he has killed anyone, Horton is still dangerous.'

James nodded gravely. 'Indeed. That much is only too clear.'

Reiner left then and James stood for a moment, absorbing what he had learnt. This, presumably, was what Rosa Bruno had wanted to tell them and what had brought about her savage death. The same applied to poor DeClichy. No doubt Reiner would have been next. The more he heard about Walter B. Horton, the more James became convinced that he was the killer. The problem was that there was not, as yet, any direct proof. All they had so far was evidence of Horton's character and that in itself would not be sufficient to connect him to the killings. They needed more. And James hoped that if things turned out as he suspected then more was exactly what he would be in a position to provide.

He went back in and moments later a hush descended as Horton strode into the centre of the room as if the limelight belonged to him by right. Following behind him was a cloaked figure, slightly hunched. Its face was obscured by an enormous hood. It passed within about a foot of James and he had to turn away from the sour stench that surrounded it. Sofia was standing next to him and he heard a clatter as the figure passed by her. She had dropped her *stuzzichini*. James knelt down to start scooping up the food onto the platter but when he stood up Sofia had gone, he assumed to get a cloth or perhaps some more food.

People started to move away from Horton who was now standing in front of a striking painting of an African chief. It seemed to James that they wore similar expressions – a sort of amused superiority. Horton took a cigar from his pocket and lit it ostentatiously. The cloaked figure stood next to him.

James looked over towards Lombroso who was staring at the figure in fascination, his eyebrows raised in surprise. Borelli stood next to him, frowning. The figure slowly turned towards Lombroso and began to pull back the hood.

'Stop!' cried out Horton. 'Not yet!'

He need not have worried. The face of the figure was almost completely obscured by a carnival mask with the features of a wolf.

'What is the reason for this, Dr Horton?' Lombroso asked.

Horton smiled broadly. 'I have brought a subject for you to analyse, Professor.'

He uttered Lombroso's title with such contempt that it was clear he thought that the professor would not meet the challenge he appeared to be laying down before him.

Lombroso gave a short bow. 'How interesting. I would be delighted to assist. What would you like to know?'

Horton smirked at him. 'We have heard you talk of your theories so often, Professor, I thought it was high time you gave us a demonstration.'

'I see,' Lombroso said, politely. 'Exactly what questions would you like me to answer?'

Horton looked smug. 'What kind of a man is this? Is he a criminal, and if so, what variety? Describe his characteristics. Put your theory to the test, Professor. Are you prepared to take up the challenge?'

The professor removed his glasses and rubbed his eyes thoughtfully. For a moment James thought that he was going to decline Horton's request. 'I always enjoy a challenge, you know that, Horton.'

There was a ripple of applause. Gemelli looked particularly pleased but not, James assumed, for benevolent reasons. Ottolenghi looked concerned and James started to wonder if Lombroso had made an error in so readily picking up the gauntlet thrown down by Horton.

'There is one thing, however. I must see the face. Otherwise I cannot identify this man's type.'

The disguised man shook his head vehemently and Horton pursed his lips in thought. 'The man does not wish to be identified,' he said. 'But what if you could feel his features beneath the mask. Would that suffice?'

Lombroso stroked his beard thoughtfully. 'Yes, I believe it would.'

The atmosphere was highly charged as Lombroso strolled around the figure. Occasionally he would lean towards him, sniffing. James was surprised that he could bring himself to get so close given the disgusting aroma that emanated from the subject. Then he began to measure him, using what looked like a piece of string pulled from his coat pocket. He pulled out the ears and flapped them to and fro as if they were bits of paper. He felt beneath the mask for the nose and mouth. Then he picked up the hands and examined them closely through an eyeglass. Finally he made the subject march up and down as if on an army parade ground.

Lombroso sighed and rocked backwards and forwards on his feet. 'May I ask the subject some questions?'

Horton nodded. 'Not too many, mind. We don't want to make it too easy.'

Lombroso went to the back of the figure and peered over his shoulder. 'Has your head ever felt heavy?'

The figure cleared its throat. 'Yes, sir, it has, particularly in the summer months.' The voice was rough with an underlying whine. It sounded vaguely familiar.

'Mmm, interesting, interesting . . . And tell me now, do you ever suffer from headaches?'

'No, but in the winter I am light-headed.'

'Have you ever killed anyone?'

There was a sharp and universal intake of breath from the audience, for that is what they had become. Horton interjected, 'Come, come, Professor. That's cheating.'

'Are you liked by your neighbours?' Lombroso went on quickly.

'Only when I'm buying drinks, otherwise they hate me.'

'And your family?'

'Them too.'

'Would you kill?'

Horton stepped forwards as if he wanted to interject again but the figure answered before he could.

'I might.'

'Enough,' Horton said. 'It's time for your conclusions, Professor.'

There was a long pause and Lombroso stood with his hands in his pockets, looking into the distance. Finally he spoke.

'From the evidence present I think that we can conclude that this man is a born criminal – a thief, in fact. This is indicated by his physical characteristics – prominent ears, large nose and . . .' Lombroso stopped and suddenly the figure cried out.

'Ouch! That hurt. Did you see that? He pinched me!'

'As I thought,' Lombroso added, 'extreme sensitivity to minor pain.'

'Huh, minor!' the figure said.

'He also has a persecution complex and a penchant for eating mouldy polenta.'

'How could you possibly know that?' Horton asked, incredulously.

'From his odour, of course, Doctor. You should know that, as a medical man. I would guess that he suffers from some kind of mental condition brought on by the disease pellagra, which can in itself be a consequence of eating mouldy food.'

'Hmm, not bad, Professor, although the mental condition has yet to make its mark,' Horton said. 'Stupidity is not the same thing.'

The figure started to mutter angrily.

'Quiet!' Horton barked. 'No one asked your opinion. Anyway, haven't you something to give to the professor?'

The figure nodded and pulled an envelope from his pocket.

'We found this on the way in,' Horton said casually.

Lombroso took it from the figure and began to open it. People started to move closer in an effort to see what was in it but Tullio gestured for them to move back.

'What does it say, Professor?' James asked.

'Yes, read it out, Cesare,' Borelli said, eagerly.

'Is it from the Pilgrim?' Madame Tarnovsky asked.

'It is indeed,' Lombroso replied. He cleared his throat as if about to declaim a Shakespearean speech and began to read it out.

'Watch out for the man who laughs and looks ahead with small mobile eyes. Thin beard and little colour, there's nothing worse under the sun. These are some of my final tributes to you, Lombroso.' He looked up, a puzzled expression on his face. 'It is signed "the Pilgrim".'

'What does it mean?' James asked.

'They are popular Italian proverbs,' Lombroso replied. 'I have cited them before to demonstrate that my ideas are not out of step with public opinion. As to why they have been used here, well, I could not say for sure.'

'Clearly it is another example of the killer's twisted admiration for you, Cesare,' Madame Tarnovsky said firmly.

'Where and when did you cite them?' Tullio asked.

Lombroso sat down heavily on a nearby armchair. 'They appear in some notes I made for an article.'

'Well, obviously the killer has read it and used it for this,' Madame Tarnovsky said.

Ottolenghi shook his head. 'I'm afraid it's not as simple as that.'

Tullio frowned in confusion. 'Why, what do you mean?'

Lombroso sighed. 'I have not yet written the article. I was going to and then I put it to one side, awaiting some further research. As far as I know the notes are still somewhere in my study.'

'Unless they were taken in the burglary, Professor,' Ottolenghi said.

Lombroso shook his head. 'No, I was referring to my study here.'

James stared at him. That meant the letter writer had been here, in Lombroso's home.

There was some sympathetic murmuring and a large glass of brandy was brought to Lombroso who sipped at it with a faraway look in his eye. His guests stood about in groups talking worriedly. Only Gemelli seemed unconcerned. James couldn't hear all of what he was saying but it sounded more threatening than sympathetic. He heard the words 'last chance' and 'sheer carelessness' as well as 'sullied reputation'.

It wasn't long before guests began to drift away, bidding

somewhat muted goodbyes to their host. Lombroso seemed remarkably unaffected by it all, despite the underlying threat in the Pilgrim's letter. In fact, Borelli looked as if he had been more troubled by it than Lombroso. Soon, just the professor's immediate circle of friends and colleagues were left behind to offer support, if indeed it was actually needed. It was only then that they noticed that Horton and his mystery friend were nowhere to be seen.

27

According to Esquirol, some homicidal monomaniacs have a quiet, melancholy inconstant and impetuous character, while others are known for their kindness. When they are violent, the catalysts include the weather, abnormal indigestion, over-excitement of the nerves, religious exaltation, imitation, misfortune and extreme poverty. Lombroso, 1889 p 272-3

James, Ottolenghi and Tullio sat for a while, trying to make some sense of the letter and its contents. Tullio seemed reluctant to leave Lombroso's side, even for a moment, and had to be persuaded to move away from him, just a little. James had some sympathy with his feelings. The threat felt more palpable than before, although he was certain that none of the professor's immediate circle could be involved. Still, they did not know the whereabouts of Horton and his behaviour was suspicious to say the least, particularly in the light of Reiner's information.

'This just gets worse,' James said gloomily. 'Did you see Gemelli's face when he left?'

'I did,' Ottolenghi replied. 'I wouldn't be surprised if there is yet another meeting tomorrow.'

'What about Horton?' James asked Tullio.

'I have sent officers to his hotel to see if he has turned up there.'

'He certainly has some questions to answer,' Ottolenghi said.

Tullio nodded grimly. 'He has something to do with all of this, I'm sure of it.'

'He must be a prime suspect at the very least,' James said. 'He brought the letter and his behaviour has been odd from the beginning. And there's more.' He told them what Reiner had revealed earlier.

'It's horrible, of course, but it doesn't prove he's a killer. And somehow he doesn't fit in with the professor's description of a schizoid killer,' Ottolenghi said. 'He doesn't seem to have more than one personality, or if he has it certainly hasn't manifested itself.'

'But isn't that the point? There's a hidden side to him that most people do not see,' Tullio said.

'Perhaps so, but I certainly wouldn't describe him as charming,' James said.

'True,' Ottolenghi added, 'and he does not appear to be hiding any of his feelings. He seems pretty straightforwardly unpleasant to me.'

'All the same, we cannot be certain of his innocence just because he doesn't fit in with the professor's ideas.' James leant forwards and spoke more quietly. 'After all, he may be wrong.'

'I agree,' Tullio said. 'We obviously cannot dismiss Horton as a suspect. He should be questioned at the very least.'

Ottolenghi sat back in his chair and drained his glass. 'I don't know about you but I could do with a drink and maybe some coffee.'

'I'll go downstairs and ask Sofia to bring us some,' James

said, happy to have an opportunity to speak to her. He went down to the kitchen, full of anticipation, but when he got down there he could only see the other girl who had been helping out that evening.

'Where's Sofia?' he asked, suddenly feeling apprehensive.

'She went out, signor,' the girl replied, 'just after she dropped the plate.'

'Did she say why?'

'No, sir, she just went, but she looked . . .' The girl hesitated.

'Looked what?' he asked urgently.

The girl frowned. 'She looked frightened. I thought at first that it was because she dropped the plate and she was scared she would get into trouble, but that's not like her.'

'You're right. It isn't.' In a few short moments he was heading towards Sofia's rooms. He had to make sure that she was all right because her reaction was odd. As he approached the small piazza where she lived he saw her in the distance. She was sitting on a low wall outside her room, her head in her hands. He was about to call out to her when someone approached her from the other side. She stood up and James saw him seize her by the shoulders, lift his arm and strike her across the face. She struggled and screamed. James shouted out and began to run towards them. The figure turned and looked at him. Its shape seemed oddly familiar but he could not see clearly in the shadows and, taking advantage of the distraction, Sofia broke free from the figure's grip. To no avail – he grabbed her again and in doing so caused her to fall as James reached them. She lay motionless on the cobbles and the figure began to run. James was riven by indecision. Should he go after Sofia's attacker or stay and tend to her? In truth, there was no choice. He could not leave her lying in the street. He knelt down and saw blood trickling from a cut on her head. He held her in his arms and looked at her, fearing for a moment that he had lost her. But she was breathing steadily enough. He lifted her up and carried her back to Lombroso's house, where he knew she would be safe.

The following morning Sofia lay in bed, her dark hair cascading over the pillow like a strange, exotic head dress. She was dressed in a white cotton nightgown with lace around the cuffs and collar, not quite a shroud and not quite a wedding gown, but a parody of each.

When James had arrived with Sofia, Lombroso had examined her. He confirmed what James had hoped, that she had simply sustained a bump on the head and would make a full recovery with rest and care. Now, he looked at her from the doorway – as near to her as decency would allow. He longed to hold her hand, to sit by her and wait until she awoke so that his was the first face she would see. But he knew that was impossible and that made him even more determined somehow.

There was nothing practical he could do to help Sofia but at least he could try to find who had hurt her. He decided to pay a visit to the victim from Tullio's past cases, the man who had been unfortunate enough to have an inverted cross carved into his flesh. His name was Angiolo Sighetti and he worked as a meat porter in the Porta Palazzo market, so James made his way there. As Sighetti had a substantial criminal record for offences of petty theft the file had included a mugshot which James hoped would assist in identifying him. He was a sullen-looking man, short, stocky with blunt features. His hair looked to be dark but with a shock of white in the centre, giving him the air of a down-at-heel pit pony. Even with this distinguishing feature it took James longer than he thought to track him down but when he finally saw him it was obvious that he had got the right man.

Sighetti was heaving the carcass of a sheep onto his broad shoulders. The day was mild and the man's shirt was open to the waist. It flapped to and fro and every now and then the ugly raised scar tissue was left in plain sight. James walked towards him, weaving his way through handcarts and housewives, stalls and stockmen as well as the general market detritus generated by all of them.

'Angiolo Sighetti?'

The man looked suspiciously at him. 'Who wants to know?'

'I wanted to ask you about your attack.'

'I've already given a statement. That's all you're getting.' He started to walk away, the headless carcass bobbing up and down on his shoulder.

'I'm not a policeman.'

Sighetti stopped and turned.

'Then what are you, a journalist?'

'No, but I'll pay you for any information you give me.'

Sighetti stared at him for a moment and then nodded curtly. 'Just wait for me to dump this. I'll meet you over there.' He nodded in the direction of a shabby bar on the far side of the market. 'You can buy me a beer.'

A few moments later James was sitting opposite Sighetti as he picked up his drink and took a large gulp. He wiped the froth from his lips with the back of his hand and grinned. 'That's better. Now, what do you want to know, exactly?'

'Just tell me what happened to you.'

'It was at night. I was on my way home from my local bar, La Capra, and someone came up to me from behind.'

'Were you drunk?' James asked.

'A bit, I suppose. But what's wrong with that?'

'Nothing, nothing. But it might have made you easier prey.'

'Perhaps. But they were quick. Even a sober man couldn't have escaped.'

'They?'

'Yes, there were two of them. One held me from behind and pinned my arms to my side.'

'And the other? What did he look like?'

'I don't know. They slipped a hood over my head and I saw nothing.'

'Then what?'

'The second man carved me. *Merda*! It was painful. Look.' Sighetti pulled back his shirt to reveal his scar. 'It's the devil's mark, isn't it?'

'That's what some would say. Did you notice anything else?'

'I've thought about this long and hard but it only came to me a couple of days ago.'

'What?' James asked, leaning forwards.

'Two things. Firstly, the man holding me from behind stank to high heaven. It wasn't the usual thing – sweat, dirt. No, it was more like sour milk. That's the closest I can get anyway. Just the thought of it makes me want to heave.'

'And the second?'

'It was something the second man said after he'd carved me. He whispered it into my ear. I've no idea what it means.'

'Tell me.'

'I can't recall the exact words but it was something like: "A good man cannot be harmed, alive or dead." '

'So what happened then?'

'No idea. One of them hit me on the back of my head and I passed out. That's the last thing I remember.'

'Just one last question, the second man, did he have an accent?'

Sighetti scratched his head. 'I can't be certain but he sounded different. Not foreign, necessarily, like your good self, sir, if you don't mind me saying. No, if anything he spoke like my lawyer does – a bit posh, educated, you might say. Sounded just like him, in fact.'

'And your lawyer is from Turin?'

'I think so. He's the best in the city, that's for sure.'

James thanked Sighetti for his trouble and, having paid him, bought him another beer and thrown in a sandwich for good measure, he left.

It seemed that Sofia was right. Their killer had rehearsed his method, or part of it, at least once. This time the carving had been done alone and on the front of the chest rather than the back, presumably to test it out. But there had been no attempt to rehearse the main mutilations, at least not in Turin anyway. The problem was that although this new information was certainly of interest it did not take him any nearer to identifying the killer, or indeed his accomplice. It sounded as if it could be Horton, who spoke Italian like a native. But then it could also be practically anyone else. Still, that comment the second man had made to his victim had a familiar ring to it. Where had he heard it before? If he could work that out then he might be able to identify the killer.

James had only intended to take an hour or so to see his witness but it was almost two o'clock when he returned to Lombroso's house. He was admitted by the maid he had spoken to last night. Her face was tear-stained and for one

dreadful moment James thought that Sofia had taken a turn
for the worse.

'What is it?' he asked her fearfully. 'What's the matter? Is it
Sofia?'

'No, sir, it's the master, the professor.'

'What about him?'

'He's been arrested! The carabinieri came for him earlier
and took him away.'

'On what charge?'

The girl began to sob. 'Murder, signor! The ones in the
paper – they said he was the Pilgrim!'

There was a knock at the front door and James nodded to
the girl to open it. It was Ottolenghi and Borelli.

'You've heard, then,' Borelli said grimly.

'Machinetti finally got his way,' Ottolenghi added.

'Assisted no doubt by the influence of Gemelli,' Borelli
said. 'This will mean the end of Lombroso's career if we can't
sort it out soon.'

'Where is he?' James asked.

'He's being held at carabinieri headquarters,' Ottolenghi
said.

'Then what are we waiting for?' Madame Tarnovsky said as
she descended the staircase to join them, having been tending
to Sofia. 'Let's go and get him released. He isn't the killer.
We all know that. We just need to persuade that ridiculous
policeman Machinetti to see the truth.'

'What *is* the truth?' Borelli asked.

'What do you mean?' Ottolenghi said. 'You're surely not
suggesting that the professor killed all these people?'

'He has alibis for some of the murders,' James said. It
seemed strange to hear Borelli, of all people, one of Lombroso's

oldest friends and colleagues, speak as if he was unsure of his innocence.

'Some, not all,' Borelli said. 'What if he arranged them?'

'Why would he do that?' James asked again.

'To allow him to solve them, of course,' Borelli said. 'You heard him last night with his schizoid killer theory. He loved it!'

'Even Cesare doesn't love his work enough to kill,' Madame Tarnovsky said, scornfully.

'Can we really be sure of that?' Ottolenghi said quietly.

James looked at him and frowned. 'So even you're doubting him now.'

'He maybe a little over-zealous in his methods at times but he's no killer,' Madame Tarnovsky said. 'Anyway, I think it is time we gave Cesare the chance to answer for himself. We need to get him released.'

They agreed to go to carabinieri headquarters to see what could be done but Borelli declined. It was as if, James thought, he had given up on his old friend.

When they arrived they found Tullio sitting in the entrance hall looking rather lost.

'Have you spoken to Machinetti?' Ottolenghi asked.

'I have, but he won't budge,' Tullio said. 'Gemelli managed to persuade him that Lombroso was bluffing and had written all the letters.'

'So what can we do now?' James asked, sighing. 'If Machinetti's convinced we'll never get the professor released.'

There was a pause and then Madame Tarnovsky spoke. 'I believe I know the best way to approach Machinetti. Could we get him to speak to me, do you think?'

Machinetti was duly summoned with the assistance of Tullio. He came bristling into the room as if ready to attack.

'Ah, Marshal, how kind of you to see me,' Madame Tarnovsky said with her usual charm.

Machinetti seemed taken aback. Charm was clearly something he was not used to. He gave a short and uncomfortable bow.

'What can do for you, signora?' he asked.

'Could we speak in private, do you think?' she requested.

He nodded and escorted her into a nearby side room. A few minutes later he emerged, blushing like a young girl, and signalled to one of his men.

'Release Lombroso,' he ordered, brusquely. And with that he left quickly, presumably not wishing to witness his prime suspect leaving the premises.

Madame Tarnovsky soon joined them.

'How on earth did you manage that?' James asked in awe.

'I simply appealed to his better nature,' she replied, a knowing smile on her face.

'He has one then?' Ottolenghi asked.

Madame Tarnovsky shrugged. 'Well, perhaps not, but he does have one feature . . .'

'What's that?' James asked.

'His vanity,' she replied. 'I simply reminded Marshal Machinetti that the evidence against Cesare was scant and suggested that it might be better to release him and put him under surveillance. That way he could be certain of catching him red-handed.'

'So not only did you procure his release but also further police protection. Bravo, Madame. Perhaps I should be recruiting you!' Tullio said in admiration.

As Madame Tarnovsky acknowledged him with a smile an officer arrived and told them that one of them would have to identify Lombroso and sign for him, so James and Otto-lenghi dutifully followed him to the cell area.

As James had expected, Lombroso was neither angry nor dejected at his detention. Anything but, in fact. As they arrived they heard laughter and there, seated on a bench surrounded by some of the most fearsome criminal specimens James had ever seen, was the professor. He seemed to be examining a set of colourful tattoos belonging to an enormous man with a shaved head and no teeth, who, he learned later, was a notorious thief and robber. They quickly identified Lombroso and he was extricated from the cell without further ado, once he had bade a cheerful and prolonged farewell to his cellmates. He didn't seem particularly grateful for his release at first. In fact, he appeared to be rather annoyed.

'You could have left it a little longer,' he said, indignantly. 'I was getting some extremely useful material.'

He did, however, react rather more graciously when he heard about Madame Tarnovsky's intervention, roaring with laughter on discovering that she had managed to provide him with round-the-clock protection, courtesy of Machinetti.

'Madame, you are a lady of many talents,' he said, a broad smile on his face. 'Now, I think it is time to go home. I hope you will all join me.'

All of them accepted the invitation and soon they were sitting in the large living room where the salon was usually held. Coffee and sandwiches had been served and Lombroso was holding forth again about his new criminal type. As he did so, something on the floor caught James's eye – a flash of colour beneath the picture of an African chief. It was a piece of red and gold card. James went over, scooped it up and examined it.

Before he could say anything the maid came in. 'There is a letter. It has been redirected from the museum, sir.'

Lombroso held out his hand but she shook her head.

'It is for Dr Murray.'

She gave it to him and Lombroso raised his eyebrows.

'Really, Murray, I do think you could have your personal mail sent to your home,' he said tetchily.

James looked down at the letter. 'It is not personal, Professor, and has a bearing on the case. Well it might, depending on the contents.'

Lombroso did not look pleased. His homily had been interrupted. He gave a dry laugh. 'I doubt that, Murray. We are dealing with criminal anthropology here, not guessing games. Science will solve these murders.'

'I agree completely, Professor, and science is exactly what I have here.' James waved the envelope.

'Very well, tell us what astounding discovery you have made.'

James ripped open the envelope and quickly scanned the contents.

'Well?' Lombroso said impatiently.

'I sent the cigar ash we found at the Ausano murder scene to Scotland, to be analysed by Dr Bell who has a certain expertise on such matters.'

'I see . . . Well, I am sure we could have done something similar here,' Lombroso said in hurt tones.

James could have pointed out that Lombroso had been somewhat sceptical when he had raised it after Ausano's murder, but he decided to err on the side of politeness.

'Indeed, Professor, but as Dr Bell has written a monograph on the subject . . .'

Lombroso nodded. 'Well, of course I have been planning

something similar myself but there has not really been time with the symposium and these murders. Go on, Murray.'

James cleared his throat and looked round. This time, he thought, it was his turn to make a dramatic announcement.

'The findings indicate that the ash is from a cigar made in Havana but available only in certain states of America – California being one.'

'Horton!' Tullio declared. 'It must be.'

'Well, it is not conclusive,' Lombroso said, clearly reluctant to move away from the notion of a criminal type.

'But it is compelling,' Madame Tarnovsky said.

'When one adds it to the other evidence . . .' Ottolenghi said.

'Such as?' Lombroso asked.

'This!' James said, holding the piece of red and gold card up with a flourish.

'What's that?' Lombroso asked.

'I think Horton left it here last night. It comes from the base of his cigar.'

'And how does that connect him to the murders?' Lombroso asked. 'Really, Murray, a piece of paper can be dropped by anyone.'

'Not this one,' James said. 'I found an identical piece of card at the scene of Ratti's murder.'

'It all fits, Cesare,' Madame Tarnovsky said. 'Look at the way Horton has challenged you from the first moment he arrived.'

'Particularly at the last salon,' Ottolenghi said. 'It was a very public challenge too.'

'Tribute equals test, Professor,' Tullio added. 'You said so yourself.'

'And then he disappeared,' James remarked. 'In fact, he

has acted very suspiciously throughout this whole affair. He was lurking in the university library not so long ago. And now we have the ash and the cigar paper left at two crime scenes.'

'And let us not forget the cigar butt from the first murder scene!' Tullio said excitedly.

'I don't think that we should get too carried away,' Lombroso said. 'After all, he does not fit my new criminal type – not exactly, anyway. But there is certainly enough to indicate that he might well be our man.' He paused. 'All we have to do is find him.'

Lombroso withdrew to his study shortly after this, saying he wanted to find some notes on the criminal type and do a further comparison with what they knew of Horton to see if they tallied.

James took the opportunity to slip upstairs to see Sofia. Madame Tarnovsky came with him for the sake of propriety. James thought that she might have guessed how much Sofia meant to him.

James gave a gentle knock at the door and poked his head around it.

'She's not there!' he exclaimed.

Madame Tarnovsky followed him into the room. 'Perhaps she has recovered a little and decided to dress. Silly girl! I did tell her not to.'

James heard a rustling coming from an adjoining room and went to see if he could find her. Instead it was the maid making a bed.

'Where is Sofia?' he asked nervously. A terrible suspicion had arisen in his mind and he hoped against hope that he was wrong.

'She was taken away earlier, sir, by an ambulance.'

'Taken by whom?' he almost shouted.

The girl stared at him, wide-eyed. 'I don't know! But there was paperwork and everything left for the professor. Oh, signor, did I do wrong?' With that she burst into tears.

Madame Tarnovsky went over to the girl and began to comfort her. Hearing the commotion the others came up and James quickly told them what had happened.

Lombroso's brows furrowed. 'I certainly did not order an ambulance.' He sighed and sank down onto Sofia's empty bed. 'It seems that the Pilgrim has decided to get to me through other means.'

'Horton,' James declared.

'Speaking of which, did I hear you mention paperwork?' Ottolenghi said.

James nodded. 'Yes, the girl here said some was left for the professor.'

The girl fished an envelope out of her pocket and handed it to Lombroso. He opened it and gasped.

'What does it say? Tell me, Professor, please.' James could hardly contain himself.

Lombroso looked at it gravely. 'It asks me to go to the top of La Mole Antonelliana at five-thirty this afternoon if I wish to see Sofia again. And then it says . . .' He paused as if he could hardly get the words out. 'It says that this is the last Tribute to Lombroso.'

28

Murderers affect gentle, compassionate manners and a calm
air among those they do not know. While they are not great
wine drinkers, they love gambling and sex.

Lombroso, 1876 p 73

They dodged Machinetti's men easily enough by the simple
device of leaving the house through a back entrance.

'So much for round-the-clock protection,' Lombroso had
remarked, sardonically.

La Mole Antonelliana was, at 548 feet, the tallest building
in Turin. When they arrived they stood for a moment or two
looking at it. It was fenced off because the building was not
yet completed. They found a side door in an alley, but it was
locked.

'How are we going to get in?' James asked.

Lombroso pulled some keys from his pocket. 'Crime sometimes pays, gentlemen. We should always remember that.'

He jiggled each of them in turn in the lock until finally
there was a click and the door opened into a large central
atrium.

'How do we get to the top of the building?' Ottolenghi
asked. James looked around but there didn't seem to be a lift
of any kind.

Lombroso sighed. 'We'll have to take the stairs.'

They helped themselves to some builder's lanterns left in the stairwell and began their ascent but their progress was slow. Lombroso was fit for his age but James could see that he was finding it a challenge. He stopped occasionally and leant on his silver-topped cane for support. Even James and Ottolenghi had to pause every now and again in order to catch their breath. Occasionally there was a creak and they stopped.

Ottolenghi smiled at the look of alarm on James's face and informed him that the earthquake that had hit Turin earlier that year had caused some structural damage. 'We should be all right though. It's still standing.'

Once he had heard that, the higher they got the more James thought that he could feel the stairs actually moving. None of this deterred them, though. They all knew what was at stake. The killer was Horton and he had taken Sofia. He had to be stopped. James tried to put from his mind what they might find when they got to the top but it was hard. All he could think of were the mutilations that he had witnessed over the last few weeks.

Finally, after what must have been at least an hour, they arrived at their destination. It was already dark and, as they stepped out onto the topmost section of the building, an observation area surrounded by stone pillars, James was momentarily struck by the beauty of the city, its lights glinting in the evening gloom. He was about to say something but Lombroso put a finger to his lips to hush him then beckoned them to follow him as he slowly made his way round the circular balcony. James looked up for a second and saw the angel at the very top of the tower looking down on them as if protecting them. He was known in the city as the 'winged genius' and James fervently hoped that he would live up to his name.

Suddenly Lombroso stopped and then James gasped as he saw her. He almost did not recognise her at first. Sofia was still alive but her beautiful hair had been shorn. She was bound to one of the pillars and a cloth had been tied round her mouth. The lack of hair made her eyes look even bigger than before. They were full of fear and James wanted nothing more than to run to her and set her free. Ottolenghi stopped him with a restraining arm and he followed his glance to the floor beside Sofia.

A figure lay there and James could just see, in the light of Lombroso's lantern, as the candle flickered in the icy wind, that it was surrounded by a pool of what looked like blood. Ottolenghi went over to the figure and felt for a pulse. He looked up and shook his head briskly. Lombroso joined him and examined the body briefly. James could see then that the cause of death was clear. He had been shot in the face. He turned away for a minute, revolted. There was almost nothing left of the man's features. But even that had not been enough for the killer. The corpse had been further mutilated as the other victims had been. This time the heart had been removed and placed carefully on the stomach. Underneath it lay a note. Lombroso took a deep breath and lifted the congealed mass of flesh and blood in order to pull the note away. He got to his feet.

'The last tribute,' he murmured.

'Well, not quite . . .' The voice came from behind Sofia and James saw a figure in a hooded cloak standing behind her. At first his eyes were drawn to the cloak's golden clasp that glinted in the fading autumn light, then he saw that the figure was holding a pistol aimed at Sofia's head. He did not seem to be on the balcony itself and for a second James thought that the figure was floating in mid air but then he saw that the man was standing in a builder's cradle suspended at the side of the tower.

'Horton, why have you done this?' James cried, unable to contain himself.

'Ah, a case of mistaken identity,' the figure said. 'It's getting to be somewhat of a habit, is it not?'

'Then who are you?' Lombroso asked. 'What do you want?'

'Don't you recognise me, Cesare? Does our friendship mean so little to you?'

James heard Lombroso gasp as the figure threw back its hood.

'What I want is much simpler than a man like you could ever imagine,' Borelli replied. 'You killed my brother.'

'I have killed no one! You are mistaken!' Lombroso protested. He appeared to be genuinely puzzled.

Borelli looked at him and shook his head. 'You don't even remember, do you? My brother was convicted of murder. He died in prison, a broken man. You testified against him. You said that he was a born criminal, an habitual killer who could not change his nature. He kept telling you that he was innocent but you did not listen.'

'What did he say?' Lombroso asked.

'"Nothing can harm a good man, either in life or after death."'

James heard himself catch his breath. He remembered where he had heard those words before. Not only had Sighetti repeated a version of them but earlier Lombroso himself had quoted them exactly during the prison demonstration, as the words of the young man he had helped to convict of murder.

421

Lombroso sighed deeply. 'He had killed someone. How was I wrong?'

'He was innocent,' Borelli cried, 'but your vanity would not allow for that.'

'He may have told you that – but habitual criminals rarely admit their own deeds, even to themselves.'

'I know he did not do it.'

'How could you know, Adolfo?' Lombroso asked.

Then there came a great roar of pain, 'Because it was me!'

There was a terrible silence as they tried to make sense of this confession.

'I murdered the old woman who lived next door to us, the miserable cow.' Borelli paused and shook his head. 'Don't you see, Cesare? *I* am the habitual murderer. I've been under your nose for years but you couldn't spot me, could you, for all your theories.'

'You killed all those people just for that?' James cried out in fury.

Borelli looked at him and sneered. 'People? They're not people. They're criminals. What do they matter? Lombroso treats them as subjects and so do I. I used to them to prove my hypothesis, like any good scientist.' He turned to Lombroso. 'Did you not recognise your work? Noses, ears, jaws, tongues for criminal jargon, tattoos, feet, a shifty gaze . . . you named them all as criminal characteristics of your beloved type and yet you could not recognise the criminal who was standing next to you. How does that make you feel?'

Lombroso was silent.

'But DeClichy was no criminal,' Ottolenghi protested. 'Why did you kill him?'

Borelli frowned for a moment. 'You are right. He was no criminal. He was a decent man with decent theories, if only

422

someone had listened to him.' He glared at Lombroso. 'I did not kill him. My victims, if you must call them that, were sacrificed in the name of science.'

'And Rosa Bruno?' Lombroso said quietly. 'You did not kill her either, I think.'

Borelli looked at him. 'I did not, though I might have done, given the opportunity. But someone beat me to it. I admit I was lucky. Even with your bumbling about, Cesare, you might just have got to me sooner than was convenient if it hadn't been for Signor Horton.'

'You framed him, didn't you?' James said.

Borelli smiled and pulled something from his coat pocket. It shone even in the meagre light available. 'Would you like a cigar, Murray?'

James gasped. 'Horton's cigar case – you took it at the first salon.'

Borelli laughed. 'I did. It was what gave me the idea of framing him. There he was, flashing his case round, handing out his largesse as if he owned the place. It was too good an opportunity to miss. I decided that he would be an excellent candidate to be your murderer, so I took the butt of the cigar he offered me and went back to the scene of Soldati's death after I left the salon and left it there in the hope that it would be found. I must thank you for your efforts, young Murray. It was largely down to you that I succeeded. You were so busy picking up the cigar butts, the little piles of ash and pieces of paper I left for you that you didn't give *me* so much as a cursory glance. Your scientific policing is indeed useful for providing evidence but don't forget that I am a lawyer. It is my job to persuade people to think black is white – and I am a master of manipulation.'

James stared at him. 'Of course! "The finest lawyer in Turin" and Sighetti was your client.'

'Ah, finally the penny drops.' Borelli turned back to Lombroso. 'You know, Cesare, that if I had killed either Bruno or DeClichy I would have followed your list of criminal characteristics, the list you so thoughtfully left lying about in your study. It was a template for my work. It wasn't easy to get hold of – I had to organise a burglary – but it was worth it.'

'I suppose your support at the meeting discussing my dismissal was all part of your plan,' Lombroso said, almost wearily.

Borelli sneered. 'Well, I would not want my challenge to be over so soon, now would I? It was almost too easy. You even helped me yourself. I had to intervene because I wanted your downfall to be complete – not just a suspension based on tittle-tattle. I had so much more up my sleeve.'

'Like the carvings?' James asked. 'What significance did they have?'

Borelli looked at him and gave an empty laugh. 'None whatsoever – they were just – now what is the expression? – red herrings, I believe. I simply wanted to make it interesting by leaving a little clue. It was the same with the so-called Solomonite scrapings in the tunnels. A little research was all it took – oh, that and some help from my accomplice here.'

He indicated the body that lay nearby. 'He did a good job for me; in some ways it is a pity he had to die.'

'Who is he?' James asked.

'All in good time, Murray. I see you are as impatient as ever. A final clue though – you know him.'

James looked down at what was left of the body, hoping that it was not Sighetti.

Borelli continued. 'I led you all a merry dance, did I not?

It was so very entertaining to watch you, Cesare, with your ridiculous ideas. There you were, puzzling over this clue and that and *still* you got precisely nowhere. Criminal expert, my eye!'

'And the letters?' Ottolenghi asked.

'I wrote to *you*, Cesare, but not to the newspapers. That was someone else's doing,' Borelli replied. 'But I'm a generous man, I don't mind lending, or borrowing for that matter, if it helps another in their work. Besides, I rather enjoyed being the Pilgrim.'

'So your experiments have disproved my theories,' Lombroso said. 'Well done. You've got what you wanted. Now it's time to stop this.'

'Oh no, I don't think so. Did you really think it would be that easy?' Borelli said. 'I have not quite finished my work.' He looked at James and sneered. 'How do you like your *amante* now? Not so beautiful inside or out, is she? She gave herself her to me only too willingly. She's just a whore after all. What is it you say, Cesare? "Where criminal women differ most markedly from the insane is in the rich luxuriance of their hair." I've taken that. And now, unless you accede to my final request, I'll take her pretty eyes to go with it.'

Again James went as if to rescue her but was restrained by Ottolenghi.

'What is it that you want?' Lombroso asked.

'I want you,' Borelli said, 'in return for Sofia – a fair exchange, don't you think?' He beckoned at Lombroso. 'Join me here and you can have her, if you think the whore is worth it.'

Borelli moved closer to Sofia and removed her gag, leaning towards her as if he was going to kiss her. She turned her face away from him and he began to caress her body with the pistol. James wanted to kill him there and then but he held himself back, afraid of what Borelli might do. The way he was looking at her reminded him of something. He struggled to bring back the memory and then all of a sudden it came to him. He had watched in an alley way as Lombroso had paid Sofia what had looked like a clandestine visit. Since then he had been haunted by the possibility that there was something between them. Now he realised how wrong he had been. It was not Lombroso but Borelli he had seen that night. James wondered then what hold he had over her that would induce her to entertain him in such a way. Despite what Borelli claimed he knew she would never give herself to such a man willingly.

Borelli looked directly at them. 'I'm waiting. We don't have time for you to produce one of your theories, Cesare.'

Lombroso moved towards him, his hands raised up as if in supplication.

'Professor, no!' Ottolenghi shouted.

Lombroso looked at him and shook his head as if to silence him. When he reached the edge of the building Borelli began to assist Lombroso to climb into the cradle. As soon as they were safely inside he nodded at James and he ran over to Sofia and began to untie her. Borelli started to lower the cradle and looked over the balcony for a moment. Suddenly James saw Lombroso take his cane and, with a well-aimed blow, manage to hit the gun out of Borelli's grip. Borelli spun round and put his hands around Lombroso's neck and began to throttle him while Lombroso waved his cane around wildly, trying to beat Borelli with it until the lawyer seized it and threw it down.

The cradle rocked precariously from side to side as Lombroso tried desperately to weaken Borelli's grip and it looked as if both men would be tipped out. On they fought, with the lights of the city twinkling incongruously in the background, witnessing a struggle for life or death. James looked round for something, anything that he could use as a weapon.

'Over there!' Sofia pointed to the stairwell. There was a piece of metal lying in a corner. It was only a couple of feet long but it might be enough, James thought, as he grasped it and ran over to the cradle. He leant over and aimed at Borelli's head but he was just out of reach. Again and again James tried until he was hanging right over the edge.

'Hold me!' he cried out to Ottolenghi and felt him grab hold of his legs. 'Now push me over!'

'James! Be careful!' Sofia shouted.

Each time he swung the metal bar it came tantalisingly close to Borelli. Then Borelli felt it just brush the very top of his head. He looked up at James and snarled and Lombroso took the opportunity to loosen Borelli's hands from around his throat, allowing him to recover slightly.

Then James was finally close enough to make proper contact. He swung the bar back for all he was worth and then brought it down as hard as he could onto Borelli. But instead of hearing a satisfying thwack he felt the bar stop just short. Borelli had seized it. He pulled at it and James felt Ottolenghi's grip on his legs weaken slightly. For a split second he relinquished his grip on the bar – but it was enough. Borelli grabbed it and promptly hit Lombroso across the head with it. The professor staggered slightly but recovered and then he too grabbed the bar. They wrestled with it in the middle of them, like two retired boxers desperate for a final shot at fame and fortune in the ring. And then suddenly it was falling away to the ground beneath in a sinister echo of what might befall either one of them. James could hear it bounce off the sides of the building as it crashed to earth and Ottolenghi pulled him up to safety. Again the cradle began to sway dangerously as Borelli and Lombroso struggled.

Both James and Ottolenghi leant over and tried to reach the cradle's controls so they could bring it back up to where they were, but before they could do so completely it tipped over so that it was hanging with one side up and one side down. Both Borelli and Lombroso were left dangling from it, just beyond their reach. Lombroso reached into the cradle and managed, by some miracle, to find his cane. He held it out and James and Ottolenghi pulled him, levering him up so they could drag him back over the parapet to safety. Then they turned their attention to Borelli. James leaned over to give him his hand and Borelli looked at Lombroso with a contemptuous smile.

'*Finito!*' he cried, and releasing his grip he fell to his death.

At first there was silence and then as James turned he saw Sofia kneeling by the corpse of Borelli's last victim. She was weeping. He went over to her and pulled her gently to her feet.

She leant into him as if all her strength had gone. 'Hush now, it is over. The professor is safe.'

She pulled away and looked at him, her face distraught. 'You don't understand. This man, he was my father.' She gazed at the poor, mutilated body and sighed. 'I hated him for what he did. You know that, but he was all that I had left.'

James pulled Sofia away as Ottolenghi approached the corpse and examined it more closely. An almost overpowering smell of sour milk mingled with the metallic odour of blood. He looked up.

'It is Vilella,' he announced grimly. 'We spoke to him in La Capra. He was the man Horton brought to the house.'

Suddenly there were footsteps behind them.

'Stop! All of you put your hands in the air and turn round slowly.'

They obeyed the command and saw Machinetti standing in the doorway holding a pistol, the plume on his hat nodding frantically.

'Ah well,' Lombroso said in a resigned tone. 'Better late than never.'

29

Once criminals have experienced the terrible pleasure of blood, violence becomes an uncontrollable addiction.

Lombroso, 1876 p 66

A few days after Borelli had plunged to his death, Lombroso invited all those involved in the case to dine at his home in the Via Legnano. It was by no means a celebration, simply a way of drawing a line under the whole affair and, unsurprisingly given the circumstances, it was a rather subdued occasion. The one piece of good news was that Ratti had unexpectedly survived, regaining consciousness in time to identify the killer. Machinetti had gone to Lombroso's home to warn him and, on finding Borelli's letter, made his way to La Mole. No doubt an interview with Ratti penned by Baldovino would soon appear in the *People's Voice* – 'The Last Survivor Tells His Story!' or some such nonsense.

For James, the occasion was decidedly bittersweet. He had received a letter from his aunt that morning, curtly informing him that his father's health had deteriorated and that he must return to Edinburgh immediately. Lucy had also written to him, begging him to come back. It was a blow. For many reasons he had hoped to stay longer but he knew that he had

430

no choice in the matter. Lucy needed him and that was all there was to it.

He looked round at his dinner companions as they sat and discussed every other subject except the one that was on all of their minds. Lombroso had, presumably in an effort to keep his enemies as close to him as his friends, invited both Father Vincenzo and Gemelli. They spoke quietly to each other about some lecture or other that was being organised. Ottolenghi and Tullio were chatting about scientific policing and its possibilities, a subject that James had mixed feelings about, given the way his own efforts had been manipulated by Borelli. Lombroso and Madame Tarnovsky were talking animatedly about a research project on female offenders that they were planning.

It was odd, James thought to himself. He had come here to find out whether or not he could have inherited his father's criminality. Now he was not sure whether the man he had intended to consult could actually give him a conclusive answer. Lombroso had seemed so sure of his theories and indeed, nothing appeared to have changed, judging from the plans he was making with Madame Tarnovsky. But surely Borelli's actions must have made him wonder why he hadn't at least suspected him?

Finally, as port and cigars were provided, it seemed that James might be about to find out as the conversation at last turned to Borelli's murders.

'I presume that the final victim was an accomplice. What was his name?' Father Vincenzo asked.

'Vilella,' replied Lombroso, sighing slightly. 'Yes, he was an accomplice. He was also Sofia's father and her mother's killer and he had been taking money from her for years in return for staying away. Borelli found out and blackmailed

Vilella into helping with the more physical aspects of the killings, although I suspect, from what I know of him, that he was a more than willing assistant. And Borelli also blackmailed Sofia.'

He looked over to James, who nodded in acknowledgement. Clearly Sofia had had little choice but to accept Borelli as a 'client'. She had lied, but only because she had been forced to do so.

'What of the woman, Rosa Bruno?' Gemelli asked. 'Did Borelli kill her?'

'Rosa Bruno knew that Vilella was Sofia's father. I believe she wanted to tell us in order to protect her,' Ottolenghi suggested. 'Borelli couldn't risk Rosa telling us in case we made the connection between him and Vilella and the murders so he murdered her and later tried to kill Sofia. He denied killing Rosa – but why should we believe him? After all, she was a criminal, according to him.'

'I don't think that is why Rosa was killed,' James said quietly.

'The whys and wherefores are not really the point,' Madame Tarnovsky declared. 'The important thing is surely that a murderer has been stopped from killing again.'

'So, Lombroso, was it really your evidence that convicted Borelli's brother?' Gemelli asked.

'Only in his own mind,' Lombroso replied, tersely. 'There was circumstantial evidence as well.'

'But in the end you were mistaken in your conclusions, Professor, were you not?' Father Vincenzo added with a thin smile. 'The brother was innocent. Borelli himself was the killer.'

'Which of us here can say that we have never made an

error in our work, I wonder?' Madame Tarnovsky said, as ever the peacemaker.

'I acted in good faith,' Lombroso said. 'I believed that I was right.'

'Hubris and folly! Did I not warn you that your work was dangerous and yet you did not listen?' Father Vincenzo said, warming to his theme.

'Indeed, and I am sure that you will accept that caution should be your watch word from now on, Lombroso,' Gemelli said with a sneer. 'The university will expect nothing less.'

James thought that Lombroso would fight back at this point, since Gemelli had taken every opportunity to bring him down over the past few weeks. But he seemed strangely disinclined to do so. Instead he sipped at his cognac and remained silent. James could not let him accept this criticism so readily.

'Professor Gemelli, with respect, you are conveniently ignoring the fact that Professor Lombroso was right about a number of things,' he said.

'And what, pray, were those?' Father Vincenzo asked.

'The characteristics displayed by the killer were just as he said – a fully functioning member of society motivated by intense hatred, a man with two faces, apparently normal and probably rather charming but with a dark side that allows him to commit his crimes without compunction. That is Borelli to a tee!'

'Dr Murray is right,' Madame Tarnovsky said. 'You must surely accept that, gentlemen.'

There was a long silence.

'We still do not know who killed DeClichy,' Tullio said.

'I thought it was Borelli?' Gemelli said.

'Borelli claimed otherwise. He said that he killed only criminals,' Ottolenghi said.

There was a pause and then Father Vincenzo reached into his jacket pocket and produced a thick envelope which he placed on the table.

'I was going to give this to you privately, Lombroso, but I think perhaps that you should see it now,' he said.

Lombroso picked it up and opened it, emptying the contents onto the table. They leant forwards as one to see what was there. There were some yellowing newspaper cuttings, some scribbled notes and an old photograph.

'What is this? Where did you get it?' Lombroso asked Father Vincenzo.

'DeClichy gave it to me. He asked me to give it you in the event of his death.'

'And you kept hold of it until now?' Tullio said, incredulously. 'Why did you not bring it to our attention?'

'It was given to me in confidence and I promised to give it to Lombroso,' replied Father Vincenzo.

'But why did you not give it to me earlier?' the professor asked.

Father Vincenzo shook his head. 'I was with you when we found out that DeClichy had died. I almost gave it to you then but—'

'But you thought that I may have been involved in his death, didn't you?' Lombroso asked.

Father Vincenzo nodded. 'I could not risk it until I knew for sure that you were innocent.'

Lombroso looked at him with contempt and began to examine the contents of the envelope, beckoning Ottolenghi, Tullio and James to join him. The cuttings were from various local newspapers in American cities and James realised that they must have been the ones removed from the volumes he had inspected in the library.

'What is it, Murray?' Lombroso asked.

'I was in the library shortly after DeClichy. I looked at the volumes he'd been examining and some of the pages had been ripped out. I thought it might have been Horton trying to stop us from finding out that he was not a real academic – which is what I suspected. I didn't think DeClichy would have done such a thing. If I had realised—'

'Never mind that,' Lombroso said briskly. 'Can you translate the gist of these cuttings?'

James nodded and read through them quickly. 'As far as I can see they are all accounts of unsolved murders,' he said. 'The victims are not of one type but the attacks seem to have one thing in common.'

'Let me guess,' said Lombroso. 'They all involved some kind of botched surgical procedure.'

'Indeed. The considered opinion in each case was that they were the work of a surgeon or doctor. Organs were removed in each case and left arranged on the body . . . Dr Death!'

'What do you mean, Murray?' Lombroso asked.

'DeClichy left some notes behind. They were just squiggles, mostly, but he had written Dr Death at the top of the page. That must have been what he meant.'

'These mutilations are not unlike the work of Borelli,' Ottolenghi said.

'Mmm, similar but not the same,' Lombroso said. 'Borelli removed body parts, not organs.'

'Like Rosa Bruno and DeClichy,' Gemelli said.

Lombroso looked at him thoughtfully. 'Borelli did say that he had not killed Bruno.'

'There is another similarity to our case,' Father Vincenzo

said. 'One of the articles is an editorial. It describes a letter that has been received by one of the newspaper's reporters from someone claiming to be a murderer.'

'Borelli wrote only to me, or so he said,' Lombroso said. 'The letters to the *People's Voice* were the work of someone else.'

'So who *did* write those letters?' Madame Tarnovsky asked. 'Was it Horton? It's just the sort of mischief he would find amusing.'

'No, it was Baldovino,' Tullio told them. 'After all, what better way could there be to sell newspapers and raise his own profile in the process? He has confessed everything.'

'So after all that the letters were not real!' James exclaimed.

'The letters sent to the *People's Voice* were forged, yes, and, as he said, Borelli took advantage of the fact and decided to adopt the persona created for him,' said Lombroso. 'But the letter sent to me personally was genuine.'

'A wonder you did not realise who sent it then,' Father Vincenzo commented.

'So there never was a real Pilgrim . . .' James said.

'Indeed not.'

'And what of Baldovino?' Madame Tarnovsky asked.

'Currently in custody helping us with our enquiries – which could take some time,' Tullio said, grinning. He turned to James. 'He had, by the way, been following you around the city in the vain hope that you might provide him with some information.'

'Was it him in La Capra and the tunnels?' James asked.

'We think it may have been, although he has not told us so,' Tullio replied.

'He probably stumbled on the body of Rosa Bruno which rattled him so much he ran away. Alternatively, it could have been Vilella, laying a false trail for his master,' Lombroso said. 'Vilella almost certainly carved the Devil's sign in La Capra and I think it is likely that Borelli realised that a fellow murderer was visiting the city because criminals tend to recognise their own type. And it may be that he encountered him during his travels abroad. At any rate, he took the opportunity to use him to confuse us still further.'

'Do DeClichy's notes help us?' Ottolenghi asked.

'A little, although I can't quite decipher all of them,' Tullio said. 'There's no name but I see he has put some initials in red. It looks as if DeClichy followed someone here because these enquiries seem to date back several months.'

'What about the photograph?' Madame Tarnovsky asked.

'Of course,' Lombroso said. 'How could I not have seen it? I think DeClichy was looking at it when we were at the prison.'

Lombroso held it up. It looked to be of a unit of soldiers from the American Civil War. An arrow pointed to one of the party sitting at the front.

'There is writing on the back,' Lombroso said.

'What does it say?' Tullio asked.

'Dr Death,' he replied. 'Just as it said on the note you found in the library, Murray. And then WBH – San Francisco.'

There was a silence as they took in this information and tried to work out its meaning. Finally Lombroso spoke.

'If you read these notes in conjunction with the rest then I think we can see exactly what happened to poor DeClichy and who was responsible.' He turned to James. 'I think you know, Murray.'

James nodded. 'Horton killed him,' he said firmly.

'Of course!' Madame Tarnovsky said. 'Walter Beresford Horton – WBH.'

'Why would he do that?' Father Vincenzo asked, puzzled.

'Thanks to your own folly and hubris we may never know for sure,' Lombroso said gravely and Father Vincenzo blushed. 'But it looks as if Horton killed DeClichy because he feared his true identity was about to be revealed. He took the opportunity provided by Borelli's slaughter to disguise his own crime, although of course he failed.'

'How?' Father Vincenzo asked.

'He did not know that Borelli had left a signature behind on his victims,' Tullio said.

'Indeed,' Lombroso said. 'Borelli left a rudimentary carving of an inverted cross, the devil's sign, on each body. There was no such mark on DeClichy.'

'Or on Rosa Bruno,' James added.

'Yes,' Lombroso said. 'It seems that Horton may have murdered her too.'

'But why?' James asked. 'And what did DeClichy discover that made Horton kill him?'

Lombroso held up the notes which he had been reading throughout the discussion. 'DeClichy started his investigation at Horton's asylum where, he suggests, there have been a number of suspicious deaths amongst the inmates. On following up his enquiries he discovered that Horton was not his real name. He is in fact a man named Beresford, an ex-army doctor who began his career by performing unnecessary procedures on his unfortunate patients. He discovered he was suspected of malpractice and made his escape, but his appetite for blood had been whetted so he then began a murder spree across America. DeClichy seems to think that he became concerned that he was being followed. To avoid detection he reinvented himself as Horton and founded his asylum as a cover for his activities. He killed because he enjoyed it . . .'

Gemelli shuddered. 'What kind of a criminal is that?'

'A born criminal,' Lombroso replied. 'A person who is born as a homicidal monomaniac whose instinct is to kill. When he does so, then his intellectual and moral powers are suspended.'

'Different to Borelli?' Madame Tarnovsky asked.

'Yes and no,' Lombroso said. 'Borelli believed I had killed his brother with my theories and that I was persecuting the innocent with my work. He had a reason for his actions, albeit twisted.'

'And Horton?' Madame Tarnovsky asked. 'He was a compulsive murderer?'

'*Is* a compulsive murderer,' Tullio said. 'He seems to have left the city. No one has seen him since your salon, Professor.'

'So Horton lives to kill again,' Lombroso said, glaring at Father Vincenzo.

'Deliver us from evil,' Father Vincenzo said, crossing himself.

'Or from the born criminal,' Lombroso said wryly, 'which in this case seems to amount to the same thing.'

30

Both born criminals and the morally insane manifest their
tendencies from infancy or puberty . . . Many of the morally
insane have mad parents. Lombroso, 1884 p 218

Later that evening, when everyone else had gone, James and
Ottolenghi sat round the fire with Lombroso, sipping brandy
in a companionable silence. It seemed to James, on this night
when there had already been so many revelations, that the
time had come to tell them his secret. Not only that, but with
his imminent return to Edinburgh there were practical considerations. He had wanted to speak to Sofia about their
future and he could wait no longer. He could feel his heart
pounding as he tried desperately to find the right words with
which to begin his story. But before he could speak Lombroso looked at him.

'I think you have something to ask me, Murray, do you
not?'

James looked at him, astounded. 'How did you know,
Professor?'

Lombroso smiled. 'You could say that I have deduced it
from the evidence before me.'

James remembered using those very words during his first

meeting with the professor, but what evidence had he provided?

'How could you have done that, based on the little I told you?'

'You did not say a great deal, it is true, but it was enough,' Lombroso said. 'For example, you spoke of your father when we first met.'

'Yes, but I did not say what had happened to him.'

'Ah, but you did, Murray,' Lombroso said cryptically. 'Let me explain. You told me he was dead but as you did so you looked away. That alerted me to the possibility that you might not be telling the truth.'

'That could have been a coincidence, surely,' he protested.

'Perhaps, and on its own it was hardly conclusive; however, there were other signs.'

'What were they?' James asked, intrigued.

'You flushed slightly and there was a thin film of sweat on your brow.'

'I do not see that this signifies anything,' James said.

'Really?' Lombroso said. 'What do you think, Ottolenghi?'

Ottolenghi nodded. "These are almost certainly physiological signs of stress, the sort of stress that can only be produced from lying.'

'I have been conducting some experiments in this regard, Murray,' Lombroso said. 'I am developing a machine that can detect such physical changes. If I am successful it could revolutionise the investigation of crime. Think how much easier it would be to interview suspects if we knew when they were lying.'

James looked at him, wide-eyed, realising that he had only begun to scrape the surface of the science of crime. Lombroso, it seemed, was not just a theorist but also a practitioner.

Perhaps he had misjudged him. But James still needed an answer to his own question.

As if he knew what was on his mind, Lombroso spoke. 'We're listening, James,' he said quietly.

Then James revealed all that he had told Sofia about his father and his fears about his own character that this experience had produced.

Lombroso listened carefully. Every now and again he would nod encouragingly and finally, when James had finished, he paused before speaking as if to allow what had been said to settle a little.

'Your father's behaviour is not unheard of, Murray. Indeed, I would go further. This is a danger for every scientist – when we allow our work to dominate our minds to such an extent that it takes away our humanity.'

'But it was *my* humanity that deserted *me*, Professor,' James said miserably. 'That is what disturbs me. And now you know everything about me, you will see me differently.'

'As I have told you, I knew of your background from the beginning, Murray,' Lombroso said. 'I hope that you have learned enough from all that has happened and all that we have done here to understand that you are just about as different from Borelli, Vilella and Horton as you could possibly be. You were angry, and rightly so. And you were going to do the right thing. It was your father who had lost sight of his humanity, not you. You are not a criminal of any kind, born or otherwise. And I should know. After all, I am the expert.'

Ottolenghi made it clear that he agreed completely with Lombroso's diagnosis, as he put it. Sofia had been right. He should have believed in her a little more. But then perhaps there was still time for that.

'Professor, I have something I need to speak to Sofia about. Would you excuse me for a moment?'

Lombroso nodded sagely. 'Of course, but . . .' He looked at James steadily. 'She has suffered more than most of us over this whole affair, so take care. Her answer may not be what you wish to hear.'

James looked at him. So he had known about them all along. He supposed he should not be surprised. Lombroso was, after all, a keen observer of those around him, even if his conclusions were not always sound.

'I will, Professor,' he said quietly.

He made his way to the kitchen where he told Sofia all that had passed between him and Lombroso and Ottolenghi. When he had finished, she gave him her usual enigmatic half smile.

'Did I not tell you the same thing? Perhaps I should be a scientist!'

James pulled her to him. They embraced for a moment and then he put her at arm's length and looked into her eyes.

'Sofia,' he said, his heart pounding as never before. 'You know that I love you.'

'Oh, *caro*,' she replied, softly. 'What am I to do with you?'

'Sofia, I have to return to Edinburgh. My father is ill.'

There was a pause as she took in the news. 'I see,' she said gravely.

'I know this is madness, but I want you to come with me, Sofia.'

'No, *caro*, it can never be.' She shook her head sadly. 'Our lives, our worlds, are too different. It would never work. You – *we* – would be shunned. You could not be the man you should be. I would stand in your path.'

'I don't care what other people think.'

'You do, *caro*. I know you do,' she said tenderly. 'You care for your sister.'

'And I care for you!'

James wrapped her in his arms, not wanting to let her go, for he feared that once he did, it would be forever. Sofia took his hands gently from her waist and stepped away from him.

'It is over, *caro*. Go back to Scotland, to your sister, be what you should be.'

She turned away but he could not accept what she had said. He went over to her and pulled her round to face him.

'No, I cannot leave you like this. Come with me, marry me!'

Sofia looked at him in surprise and then with a small smile she shook her head. 'No, James.'

It was as if someone or something was stabbing at his heart. 'Sofia, please . . .'

She sighed and pushed him away firmly.

'James, it was good, what we had together, but now it is finished. You must understand this. My life is here. I do not want to go with you.'

He opened his mouth to speak but before he could Sofia stopped him.

'I am only a servant . . . You, you are a *brava persona*, a gentleman. What you ask can never be.'

'You cannot mean it! We can make it work, Sofia.'

He reached out for her hand but she snatched it away from him.

'Please . . . do not make this harder than it needs to be. It must end, James. There is no other way.'

'I don't believe you would give up so easily.'

'You must believe it. Now go back to Scotland, where you belong.'

She turned away from him again with what, for James, seemed like a terrible finality. He knew then that there was no choice but to obey her. He started to head towards the door but something made him turn back. Sofia was looking at him with tears in her eyes and he understood everything. She *did* love him and that was why she was telling him to go.

He went to her and held her to him. This time she did not resist. He looked again into her eyes. There was so much he could say but for moment or two he could not speak.

'*Caro*, forgive me,' Sofia said, 'but I had no choice.'

'I know,' he said quietly. 'But now I understand and there are two things I am sure of.'

She gazed back at him. 'What are they, *caro*?'

'Firstly, I will come back to Turin. This city is in my heart because of you, and I have no choice in the matter.'

He put his hand up to her tear-stained cheek and she put hers over his as she had done all those weeks ago.

'And the second thing?'

'When I do come back, we will be together.'

Sofia started to protest but he put his finger on her lips. 'Hush now. You must trust me. I will find a way.'

He held her in his arms and as they stood there together he knew that for the first time in his life he was certain of something. It wasn't science or criminal anthropology – he was certain of himself.

When James rejoined Lombroso and Ottolenghi the three of them sat at the fireside, lost in their thoughts. James looked at Lombroso's face, which was full of sadness, almost reflecting his own feelings.

'Are you all right, Professor?' he enquired.

Lombroso turned to him. For the first time there was a

glimmer of uncertainty in the older man's eyes. He sighed deeply. 'I wonder . . .'

'What?' James asked.

'Could we have prevented any of these deaths if I had not been so stubborn? Perhaps if we – if *I*,' he corrected himself, 'had not been so intent on following my own theories then we might have established the identities of the murderers sooner.'

Ottolenghi shook his head. 'You must not think like that, Professor. Perhaps if the crime scene had been better preserved and some system of scientific examination introduced then there could have been a swifter resolution. There can be no doubt that we were hampered by Machinetti's chaotic handling of the whole affair.'

'Perhaps, Ottolenghi, perhaps, but I cannot help wondering if my theories led us astray and cost us valuable time.'

'No, Professor,' James said. 'You did all you could.'

Lombroso sighed. 'Yes, but it was not good enough.'

James shook his head. 'If I had realised the significance of what I found in the library sooner then perhaps I could have saved DeClichy and Rosa Bruno.'

'But still,' Ottolenghi said, 'how could we have known that there was not one but two criminals amongst our number? We would not have made the necessary links. Besides, both men called themselves experts in crime. It was almost inconceivable that they were experts in the practical application of violence as well as the theoretical.'

'But the question remains in my mind,' Lombroso said, 'could these crimes really have been prevented by the application of criminal anthropology?'

James hesitated. Should he say what was really on his mind? He took a deep breath. 'No, Professor, in this case

I don't think they could. I think we must accept that the criminal type is not always the answer.'

Lombroso looked over to him, his face a picture of inner torture. 'Then I have caused people to die?'

Ottolenghi interjected. 'No, Professor, you have not. They may have been affected by their upbringing, but they may also have been born criminals. Horton, in particular, fitted many of the physical characteristics that you have named. But we know nothing of his childhood and the effect it may have had on him.'

'Ottolenghi is right, Professor,' James said. 'We cannot know everything about the human psyche. Science cannot be the answer to everything. What is in the human heart will always be something of a mystery.'

Lombroso stared into the firelight and nodded slowly.

'Those are wise words indeed, Murray. I promise you that I will not forget them, my friend.'

James looked at Lombroso and Ottolenghi sadly. 'There is something more I must tell you.'

They looked at him expectantly.

'I know I have more to learn, but I cannot stay here. My father has been taken ill and I must return to Edinburgh, for the time being at least.'

Lombroso nodded. 'Of course, we understand.' Then they all stood and he seized James's hand in both of his and pumped it up and down vigorously. 'Take care, Murray. I hope you'll be back with us before long.'

'I hope so too, Professor. You have taught me more than I can say,' James said gratefully. 'Despite all that has happened, I would not have missed this experience for the world.'

'And neither would I, Murray. We have both learned much over the last weeks, I think,' Lombroso said.

James turned to leave.

'Before you go, Murray, there is something I should say to you,' Lombroso said very seriously.

'What's that?'

'We must all be vigilant. Horton is still at large and we know him better than most. He is an habitual killer and his appetites will not be sated by his actions here for very long. If any of us see or hear anything that may indicate his whereabouts then we should meet at that place and ensure that he is apprehended once and for all. Are we agreed?'

The three men shook hands solemnly at this and James finally made his departure.

A few days later James was walking down the Via Legnano for the last time. Before long he would be back in Edinburgh with Lucy, telling her of his adventures. He had missed her terribly and it would be wonderful to see her again, despite the circumstances that had forced him to return to her. But their reunion came at a cost. He had to leave behind the woman he loved.

James felt a familiar jolt of pain in his heart as he thought of Sofia and the distance that would lie between them. But he had a duty as a brother, and indeed as a son, and that had to come first. There was no way to resolve his dilemma but perhaps one day there would be. That little nugget of hope would have to keep him going in the months to come.

He took a detour and made his way towards the museum. As he did so, it seemed to him that the atmosphere had changed. With the death of one killer and the departure of another it was as though a pall had lifted. Even the air smelled sweeter and he felt as if he could finally breathe deeply again. The place was not completely devoid of its shadows. There were plenty left there, hoping to re-emerge as time went on, as there are in any city. But for now they had withdrawn into the darkness. And if they stayed there, even for a while, then that really would be a more than fitting tribute to Lombroso.

Author's Notes

Cesare Lombroso (1835–1909) is known as the father of modern criminology. His theory of the born criminal dominated thinking about criminal behaviour in the late nineteenth and early twentieth century. Essentially he believed that criminality was inherited and that criminals could be identified by physical defects that confirmed them as being atavistic

or savage throwbacks to early man.

Lombroso studied medicine at the Universities of Padua, Vienna and Pavia, and shortly after graduating he volunteered as an army doctor and was stationed in Calabria. It wasn't until the 1870s that he began to focus on the study of criminals.

In 1871, on examining the skull of one Giuseppe Vilella, an elderly Calabrian peasant who had been imprisoned for theft and arson, Lombroso wrote:

At the sight of that skull, I seemed to see all of a sudden, lighted up as a vast plain under a flaming sky, the problem of the nature of the criminal – an atavistic being who reproduces in his person the ferocious instincts of primitive humanity and the inferior animals. Thus were explained anatomically the enormous jaws, high cheekbones, prominent superciliary arches, solitary lines in the palms, extreme size of the orbits, handle shaped or sessile ears found in criminals, savages and apes, insensibility to pain, extreme acute sight, tattooing, excessive idleness, love of orgies, and the irresistible craving for evil for its own sake, the desire not only to extinguish life in the victim, but to mutilate the corpse, tear its flesh and drink its blood.

From the Introduction to *L'uomo delinquente*,
Cesare Lombroso, 1909 edition. xxiv-xxv

RÉVOLUTIONNAIRES ET CRIMINELS POLITIQUES. — MATTOÏDES ET FOUS MORAUX.

This, he claimed, was a turning point for him and inspired his life's work in criminology. He was appointed as a Professor of Legal Medicine and Public Hygiene at the University of Turin in 1876. Over the years he became one of the most well-known and prominent thinkers in Italy, writing prodigiously and performing many experiments using some of the equipment described in *City of Devils*.

He was endlessly curious about crime, criminals and their motivation for offending, as well as their culture, and this led to two things. Firstly, Lombroso collected artefacts created by and belonging to prisoners he had encountered in his long career as well some more bizarre exhibits, such as carnivorous plants and a mummy, as described in the book. These he housed at the University of Turin, informally at first and then later in  1892 as a museum open to the public. This closed in 1914 but has recently reopened. One of its most prominent exhibits is the head of Lombroso himself in a jar of preservative, a legacy he kindly donated on his death in 1909.

So what kind of a man was Cesare Lombroso? Reading between the lines of his work he seems to me to be a basically kind, occasionally capricious and always ebullient man who believed in the essential rightness of what he was doing. He was a national celebrity during his lifetime and as a result his lectures often played to packed houses. His opinion was sought on all kinds of subjects, probably because he was not afraid to court controversy. He had a theatrical turn of phrase and was, perhaps, something of a showman. If he was alive

today, doubtless he would be an avid user of Twitter, a frequent blogger and perhaps even have his own television show.

Notwithstanding his celebrity status, as a scientist he was disorganised and even chaotic and had a tendency to buttress his less successful results with the use of anecdotes, proverbs and literary passages. He was also not above bending his findings to fit his theories when occasion demanded. This was food for his many academic critics but also made his work more accessible and therefore even more popular with the public.

Until relatively recently his reputation as a criminologist was somewhat tarnished, not only by his rather slapdash approach to the collation of data but also by his attitudes to women and certain racial groups. In addition, much of his work was never adequately translated into English. Perhaps as a result of these things, both the man and his work were at best misunderstood and at worse largely forgotten. However, with the translation in the last few years of his two major works, *Criminal Man* and *Criminal Woman, the Prostitute and the Normal Woman* (Rafter and Gibson 2004/6), and the reopening in 2009 of his famous museum in Turin, this is beginning to change.

I would argue that he should be judged as a man of his time. Although one might not agree with his conclusions and views on various matters, they did, to some extent, reflect nineteenth-century attitudes. For all his flaws as a scientist and researcher, it is clear that Cesare Lombroso made a huge contribution to the understanding of crime and criminals and inspired many others to examine the topic of crime from a scientific perspective.

An enthusiast, a collector and an innovator, Lombroso achieved much in his life worth talking about, not least the invention of a proto-type for the lie detector. But if I had to sum him up in a phrase I would turn to his recent translators who described his work in their in-troduction. It was, they said, 'a magnificent tangle of brilliance and  nonsense,' (Rafter and Gibson 2004 p 31) just like the man himself. I found him as a character to be both infuriating and endearing in equal measure. Whatever you may think of his eccentricities, he was never anything less than fascinating.

Salvatore Ottolenghi (1861–1934) was Lombroso's assistant from 1885 to 1893 and went on to found the first School for Scientific Policing in Rome in 1903.

Bibliography

Lombroso, Cesare (2006) *Criminal Man* (M. Gibson and N. H. Rafter Trans) Durham and London, Duke University Press. (Original work published 1876–97).

Lombroso, Cesare and Ferrero, Guglielmo (2004) *Criminal Woman, the Prostitute and the Normal Woman* (M. Gibson and N. H. Rafter Trans) Durham and London, Duke University Press. (Original work published 1893).

Gibson, Mary (2006) 'Cesare Lombroso and Italian Criminology: Theory and Politics'. In P. Becker and R. F. Wetzell (Eds), *Criminals and their Scientists* (pp 137–158) New York, Cambridge University Press.

Gibson, Mary (2002) Born to Crime: Cesare Lombroso and the Origins of Biological Criminology. USA, Greenwood Press.

Horn, David (2003) *The Criminal Body: Lombroso and the Anatomy of Deviance*. London, Routledge.

Acknowledgements

The idea for this book came on a rainy Monday afternoon in a seminar, with a question from a student. Thank you for asking it.

It was further developed with the help and support of my tutors on the MA Creative Writing course at the University of Portsmouth: Sam North, Dr Alison Habens and Dr Stephen O'Brien. Thanks also to my fellow students who made it such a joyful and life-enhancing experience, especially my dear friends Carolyn Hughes and Claire Holland. Without your fearless critique and constant support I'd be lost.

You also gave me the confidence to take the next step – entering the *Good Housekeeping* Novel Competition. Thank you so much to the judges: Kate Mosse, Luigi Bonomi (now my agent), Kate Mills from Orion Books, *GH* editor Lindsay Nicholson and features director Andreina Cordani, for choosing my story and giving me this wonderful opportunity.

Thanks to Nicole Rafter and Mary Gibson for allowing me to quote from their excellent translation of Lombroso's work.

My colleagues at the Institute of Criminal Justice Studies in the University of Portsmouth have been a tremendous source of expertise. In particular, my thanks go to Dr Paul

Smith for making sure that my forensic knowledge was up to scratch, Dr Phil Clements for his support, Ann Treagus and Brenda Newman for their input on that all-important synopsis, and Mandy Curnow for making sure my competition entry got into the post tray on time!

One of the most important things that I have learned is that a writer is nothing without a good editor and I have been truly blessed in this. Jemima Forrester has been everything that a new author could wish for and more. Thank you so much for all your patience and brilliant insight.

Finally, heartfelt thanks to my wonderful husband David, without whose advice and encouragement I would never have started, let alone finished, this book.